"BURN HIM OUT!"

Clay Monroe's mind went as cold as the keening wind. The half-starved and drunken oil workers had found out that he'd been working with Henry Flagler and John D. Rockefeller—and identified him with them as the cause of all their troubles.

Monroe opened the door and brandished his unloaded gun; the mob hesitated a moment, then surged forward.

"He won't shoot," someone shouted. "Remember, he had the Pinkertons do all the killing for him and the big-money boys."

Few heard the carriage come thundering down the street, or paid attention to the licking fire that someone had started in Clay's shanty.

Clay fought off a tall man swinging a length of pipe, seized the pipe and started battling his way through the mob. Then he saw the fast-moving carriage. Desperately warding off his attackers, he leapt up on the running board of the carriage and burst inside.

There was Eugenia Packer, in sables, face pale against her golden hair.

"We just passed Flagler's house."

"The train will be safer," she gasped. "God, Clay, this is the end of the world!"

The Making of America Series

THE WILDERNESS SEEKERS
THE MOUNTAIN BREED
THE CONESTOGA PEOPLE
THE FORTY-NINERS
HEARTS DIVIDED
THE BUILDERS
THE LAND RUSHERS
THE WILD AND THE WAYWARD
THE TEXANS
THE ALASKANS
THE GOLDEN STATERS
THE RIVER PEOPLE
THE LANDGRABBERS
THE RANCHERS
THE HOMESTEADERS
THE FRONTIER HEALERS
THE BUFFALO PEOPLE
THE BORDER BREED
THE FAR ISLANDERS
THE BOOMERS
THE WILDCATTERS
THE GUNFIGHTERS
THE CAJUNS
THE DONNER PEOPLE
THE CREOLES
THE NIGHTRIDERS
THE SOONERS
THE EXPRESS RIDERS
THE VIGILANTES
THE SOLDIERS OF FORTUNE
THE WRANGLERS
THE BAJA PEOPLE
THE YUKON BREED
THE SMUGGLERS
THE VOYAGEURS
THE BARBARY COASTERS
THE WHALERS
THE CANADIANS
THE PROPHET'S PEOPLE
THE LAWMEN
THE COPPER KINGS
THE CARIBBEANS
THE TRAIL BLAZERS
THE GAMBLERS
THE ROBBER BARONS

THE ROBBER BARONS

Lee Davis Willoughby

A Dell/James A. Bryans Book

Published by
Dell Publishing Co., Inc.
1 Dag Hammarskjold Plaza
New York, New York 10017

ISBN: 0-440-07441-X

Printed in the United States of America

First printing—December 1983

Chapter 1

For two days, while the sleet storm had raged over Lake Michigan, the heat and the smell of the oil lamps had only added to Clayton Monroe's mood of depression. After coming all the way from England on the strength of a mysterious message from his family, he'd barely made the *Lady Bristol* at Buffalo, only to discover that his destination, the port of Milwaukee, was frozen over, and that he would have to debark at Chicago.

Impulsively he grabbed his tweed cloak and cap for an escape from the cabin. On deck, reeling from the impact of the wind, he wondered if he had been too impatient to be the first one out for a breath of fresh air. He gripped the rail and allowed his tall frame to sway easily with the pitching of the vessel. The icy gale, laden with tiny crystals, stung his cleanshaven face and high forehead. Still it was a welcome change from the stuffy cabin. He pulled off the tweed cap with a large hand and let the wind play havoc in his long, curly hair.

Then, a slight smile played at the edge of Clay Monroe's firm, determined mouth. A feeling of exultation filled him. The Great Lakes steamer was now, he saw, moving toward the protection of the shoreline—a shoreline of grassy winter-brown meadows interspersed with growths of maple, cottonwood, oak, ash, cherry, elm, birch and hickory.

Trees meant home, even though, as the youngest son of Barrett Monroe, the great lumber entrepreneur who had constantly moved his sawmills westward to keep securing vast patents to the great elm, pine, and oak forests, Clay had never really been a part of the family business.

"You're in for a shock," came a voice to him on the

wind. He did not have to turn to know who was addressing him. Having shared cabin and alternating bunk space had left little for him not to know about Harrison Dole. In fact, Clay felt he knew too much about the nephew of George W. Dole, one of the original incorporators of the town of Chicago and partner in Newberry and Dole.

Still Clay turned to look at the stout, pleasant-appearing little man of his own age. Before he could respond to the curt remark, Harrison roared on over the wind.

"Left the country in forty-and-one, I believe you said?"

"Fifty-and-three! The other is the year of my birth, which you have finally wangled out of me." His severe tone was no mean accomplishment in the face of the gale.

There was a short silence. Harrison, as an agent for Newberry and Dole, seldom found himself in the position of having to be corrected, even when he was fishing for information.

"Still," he said, "Chicago was even then just a lake-front community, with Fort Dearborn as its most commanding feature."

"Surely it hasn't altered that much?"

"Just you wait and see," counseled the Chicagoan. "The population was about four thousand on your departure and now, in 1865, it's over one hundred thousand."

Clay laughed in disbelief. He put all of his geniality, all his bluff charm, into that laugh. He had learned from the moment of meeting him that Harrison Dole craved center stage in all situations and would rant on about the town's growth whether Clay wished to listen or not.

He did not want to cloud his brain with useless facts when it was packed full of so many vital matters, but his eyes were beginning to tell him as much as Harrison's words. The steamer was passing through the harbor basin, which had been deepened before he was born to allow vessels of this size to leave the lake and enter the river adit. To the left, where the neatly kept, whitewashed stockade and buildings of Fort Dearborn had stood, the shore was nearly strangled by streets of houses, stores, and inns. The river's edge, as far as the eye could see, was lined by wharves tightly packed with vessels in the busy process of loading and unloading. On the right, where he recalled green fields and patches of forest, were acres upon acres of log, clapboard and shingled structures of hodge-podge design and construction. Nothing was recognizable from the past.

His momentary excitement turned again to depression. Even the squalor of India was impressive in comparison to this city of hovels.

As though willed by Captain Wilkins, the wind began to subside as they pulled into the main stream of the river. The steam engines slowed to inch them along to the old section of town and the Newberry and Dole dock off Rush Street. There was a tangle of excited tongues on the deck below them; there was talk in German, and Clay caught a few words in French. The English-speaking voices he heard were not British.

"Whatever is there for all of them to do?" he mused aloud.

Harrison raised his hand as though it were a question he would rather brush away. "Up until recently they would have been met at the eastern docks and the men among them offered a goodly sum to replace men of American birth in the draft army. Better they as cannon fodder than young men of talent like us, don't you agree?"

"Up until recently doesn't answer my question about the present," Clay said curtly, purposely avoiding the question. The manner in which he'd missed the war was no concern of Harrison Dole.

"Oh," Harrison said slowly, knowing full well he had hit a nerve, "some of these immigrants will be absorbed into the vast number of cottage factories that have sprung up because of the war; others are bent on homesteading hereabout and farther west. We carry many from Cornwall who have pre-paid passage to become lead miners in Galena. Of course, as you must be aware, the German families are all Black Forest people who were destined for Milwaukee and your father's sawmills. Now they will have to be transported back to Milwaukee by other means. It will cause problems, I am sure. Not a wise thing to make Monroe & Sons pay the passage back north."

There was no answer. Again Clayton Monroe could hardly comment on family business matters he knew nothing about. Not only had he been divorced from such knowledge for twelve years, but he had only a vague memory of it before that time. It was one of the prime worries on his mind, but not one to be discussed with Harrison Dole.

Harrison smiled to himself. Another nerve pricked. From the corner of his eye he studied Clay anew. Up to then he felt he had read the man astutely. His aloofness was quite typically British, but that could come from having been around them during all of his formative years. The big handsome face, however, did not possess the English pallor. In it was power, and turbulence, and great intensity.

Harrison admired tall men, muscular men. His stout little frame, more than his talents, had induced his family to keep him out of the war. Clayton's virility and strength of body were the very image Harrison had of true masculinity. The manner in which the man had stood up to Captain Wilkins dismissed any question of a coward's streak. Yet something had kept him away from America during the war years.

A dandy? Harrison hardly thought so, although he loved the fashion in which Clayton Monroe's long, high-split traveling coat fitted his broad shoulders and his narrow compact waist, the tight elegance with which the tan flannels molded themselves over his muscular long legs. The unspurred boots were of the finest polished kid, and though they showed no sign of ever having been worn on a fox hunt, they still reeked of English gentleman. Would that he could wear clothing in such a casual manner, or even afford it. Harrison figured that the silk neckcloth and contrasting shirt would have been equal to his monthly salary. But then, Barrett Monroe could well afford to keep a son in such a gentlemanly fashion.

Clayton Monroe would have roared with delight, had he been able to read the man's mind. His silks had been haggled down below the local market price in Calcutta, and his coat, breeches and tweeds he'd acquired at a funeral auction in Soho. Four years' mastery of whist in India had helped to separate a naval officer from the fine boots during the Atlantic crossing. After paying his ship fare, his worldly possessions consisted of a carpetbag, a change of shirt and undergarments, and two dollars American. What the future—and his father—held in store for him was another of his worries.

"Well, Clayton," Harrison said at long last—this was the first time he had called his traveling companion by his first name—"that should make you feel proud. War or no war, Monroe & Sons have helped make Chicago the lumber capital of the world."

"I have never seen such a lumberyard," replied Clay slowly, overlooking Dole's sudden familiarity. "It is several city blocks long and looks like a city itself. Why are they loading the lumber onto flatboats?"

"You have been gone awhile," Harrison laughed. "The Illinois and Michigan Canal links Chicago with the Mississippi. New Orleans has been back in the Union for nearly three years. Didn't England print any of the war news?"

"They must have, but . . ." He hesitated. "But I have been mainly in India these past years. Out there, even news of England was several months old. We heard little of what was transpiring here."

"Not even from your family?"

"More so during my school years in England, Mr. Dole," he said. "The mails from Milwaukee to India, via London, are hardly an overnight matter."

"Milwaukee? Oh yes, I understand. I keep forgetting the length of your absence and the move of your parents north. I, of course, am only acquainted with Cy in a small way and have never been invited to Old Jonathan's home. Was that your home as a youth in Chicago?"

Clay was momentarily bewildered. "Cy?" he questioned, curious but unable to answer the question as directed.

"Cyrus Monroe. Old Jonathan's second son. He's the transportation clerk for the immigrants and deals directly with Newberry and Dole. If I am not mistaken, he is near our own age."

"Six months my senior," Clay said, almost too quickly.

"I was an uncle twice before I was even born. There were five Monroe boys before me—Jonathan, Hershel, Ivan, Henri and Carter. Henri—not Henry, as my mother is French—was to be the last. My father is Germanic, as you probably know, and needed more loggers. Carter came six years later, and I ten years after that." He stopped, abashed. He had revealed quite a lot of family history in just a few seconds—and to a comparative stranger. A moment more and he would have been blurting out all of his secret family fears.

After four days of probing, Harrison reveled in these disclosures. Clayton Monroe had to be a black sheep crawling home as a prodigal son. He loved it and wondered how he could turn it to his own advantage. He actually despised the Monroe clan and people of their ilk. He was a Dole, one of the twenty-eight family names who incorporated Chicago—one of the traditionalists. The Monroe money and power he classified with the arrivistes, late-comers who would steal Chicago away from them and put their own mark on progress.

"Ah, we are about to tie up. Come with me and we will use the Captain's private gangplank to avoid being crushed by the riffraff. I declare, all of Europe seems bent on coming to America. The dock will be bedlam. If Old Jonathan has not received word on your change of destination, I shall arrange carriage service for you. It is the least Newberry and Dole can do after all of the uncommon delays."

Clayton followed without really listening. *Old* Jonathan, he kept thinking. His eldest brother had been twenty-two at his birth, which would make him presently only forty-six. Hardly ancient, he considered. Still, his own father had been forty-two at the time of his birth and he had always considered him a very, very old man. And suddenly, as he started down the gangplank, he could not even bring the image of his father's face to mind. He shivered, but not from the February temperature. He was returning to America because of an urgent family order. The message had been cold, cryptic and unsigned. He was not sure if it had come from his father, mother or some other member of the clan. And therein lay his greatest worry. If a family tragedy was in store for him at the end of the journey, he wished not to learn of it from a total stranger.

It was worse than bedlam. Down the gangplank the immigrants streamed—shouting, laughing, squealing and weeping. From the hold came their livestock to add to the cacaphony—cows, horses, hens, cocks, geese, hogs, dogs and cats. The men cursed under the weight of heavy trunks and household possessions. Children who had become friends during the four days gathered in knots to gaze at their new surroundings.

"Look out!"

The warning had come too late. The board flipped upward under Clay's weight and his feet sank into a hole in the river bank. Harrison had jumped aside after giving the warning. Clay was pelted from head to toe by globs of mud.

"The ground is not winter-hard yet," Harrison laughingly observed, as Clay wiped his mud-splattered face and shirt. Illogically, he thought how fortunate he was not to have donned his last clean shirt and brocade vest that morning.

"Come into the office and wait for someone to meet you."

"They were expecting me in Milwaukee."

"We are no longer in the wilderness," Harrison laughed. "By telegraph Chicago probably knew of the frozen port before Captain Wilkins. I'm sure your brother Jonathan is well aware of your arrival."

Avoiding mudholes and putting his weight firmly on the middle of each plank, Clay followed his rotund little guide to the large warehouse that stretched along the river and fronted on Rush Street. Before they reached the office door, a man, shorter and rounder than even Harrison, approached them. His calf-high boots were mud-caked, his tucked-in trousers splattered. His keg-like chest was clad in a lumberman's mackinaw and the winter flaps of his cap drawn down over his ears.

"Pardon," he mumbled, removing his cap and nodding his head deferentially, "but I recognize you, Mr. Dole. Would you by chance be escorting Mr. Clayton Monroe?"

"I would be."

"Fine it is then. I'm Ferguson and have been sent for himself and his trappings."

"You see, Clayton, you have been sent for. Ah, and here is a cabin boy with our bags. The carpetbag is Mr. Monroe's only luggage. Clayton, I will not say good-bye. Later today I shall send a note around to your brother's house to see when it would be convenient for you all to dine with me before you head north."

"I'm to take him directly to the railway yard, sir," Ferguson cut in quickly.

"Railway yard?" repeated Clay, slowly, feeling as though he were an object to be considered no more than the carpetbag.

The old man's face darkened and wrinkled further. "I'm only following the orders I got from my foreman, Mr. Monroe. I've got a lumber wagon right over there, you see."

Harrison stared. Lumber wagon! Ah, he had been quite correct. The black sheep returns and no open-armed welcome greets the prodigal—no family, and the orders come from a foreman. It was deliciously insulting and he loved it.

Clayton was silent for only a second. He wet his lips to keep either man from seeing that they trembled. His heart was pounding with fury and hurt. Twelve years of loneliness had taught him not to show his emotions outwardly, and he would not crack under this humiliating situation.

"Then I shall say good-bye, Mr. Dole," he said evenly. "As I am unsure of my future whereabouts, you may save your note-paper. My thanks, though, sir, for sharing your berth with me."

They shook hands solemnly and Clay walked stiffly toward the wagon. Harrison Dole watched the retreat and now wondered how he could use the man's bitterness and resentment to his advantage. He was a patient young man and instinctively felt that this was not the last he had seen of Clayton Monroe.

Clay sat the wagon tall and proud. He had already reasoned that he would get no significant information out of Ferguson and so remained silent. He concentrated on the city, jammed with people, all sorts and conditions of people pushing and shoving on the boardwalks, dodging to avoid the showers of mud from the wagons and carriages. The stores had been carved out of the walls of large frame buildings that had once been warehouses. It was hardly London's Haymarket.

There was a bump and the wagon ride grew smoother. Clay looked down to see brick paving and looked back up to find a different world. To the right and left were imposing mansions he did not recall.

"That be ole man Newberry's place," Ferguson said sourly. "And the one that covers a whole city block belongs to William Butler Ogden."

The name rang a faint bell in his memory. His face reflected a genuine puzzlement that made Ferguson laugh.

"The man who built the Galena and Chicago Union Railroad west into the prairie land before we had a line from the east."

Clay nodded, remembering. The line had not been completed before his departure.

"Then why am I being taken to the railyard?" he finally asked, because it had been a puzzlement all along.

"For a train, I assume. Ain't the only line now, Mr. Monroe. We're now the hub of ten main railroad lines with nearly one hundred trains arriving and departing daily. Most of our winter lumber comes down from Milwaukee by rail. I'll be taking back a wagonload from a boxcar after I drop you off."

All of a sudden it struck Clay as very funny. Jonathan Monroe was proving to be as penny-pinching as their father. Why waste costly carriage horses when a wagon was traveling in the same direction?

"I'm amazed," he laughed, "that my brother Jonathan did not give your foreman orders to have me help with the loading."

Ferguson leaned towards him and spoke in a soft and confidential voice: "I'm with the company ten years now, sir, and we ain't seen that much of Mr. Jonathan in the past two. I'll tell you, sir, just between us two, wot the yard men say to it. Ain't his sickliness that keeps him away as much as his break with his sons. In a way, it don't sit well in the men's bellies that his long-standing rules can be altered on a whim by Mr. Jon or Mr. Cyrus. You must have seen Mr. Cyrus rounding up them German men off the boat? Every time he brings in a new bunch, *Mister* Jonathan Junior cuts our wages. With him as foreman we have to accept it or look for another job."

Clay pursued hurriedly, as if he wished to change the subject: "You mentioned my brother's sickliness. Is it anything serious?"

"Ain't been close enough to him in six months to ask personally. Once upon a time any worker could go to the Huron Street house and be received with a hearty glad-hand. That's when your Mama still lived here in that house with him. Fine woman, your Mama. My own Ma was French-Canadian and I always appreciated your Mama speaking to me in French."

"It was her natural tongue." Clay laughed. "As a boy I had to speak French with her, German with my father and English with my brothers. Sometimes it got very confusing."

"Hold on, sir. It is going to get a little jarring going over all of these tracks."

"But I remember the depot being off Canal Street."

"Still there, plus this one and another for passengers over on North Dearborn Street. This one is mainly for freight, but I'm to take you to that siding over there."

On a spur sat a string of private railroad cars without an engine attached. From each, smoke rose from a pipestack as though to announce that they were inhabited and cozy and warm. Clay was used to the railway cars of England—utilitarian in design. These cars were some sixty to eighty feet in length and held the sheen of polished wood, metal and brass. Two had domed tops that towered fourteen feet above the axle base. Each seemed to have a character all its own. The first was windowless for half its length, but sported five oversized smokestacks on its roof. Heavy drapes were drawn over the windows of the next two cars and gave no clue as to their interior. Between the two domed cars was one of normal height that afforded Clay a view of uniformed servants setting out silver and crystal dinner service.

"What am I supposed to do?"

Ferguson shrugged. "All I know is that this is where I was supposed to drop you. Last car in the line. Good luck. Fanciest rolling stock I've ever seen."

Their elegance was enough to make Clay aware that they were not owned by Monroe & Sons.

Chapter 2

A moon-faced black servant opened the back platform door before Clay had a chance to knock.

"Mr. Monroe," he said, and grinned. "You are expected, sir. Let me have your valise and follow me."

Clay had seen many "colored" servants in India. He was familiar with their sing-song voices and subservient attitude, but this large man's booming bass was crisp and articulate, friendly without being submissive, and he moved out of the little marble-floored foyer with easy grace. He was the first American black Clay had ever had an opportunity to meet—and he was impressed.

The foyer archway was draped in velvet. Clay stepped through and stopped short.

He found himself in a large, warm office, where a fire burned in a black marble hearth between two wide and luxuriously curtained windows. He stood on a thick, soft Oriental rug, its pattern dark crimson and white. The walls were paneled in gleaming hardwood, along which were placed a few heavy, tufted chairs covered with crimson velvet and accented by white tassels around the armrests and skirted bases. Silver and spun-glass wall sconces bordered the fireplace and the panels between each of the other windows. The rosy glow cast down on this sumptuous room came from a series of half-moon Tiffany stained-glass windows set in the dome, its curved ceiling intricately patterned in filigree. The far wall of this section was a floor-to-ceiling mirror, bounded by another draped archway that opened onto a hallway leading to the other end of the car.

At an angle, in front of the mirror, stood a great mahogany desk, richly polished and littered with papers and silver objects. At the desk sat a tall, craggy-faced man with unruly white hair. His head and hands seemed to move in unison as he busily signed letters under the bright light of a hanging crystal chandelier.

Clay stood in stupefaction. A slight touch at his arm told him that the servant wished to take his cloak and cap. He removed them, but was hardly aware of his own action. Never before had he beheld such luxury. It had always been the rule of his father to put money into articles for use and not for show. This office alone, he was quite sure, had cost more than all he had earned in his twenty-four years.

The servant bowed, whispered softly in the man's ear and departed through the archway.

The white-haired man at the desk started, then looked up with the sharp and piercing glare that distinguished him. He came up out of the padded swivel chair in sections, as though wires held him together and some invisible puppeteer pulled him up. Coming around the desk, he took in every aspect of Clayton Monroe, then smiled thinly, but his pale blue watery eyes gave no hint as to what thoughts were churning in the chambers of his brain. He extended a cold, dry hand with a quick thrust.

"Well, well!" he exclaimed, in a hoarse and even-pitched voice. "So, you are the product that developed out of the brawny little child that was sent to England. I would not have recognized you, but I can see from your facial expression that you, likewise, do not recognize me. I am Harvel Packer. Your father and I were gold prospectors together in California when you were about eight years old. Of course, your father stayed only long enough to secure enough of a nest egg to invest in additional sawmills. I stayed until I could be assured of having my first million."

Nothing the man had said so far had stirred a memory in Clayton's brain, but he was under the immediate impression that the man was uttering straight facts and in no way bragging.

"So," the man continued, "you have returned quite quickly. I was that amazed to receive your father's telegram. He anticipated that you were still in far-off India. Sit down, my boy. From the look of you, the trip has been an ordeal."

His eyes bored into Clay's glassy gray ones, which were rounded in wonder. Carefully lifting the tails of his coat, Clay sat down and placed his large hands upon each thigh.

"If I am pale, sir," Clay said honestly, "it is because I have never had an opportunity to view a room such as this. It actually takes one's breath away."

Packer chuckled drily. "It is a marvel, isn't it? Designed by a business associate, Philip Armour, who had yet another business associate, George Pullman, build it and the other cars. These are prototypes and are called hotel-cars. I shall show you all of their marvels after we have had a drink."

At the slightest touch, a portion of the mirrored wall popped open to reveal glass shelves, racked bottles and silver service. Mr. Packer brought forth a crystal decanter of brandy and two little silver snifters. He filled them carefully, not a golden drop too much or too little. He handed one across the desk to Clay.

"We shall drink to your safe return, my boy."

"As you wish, sir," Clay said candidly, "but I am most curious as to why I am here and not on my way home."

Packer sat down slowly, never taking his hard stare from Clay. His gray lips smiled faintly.

"What message did your father send you?" he said.

"A puzzling one, sir. It was held in England by Hammershell & Barnes, as they were aware that I would be returning within the fortnight from my four years' apprenticeship in India. Frightening, too, sir, for it told me nothing. So short that I have memorized it. 'Winter or no, imperative you return home immediately. Divest yourself of all obligations there and advise of arrival this side.' Tell me, sir, I pray you, have you been assigned as an agent to soften some tragic blow for me? I was not even met by family at the wharf."

"Blundering idiots," said Packer in a sarcastic tone, "from your pig-headed father on down. No, my boy, your family are all quite well, except that Jonathan suffers greatly from gout and chronic overweight. You are to see your family here for dinner tonight. Can no one express my messages in a simple and direct manner?"

"In this case it would seem not, for I am still quite in the dark."

Harvel Packer was a gentleman, and a third-generation American. It was not necessary for him to invest his money in various schemes, but in so doing he had vastly multiplied his original million. It infuriated him that such as he had to wait on lesser minds to catch up with his simplest notion. At that moment he was striving hard to keep from losing his temper.

"Shall we start back at square one, eh?" said Mr. Packer, trying to smile agreeably. "Background! I will leave out all of the bullcrap that you will be able to read about me later. I married late in life, the year you were born to be exact. Two years later, my wife presented me with a girl child and lost her own life in the presenting. I did not remarry. Business became my mistress. When I invested in land, it was through Will Ogden. He was also my contractor, and Harry Hart Horner the architect for the stores, offices and homes we desired for this, our adopted city. Naturally, the wood contracts went to Barrett Monroe. When Will Ogden wanted me to invest silently in railroads, you do not need a crystal ball to determine who supplied the ties, bridge trestles and the like. Simple and direct—we tried to keep Chicago money in our territory. Territory, son, meaning north to Lake Superior and west to the Mississippi. Lumberlands, farmlands, dairy lands, waterways, railways and something the Jesuit missionaries found three hundred years ago on the shores of Lake Superior—the richest beds of native copper and iron in all the world. I had a finger in each of these pies, along with a few others, and the Civil War caused me to push in a full fist. What do you think of that?"

He threw himself back in his swivel chair, and gazed at Clay with a look that hardly ever failed to intimidate. But Clay was not in the least intimidated, because he was still totally confused.

"I am impressed, sir, but in doubt as to why you recount it for me."

Mr. Packer coughed roughly. "I am at the disadvantage,

Clayton,'' he said ironically. ''Why did your father send you away to England?''

''If the truth be known, sir,'' he answered more sourly than he intended, ''it was not the wish of my father, but the constant prodding of my mother. Her dream, if you wish to call it that, was to have one of her six sons an educated man. Knowing our family, as you seem to, sir, you know where I am on the ladder. As the youngest, I was the logical choice for education and business apprenticeship in England.''

''Do you regret their choice?''

''The thought has never entered my mind, sir,'' he said coolly.

There was no sound in the car but the dropping of the log on the grate, and then the dry, quick rustle of a paper Mr. Packer pulled from a stack and perused silently.

Finally, he exclaimed in a tone of intense satisfaction as he slapped the paper, ''Then I must be reading of an entirely different person. Intensely studious in preparatory school; a quiet undemonstrative, boarder; a top fellow at Eton with the scholastic ability to complete advanced studies by the age of twenty. Hammershell & Barnes, never ones to laud any man, give one Clayton Monroe full credit for many innovative changes in their India operation. They were most reluctant to bring you back from India and to let you go. You know, of course, that old English thief Hammershell made your father pay a stiff price to buy up the last two years of your employment contract.''

Clayton was startled. He raised his eyebrows with injured innocence. ''I know nothing, sir. The communication I quoted is all the knowledge I possess. I was dumbstruck, confused, and I made a proper mess of closing out my affairs and sought counsel from no man—including Mr. Hammershell. The paper you possess and the conduct of my father in this matter—whatever matter it seems to be—greatly distresses me. I am still being treated like a barefoot boy of twelve with snotty nose and a brace hanging loose.''

Clayton was very wrought up, and leaned towards Mr. Packer with a face expressing indignation and disgust. But

Mr. Packer merely leaned back in his chair, smiled pleasantly and waved his hand.

"For a year your mother has warned of this reaction, but your father and I had to be steadfast in our course. Our reasons cannot be put in a simple phrase. This war has opened a floodgate of change in the north and west, and has brought forth the world's best business opportunities. It is only the beginning. I would make a pact with the devil if I could take thirty years off my life. But, being a staunch believer in reason, analysis and logical decision, I know that an impossibility. Education is a remedy, but not at my age. Efficiency is my god. Old-fashioned methods are suspect, unless they can be altered to be efficient—something that you did in India. In short, your talents would be wasted in the lumber industry where your father already has sons and grandsons fighting over the slices of that pie. Your father and I do not quite see you getting into the middle of that fray."

"How nice that I am being so considered. I feel like a pine that has been left standing for twelve years to gain greater girth. The woodsman stands with axe poised, but the tree does not know if it is to become house, ship, or firewood."

There was a deep silence in the room, as wary old eye and baleful young eye engaged each other.

Then Packer, chuckling ruefully, reached forward to pat the papers. He winked. "You forgot that the log could also be ground into fibrous pulp to make this document. But enough for now. Come through to the dining car for a bit of lunch. After all the ship fare you should be ready for some fresh food."

Clay really had no appetite, but his curiosity was insatiable. The man was still a mystery to him, and why he was there an even greater mystery. He could despise his father for pulling the strings of his life in such a fashion, but that would be a wasted emotion without the man present to feel the waves of his anger.

Anger? Following the lean man down the hallway of the car, he was amazed that such a word had entered his head. How could he feel anger at someone who was such a vague part of his memory—at a burly woodsman who slipped in and out of his first twelve years like a ghost at a seance? Rarely did they see him in his mother's "civilized" winter home in Chicago. Jonathan had been more father than elder brother. Even in the summertime tent-city at the lumber camps he had run to Jonathan with every problem, scrape or bruise. Barrett Monroe was always off on some fresh new scheme or hacking out another clearing in the wilderness for a sawmill.

He was well into preparatory school before the stork myth was exploded. Even as his schoolmates made much over his naivète, he remained in doubt. How could such an errant visitor have conceived him? Exact two-year spans separated Jonathan, Hershel, Ivan and Henri. Because boarding school boys encountered no daily family life, he developed the notion that his mother had been solely responsible for himself and Carter. That fable had to be erased when he was seventeen and a first hat at Eton. His roommate became the unwitting father of a child by the scullery maid and Clayton the pop-eyed father-confessor to the terrified friend. The manner in which a child was conceived at once became, in young Clay's eyes, an evil that deserved avoidance. Without a mature man about to counsel him properly, he closed his ears to school chatter and slowed his climb toward manhood. He became quite a loner.

Even in India, because of his brawny frame, he was considered eccentric, but his manliness was never suspect. He gambled not, drank little, smoked never, fought only when necessary, and wasted no time with the pleasures available from the native women. He was, therefore, almost as naive as the day he had departed Chicago.

"Ah, Philip is busy at the oyster bar," Mr. Packer said, bringing Clay out of his reverie. "Not a good time to make the proper introduction. This is my table. Sit you down."

At the far end of the dining car the black servant who had greeted Clay was helping a somberly dressed young man select oysters from an iced bowl and crack them open. Seeing them, the servant came forward with a smile.

"Everything is in order, Mr. Packer," he said, holding a high-backed window chair for the man. "Miss Eugenia will be along shortly."

"Thank you, Morrison. Oh, I was remiss earlier. Clayton, this is the proudest gem in my staff. If there is a food, wine or service that Morrison does not know about, then it has not been conceived. Whatever your desires, let Morrison know of them."

Clay looked back at the end of the car; he was confused. Packer saw the look and immediately understood.

"No, my boy, that is Philip Armour, another associate of mine from the gold-field days. Philip made his first million in hogs, but that is his own story to relate. You must forgive him. Philip is a tireless workhorse who prefers to eat a very light midday repast quite alone."

Clay took his seat slowly. He found it incredible that the man at the far table was a millionaire. He seemed no older than Clay himself, with hair and beard as dull a brown as his drab dress. The uniform and style of a minor clerk, Clay could not help but think. Philip Armour devoured the oysters one at a time, without a trace of emotion on his face.

The outer car door opened and a girl came gliding through, with the lithe grace of a ballet dancer. Clay saw Armour immediately rise. Clearly, there was an expected pleasure in the meeting, for Armour's face was instantly aglow with animation.

"So," Eugenia Packer said impatiently, "you are going to eat alone and scoot again?"

"Sorry, Miss Eugenia," Armour said. "It's the smell of the stockyards on my clothing that I fear would offend your appetite."

His rich and deep voice traveled the length of the car easily. Clay looked at him, a little startled. He had expected a mousy voice to match the attire. He glanced at the hands that gestured as Armour talked. They were strong hands, work-hardened and demonstrative—not clerk's hands, like his own. Clay was forced to revise his initial impression of clerkishness. As the arms moved, Clay could see the outline of solid muscular arms beneath the ill-fitting sack coat. True, Armour was probably quite brawny under the suit, but it was the brawn of a graceful gentleman who'd been heir to generations of proper breeding, he thought.

"Eugenia, we are waiting," Packer called out.

Clay took it as a cue, and was on the point of rising when he looked again at the girl bidding her adieu to Armour.

He had been remiss in not noticing her loveliness before. Her honey-blond hair was like finely spun gold, brushed all to the right and twirled into five massive curls that cascaded off the shoulder and rested gently on a high, supple bosom. Her full red lips molded each word so carefully that a deaf man could have followed her conversation with ease. With a wave of her hand she turned and swept toward them. In an exquisitely tailored midday-suit her hour-glass figure moved like a feather. She floats, Clay caught himself thinking.

Then he became aware that he was being studied through golden lashes so long they seemed a gauzy curtain over each snapping sea-blue eye. And why did she seem so amused in her study, he wondered.

"Sorry to be late, Papa, but shopping in Chicago is utterly impossible."

She kissed her father lightly on the cheek and allowed Morrison to seat her next to him. Harvel Packer's face softened to paternal adoration as he again took his seat.

"My dear, do you recall Clayton Monroe from your youth?"

"The question is, Papa, does Clayton Monroe recall me from his youth?"

Clay's eyes went round with astonishment. He had not as yet fully pinpointed Harvel Packer in his memory, let alone his daughter.

"I'm afraid not," he murmured, clumsily taking his seat.

The girl cast him a glance across the table that was filled with amused contempt.

"Of course, *he* has done a bit of filling out as well. Don't you dare give him a clue, Papa. I intend to be as mean to him as he always was to me. Morrison, I am utterly starved. Wherever did you find oysters in February? I will start with a half dozen before I learn what other delights you have in store for today. Oysters, Mr. Monroe? They are heavenly with a dash of champagne to wash them down."

"I've never tasted them before," Clay stammered.

"Then you must," she laughed, as though preparing some great practical joke.

It was not the laugh which disturbed him, but her voice. It was a soft, melodious purr that sensually suggested she knew some secret about him that he could not recall. He glanced quickly at Harvel Packer. The old man was nodding some non-verbal message to Morrison, who instantly spun away to extract a chilled bottle of champagne from a silver bucket. He expertly popped the cork and served the sparkling wine.

Eugenia raised her glass, took a dainty sip and played the moisture around the oval of her lips with the tip of her tongue.

"Don't be afraid of it," she teased, taking another sip.

Clay felt heat begin to rise from his neck to cheeks. Normally he allowed nothing to embarrass him, and he was damned if he was going to admit never having tasted champagne. He followed her example of holding the glass and sipping.

He nearly choked. It was tart to the taste, tickled his nose and watered his eyes.

"Aren't the British used to drinking champagne?" she simpered.

"Not in my social class," he whispered, and looked down at the plate Morrison had silently set before him. His eyes widened at the gray objects lying on half-shells of mother-of-pearl. Eugenia's firm little chin trembled and she loosed her laughter.

Harvel Packer jumped at the sound.

"Will you stop badgering the boy," he snapped.

"Really, Father," Eugenia smiled. "This is hardly any different than the time when Clay and Carter blindfolded me and forced me to eat a worm, which turned out to be nothing more than a wet noodle."

"Is this another of your tall tales?" he scolded. "I recall no such happening."

"How could you?" she chuckled. "You and Mr. Monroe were off in California and I was left in Marti's care."

Clay turned brick-red.

"The orphan girl!" he gasped. "But you were a grubby little mite with pigtails."

"I still wear pigtails at night," she purred, raising her glass and looking at him over the rim. "Would you like to see them some evening for comparison?"

"*Eugenia*!" Packer rasped. "I have spent a small fortune training you to be a lady, so conduct yourself accordingly."

In his dismay at her conduct, Packer took his small fork, raised an entire oyster to his mouth, chewed and swallowed.

To keep out of this trend of conversation, Clay followed his example. He nearly gagged. It was not the taste that was unpleasant, but the contact of the slimy portion of shellfish as it slid down his throat. His stomach wanted to immediately reject it, but he fought valiantly to keep it down. Stubbornly, he scooped up a second oyster and devoured it. He had been forced to eat and like many exotic foods in boarding school and in the restaurants of India. Taking his third oyster, he was determined not to let Eugenia Packer make him a laughing stock. To emphasize his point, he looked her square in the eye as he chewed and swallowed.

He had, he saw at once, struck the right attitude. She smiled, after eating one of her own oysters, and followed it with a sip of champagne. He followed suit. He was amazed. The wine did serve to wash away the fishy flavor and now seemed quite sweet and enjoyable.

"Perhaps there is hope for you," she whispered sweetly, so that her father wouldn't hear—"in some respects."

Clay colored anew. He wasn't used to women with so much wit and guile. He wasn't used to women of any sort, nor such rare food and drink, nor such plush splendor.

At that moment, however, he was pleased to see that one person had taken his plight into consideration. Morrison had intelligently put only three oysters upon his plate and now deftly whisked away the evidence and replaced it with a steamy cup of beef broth. Morrison hesitated a moment and then served the father and daughter.

They ate the soup in silence, although Clay was aware he was still being carefully studied.

Morrison replaced the soup and champagne with a cold luncheon plate of boiled ham and tongue, pressed corned beef, sardines, turkey slices and hard-boiled eggs, which was accompanied by side dishes of Lyonnaise potatoes, stewed tomatoes, crisp Albert toast and goblets of a clear, dry white wine.

"Quite adequate," Packer said approvingly. "I knew you would not overshadow your homecoming dinner surprise, Morrison."

"Father has been planning this for some time, you know." The statement was supposed to explain everything. But seeing that Clay still did not understand, she added quickly: "Didn't he explain that he has you pegged to be his administrative aide-de-camp?"

"All in good time, my dear," Harvel Packer said expansively. "The mind accepts change better on a full stomach."

Clay nodded as though he were in perfect agreement, but was stunned by her words. What she suggested was incredible. Had he missed some nuance in his conversation with the man because he had been so awed by so much magnificence? Still, he could not repress the feeling that she was still out to avenge her childhood hazing at his hands, although it was a vague memory to him. Then, midway in a bite of corned beef, a flashback crossed his mind. The pigtails were there, but not the Chicago scene. It was summertime and the family was in a logging-camp tent. Ages he could not recall, but a tremor in the pit of his stomach suggested many unhappy circumstances that he had banished from thought. Nuisance! The word would not leave him and he tried to picture her as a nuisance. It was hard to do, seeing her now. Never had a woman been able to so unbalance him and leave him looking like such a stammering fool. He resented it and fought vainly for more information from the past. It came so suddenly that he blurted it out with his mouth full of food:

"Jeanie!"

"Enough!" she exploded, banging her fork down on the table. "It is *Eugenia*! I have never allowed a single soul to shorten my name since you two urchins made such a mockery of it!''

Clay's gray eyes sparkled. His memory had at last found a gap in this young beauty's armor. To open his mind more, he would plunge the knife in full and twist.

''Mockery?'' he said, his voice calm. ''I hardly see that as possible. It still seems to fit you, Jeanie.''

''And a capital B seven-letter word fits you,'' she snarled. Packer's head came up from his plate, his mutton chop whiskers bristling. Ignoring him, she went on before he could speak. ''You and Carter thought you were so clever making my name come out *Genie*, as though I were something that popped out of a bottle in a puff of smoke. Oh, how you made me hate the name!''

Clay began to laugh, and it was taken up by Harvel Packer.

''The things you learn about your child,'' Packer chuckled, ''that you've never known before. At times, my dear, you are rather like a genie popping in and out of a bottle, but, frankly, making demands rather than granting wishes.''

''Stop it! Both of you!'' she cried, and her voice was genuinely angry.

So, Clay said to himself, she's just as spoiled as ever. He found the thought oddly displeasing. He was suddenly remembering her screaming tantrums and the far-fetched tales she carried to his mother. Carter always seemed to bear the worst for it, because Clayton was too young and innocent. Then, later, he would feel the brunt of his due from Carter's pounding fists. Yes, the memory of Eugenia Packer was coming back quite strongly.

''Delightful,'' Harvel Packer laughed, ''utterly delightful. You're all right, Clayton. The only emotion my daughter has shown of late is an anger toward Marshall Field for carrying merchandise suited only for the middle class. Sorry she let some of the cat out of the bag. Briefly, Clayton, my offer is this: I need someone to see after my various investments and help improve them. Why you? Several reasons. The minnows spawned before the war have become giant whales of business and industry because of it. Like Armour, the majority of them are young men in their thirties. I am hardly senile, but I need a sharp mind to help me match wits with them. My boy, I want Chicago, not New York, to be the financial as well as transportation hub of this nation. With an Illinois boy in the White House, it gives us a voice in government. And with an Illinois boy like Grant heading the army, it gives us a voice in the military—and the military will have a strong say in the West and South when this war is over.''

He paused and stirred thick rich cream into his coffee, then laced it with sugar.

''This is becoming a truly American drink. The beans come from Brazil, the cows originally from Switzerland and the sugar from recaptured Louisiana. A mixture of the best, just like ourselves. My family were originally English, your people German and French. We can blend together just as the sugar and cream in the coffee. Your father possesses five sons, I but a daughter. You would become more son than an employee, although I will go ten percent over your Hammershell & Barnes wage.''

''You said they were horribly stingy, Papa,'' Eugenia said calmly, forgetting that she was supposed to be mad at both of them. ''He's worth at least double their wage.''

Packer's face scowled at her interruption, but after a moment he recovered.

''Granted,'' he admitted, ''but he will have to prove his worth.''

Clay was not sure he had heard correctly. It would put his wage at two hundred dollars a month. He was about to open his mouth to accept, when Parker went on.

''Your first assignment is to work with my colleague, Mr. Armour. You will start in the morning, because Philip wants to get to New York as soon as possible. You can arrange for accommodations after our return.'' He turned to his daughter. ''Eugenia,'' he said, ''you might counsel him on proper attire. Philip can afford to look the stockyard vagabond, but I expect Clayton to look affluent when he represents me.''

''Yes, Papa,'' Eugenia said. ''But don't you think you'd better ask him if he wants the position?''

''Well, why wouldn't he jump at it?''

Clay suddenly felt a stir of uncertainty. He knew next to

nothing about the man's affairs. He had studied Hammershell & Barnes in depth just to gain an apprentice interview. He frowned. Not once during the discussion had his personal wishes been taken into consideration.

"I am quite honored by the offer, sir," he said slowly, feeling guilty that he had to put a reservation on it at once. "I have come a long way and have not seen my family in twelve years. I strongly desire to go to Milwaukee before commencing employment."

"Not necessary," Packer said sternly. "Your father is well aware of my need for speed now that you are among us. He agrees that there will be plenty of time for a family reunion after our return from the East."

Clay did not answer him. But through his heart passed a burning sword and he felt new enmity and hatred. Packer might not have been aware, but he saw his father's eternal vengefulness in the words. The arrogant, domineering man had not been able to turn him into a lumberjack and would now stop at nothing in pulling all the strings to make him a businessman. He felt naked and powerless. He had no choice.

"There is little I can do about proper attire here in Chicago," Eugenia said, as though everything was cut and dried.

"I will leave that in your capable hands," Packer said, rising. "I now have some paper work to complete. We shall meet between three and four, my boy, prior to cocktails. Dinner will be at five to make a short evening of it, as you will be at the stockyards with Philip at dawn."

"Genie," he murmured, then was silent as Packer departed.

He saw her smile, a smile that told him she knew he had not called her name. She knew he was bemoaning the fact that he was in the hands of a genie who made things happen by words and not by magic. Then, without a word, she rose and glided away from the table. He watched her and then followed. Her narrow back was so straight, the gentle curve of her hips so seductive. Her exquisitely formed head was high and haughty.

In the next car, Eugenia turned. "This way, Clayton,"

she said. "We have to pass through Philip's car to get to yours."

Something in the way she said Armour's name disturbed Clay. Slowly, as he walked behind her, he turned the matter over in his mind. It came to him as no great shock that it was said with loving adoration.

"You will note that Philip's car is quite different from Father's," she called over her shoulder.

Clayton nodded in perfect agreement. The hallway ran down the right side of the car with three large sitting compartments on the left. The center compartment contained a paper-littered table, which Clay assumed was the man's working-office area. The hall opened into a living room space in the final third of the car. It was incredibly crowded. All the woodwork was carved in tortuous Moorish designs. The tables and chairs were not in harmony, as were Packer's, and they were draped with fringed chenille throws. Here, too, was a marble mantelpiece, over which hung a Currier and Ives train scene nearly dwarfed by its massive frame. Just as massive, on each and every table, were lamps and shades of every conceivable size and color.

As before, Clay was awed by the luxury, though he considered it a little more livable than the Packer car. He was, therefore, taken aback by Eugenia's retort.

"The next car returns us to sanity," she chuckled, opening the door to cross the connecting platform. "Philip's car is an exact duplicate of his hodgepodge home."

The platform was curtained to protect them from the wind. Clay held his comment until they were in the sleeping-car vestibule.

"Perhaps that fits his bachelor tastes."

"Hardly *his* tastes," she said with icy passion, "but those of his wife, who refuses to accept wealth graciously. She remains a housewife and little more."

"What is so terribly wrong with that?"

"Clayton, let us be frank. I have nothing against middle-class women and their heavy emphasis on housekeeping and Sunday school. More to the point, if they demand Victorian sexual standards from their men—taking control of their bodies, limiting the frequency of intercourse and demanding separate bedrooms—I don't give a damn. But we of wealth have an obligation to present quite a different picture.''

He was astounded. Her words were shocking, intolerably affronting to him, and indecent. Such casual reference to bodily contact between husband and wife he had never heard from a woman's lips before. He was too aghast even to comment.

''In the East,'' she went right on, ''a phrase has sprung up around the men who have developed vast wealth—robber barons they're called. I find it quite contemptible, but Papa laughs it off with a stern expression. How can you call a man a robber when he pours his wealth back into more and more industry for the country?''

''What does it mean?'' he stammered, because he could think of nothing else to say.

''It is bound to be one of Papa's three o'clock lectures to you. Here is your compartment.'' She slid back a door and stepped in.

Clay stood looking in, his gray eyes unblinking. It was very elegant and yet totally masculine. Two horsehair sofas sat before the inner walls of polished redwood. A table jutted out of the space between the two windows, which were draped in forest-green velvet. On the back of a narrow door the few possessions from his carpetbag hung on brass hooks.

''The door is to your own private lavatory, although the water 'spring' closet for bathing is at the end of the car. You will have to arrange with Morrison for its use, for it never seems to have ample hot water. I so hate the contraption that father took a compartment in our car and turned it into a full bath. If you prefer a bath, I might be talked into sharing it with you.''

Again he took it as a bawdy suggestion and quickly changed the subject.

''Where do I sleep? The sofa seems a little short for my length.''

''That curved section over the windows drops down into a bed. Morrison will do it for you, but if you wish to try it now, I know how to operate it. It is not as if I have not seen you in a prone position before.''

"I don't think you need to show me the bed," he said quietly, the heat rising in his face again. "And I hardly recall you seeing me in any such position."

Eugenia stood quite still before him, her blue eyes dancing with mischief. Then, very softly, she began to laugh.

"You *are* forgetful," she said. "Don't you recall the three of us playing Indian in the woods? Naked? Of course, we blamed the burning up of our clothing and half the forest on Carter, because he was bigger—in all respects."

Clay turned slightly redder than the woodwork and wanted to deny it all.

Eugenia calmly took a step closer. When she spoke, mischievous laughter bubbled up through her voice.

"Carter and I often laugh about it," she said. "We should too, as long as we are going to be so close again."

She was close enough to put up her arms and wrap them about his neck. Before he could protest, she bent down his head and found his mouth. She kissed him lightly, suggestively, lingering upon the touch. Against the surprising strength of her arms, he was powerless, unless he wanted to turn brutal. He tried deliberately to turn his head away, but she pressed the curve of her body and mouth hard against him in an attempt to force his arms to enwrap her. Instinctively they did, and she immediately turned gentle to capture the response she desired. He felt the tremor of her high young breasts. Her eyes closed, and her lovely face tilted upwards, she pressed her tempting warm lips on his reluctant mouth until she felt his lips part.

Eugenia found herself thinking, my God, he's still an untried and untrained baby. Maddeningly she dug her fingers into the hair on the back of his neck and daringly explored beyond his lips with her tongue. His head jerked convulsively in disgust. Just as quickly, she contemptuously drew away her mouth.

"Eugenia," he gasped, "I—I—"

"Have never been kissed like that?" she growled. "That truth is quite obvious!" She grinned up at him wickedly and watched the color drain from his face. "But don't start getting the wrong idea over a single kiss. I have set certain standards for the men I deem worthy of courting me, and you are greatly lacking in almost every category. Every category! Pray, don a clean shirt for Papa, as it seems to be the only change you own."

Eugenia turned and sauntered back to the railway car door. Clay watched her go, the anger boiling in him. Then he turned back into the compartment and slid the door shut behind him. He felt so unbearably desolate. She had baited him, tempted him and then cast down the supreme insult. He was unworthy. The cold naked truth put fury in his eyes. He sat and thought about the past with deep earnestness.

He could not recall the incident, although in her words it was often recalled by Eugenia and Carter. Carter? He recalled his brother as a devil-may-care, selfish young barbarian who charged up the steps to manhood.

Laughter suddenly rumbled in his throat. Carter was twenty-two when he'd left home, and fully grown when this naked cavorting was supposed to have transpired. Little wonder that she could make her nasty comparison. That she had even looked he would put down for the moment as youthful curiosity.

Then he thought of her in her present womanly state. Or was she still a spoiled child with a lovely woman's body? Pretty as a picture, he had to admit. It occurred to him that her frivolity could best be kept in check by a sound spanking. As he recalled, the "orphan girl" always stood out of harm's way when punishment was meted out. His memory, again, did not serve him well in recalling how she came to be motherless. If Harvel Packer had mentioned it earlier, it had gotten lost in the jumble of too much happening too soon.

He removed the soiled shirt and opened the door to the lavatory. Immediately he was face to face with his own image in a rectangular mirror. There was nothing there to be ashamed of—or make him question his lack in any category. A faint smile played on his firm mouth. Had Eugenia ever once questioned that she might be lacking on the standard scale he had for a woman?

Then he knew that he must be ruthless in keeping her out of his life. He was there to work for Harvel Packer, not to become Eugenia's pawn and plaything.

Chapter 3

Mr. Harvel Packer had not been able to multiply his million without the quiet and questioning, yet intrinsically shrewd understanding of his fellow men.

He was a dreamer, but with a practical plan. His plotting for the past fifteen years had the outward appearance of a child playing with new Christmas delights until they were broken or forgotten because of a newly unwrapped delight. Eastern money men never saw his schemes as nefarious, sly maneuvers to bring confusion or ruin among them. He simply followed a course that would bring the largest possible profits to himself. As they pursued the same, he was never considered a threat. Nor, to their frustration, were they ever allowed to learn how many strings he held at any one time.

When Clay learned the vast extent of Packer's holdings, he was dumbfounded. The first half hour of their meeting was a maze of facts, figures and company investments. To the penny, Harvel Packer was well aware of the placement of every cent he owned.

"I have always been one to help my friends, Clayton," he said proudly. "That is why you see such a wide range—from cottage factories to copper mines. Windfalls on many of them, penny profits on others. An augury, if you will, of the economic revolution which has been rising during the war. But what after the day of the war's end?"

"My experience with postwar economic trends is limited, sir." Clayton's face furrowed. "The suppression of local resistance in the Sepoy Rebellion was well in hand by my arrival time in India. It did, of course, bring about the ending of the East India Company as the supreme voice and force upon the other companies' rather harsh business laws."

"A point that intrigued me in the Hammershell & Barnes report," Packer chuckled. "When it comes to law, we Americans have a penchant for running home to Johnny Bull to see how he handles a legality. I smell the same happening after our civil upheaval. Congress will become the hunting hounds of disgruntled and howling merchants fearing they were not invited to the slicing of the pie. With injured innocence those of little intellect are already using the onerous and disagreeable words 'robber baron' against the men who alone were prepared to place their capital on the line in the hour of danger and confusion when it appeared the South would make good their promise to win the war in the first year. The present laws do not scare me, Clayton. I have been skating on that thin ice for five decades. You are privy to British law. In New York, I want you to purchase every book available, and to acquaint yourself with every factor on which you are not yet on knowledgeable terms. Then keep your olfactory organ pointed toward Washington so that we can smell out the first whiff of change. There are now no laws that say monopoly practices are illegal, and we shall keep it that way."

Clayton did not comment, for he understood the man's points quite well. He had been the "nose" for Hammershell & Barnes, had sniffed around the taxation laws and found the unwritten loopholes.

Now Packer gazed at him thoughtfully, and his smile took on a curious quality, as if he seethed to get on with a new project. "I have for you here a list of names," he said in a strange and mysterious voice. "I intend to tell you little about these gentlemen, and I assume that you know nothing about them at present. In New York, at various times, you will have the opportunity to meet them face to face and prepare your own judgement. For the most part, they are aggressive Yankees still in their early twenties, except for Mr. Jay Cooke, who is almost forty. If I told you the shape of each man's bow, and the number of arrows in his quiver, you would have the name of every major corporation in America, but no knowledge of the man. Most of them, like myself and your father, come from a childhood of utter poverty. They have all made their own way, some to a greater degree than others. They consider me an old man—and treat me as such. We shall have to wait and see how you are treated. I deplore the term 'assistant.' It has the onerous implication that you follow me about to wipe my butt. 'Associate' will be the manner of your introduction, but don't be swayed by a title. I bear none other than 'mister.' Ah, there is Morrison's bell. Our guests are arriving. You go on through and I shall join you shortly."

Through the door of the dining car Clay could hear voices. One was Jonathan's, while the other Clay recognized, after a moment, as that of Carter. He peeked through the narrow panel of glass to ascertain the time-change in his family. All he could see were seated legs. Morrison had transformed the near end of the car into a cocktail lounge, while at the far end the tables had been pulled into the center banquet-style.

Quietly he entered to face them. The mauve satin knees belonged to Mary Louise Monroe. He remembered Jonathan's wife as a plump woman. She was a plumper matron, hiding her girth under yards of glimmering mauve satin and gigantic hoops—with a froth of white lace choker to mask the triple chins.

"Clayton!" she cried boisterously, stretching out her big warm hands with joyous pleasure. He took them quickly and gave her a kiss on each plump cheek. He recalled her as rather dull and quiet—a shadow in the household that was dominated by her mother-in-law. Where the hoarse, booming quality of voice had been acquired he was unsure.

"Welcome home!" roared Jonathan, waving Clay over to where he sat.

Clay started, and stared at the almost unrecognizable man. Jonathan had gone totally bald and his large belly sloped down toward shanks that seemed swollen and disfigured. A wooden cane rested beside each leg. But although the face was fat and puffy, the eyes still glowed with joy at his return.

"My sons, come and greet your uncle!"

The two bowed ceremoniously, but furtively eyed Clay

like young pit bulls. Clay, after one brief appraisal, decided that he liked neither of them. Jonathan Monroe, Junior, was twenty-five, a plain man of florid color, with deep-set smiling blue eyes. He had a big and fleshy body, heavy with muscles, and was dressed as though he'd come directly from the lumberyard. He was quick to announce that his wife was about to make Clay a great-uncle again and sent her regrets.

But it was Cyrus Monroe that Clay instinctively detested. He was a few months older than Clay, and slightly taller, very thin, almost lathe-like, and dressed with exquisite taste. His face was emotionless, long and thin, with a narrow, ridged nose and thin, tight lips. Under mousy brown eyebrows his eyes were a curious green. Cat-like eyes, wicked and amoral, Clay figured. He recognized the eyes at once as being the same as his own father's—unfathomable and cold.

Cyrus' aloof glance warmed, after a cool greeting, to Clay. "I say," he murmured, "it has come to my attention that you have made a friendship with Harrison Dole."

"We were but cabin mates from Buffalo," replied Clay.

His gray eyes were piercing, but Cyrus allowed no thought at all to touch his green eyes, and while he did not yawn, he gave that impression. "Beastly social climber, Harrison," he murmured. "But then that sort is all Chicago is full of any more."

Jon laughed his rich and rollicking laugh. "Then why do you constantly associate with them?"

"I shan't after next week." He dropped his hooded eyelids and averted them from his brother. "I've decided to take an executive position with a gentleman associated with the Vanderbilts and their railroads. At last my superior talents will be put to proper use."

"Cyrus!" cried Mary Louise. "You've mentioned none of this! You are too young to live alone in New York!"

Jonathan said nothing, but his eyes became reflective for a moment.

"Older than I when I married," Jon said with a complacent grin.

"Hardly the point," said Cyrus with much ennui. "It is vulgar to marry and bring brats into the world until you can afford them. I will not be a poor rabbit like the peasants we hire."

"Vulgar," said Clay, mimicking him exactly. "All their children do is grow up to be the next generation of lumberjacks."

Cyrus turned to him and stared with eyes suddenly murderous. He tried to hide that look from his parents, but Jon saw all. He laughed loudly. He took Clay by the arm and shook him. "I like that statement!" he cried.

"Then keep it in mind when you consider cutting their wages again," said the senior Jonathan coolly.

"I thought I heard Carter," Clay said quickly, not wanting to be part of any family business discussion.

"He went to escort Miss Packer," breathed Mary Louise with a romantic sigh. "They would make such a lovely couple."

"Carter isn't married? I thought sure mother wrote me of a marriage a few years back."

Mary Louise clapped her hands to her ears and looked horrified. "What a family disgrace! Left literally at the altar, he was. Turned him into a perennial bachelor."

"Who has tasted so much of the apple of life," Cyrus said snidely, "that there is little left but the core."

"And half a worm," Jon boomed.

A loud burst of laughter, accompanied by a feminine giggle, sounded from the end of the car. Carter Monroe masterfully entered as a cavalier with lady on arm.

Carter, elegant in royal blue broadcloth, moved with a grace equal to that of Eugenia Packer. They appeared like two joyous dancers coming center stage to take their curtain call. At last, Clay reflected, here was a person almost unchanged. His golden hair, shining as though painted on his narrow skull, caught rays from the lamps Morrison was beginning to light. His blue eyes gleamed in a keen face that seemed a decade younger than his thirty-four years. His delicate mouth was a constant grin, as though he wished the whole world to think him happy.

The eyes of the brothers met for a long and inexorable moment. Then Carter threw out his long, sinewy arms and pulled Clay into a back-slapping bear hug.

"I hear you've been a naughty boy already," Carter whispered on a chuckle, "and with my girl."

Clay pulled away and looked at Eugenia. She was ravishing in emerald green chiffon, with matching ribbons laced into her over-the-shoulder curls.

"Do I get a greeting?" she purred. Mockingly she extended her hand to him. He took it into his own, although Carter's words had rekindled his anger. Gallantly he raised it to his lips, but his eyes offered no warmth.

"Always the tattletale?"

"If it helps me gain my desires," said Eugenia in a frigid voice. Then she spun away merrily to greet the others.

"Is she really your girl?" Clay asked.

"It's a standing joke between us." Carter laughed, but only with his mouth. Clay detected a frozen misery in his eyes.

Morrison started serving drinks as soon as Harvel Packer arrived. He became the center of attention and conversation. Mary Louise and Jonathan treated him with fatherly respect. Carter was able to joke with him as an equal, whereas good-natured Jon seemed to grow sullen and purposely ignore the man. The aloof Cyrus, in turn, became quite animated and fawned over the man until it was almost embarrassing. Eugenia bubbled into every conversation, as though vying with her father for some of the attention. Clay remained silent.

Only a single drink was served before they were seated. Packer headed the table, with Jonathan to his left and Mary Louise to his right. Clay was seated next to his sister-in-law, with Jon and Cyrus to his left. Across from him was Eugenia and then Carter. The foot was left vacant for the absent Philip Armour.

The meal was excellent, but the conversation as if from a prepared script. Each in turn seemed to feel responsible for bringing Clay up to date on some aspect of the war—as though those were the only years that he had been absent. None of them hesitated to highlight their own individual efforts toward the cause and make him feel the slacker for not having been around.

Most of it fell on deaf ears, for his attention was pulled time and time again to Eugenia's intrigues. She played

Carter and Cyrus against each other like a coquette unable to make up her mind between them—while at the same time she rubbed a slippered foot against Clay's boot until he could find an excuse to move his foot.

She was a devilish pixie in her taunting—witty, sly and suggestive. Cyrus responded elaborately, using the chic society jargon of the day that delighted Eugenia—and that Clay did not understand. Carter did understand, and with determined courage he tried to be as au-courant as they, and even to outdo them.

It was a new Mason-Dixon line, eternal elders against eternal youth, with Clay not being a part of either. He felt that he had totally lost contact with his family. When Harvel Packer made a business point to Jonathan, Mary Louise prattled on to Clay about family matters that his mother had never put in her correspondence. Horribly, he found himself quite indifferent and bored by the family gossip. It was little more than news about total strangers. He got confused keeping the wives and children of Hershel, Ivan and Henri straight in his mind.

Only Carter, the eternal child, seemed the same. And Clay could not help but feel pity because of it. He felt he had a rudimentary knowledge of Eugenia now. She had the cunning and shrewdness of a British officer's wife. Flirting with a younger officer to tickle his vanity, then sending the young scoundrel away with his tail between his legs when he became too amorous—or when a new challenge had come on the scene. She would hurt Carter, he foresaw, if she had not already done so many times over.

Never had he been so glad for a meal to end. On parting, Jonathan gave him a lecture, which he sensed had come directly down from Barrett Monroe in Milwaukee, on the proper reverence the family expected him to accord to Harvel Packer. Mary Louise kindly told him simply to use his common sense. Jon nodded agreement and Cyrus shrugged wryly.

When he returned from seeing them to their carriage, only Morrison remained in the dining car.

"Mr. Packer has retired, sir," he was told, "and Mr. Carter Monroe has escorted Miss Eugenia back to her compartment. Good night, sir. I shall call you in time to be ready for Mr. Philip in the morning."

When he was back in his own compartment, Clay experienced an odd depression of spirit. With the berth-bed down the compartment seemed insufferably small. It gave no room for him to pace and work out his turbulent thoughts. He flung himself upon the berth, covered his face with his hands. Everyone had their own plans for Clayton Monroe, except Clayton Monroe himself. He tried to put everything out of his mind and allow a lassitude to enter.

The wind increased outside. A chill pervaded the compartment, but he ignored it. In another compartment a clock faintly chimed seven. A carriage rolled over the gravel and stopped. He assumed it was the return of Philip Armour. He also assumed that sleep would come quicker if he were properly undressed, but still he did not move.

Then, after a long moment, he sprang down from the berth. On an impulse he grabbed cloak and cap from their hook and dashed out. He would walk until he was tired enough to sleep.

The wind hitting his face was refreshing. The sky held the halo from Chicago lamplight. Across the many tracks an engine chugged and belched into the freight yard.

He turned to walk along the car and noticed that the carriage still sat next to the siding. The breath jetting from the horses' nostrils and the coachman huddled down into his greatcoat like a frightened turtle were evidence enough that it was awaiting a returning passenger.

Clay started to circle out around the vehicle when his attention was arrested by three lighted windows in the car. With the shades pulled down, the interior illumination turned them into screens for a shadow show. The figure of a woman in one panel was unmistakable. The profile was clear and crisp, the flow of her long hair diffused and ethereal. The filmy dressing robe seemed draped like a bridal train. She disappeared for a moment and then glided silently into the center panel. A male silhouette came to join her and their hands entwined. Something he said must have amused her for her head tilted back as though in merry laughter. The male took immediate advantage of the situation and pressed his lips to the exposed neck. She displayed a momentary start, but he quickly moved his head down to the cleavage and arched her further back.

Clay tried to pull his eyes away, but he was mystified. He was under the assumption that Eugenia's compartment was in her father's car and that Philip Armour had a car of his own. There was no other woman on the train, as far as he knew. Who then could these people be?

With a single motion the man tore down the dressing robe from her shoulders and exposed her breasts. As the man moved his head from breast to breast, she dug her fingers into his hair. It was hard to tell if she was attempting to push him away or draw him into closer contact. Her head and mouth were moving rapidly, but no sound escaped from the car.

When the head moved below the silhouetted breast, her scream did pierce through to the exterior. Without thought Clay spun back toward the car steps. The coachman remained in his turtle pose.

Clay raced down the center hallway, momentarily confused as to which right-hand compartment door he should pound upon in order to offer his assistance. A shrill voice brought him to a halt in front of one. There was now no mistaking the voice, and it baffled him.

Eugenia's pleading tone turned to cold contempt and reproach. The man's laugh was even more contemptuous, and followed by the echoed sound of a slap.

Clay didn't hesitate. He quickly burst through the door and took in the situation.

The compartment, three times as large as his own, was fashioned as an elegant library-sitting room. The walls were mainly black wood bookcases, the molding intricately carved and the shelves boasting formidable tomes in red leather jackets. Near the door sat a small, antique mahogany desk with lighted lamp and open book. At the far end of the compartment were matching lounge sofas with a dual lamp table between.

Eugenia sat upright on a chaise, where it was evident that she had been slapped into a reclining position before the interruption. After a fearful glance at Clay, she pulled the dressing robe over her nakedness. She seemed suddenly small and terrified.

The man kept his back to the door and did not rise from his kneeling position in front of the chaise.

By the man's clothing Clay knew at once that it was not Philip Armour, and he felt a little ill that Carter Monroe could be so despicable with the young woman, even if she had been a tempting vixen during dinner.

"Eugenia," murmured Clay, to cover the awkward silence. "I—I could not help but hear you scream."

"And thus had to play the gallant," cried the man vigorously. "Away with you! There is nothing amiss here!"

"That is for Miss Packer to say," Clay said coolly.

"Tell him, Eugenia. Tell him I came back at your invitation. Tell him to depart," he added hastily, cringing a little from her expected rejoinder.

"You may answer quite truthfully, Eugenia, as he seems coward enough to keep his face hidden from me."

At the sound of his reassuring words, Eugenia sprang from the chaise eagerly. The disks of her blue eyes were suffused with sudden tears. "It is you I wish to leave," she cried to Clay.

With a sardonic laugh the man sat down on his rump and spun around. "Well, well, well," Cyrus chuckled. "Home but a few hours and already a pain in the butt."

Clay stared. That it might be Cyrus had not crossed his mind. Because he was so shocked, he said nothing.

Cyrus rose slowly; his face a mask of superiority, he indicated the door for Clay with an inclination of his head. "Your exit, uncle dear. I am not aware of how such matters are handled in the old colonies, but the lady made it most obvious during dinner that she sought my favors. Being a lady, she naturally had to demur and protest. That being over, we can now proceed to the next step and without the presence of a third party."

Again Clay did not speak. He bit his lips impatiently, and scowled. His own experience with Eugenia made him wonder if he was not indeed playing the fool as her cavalier. As if he had spoken, she trembled, gazed at him with sudden pleading.

Then Cyrus, unable to contain himself, burst out savagely:

"You will not ruin this for me, as you have ruined everything else. I was the one that grandfather thought was best suited to fill the needs of Mr. Packer. *It was to be my job*!" He involuntarily uttered a shrill cry. "You stole it from me, you bastard!"

"Silence!" said Clay with stern disgust, and his voice was like a whip. "You defame your own grandmother by trying to insult me."

"Defame?" he chortled. "What has the woman done to me but benefit you? You who were tutored, while I was not! You who were sent to England for an education, while I was overlooked as a stumblebum? You are obtuse! The woman does not have sons and grandchildren! The woman has but a single pet that she made sure would be brought home to reap the Packer position. Her grey-eyed pet, in a family of all blue eyes."

"What have my eyes to do with all of this?" Clay asked with the strangest and mutest of expressions on his face.

"You don't know?" said Cyrus with low bitterness and hatred. "No, I can see that you don't know and your egotism would never allow such a thought to enter your head. But then, you always were an irresponsible and weak child. You were pampered just enough so that you never saw that grandmother was a most horrible woman, a really terrible woman, a tyrant dominating and terrorizing her husband, her sons, their wives and children. Deep in you, you must know why you were loved by her alone, and kept an ocean length away from us all these years. So you see, my name-calling is not in error."

Clay took a step towards him, as if shaken to his very depths, and regarded Cyrus darkly. "I thought you were a man, Cyrus. I will not now utter the bitter and disdainful thing you really are." Like a shot, he reached out and grabbed Cyrus by the lapels, easily lifting him off his feet and with a single motion spun him about and heaved him out the open door.

He turned back, as if shaken to his very depths, and regarded Eugenia with concern.

"Are you all right?"

"He's such an impossible little prig," she sniffed, affronted.

"Then why in the world invite him back?"

She shrugged, as though it were a minor manner. Three steps took her to the desk, where she bookmarked the page she had been reading. All her movements were measured and calm.

"This library is my private haven," she purred. "You might see the light on until the wee hours of the morning—if you ever care to check on me. Good night, Clayton."

She melted out the door and was gone.

He stood for a moment, silent and confused. No thank you or explanation! He put out the lamps and closed the door. In the corridor he was overcome by a mortal fear. Cyrus had all but openly called him illegitimate. A preposterous lie, he knew, but enough of a devastating suggestion to make him wonder why Cyrus would raise the issue. Nor did Eugenia comment on it either way. This he put down to her greater concern over Cyrus' indecent behavior. Then he wondered how great was her concern. The woman certainly was a hard one to figure out.

Now he did need fresh air to clear his head. If this job was to have gone to Cyrus, why hadn't Mr. Packer mentioned the fact? And was it possible that his message had come from his mother and not his father? Harvel Packer had not made it sound that way.

His mind was so absorbed that he did not see the carriage until he was directly upon it. The coachman had his turtle head out of the greatcoat and his whip in hand. A dark suspicion began forming in Clay's mind when he saw Cyrus peeking out of a carriage curtain, but he had no desire for further confrontation with his nephew.

He turned back, but too late. The coachman flew down from his perch like an avenging Jove. The whip cracked out, delivering stinging blows. Clay's head snapped as the tip end circled to open a gash on his cheek.

He pivoted back on his left foot, leaned forward to give the whip only an aim at his cloaked back, then put all his weight behind a charge at the man. His great fists pumped out, he warded off the snapping whip and attempted to capture it. The man was twice his girth, and when Clay was close enough, his hammer blows seemed to bounce off the man.

Then the coachman did an odd thing. He captured Clay's arms and pulled him close.

"Struggle with me, lad," he whispered. "I'm only doing this under orders."

"Then unhand me so I can go after the order-giver."

"Please, lad," the man begged. "I'm the best whip in Chicago and am ordered to leave you dead."

Then, to Clay's astonishment, the man pushed him away and hooked upward a fist that would have taken his head off, but it landed on his chin like a feather. Clay took his cue and crumpled like a suddenly emptied sack of flour. The man cracked the whip down onto the ground around Clay several times, then made a dash for the carriage. Wildly, without comment to the passenger, he careened the vehicle away from the siding.

Clay lay still until he no longer heard wheels on gravel. His astonishment was a strange mixture. What devilish sort of man was Cyrus to order his cold-blooded murder?

Slowly he rose and entered the railway car. The night held no answers to his myriad questions, but he was determined that the next day would reveal all.

Chapter 4

Outside the train window, a dirty, cold drizzle was falling. The pre-dawn had been slate-gray and ugly, and the gusts that had blown through the stockyards bitter cold.

In his parlor car, P.D. Armour, as he had asked Clayton to call him, sat sprawled in a fireside seat with his big frame loose-muscled and relaxed, his face a studious mask.

"What did you gain from this morning's venture, Clayton?"

Clay hesitated, warming himself at the fire. He had gained quite a different impression of Philip Danforth Armour, that was for sure. The drab costume and dull brown hair of the day before now seemed like so much stage make-believe. This was a handsomely attired young man, powerfully built and reddish-headed with the yard dust washed out of hair and beard, who had used the fewest words possible to educate Clay on his personal history.

Had Eugenia purposely misled Clay about the man? He was an extremely happy married man, who talked of his Milwaukee home and two-year-old son with almost womanly tenderness. The parlor car was a joint venture between himself and two brothers, and the wife of the Chicago grain dealer, Joseph, had furnished it. It mystified Clay.

"I gained a very strange picture, sir," he said at last. "Why did only one man bid on the available cattle and you seem uninterested in the hogs?"

Armour grinned. "Glad you noticed. Clay, between Milwaukee and Chicago there are forty-five packers. Prior to the war, the best price was determined by who was up first in the morning and out to the farms. We would wallop each other with a smile because we only needed a few animals a day on the hoof. To feed vast armies with smoked and salted meat meant larger numbers for the daily slaughter. The farmers became grasping and the prices soared. The present system came about without conspiracy intended. The first man offers a low price, which puts the next man in a position of not being interested and so on down the line. Tomorrow will be another packer's turn to start the low bidding and the rest to remain uninterested. As for the hogs, I saw most of them come off the *Lady Bristol* yesterday. All they had was squeal. I cannot make a cent off a squeal. That is a fact you can take to the bank and not get money on. Now to the point. I've hired you for the next two weeks."

Clay stared at him, his jaw dropping.

"You've hired me? But I haven't even started for Mr. Packer."

"The two will go hand in hand. We shall be dealing with many of the same men he wishes you to learn about. What do you know about the price of pork a barrel?"

"Nothing?"

Armour sat there, gazing at Clay's frowning face and then out the car window. His voice was that of an Eton lecturer.

"John Plankinton is my partner in Milwaukee. We have both been bulls on the Union and Grant. Pork is forty dollars a barrel now, but with peace it is going to break. What would your English merchantmen do in such a case?"

Clay chuckled. "First you must realize they possess icewater for blood. They would sell short without a thought of being the blackguard or scoundrel. But then, they are not ethical like you."

"Ethical people are unpredictable," Armour growled.

"Granted. But unethical people rely upon more than hunches in the world of English trade."

Armour grinned. "Clayton, I am going on more than my avowed belief in the divine management of the world. If the bull market is on the side of the expanding will of God, and the loss and destruction of a bear slide favored by the Devil, then I would always be for the former. I'm not for selling short as a general thing, but there are times, and this is one of them. Have you heard of a Mr. Jay Gould?"

"Mr. Packer mentioned him, and he is on my list."

Armour grunted. The jabbing sound may have held all the contempt in the world, but it was not without admiration.

"I am not a thief, but I borrowed one of his best plans from the war—the use of the telegraph and a band of agents to keep me informed of the daily progress of the war. This allowed Plankinton and Armour to save vast shipping charges by getting pork barrels to the army by the most direct route and, on occasion, holding up a shipment when it appeared it might fall into the hands of the enemy. I should have been running the army. The telegraph has told me from the first that while the South was winning battles, it was losing campaigns. Gettysburg was more than a Union victory. It was the beginning of the end. Now, unless I have been lied to more than General Lee, Grant and the Union are going to win very soon."

Clay puzzled. "Do you not have an eastern business outlet to handle this for you by telegraph?"

"I would sooner oversee the deal in person—with your help."

"I hardly see my usefulness."

"When properly attired, you will still reek of Hammershell & Barnes. I fully anticipate that Wallace and Wicks will wish to remain bullish. That I have an English agent in tow will set their teeth grinding. Now, I took the liberty of spending last evening with Marshall Field securing a few articles of clothing that Miss Eugenia and Morrison wish you to try on."

"You were bloody damned sure of me, weren't you?" Clay growled.

"Of course. Eugenia was still up when I returned last evening and gave me a rather detailed account of your evening—even to the reason behind that nasty gash on your cheek. You were the gentleman, Clay, although at times Eugenia goes a little off the perfect lady. But that is a personal matter for you to handle. I do not believe in luck. You did not steal the job away from Cyrus or gain it by luck. Harvel studied you like a new business venture. Your ambition and pride showed through your work in

India. Personally, I do not trust Cyrus. The man who cheats the other fellow is a thief, but the man who cheats himself is a fool. Cyrus is both. He is the perfect amphisbaena—a creature with a head at each end of its body and each facing in a different direction."

Clay felt nearly the same, pulled in two directions, as the private train sped eastward. A compartment in the Armour car was converted into a working office for him. Every ledger of every Packer enterprise passed over his table, although he had little personal communication with the man, except at meal time. Then it was Eugenia who reigned supreme; alive and glowing, almost a little unreal in her charm, she avoided any mention of the scene with Clay and Cyrus.

His mind became so ensnared with facts and figures that when she did mention the episode in private, it seemed to have happened a thousand years before.

"There's a very good reason for what you saw," she said, during a fueling stop, when Armour and her father had gone to the depot telegraph office. "I have wanted to tell you from the start, but sensed you were too bull-headed to believe me."

"Bull-headed? About what? You and Cyrus? It doesn't concern me."

"But it does concern you, Clay—it does! Carter told me Cyrus was spoiling for a fight when he came to escort me to dinner that night. We went to my library and had a long chat on it before cocktails. Carter couldn't let that happen."

"Then he should have forewarned me."

"He feels like a stranger toward you," she said, letting her eyes fill with somber lights. "The poor dear fears Cyrus. It was Cyrus who ruined his near-marriage. I have proof; Cyrus admitted it to me himself! That is why Carter thought I could get some truths out of Cyrus!"

She had his attention now. He looked at her, his eyes widening in a strange emotion.

"Is bedding with him the only way to gain his truth?" he muttered thickly and averted his face.

Eugenia gave a little laugh. "He never would have gotten that far. I am very knowledgeable on when to put a proper stop to a full advance."

"The manner of his kissing that I saw in silhouette leaves that statement in great doubt," he snapped, coloring over the fact that he had dared even reveal the truth of his knowledge.

Her laughter grew to delighted mirth. "You saw! How perfectly delicious. I thought you had come to my rescue only on hearing me scream. Of course, you could not have known that Morrison was primed to do the same."

"Morrison!" Clay got out, the name strangling in his throat. Again he was filled with rage at the woman and the games that she played.

"Naturally! He would do anything to protect Father."

"And what in the bloody hell has your father to do with it?"

She came to stand behind him, a quiet hurt in her face. "This plan has been in the works for nearly two years, Clay, between Marti and Father. I am supposed to know little, but actually know a lot. If Cy tries to ruin you, it would ruin all of Father's plans."

"You mean with that hogwash about my birth? It's a despicable lie!"

"It doesn't matter," she whispered, putting her hands on his shoulders and leaning her cheek against him. "It doesn't matter that your father pushed more for Cy than you, until Father made him see the light."

Suddenly, convulsively, he came straight out of the chair and broke her grip.

"It matters to me!" he said hoarsely. "Everybody seems to know something on this score but me!"

"That's right. But the majority of everybody does not form their opinions from rumors." She hesitated a moment, then laughed. "I have decided, though, to make a friend of you. Most men take a single look at me and reveal their huge appetites and uncontrollable lusts. You are different, like Philip. Neither of you fall at my feet or attempt a bedding. I think I should hate you both for it, but it's rather an amusing challenge. Do you think you could love me, Clay? Tell me, do you?"

"Yes," he muttered. And in an oddly curious way he knew he could love her beauty with total happiness and yet would always feel at a disadvantage because of her advanced notions of love and marriage.

"Good," she chuckled, "and that starts the friendship on a truthful note, on your part. My part, you already know. Handsome as you are, I don't desire you as lover or husband. Oh, we are moving again. Better not let the slave drivers know we have been wasting their time on personal matters."

Personal matters? Her words infuriated him anew, but she sailed away before he could remonstrate. Her idea of friendship seemed very odd. Was this the way of all American women? His new-found friendship with P.D. Armour was not the same. Was it because they were both men? Or was it because he found in Philip Armour a straight-talking man who refused to mince words?

"Waste is criminal!"

Clay knew he would live to a hundred before the sharp retort or the following action were burned from his brain. After that first morning visit to the stock yard, he had left half a sausage link on his plate. Armour had snatched it up, made the comment, popped it in his mouth and chewed vigorously.

That had also been their last "sun-up" breakfast.

Thereafter Morrison would arouse Clay at five o'clock in the morning, and by the time the engineer and fireman's light were shining in the caboose about six o'clock, or a little later, Clay and P.D. were having some of the Armour products laid before them for breakfast in the dining car.

"Why must we sit the siding and sleep at night," Clay had asked, "when the freight trains seem to go right through?"

"Why indeed?"

That day an extra crew was taken on board down the line and the train rolled on through the night. The expense of an extra crew was less expensive than the wasted time of Philip Danforth Armour. The siding time waiting for the return of telegraphic messages was not wasted time. That was incoming intelligence to bolster his hunches.

The breakfasts became the crowning hour of Clay's day. Vast ledgers were giving him a "figure image" of Philip Armour. Verbally, he was able to piece together the genius of the man just nine years his senior. Mentally, he calculated the Milwaukee pork figures until he was convinced that Armour would have been a fantastic success even without the Civil War. But some of his shrewd war contracts made Sir Damion Hammershell look the novice at sixty-eight. Philip had more than a dream; dynastic as a Tudor, he would bring sons into the world for the training for their royal responsibilities to the House of Armour.

"My family is different," Clay said. "A cow, at least, reproduces itself before it is slaughtered. A felled forest leaves a swath of wasteland that takes Mother Nature a century to replenish."

"The waste, the waste!" Philip sighed. "Oh, I speak not of trees. I know little on the subject. Clay, I am called the greatest swine-slayer of the war, but never yet have I stuck a pig, gleefully slit the throat of a sheep, or laughingly stunned a frightened steer with a hammer blow. I am a merchant and not a worker over the lifeless carcass upon the blood-soaked killing floor. But that still haunts me. I loathe waste and it costs me five dollars a load for men to cart the heads, feet, tankage and offal material out upon the prairie and bury it in pits and trenches. That is really the greater part of the hog and cow."

"The cow is sacred in India," Clay mused. "We were allowed only to bring in lamb."

"But the dead cow. What becomes of it?"

"Without being eaten," Clay laughed, "it's every part is turned into some form of sacred item. The Eastern world wastes very little, because they have so little to waste to begin with."

"Nor do we, if we really knew it."

Clay could see a sudden excitement in Armour's face, but he did not guess its cause. Morrison came to announce that they were arriving in Pittsburgh. P.D. bent forward over the table and looked at Clay as though he were the genius.

"On this subject we shall talk again, but now to the first name on your list."

* * *

Harvel Packer breathed deeply. Unashamed, he gloated over his triumph. At forty, Jay Cooke was one of the leading counselors of the war government. The patriot-banker, rising from obscurity, had gone against the old cliques of the financial world and with new techniques had come literally to hold the national purse-strings. For him to board the train secretly at Pittsburgh, for the trip to Philadelphia, was a mark of his unquenchable belief in men like Packer.

Tall, handsome, with clear, ruddy complexion and keen blue eyes, he seemed comfortably at home in the "palace" car. He bent forward to accept Eugenia's hand, with the clear intent on his face that he wanted her to think that she was the most beautiful woman in the world.

It was the first time Clay was introduced as an "associate." To his utter surprise, Jay Cooke looked at him with wide-eyed admiration.

"You must be one smart young man, Clayton Monroe! This old goat plays things so tightly that his right hand never communicates with the left."

"That's why my fingers have become stiff," Harvel chuckled.

Over a glass of sherry, Packer continued to chuckle and keep the banter light and away from business and the war. It seemed to suit Jay Cooke's mood. His hands constantly moving, as though drawing the blue-prints in mid-air, he went into raptures over the million-dollar palace "Ogontz" he aimed to build outside of Philadelphia after the war. To hear him talk, it would be a dwelling such as the New World had never seen before.

His enthusiastic rambling gave Clay a goodly time to study the man. Talk of a million-dollar private home might have astounded him, had he not been already astounded in his study of Packer's "bond" ledger. Harvel Packer had not only been a large and steady purchaser of war bonds from Jay Cooke & Company; he was one of Cooke's 2,500 sub-agent "minutemen" in the selling of the bonds. Even at a commission of .5 percent, Clay could quickly calculate, Cooke's earnings stood at over three million dollars a year, because he was most aware of Packer's earnings on his ten-million-dollar bond investment and sub-agent earnings.

After lunch Clay was to learn that Packer's bonds were but a drip in a very large barrel.

"My firm alone raised nearly three billions in four years to support the army at the front."

"And largely on greenbacks," Harvel mused.

The thought of it made Cooke laugh—and then sober up. "Every time the old bankers sold the dollar short, to the strains of Dixie, they did so to raise the gold premium. Judge Mellon sits in his Pittsburgh bank and gloats that it is over 150 percent, while refusing his son speculation money for wheat. Well, his gold is in for a shock."

"Not a plunge," Armour demanded, who had remained quiet and studious.

"Gentlemen," Cooke said expansively, "Secretary Chase dreams of replacing Old Abe after the war. His national banking legislation puts the government in the position of complete redemption of all its depreciated obligations in solid gold. Except for a few of us with large financial reserves, who holds our bonds? Ministers as well as laymen, women as well as men. Except for the women, all voters. His aspirations to the Presidency will not allow him to renege on the bond redemption and anger that many voters."

"Still a plunge," Armour repeated. "It will be almost like a run on the bank at war's end."

Clay sat away from the three men and studied them with his grave eyes. He knew that Armour anticipated a plunge in pork if he sold short, so why not see it could mean a plunge in everything?

"Bound to happen," Cooke said, as though it mattered little, "and my main reason for being here. Our nimble friend Gould has also busied himself since the opening day of the war with buying gold and selling the dollar. But what has he been buying with his gold in the electric marketplace? Ah! He may think himself tight-lipped, secretive and alert, but I also have a small, if immodest, voice in the stock exchanges."

Harvel Packer hid a smile behind his hand. Immodest was the last word he would use for the strong guiding hand Jay Cooke had in the stock exchange, in the press and over government contractors.

''Notwithstanding,'' he went on, ''while we have kept our eyes glued to the war, he has used his brokerage house to buy up little railroads, banded them together to look like a prosperous line, and then forced them onto the railway giants for a trade in shares. I propose that we borrow his infallible recipe and improve upon it. That is what makes one chef great and another mundane. They all, you must agree, have only the same basic ingredients to start with.''

''Jay, Jay,'' Harvel laughed, ''you are forgetting one important ingredient in scope. Jay Gould not only has his own money, the brokerage backing of Smith, Gould and Martin, but the aid of his father-in-law, a man of some means. Ready money they can float about willy-nilly. Look at the three of us. Our means are diversified and large chunks are in stocks and bonds. We can't hope to see a single payment on the war bonds until Chase sets a date for payment after the war. Our few millions are paltry next to his resources that can be decupled, centupled, multipled at will.''

''Sir,'' Clay said timidly, ''might I venture a question at this juncture?''

''But of course, my boy.''

''My mind goes back to your railway ledger, sir. Please forgive me if I have to bring myself up to date, but I have only figures to give me an historical view. You possess stock in the various lines that were consolidated into the Northwestern and . . .'' A crusty raised eyebrow made him skip over the fact that Packer also held two hundred of the thousand-dollar shares of the still-to-be-completed Union Pacific. ''. . . and my point, sir, is that it is still pulling itself out of the cash shortage panic of 1857, because of the slow payment and non-payment on their government contracts. Are other American roads in a like position?''

Jay Cooke beamed at him. ''An excellent question, Clayton. Some of the larger carriers are back on their feet.'' He laughed. ''A better pun would be that they are back on their tracks, but the majority are still in the slough and a lot near eclipse. Your question, I take it, has a reason behind it?''

"Perhaps," Clay murmured, which brought a scowl from Harvel Packer. Clay cleared his throat, knowing that, as an "associate," he was expected to be more positive. Only "assistants" remained as quiet as Nubian slaves.

"It would seem to me," he went on, a little firmer, "that the war bonds are of more value now, while at their premium market par, than at a future date when the war's end is bound to make them return to a one-hundred percent level or less. Would not a railroad, taking them in exchange for shares, be able to borrow forty to sixty percent against their market value?"

"And still not get hurt if the market dropped," Cooke cried in glee. "I like the way your new boy thinks, Harvel! Watch it or I'll steal him away."

"Humph! I want him thinking soundly on my investments and not on wild speculation. I have yet to see my first penny back from any of Will Ogden's railway schemes."

"But it will come," Cooke grinned. "I have $200,000 riding on the Union Pacific and $200,000 with Collis Huntington for the Central Pacific. It will be another five to ten years before they start paying off, but they will."

Packer looked impatiently at his fob-watch. "Time for my nap," he snapped with crusty indifference. "Fill his young head with your pining for greater projects and new empires to seize. My mind is suddenly bottomless."

Clay was aghast. The moment he had voiced his opinion, he was sorry. The title did not make him any different than he had been in India—a servant who shared his brain with the boss in private and let the greater man look brilliant in public. And what good would it do for Jay Cooke to fill his head with anything. He could only listen and not act upon it.

Philip Armour leaned close to whisper before rising. "Pick his brain, Clay. That's what the old man really wants."

Chapter 5

After Philadelphia, Clay paced the train from end to end. And though Jay Cooke was gone, he seemed to be everywhere about him and his voice echoed constantly in Clay's brain. Abruptly, during their conversation, in a blinding flash of clairvoyance, he knew the tack Cooke wanted him to take with Packer and Armour. They were to be the "stalking horses" while the "shark" was apparently sleeping. Drew, Vanderbilt, Fisk and Gould would never suspect these "western merchants" of being financially clever. They were names on his list that were beginning to take intelligible form without his meeting them. Would they be anything like Jay Cooke? Few men in life had ever impressed him. Cooke had affected him quite strangely.

An apprentice doesn't aspire; he perspires. He had never really thought of his own furtive future. He had been a cog that ground Hammershell & Barnes to greater glory. British to the nth degree. Jay Cooke was his first real encounter with American business ambition. This he did not consider a blasphemy against Harvel Packer or Philip Armour. The former was too in line with his parents and the latter an individual genius in his own realm. He realized suddenly, with a misery he had never known before, that he wanted to be "as rich as Jay Cooke." It seemed far-fetched, as he had less than two dollars in the pocket of a borrowed suit.

The next afternoon, with a twenty-dollar advance in his pocket, he left the St. Nicholas Hotel on Broadway, looking like an English nobleman. Without warning, Morrison had stripped his room of all clothing that morning and come back with a battery of tailors. His original clothing had been sent ahead by freight for measurements and Eugenia had wired her fabric selections. He waited impatiently while his large body was expertly repinned and the needles flew.

Eugenia came to select the proper hat, cravat and walking cane. She looked on wonderingly as he used it as a mere extension of himself. Clay was much better at play-acting the role than they had imagined, for he had twelve years of stuffy example to follow.

What baffled Eugenia, what she could not fathom, was the sudden terror that beat about her heart. This was not the Clayton Monroe that she knew. The clothing had transformed him into someone close to her ideal male. That was wrong, she knew, wrong, wrong, wrong . . .

"I feel like a fop," Clay groaned. "This is crazy, P.D., and you know it."

"Did you look at this buggy?" Philip said, ignoring him in his awe. "Do you know that this Goddard buggy is built by the Studebaker Brothers of South Bend, Indiana? Have you ever seen such beauty and such excellent fast trotters? Next door, Clay. South Bend is just next door to Chicago and we have to come to New York to learn of this excellent vehicle. That's my point. Everything must come east to make it worthwhile before we see it in the West. Bah! I want one of these for myself and for each of my brothers. Now, are we set in our script or shall we have another rehearsal? Pull this off, Clay, and I will pay you a commission rather than a salary." It was not humanity that moved Philip Armour, but hardheaded business sense.

Clay nodded that he was ready. If he pulled off this coup, they could not doubt the silent plan he had been formulating on the Cooke affair.

The Wallace and Wicks offices were a kind of *deja vu* for Clayton—a gritty, skylighted cavern, lined with the high desks of bookkeepers, used-up men who would never rise higher than the stools upon which they sat.

"Gentlemen!" Armour roared, and brought no visible reaction. Ghostlike, the senior accountant rose and wordlessly went to announce their arrival at an inner chamber door. Just as noiselessly he waved them forward to a second door.

Wallace and Wicks shared an office and twin desks like Tweedledee and Tweedledum. Each short and chubby, they sat at the entrance with piggish alertness and shared contempt for any intrusion.

"Gentlemen!" shouted Armour again, recalling that each claimed to be hard of hearing. "You seem not to recognize me, although your man didn't request my name."

"We're aware," Wallace sniffed.

"Quite," Wicks echoed the sniff.

'Then let's not waste time, except on business," Armour said in a toneless voice. "I have come in person to tell you that all the mess pork that Plankinton and Armour carries on your books as a commodity item is for sale."

"Well, well," said Wallace, smiling grimly, "the bull market will snap it up at forty dollars a current barrel."

"Snap it up," repeated Wicks, smiling faintly.

"Sell it short," Armour said quietly.

"We don't make jokes here," Mr. Wallace said in a sarcastic tone. "We are busy men."

"And it is a terrible thing you suggest," Mr. Wicks wheezed. "We expect it to rise by twenty dollars in the next month."

"And my British agent here says it will fall."

"To a low of five dollars," Clay said, in a suetty British voice, carefully balancing his cane against the desk and crossing his elegantly tailored legs as he took an unoffered seat.

"Impossible!" said Mr. Wallace, trying to smile pleasantly, but only succeeding in looking at Clay as though the Devil had suddenly entered his office.

"This is not our way of doing business," Mr. Wicks said, his face purple with wrath. "It is immoral and hardly respectable."

Clay threw himself back in his chair and gave both men a look that never failed to intimidate. "Gentlemen, I believe you represent a certain Simon Stevens, who used your offices to get Mr. Morgan to advance money options on five thousand British Hall carbines. Carbines owned by the government at $17,486 because they were defective, and yet a day later sold right back to the government for $109,912 without ever leaving their original warehouse. A

Wallace and Wicks warehouse? Immoral and yet . . . respectable?"

Mr. Wallace coughed roughly. "Hardly a matter for the British to concern themselves with. But on the other hand, Mr. Armour, your idea is against the judgment of the best men in New York. In fact, in the last few days a pool has been formed to bull the strong market in pork, to hold on for better prices than forty dollars a barrel. Sir, wouldn't you be best served by joining that pool?"

"I have a partner and do not know his wishes at this far distance."

"But wouldn't you like to meet some of the men in the pool," Wicks put in smoothly, "and then report back to Mr. Plankinton. One James Fisk, Jr., is having a gentleman's evening at the Louvre this very evening. Our good offices could get you an invitation in no time."

Armour hesitated, because it was his policy never to refuse to listen. Then he looked down and saw the impatient tapping of Clay's highly polished boot.

"Of course," he said, "I am in town with guests. Mr. Clayton Monroe and Mr. Harvel Packer."

"Ah, yes," said Mr. Wicks softly, scribbling their names onto a note pad, "they shall be included." Clayton Monroe meant nothing more to him than the overdressed snob at his desk, but the name of Harvel Packer satisfied his "loose money" ego. He was a gentleman of far greater means than this brash small-town trader from Milwaukee.

A "gentleman's evening" had suggested something quite different to Clay. He was hardly prepared for the elaborate, costly and refined concert salon.

The Louvre was vast, covering the greater part of a city block on Broadway. Several parties were already in progress in spacious rooms, but none as yet hosted by Jim Fisk.

A maitre d' hotel guided the trio to the grand drinking hall with its great, ornate, mirrored bar and sparkling fountain. Several hundred in the hall seemed but a few under the massive glittering crystal chandeliers. Tall marble columns gave it the feeling of a palace, with walls paneled in gold and emerald and frescoed with baskets of luscious fruits and bouquets of vivid flowers.

The hostesses were the prettiest in the city, and even though the evening was quite young, gilded youths were already vying for their after-hours favors.

Among the older set, Harvel Packer was hailed from several quarters, which he acknowledged with stiff little nods of his head. Once seated, he expected the gentlemen to approach his table and not bellow halfway across the hall. For just such a moment he ordered champagne and extra glasses. Clay still did not like its taste and Armour's glass remained empty. Tobacco and liquor he never touched, and he was only in attendance at such an establishment because it was for business.

At the next table two evening-suited young swains were boisterous in their unabashed bidding over their hostess.

"How can they be so brazen," Clay gasped, "with so many ladies about to hear?"

Armour purposely ignored him and Harvel Packer roared with mirth. The Louvre was not new to him. In fact, it was one of his favorite "sights" in visiting New York.

"Clayton," he chuckled, "this place is especially celebrated as the habitual resort of New York's most expensive, fashionable and beautiful *demimondaines*. What you possess in your pocket would not even buy a quarter-hour of their time."

Clay was astounded and could hardly believe it. The bevy of ladies were elaborately gowned and begemmed, fluttering their fans and conversing in bright twitters with elegant middle-aged gentlemen in expensive evening attire.

A hostess brought Philip a note and stood politely waiting for a reply.

"Fisk is in the billiard room. We are asked to join him there or wait until his lounge has been prepared. It seems that Wallace and Wicks have declined for the evening."

Packer shrugged. "Best that I wait for the lounge meeting and not look a part of your hog deal. Ah! There is Daniel Drew leaving the billiard room. I'll wave him over for a glass while you two see to Mr. Fisk. Young woman, please invite Mr. Drew to my table. The gentlemen will take their own reply back."

They did not need to reply; they were greeted heartily the moment they stepped into the spacious room. Clay stayed back, awaiting an introduction and viewing the second name on his list.

The man was big and florid, with blond hair, curling mustache and strange attire. The flamboyant tail coat was bright cherry red, toned down to a degree by a pearl-gray ruffled shirt and trousers. But two Jim Fisk trademarks took away the toning down. He may have had a love for vests, but his choice that evening of a burnt-orange velvet was shocking. Few, however, took real note of his clothing, so spellbound were they by the fat hands covered by rings of several gems.

"I was under the impression a pool was being formed," Armour said, wishing to get right to the point so that he could depart the salon.

"Why get into a debate with many gentlemen, when Fisk & Belden can talk for all?"

Armour smiled to himself. The almost unknown brokerage firm had a reputation of executing secretly large market orders for Drew and Gould without the knowledge of rival speculators. "Do you also speak for certain Cincinnati gentlemen, Mr. Fisk?"

"You aren't, by chance, Mr. Armour, making game of me?" he asked, in his booming and disdainful voice. He rolled the billard cue in his hands as though it could become a weapon. "Let us be frank, Mr. Armour. You are not the only packer in America."

"Nor did I make that claim, sir. I speak only of my mess pork assigned to Wallace and Wicks."

With a hearty laugh Fisk concealed a native shrewdness. He had not deluded himself with false evidence. The eastern packers were decreasing because the livestock available to them had to be shipped in from the Midwest and West. He didn't have any Cincinnati packers in the pool, not yet. He mentally thanked Mr. Armour for the excellent suggestion.

"Mr. Armour, sir, you would best be serving your country by joining this pool. Especially with rascals and thieves from other countries trying to get your pork for less."

Clay ignored the personal gibe, but the hypocrisy of the statement nearly made him laugh. Fisk, he had learned from Cooke, had run contraband cotton for a Boston firm, had sold army blankets at prodigious prices, and engaged in a thousand other projects that served Jim Fisk and not the country.

"Mr. Monroe is an associate of Harvel Packer."

Clay couldn't quite understand Armour's sudden change in direction. Fisk, too, looked puzzled.

"So," Armour went on, "I have no desire for your pool. Wallace and Wicks will be so informed. Goodnight, sir. Clayton, will you inform Harvel that I have returned to the hotel to retire."

"A moment, please," said Fisk, his voice falling to a low whisper. "The pool already has a large portion of your paper to hold for better than forty dollars a barrel. I think we would like to take another lot of that mess pork."

"I'll sell you one thousand barrels, if you want it."

Fisk tried not to change expression, but his wide nostrils dilated and his glacial blue eyes widened. He felt as though he were back at his shell game in the traveling menagerie and had a rube in tow.

"When pork is sixty dollars a barrel, you will want to get the one thousand back," Fisk chuckled.

"I will deliver you that pork when I can get it at eighteen dollars a barrel," Armour retorted and waved Clay to follow his departure.

They avoided the main drinking hall and went to the cloak room in the foyer.

"I want to be at Wallace and Wicks first thing in the morning, Clay, but you stay with Harvel. Jim Fisk tipped his hand, and so did I about you. I am not a gambling man, but I'll bet that Fisk has no other pool than Drew and Gould. His request for one thousand more barrels means he wants more than that. I wanted him free to pump you for information and you are to give it freely. Of course, it won't hurt you to learn some more about the Erie Railroad for us."

What Clay did not learn at once, he learned in pieces. It became too much to hold within his head, so he developed a portfolio on not only his listed names, but the "old turks'' as well. He began to haunt the newspaper ''morgues'' and back issues. If a Commodore Vanderbilt was in a pitched stock battle with a Daniel Drew over the New York Central, he wanted to know the origin of the feud. He also wanted to know the fine print. If the old Dutchman could raise five million dollars in a single morning from a ''pool'' of associates—who were these well-heeled associates?

Personal meetings were showing him only masks. Harvel Packer liked Daniel Drew. Clay found him elaborately imperialistic and sly about his dealings with Fisk and Gould.

That Vanderbilt and Drew could be friends and rivals at the same time did not surprise him. Vanderbilt and Packer were near the same, although the seventy-one-year-old tycoon treated Harvel like a snot-nosed boy, whereas Clay was treated as a near equal because he would give his undivided attention to playing a rubber of whist.

Harvel fumed over this wasted folly, but it gave Clay a measure of the man few understood. He kept the whist tally sheet in his head and never cheated. Slyly Clay learned that this captain of industry also kept his books in his head and was never known to lose a day's interest on the smallest sums. The card game showed Clay that the man was prudent as well as bold. Here was not the thought of retirement, but a determination for newer and bigger projects. Clay studied him like a beetle under glass.

His studies began to upset Harvel Packer.

''What am I paying you for?'' cried Packer indignantly. ''We have been here for over a month and what have you really accomplished?''

''I don't think you are being fair!'' It was the first time Clay had talked back to the man. ''My first obligation was to be a foil for Mr. Armour. That is now a sit-and-wait proposition. Because of my whist playing you were able to get Hudson River Railroad stock at twenty-five dollars and it closed yesterday at one-hundred-fifty.''

Packer drew a deep and audible breath. ''But none of that helps Chicago.''

''Sir, I don't think you are seeing the future clearly. What is this fight between them but a manipulation of small railroad stocks to gain control of roads running all the way to Chicago? Why do you think Jay Cooke is concerned about Mr. Carnegie doing the same out of Pittsburgh? Couple enough lines together to join the industrial heartland with the East and you can levy such tariffs as you please. Use your bonds now, he advises. He also is awaiting your answer on the Titusville oil proposal."

"Too many problems in that infant industry, Clayton. Twenty dollars a barrel to ten cents and back up to fourteen dollars."

"And back again to four dollars yesterday."

"Have you not answered Jay Cooke's question?"

"Not fully." Clay hesitated. "Of late, Miss Eugenia has been accepting more and more invitations from John Washington Steele."

"What has that to do with it and who the hell is he?"

"Steele was an orphan adopted by one Mrs. Sarah McClintock who died last year. She owned a two hundred acre farm strategically located on Oil Creek, whose wells have been paying more than two thousand daily in royalties."

"A handsome sum, to be sure, but it still leaves my questions hanging."

"Eugenia will call this treachery, of course, but his actions about town caused me to do a bit of discreet investigation on your part. I'm sure you're aware of whom I speak if I mention the name Coal-Oil Johnny."

Packer lifted his head. His countenance was one of dismay and disgust. "That fool of a playboy? That idiot who tours the street in that outlandishly huge carriage with an oil derrick and flowing well emblazoned on the doors? *Good God*, he is far too young for Eugenia!"

"Just turned twenty-one, plus he has a timid little wife *back* in Oil Creek."

Packer thrust an extravagantly shaking hand in Clay's direction. "Get Eugenia in here—at once! I will put a stop to this folly!"

"First, hear me out in full, sir," Clay said quietly. "I do have a plan, of which it would be best not to inform Eugenia at the moment. Briefly: the man came here with something over $300,000 in gold and currency. He has signed various disastrous business documents under the influence of brandy and champagne, among which was the purchase of a minstrel show and the Continental Hotel."

Packer controlled himself. He forced himself to lean back in his hard chair to hear what Clay had in mind, but his interest was piqued. "Where have you gained all this information?"

"Chance statements dropped by Jim Fisk in a ribald fashion at the billiard table or on occasions when I've run into him in Wall Street. He, of course, just happened to be the agent to sell the man the nearly broke minstrel show and the questionable Continental Hotel. A check of the city records showed that one of the former owners was William Marcy Tweed. A check of the newspaper gossip columns gave me all of the man's personal background. One need only stand in the lobby of this hotel nightly to see his carriage fetch Eugenia. Then, a wire to Philadelphia brought me the last bit of evidence I needed from Jay Cooke. The vultures are beginning to circle over his head. Mrs. McClintock's brothers-in-law have been able to get a court order to tie up the royalty payments in Cooke's bank and agents of the Internal Revenue are demanding the unpaid ten percent wartime income tax. In short, the princely fortune is gone."

Packer began to tap his desk with his white and slender fingers as he regarded Clay intently. "Their court order will also tie up the two hundred acres, will it not?"

"To be sure." Clay smiled an enigmatic smile. "Until the woman's death he worked as a teamster for an oil-rig company in Pithole. They were on a shoestring and paid him in stock. When he became the first oil-rich playboy, he gallantly bought up all their stock and let the company go idle. I personally believe he has forgotten this asset."

"But how can you get close enough to him to find out and not let Fisk grab it?"

"I hope through Eugenia, but without her finding out. A placard was put up at the Continental Hotel this morning. I saw it coming back from the newspapers: 'Open House Today. Everything Free. All Are Welcome.' I shall just happen to be one of the 'all,' and just happen to run into

Eugenia for an introduction. From there I shall just have to out-Fisk Fisk."

"I don't like involving Eugenia in such a business matter."

"Why is this any different than you seating her next to Pierpont Morgan at dinner to engage him in conversation about his lucrative deals in banking?"

After a moment's lofty and severe delay, Packer avoided the comparison. "How much?"

"I'm not sure exactly, but I think cash will talk louder than bank bonds or promises. 'Free today' suggests to me that he holds no hope for tomorrow. Perhaps you would care to handle the matter yourself."

"No," he snapped, almost too quickly, "I have other plans for the evening." He opened a desk drawer and pulled out his private strong box. "I am not prone to invest too heavily in this affair, Clayton. Ten thousand dollars shall be my limit."

Clay nearly laughed. During their stay Harvel Packer had lavished over six thousand dollars on the Louvre ladies-of-the-night and more than likely another one was part of his plans for the evening. In a weak moment he had even offered to purchase one for Clayton, quickly withdrawing the offer when he saw Clayton's revulsion at the two-hundred-dollar price.

Clay cared not what his mentor did with his money. He had even come to find the Louvre women highly intelligent and attractive, but not for bedding. That was still an area he could not bring himself to accept. But none of that now mattered. He was elated that Harvel Packer would be so occupied for the evening. This would be his opportunity alone, but he would have to handle it with great subtlety and restraint.

Chapter 6

Clay was appreciative of the spring weather that Saturday evening. The air was like cool wine. He breathed deeply, a bright delirium making him feverish, joyous, hopeful.

What an afternoon it had been—and what an evening he anticipated. He would walk to the Continental Hotel, if only for the sheer joy of walking. There was no hurry, for he was now expected. He could hardly believe the turn of events or his good fortune.

No sooner had he left Packer's suite than he had been sandwiched in the hall between Philip Armour and Eugenia. Armour was nearly swaggering and Eugenia in a mood of crushing gloom.

"Quickly, into my room," Armour gasped, "I have news."

But Eugenia, as always, felt her mission more important. "Please, Philip, you must come with me to see my father. A dear friend is in great need and you are able to talk father into anything."

Without another word she barged into the suite, towing the two men behind her. And without preamble barged into the plight of John Steele, before Harvel Packer could stop her.

Patiently he listened and nodded gravely, never once casting a glance at Clayton. With fatherly concern, he soothed her fears and announced that he would send Clayton along that evening to see the man, if she would set up an appointment. To Harvel's surprise, but not Clayton's, Eugenia burst into peals of laughter. Then she quickly sobered and agreed. Only Clay caught the devilish gleam that came to her eye, and he read it correctly. She assumed that he would be unfamiliar with Coal-Oil Johnny and the general debauchery that surrounded him. What a delight it would give her to see the puritan totally embarrassed.

Her torment over the man had grown with each passing day in New York. Among her set, Clayton was as much a topic of conversation as John Steele, but in opposite terms. Every woman she knew openly admired his dignity and his pride, and privately coveted him as a lover. They envied Eugenia always having him about. She tried to tell them that he was simply a servant, an object for her father to snap his fingers at, a being that never crossed her mind. But his youthful litheness, the innocently provocative way he would tease her over her teasing, his grace which roused her all too easily awakened carnality were all driving her mad. She would have liked having him as a toy, but the possibility of that was not great. And like every spoiled child who could not have a toy for their personal plaything, she'd just as soon break it as allow its pleasure to others.

But for the moment Philip Armour's news had taken away all thoughts about John Steele from Eugenia's mind.

One of Armour's agents had been able to get a coded message sent from Virginia before General Grant imposed a censorship blackout on the telegraphic wires. Grant had received a Confederate courier with a written message from Robert E. Lee.

Armour smelled victory and would not depart his room until further news reached him. But his elation was also due to having outsmarted Jay Gould. Gould's agent had not been able to wire a message before the blackout, and Armour had quickly run to Jim Fisk to sell him another thousand barrels of mess pork before the news leaked out.

The Continental Hotel gave Clay every reason to believe that the news was now general knowledge. The placard had been taken literally by every person Coal-Oil Johnny had ever met, from every parlor house, pleasure house and saloon in New York. His false friends were going to bilk him out of his last ounce of champagne and morsel of food.

Clay could hardly shoulder his big frame into the lobby. It was total disorganization and cutthroat competition. Even as Clay tried to enter, a man pushed his way out with a gilt-framed oil painting over his head. Clay was forced back into the street, just as a joyously screaming woman was being suspended from a third floor window by her ankles. Before he could fear for her, she was pulled in through a second floor window by the arms.

He knew now he would have to be as brash as those within. He plowed his way in, unmindful whether it be men or women he shoved out of his way. In the saloon doorway it was impossible to recognize any face among the packed mass, except for the girls dancing on the marble tabletops.

A waiter passed with an empty tray held high. Clay grabbed him by the arm and spun him back.

"Hey, bud," the man snarled, "can't you see I ain't got nuthin'?"

"I'm only looking for Mr. Steele," Clay shouted.

The man gave Clay a quick head-to-toe scan. "Private party on the fourth floor. A guard will have to clear you."

After the climb Clay wondered why there was need for a guard at the floor landing. The same manner of people seemed to pack the suite of rooms as had been below—and possibly even worse.

The carpets were soaked with spilled champagne; silk stockings hung like Christmas streamers from the chandeliers, and one woman stood stark naked at the marble fireplace chatting with two men as though she were fully clothed.

His name was shouted across the room, and Eugenia put out her arms to him. She came towards him, but just out of reach of his outstretched hands, she stopped.

"That was not the reaction I expected."

"When in Rome . . ." He let it dangle and looked at her. Yes, she was the one surprised, just as he had planned. He stepped forward, taking her, none too gently, into his arms.

Her surprise turned to disbelief and she tried to push hard against his chest. But Clay, forcing laughter from deep in his throat, was going to make her look the helpless captive.

When his laughter had captured an audience, he bent

down and found her mouth. It was hot and sweet with the taste of wine. With such an opportunity at hand, she relaxed in abject surrender.

The sound of Coal-Oil Johnny's drunken laugh was so soft that Clay had the impression at first that he had imagined it, but when he turned, the handsome playboy was there.

"Eugenia," he said sadly, "I expected your father's associate . . ."

Eugenia turned, staring at his reddened eyes.

"Yes," she whispered, "so did I. Forgive me, Johnny. But this is Clayton Monroe."

"You might have told me that you were powerfully attracted to one another," Johnny said gravely.

Eugenia turned again to Clay, her eyes wide with questioning.

Clay's smile was mocking.

"Private matters," he said softly, "should not be aired in public. Nor should business. My time is limited."

"Oh? I—" Eugenia whispered; then, very quietly, she motioned both men toward a closed door, as though she were the hostess of the affair. But once they had entered the bedroom, she altered her original plan and left them alone.

"Thank you," Johnny said, suddenly dropping the grave formality of his tone. "She has been a dear friend, but I hope you comprehend it has been no more than that. Every headstrong woman in town claims to have shared my bed. Frankly, my morning headaches don't let me know if such was the case or not. Besides, she is, sadly, a lady—the only lady among the trollops and the only true friend I have made in New York. Therefore—"

"Therefore," Clay said gruffly, "the first to ask for money. That's it, isn't it, Johnny?"

"That's it," Johnny said.

Clay stood there, looking at the dissipated man for a long minute. Suddenly, impulsively, because the answer was so quickly honest, he pulled the money packet from his inside breast pocket.

"Then let's get right to business," he said quietly. "We anticipated cash would be best."

Johnny hesitated, searching Clay's face. Then, quite suddenly, he was sure he was not dealing with a Jim Fisk. He viewed the size of the packet with relief.

"Thank you," he sighed, "but I must be honest. I cannot accept, it suddenly dawns on me. Perhaps you are finding me in a more sober moment than most. Such was not the case this afternoon . . ."

He paused, looking at Clay. "I leave you to shut me off if I bore you," he said. "This afternoon relatives of my wife arrived to beg me to sober up and come home. I played the real bastard and right in their face ordered more pickled oysters and champagne. I told them I was having too much fun in New York and sent them home, knowing you would be here with money tonight. With it this close at hand, I am ashamed to put out my hand to accept it. I cannot promise its repayment."

That's so, Clay full well knew, surprised at the man's honesty. "Nor did Mr. Packer plan on making it a gift. Have you ever considered putting up your Pithole stock?"

Johnny put his face in his hands. For a moment Clay thought he was crying, then he realized it was laughter. "Oh, Clayton Monroe, a scally-wag by the name of Colonel William D'Alton Mann printed that oil stock in carload quantities and sold it in the Pithole and Titusville saloons for twenty-five and fifty cents a share. When I had my windfall, I bought them back so that my old friends would not be stuck with them. I sit with one hundred thousand shares of worthless paper. It is two hundred acres that is not even farmable. Not even Mr. Harvel Packer would buy such a pig-in-a-poke." He laughed sadly. "The last offer I had was from a Mr. Rockefeller in Cleveland. I even turned him down at a penny a share. I put him on to Colonel Mann who still has a hundred thousand shares of stock in Ohio land."

No, Clay thought, I will take this gamble. Cooke had mentioned this John Davison Rockefeller in passing. Why would a Cleveland merchant show interest, unless it was worth his interest?

"One way or another," he said gently, "the money is to be yours. Worthless or not, show your good faith and sign it over. I have here ten thousand dollars."

"Do you advise me so?"

"I so advise."

"It is my only answer," Johnny said drily, going to a writing desk. "I don't rightly cotton to fools, but you advised me."

Clay stood there, watching him, while the bill-of-sale on the stock was written out. He knew he might end up being a fool, but this was his first venture alone and he had to gamble.

"Now, what the hell," Steele roared, handing Clay the paper and racing to the window. Outside, the world had erupted into clanging bells. Curiosity pulled Clay right to the window with him. Below, the street was filling rapidly with paddy wagons and uniformed policemen.

"My God!" Johnny screamed. "They are raiding this place! This is impossible! When Boss Tweed owned it, it was never raided. Fisk assured me it never would be raided!"

Clay was no longer listening. He tucked the bill-of-sale in his pocket and went in search of Eugenia. He suddenly felt an obligation to keep her from being hauled off to a precinct cell like a common whore.

The main room of the suite was a screaming bedlam. He found Eugenia staring out a window as though it were a wondrous sight below.

"Come on," he growled. "This had to be a planned thing, and I smell Fisk."

"Don't be a silly goose," she chirped, clinging to his arm possessively, "we don't have to budge an inch."

"They are bound to arrest everyone here."

"Fiddlesticks! They don't arrest ladies and gentlemen who haven't done anything."

"In a place like this, Eugenia, they don't ask questions. Right now you don't look any different to them than one of those whores."

"Well, bless my soul, Clayton Monroe, you almost made that sound like a compliment."

Coal-Oil Johnny was leading the charge to vacate the suite and settle matters with the police. Clay mirrored in his mind the man's bedroom and made a quick decision.

"Get in there," he barked, "and take your clothes off."

She smiled wickedly.

"And don't get any funny ideas! This may be the only way to save your hide."

"Clayton Monroe!" Eugenia said wrathfully. "Why must you always spoil things?"

Damn her, Clay thought, the minx is more of a hindrance than a help. Alone, he was sure that he could have eluded the police. Once inside, he locked and bolted the door, then studied the room as the police might view it. He thought it might work. Several food service trays still sat about and the chairs were piled high with various articles of men's and women's clothing. There was no fire in the fireplace, so the chamber had the right chill.

"Help me unbutton," she said.

His hands upon the buttons were clumsy and stiff. With the back of the dress released, she let the silk slide to the floor and stood in stockinged feet and a chemise of a gossamer fabric.

"Get into the four-poster."

"Turn your back, so I can do it properly."

When he looked again, she was propped up among the pillows, her hair unbound so that the giant curls spread down over each shoulder and the sheet that she'd demurely pulled up to her chin. There was ribald laughter in her eyes.

Goddamn, but she's pretty! he thought. Wonder why in the bloody hell I don't find her exciting?

"Now close your eyes."

"Blessed if I know what you are up to," she said, as he quickly undressed and crawled into his side of the bed.

"Simple. We are going to make it look as though you were not a paid-for lady-of-the-night."

"Clayton Monroe!" Eugenia said again, but there was much less wrath in her tone.

Within seconds they heard heavy feet pounding into the suite and then came a knocking on the door.

"Go away!" Clay called. "We said we didn't want to be disturbed."

"Open up in there!" a man with a heavy Irish brogue

shouted through the door. "Up ye'll be getting and open in the name of the law."

"Police?" Clay growled. "What in the bloody hell do you want?"

"Just be coming to see, laddie," the voice came back. "Just be coming to see."

Clay got up from the bed and took the coverlet to wrap around his nudity, but not before Eugenia got a fleeting glimpse of him in profile.

What a man, Eugenia thought, what a full-bodied man! How long have I dreamed of seeing him like this? Twelve years had certainly made quite a change. And now it was for naught but play-acting.

Clay purposely fumbled with the lock and bolt, as though frightened and unsure of what was transpiring. He cracked the door but an inch.

"Lord Bessie's bloomers, it is the bobbies." He flung the door wide. "I do say, officer, what is the bother?"

His heavy British accent took the Irish policeman by surprise. He looked within, taking in all in a single glance.

"Who might you now be?" he asked

"Clayton Monroe of Hammershell & Barnes, London. The missus and I are over on our honeymoon."

"How long here?"

"Four or five days. What day is it? I've lost all count."

"It be Saturday evening, eight of April, sir."

"Blimey," Clay gasped in amazement. "Then it is our sixth night here."

The food service trays helped attest to that possibility, but the policeman was still sorely puzzled.

"Did ye not hear all the party palaver going on?"

"Oh, right," Clay chuckled. "Isn't New York full of sparkling effervescence. Certainly is different from the crushing gloom of London in its bloody fog. Of course, you must realize that we were never invited to partake and had matters of our own that kept us apart."

The policeman suddenly grinned with a benevolent air and reached for the door handle to pull it to. "I'm recalling me own nuptial nights, lad. Didn't hear a thing either, I didn't. Well, I would be advising you to stay put the night again. We've had ourselves a bit of a ruckus here that shouldn't concern you. I'll be telling the other lads, so you'll not be disturbed again. Good luck and God bless."

With the door closed, Clay relocked and rebolted it. He went to the window just in time to see a bellowing Coal-Oil Johnny carted away.

"At least your friend is not going to come and demand his room back."

Eugenia was looking at him with wide-eyed admiration. "You were marvelous."

"Just pray that they don't check the hotel register. Best that we stay put until the street calms down."

"Aren't you cold?"

"A little." He crawled back into the bed, but kept the coverlet around him.

Warmth returned. Even through the coverlet he could feel the force of her body heat. It was comforting and maddening. He had never been this close to a naked female body before. He did not need her devilment to create a devilish thought of his own. Thoughts as never before crossed his brain filled it with a wild medley of desires. He lay stunned at what he was considering. He recalled her lips and knew that she would be willing for them to be used as a starting point. But was he capable of turning to her and starting the kiss?

"I'm tired," she murmured. "Can't we just dress and say that we are going out?"

"It might work if we could find the same policeman."

They left the subject dangling. Her desire to leave, Clay saw, had dampened his ardor. He was in full possession of himself again and relaxed to listen to the street noises. There was scant chance that it would have happened, he told himself. They didn't even live in the same world. She was a princess and he still a servant. She was champagne and he was small beer.

He was not aware of drifting off to sleep or for how long. The world was so quiet that he might still be sleeping. It still was like a dream. The coverlet had been unwrapped from his frame and never had he known such arousal. He raised himself up on an elbow.

There she lay, in the soft down of her pillow. She was on her back—her one arm outstretched and the other crossed on her forehead, her one leg flat on the bed and the other drawn up with her knee in the air.

He studied her as he did a column of figures—looking for an error. Everything was quite in order. The sheet molded her breasts as though a clothier had been at hand making a gown. The soft cotton sheet was tentpoled by her knee to give him a view of the rounded heel and shapely leg in contact with the creamy flesh of a buttock.

Even though he had suggested it, he was still amazed that she had divested herself of all underclothing and that it now revealed the feminine treasure of her lovely golden triangle.

Clay was frozen in fear and awe—fear of the direction in which his thoughts were traveling again and awe at her utter beauty. Asleep, she was not the "orphan" brat from his youth. He shivered at the enormous stimulus to his male juices.

A portion of his brain said it was time to shake her to gentle wakefulness and prepare for departure. He could not bring himself to do it. He turned and sat on his heels and gazed at the sublime beauty of her dimpled knee. Gently he folded back the sheet so that he could view both gleaming satin thighs and the full forest of curls which formed a cleft hill at the base of her flat belly. He had thought that all such small waists had to be helped along by stays of whalebone. Hers was delicately natural.

Again he hesitated in replacing the sheet, deeming this the only opportunity that might be afforded him to see her full beauty.

Now he did want to kiss her. On an unthinking impulse he leaned over and kissed the dimple of her raised knee. Like her lips, it was wondrously soft and warm, and invited him to trail his lips down the slanted thigh and be enchanted by the lingering essence of her unusual cologne.

He knew not what he was about; bachelor barracks talk never seemed to include him on discussions of this depth. A musky scent began to overpower the cologne and magnetically pulled his cheek to rest upon the feathery curls.

He had thought he had been ever so gentle, but she stirred and he sat back quickly for the wakening discovery.

"Ohhh," Eugenia moaned from her own dream world. "Your finger, Carter . . . only that . . ."

It sobered Clay quickly, and he stared at her as though she were again in pigtails. He stared at his engorgement with almost boyish awe, as he had once stared in awe at his brother's manhood.

Bloody bastard, Carter! . . . *He was still using his finger on her*!

At first it was like a new discovery. But hadn't the implication been there all along? Now the part that had always been a damnable affront to him came back! Carter forcing him to lie between her legs and her giggling over the fact that it did no more than tickle her. Just as that thought crossed his mind, Eugenia moaned again and spread her legs wide.

He didn't even think. He moved to kneel between her legs and, with no experience to guide him, entered almost timidly and gently. The hesitant thrusts were so cautiously implanted that it aroused Eugenia only momentarily.

She was still deep in sleep. The moonlight filtering through the lace curtains helped to retain the dreamlike quality of her mind. She felt the male member, but the movements were so slow and prolonged that it seemed hardly a sexual encounter at all. She looked up and saw the mass of curls, but felt no body weight. The man was supporting himself above her and allowing only the organs to mesh. It, too, added to the dream. Every man she had known had been a raging brute, nearly crushing the life out of her lungs with their animal rutting. And, as in every wonderful dream, she wanted to clear away the cobwebs and see the man's face.

Clay's never-used dormant passions rose and burst quickly.

Shaking, he pulled away, tugged the sheet over her body and stepped to the floor. He was rather unsteady on his feet for a moment, then came the crushing guilt. His head swam and he felt as though he were going to be sick. He took two giant leaps to a chair and quickly began to get dressed. The clothing felt like it was being put upon the most unclean skin in the world. He was so ashamed and mortified.

Barker Manville had come back into the barracks singing the praises of love. He did not feel the same. This had not been love, but only a moment of carnal lust. He felt so disgusted with himself.

"Eugenia," he called. "I think it is time for us to leave."

Her eyes opened and, after fluttering a bit, remained open. She sat up, without trying to keep the sheet about her chin. With a yawning stretch, she flung her legs off the bed and rose. He quickly turned away and she let her eyes rove up his back to the curly locks. She nearly giggled upon realizing it had not been a dream.

Silently she dressed, and they did not speak until they had gone through the vacant lobby and were upon the empty street. Here she noticed that it had not been moonlight through the lace curtains, but only lamplight that was now being extinguished. The sky was pearling gray with dawn. There was no hack around and they had to walk back to Broadway and the St. Nicholas.

Before entering, she stopped him short.

"For your sake, for both our sakes, it might be best to let Father know little of the evening—especially what you did before I awoke."

There was devilish triumph in her eyes as she noted his utter reaction. His face burst into flaming, heated color.

"But . . . if you were asleep . . ."

"Don't be naive, Clay," she said with a strange smile on her face. "A woman knows, awake or asleep."

She was taking it in such a calm manner that he regained his poise.

"Well, awake or asleep, it shall never happen again."

"Oh, but it shall," she corrected him automatically and sternly. "I have just decided."

"Oh, Eugenia! You don't know how guilty I feel. It can never happen again."

She grinned slyly, as if thinking of some secret thing, then looked directly at him with cold, hard eyes.

"Never is a long time and one gets over his guilt."

From far off, then growing closer, church bells began to peal.

"Perhaps that is where you should go," she said mockingly.

"It would cave in on my head," he groaned. "Please, talk of anything else but my sin."

She said nothing, but she sensed the struggle in him. There was a challenge now in the pit of her stomach, and her palms were moist with excitement. It was ridiculous of her to let him suffer with such guilt, and still she couldn't help it. She wanted him again, could have taken him that very moment, but she wanted his guilt over their sexual encounter to keep him away from every other woman. As they'd walked back to the hotel, the course of their relationship had come to her. She had been looking for the well-molded man and he was not to be found. But Clay had all the right ingredients for her to do her own molding. Oh yes, she would have Clay again—as a husband and under her rules.

Fire and police bells now joined the deep-throated church bells and a man came racing up Broadway.

"It's over! It's over! It just came through on the wire that Grant and Lee will meet today to sign the peace terms. We've won! We've finally beat the Secesh government!"

New York became one big party. Boss Tweed didn't even bother to check with the mayor and ordered the saloons opened, even if it was Sunday.

"Let the church folk praise the Lord in their manner and my working folk in theirs—with a pint in their hand!"

"What do you want to do about the people from the Continental, Boss?"

"Set them free! Jimmy Fisk already has the hotel back in my name and sent Steele packing toward Pennsylvania. But let those lovely ladies and boisterous gentlemen know that they are free out of the kindness of William Marcy Tweed's heart—and not to forget that fact when next they go to vote."

In certain St. Nicholas suites the celebration was subdued. Philip Armour rotated between chewing his nails and sending bellboys racing off to bring him back the latest wire news coming in.

The bedroom doors of the Packer suite did not open throughout the day or evening. It was Eugenia's habit to sleep through a dull Sunday after any Saturday night. Harvel slept because New York was finally catching up with him. Among the *demimondaines*, he had won many new friends, but cultivated none in the art of real happiness. Even if the war had not been over, he knew he could not crawl into another female bed if his life depended on it.

Clay was delighted and relieved over the closed bedroom doors. He now felt the double fool. Not only had he acted rashly in getting the stock letter from Steele, but in the haste of the transaction, Coal-Oil Johnny had made the transfer out in the name of Clayton Monroe. To fully answer that mix-up was bound to raise the question of why he was standing outside the St. Nicholas hotel with the man's daughter as Harvel clattered home in a liveried carriage. At the time no question had been raised, because Packer was too tired to think. But the steel-trap mind of Harvel Packer would get back to it sooner or later. Clay prayed that it would be much, much later.

Toward evening Armour burst into his room, his grin a gleam of triumph.

"All day nothing but people patting each other on the back," he chuckled, "and finally some meat and potatoes. Old Abe has promised a quick return of the boys—a million strong. Edwin Stanton was not about to let him have the last word and released a list of those state militia regiments that could start traveling back home today."

"The railroads will be swamped."

Despite himself, Armour could not keep from laughing.

"Swamped with what? For once I prize the parsimonious nature of Stanton and his War Department. All war contracts, with a back order date of thirty days or more, are hereby null and void. That, dear friend, includes the majority of our mess pork. I will be the first in the market tomorrow to listen to the wailing, but before that, some business between us. Clay, I stand to gain between $500,000 and $1,500,000 by selling short. Here. I know it is not the final figure, but you know me to be an honest man."

Clay took the money packet and, for an odd little moment, felt as guilty as the night before.

"I . . ." He gasped for the right words. "I have done nothing really to earn this."

"Nonsense. You have been the perfect shill to keep them from seeing me move the peas around. They laugh at us and even take our war bonds, as you suggested. They have millions, Clay, but it is gilt-edged paper. When we begin to pinch at their testicles, we will only accept hard cash or secured stock. Before the week is out, the 'robber barons' are going to question what new highwaymen have ridden through their Sherwood Forest."

For reasons that Clay could never explain, even to himself, he did not count the money packet until the next morning. Then he did another impulsive thing, one that he feared he would always regret. He took ten thousand dollars from that packet and transferred it to Harvel Packer's empty packet. Then, before he could change his mind, he rushed across the hall to the suite.

He had been prepared to be berated at once, but one look at the man stilled that fear.

"To market, to market, to kill a fat pig?" Harvel's face was sunken and blotched from his almost constant drunken and lascivious life-style. Clay had not been aware, but he had lost nearly thirty pounds. The grand and ruffled collar was far too large.

"I will not be with you on this day of glory," Harvel said pathetically. "You will be on your own, with Philip. However, there is a problem that has come up which we both must face."

Clay stood rigid, waiting for his terrible actions against Eugenia to be voiced anew. Once, twice, he took deep breaths. Then he focused a murderous gaze on the newspaper headline before Harvel on the desk.

MORAL CRACKDOWN! MORE RAIDS PROMISED!

200 ARRESTED AT CONTINENTAL HOTEL!

"Eugenia has told me all!" Packer growled.

"I have no reason to lie about the event," Clay stammered. "Even if it ruins my future."

"Future?" he roared. "To hell with your future. I am more concerned with the manner in which you saved my daughter's future and my embarrassment. Thank God, you, a gentleman, were there to act in a rash manner. From her story, the playboy would have thrown her to the wolves with the rest of his play friends. I hope you protected my money in a like manner?"

Without wanting to comment, Clay laid the money packet on the desk. Packer clutched it to his breast, like a miser protecting his last worldly possession.

Clay spun and left the suite. His non-comment made him feel more guilty than having exposed the truth. After a moment he realized that Eugenia had told her father the truth—if perhaps not all of it. Oddly, that increased his guilt. He had saved her from being arrested as a whore and then had used her like one. He had saved Packer's money from a questionable stock deal, but only at his own loss. He had never possessed ten thousand dollars before in his life, and might never again. The five thousand left in the packet he didn't feel rightfully his until Armour was sure of the market trend.

He began to curse his return from India, where life was on a very rigid schedule.

He cursed his schedule even more in the next few days. Everywhere was a business panic of a different sort.

Throughout that Monday morning the provision commodities, including pork, began to slide. When it dropped to eighteen dollars, the figure Armour had mentioned to Fisk, Jay Gould moved to counter it with gold. He forced Pierpont Morgan and Edward Ketchum to reveal that they had shipped away to London $1,150,000 in gold two years before to cover such a drop. Pork shot up to sixty-eight dollars and gold to $285.

Tuesday morning Armour thought himself a ruined man and Clay worse than ruined. It would take him a lifetime to repay the ten thousand dollars. But $285 was not a figure the Gold Room in New York could afford to handle, so they took a "holiday" to celebrate the war ending. By noon gold was back at 171 and pork at forty.

Then Wall Street was rocked by a leaked report from a close associate of Pierpont Morgan. The shifty young Edward Ketchum had deeply involved the company at the higher gold figures. During the night he had absconded with money and securities from the bank, as well as large sums belonging to Morgan personally. The closing of the Gold Room was seen as part of the scheme and brokers began screaming for the erection of scaffolds to hang all the gold speculators.

Philip Armour and Clayton Monroe sat back and watched gold dip to a par with the dollar and pork sink to five dollars a barrel. For the majority it was a "Black Tuesday." Their market symbols told Philip that the majority of Fisk's Cincinnati packers would have been wiped out at anything less than eighteen dollars. The grain merchants who supplied the feed were now looking at penny-a-bushel wheat, rye and corn.

Jay Gould, dark and brooding, came to sit with them.

"You may stop pinching, Mr. Armour of Milwaukee. It is hurting bad enough."

"I am not out to ruin the whole system, Mr. Gould, and never dreamed of this deep a drop. No matter this price, I leave for Milwaukee in the morning and will cover all my short contracts at a stable eighteen dollars a barrel."

"And if it goes back above that, sir?"

Armour eyed him coldly. "What is your opinion, sir?"

"It shall not," he sighed, "but your act shall cause me to sing your praises in the highest of financial circles. These poor fools. But then, it should be stated that he who sells what isn't his'n must buy it back or go to pris'n." He sighed. "Why do I call them poor fools? This will make grass grow up and smother the railway tracks across the land."

"I don't see why," Clay spoke up. "The soldiers still need transportation home and people must still eat."

"Clayton," he laughed, "why don't you stick with playing whist with the Commodore? He is the only one left with enough gold to keep his railroads out of the red."

"The government has gold," he said slowly, "and many have war bonds backed by that gold."

"Come, come, Clayton, they are near worthless until Stanton declares a redemption date."

"As a money broker what would you lend against them?"

"It depends," he shrugged.

"In playing whist with the Commodore," Clay said, as

though starting a new conversation, "I have learned much about his battle with Mr. Drew. Also—" and he let the word hang in the air—"your own railroad interests. The minor Ohio lines were very helpful to the Pennsylvania during the war, were they not?"

"No one knows of that," Gould started to protest.

"But I seem to, and I am only an associate. To me it seems as if war bonds would be remarkable trade items for stock, on a day such as this. By tomorrow morning they could well represent a fifteen to eighteen percent cash flow."

"Clayton," he chuckled, growing tight-lipped, "I harbor the knowledge of knowing the worth of most men in America. I trust you are speaking on the behalf of Harvel Packer. His war bonds, even at fifteen percent, would garner me less than a quarter million. The accounts payable on building the little Albany & Susquehanna line would eat that up in a day."

Clay shivered, more from excitement than fear. He had feared a ten thousand dollar transaction for Harvel Packer, but compared to what he was about to say, that seemed mere child's play.

"I was speaking more in the range of forty million in war bonds."

He had said it so calmly that he had amazed even himself. Armour looked totally stunned and Gould turned ashen.

"From where?" he croaked.

"That you will find out if we can consummate a deal without Mr. Fisk. And on top I want five thousand dollars in Albany & Susquehanna shares for myself."

Philip Armour began to smile. Clay was learning fast—'always get something for yourself in the deal'—and it was obvious that he was a man who could keep a secret and had gained the confidence of Jay Cooke.

"We deal," Gould said.

Armour started to ask a question, but Clay cut in quickly.

"We deal, but across the board. Face value of the bonds, with gold backing, as against issued stocks. There will be no 'watering' or we need not go any further."

Reluctantly Gould agreed. He had to. After he left, Philip Armour was still a bit puzzled.

"Now I learn from you, Clayton. What was that last bit all about?"

"An old Hammershell & Barnes trick, P.D. Quietly they would acquire a small trading firm, for say a quarter of a million. Against those assets, with splendid imagination, they would print and issue two million in shares. At the same time they would lease back the smaller firm to the parent organization, making the buyer think they were acquiring H & B capital stock."

"And you think that is their game?"

"You learn a lot playing whist," he said calmly. "One night the game went into morning. The Commodore refused to end the game and kept his business associates waiting in the foyer—including Jerome Plummer, who seemed quite determined to let Vanderbilt know that part of a large reserve supply would be offered that day. A large reserve supply of what I did not know, until the Commodore got clever. Furious that he was being disturbed, he scrawled a note on the unused tally sheet and had the butler deliver it to Plummer. He had pressed so hard, that between rubbers I could still make out the impression. 'Buy E.' The only 'E' I could think of was Erie."

"I'm glad you are on my side," Armour chuckled. "What a day! You stand to make quite a commission on this deal."

Clay held his silence. He did not expect to reap a single penny from Jay Cooke and only salary from Harvel Packer. If he was some day to be as rich as Jay Cooke, he wanted the man as his friend and in his debt.

An approaching cyclone kept him from having to discuss the issue further.

"You bastard!" Cyrus screeched, rushing up to them. "You utter incompetent bastard!"

"Hello, Cyrus," Clay said coolly. "Philip, I believe you know my nephew, Cyrus Monroe. He is working here in New York for Mr. Jerome Plummer."

"Perhaps not for long—thanks to you two. *He* went heavily into mess pork, on my advice," he groaned.

"Bad advice," Clay smiled quietly. "You should have stuck to your field—transportation."

Cyrus was trembling all over as though he had the ague.

"It was my field. I wasn't just shipping lumber and immigrants in and out of Milwaukee and Chicago. Right, Mr. Armour? Tell this bastard that Monroe and Sons also made your barrels for you."

"A company run by your brother Ivan," Armour said indifferently.

"Nine hundred thousands barrels!" Cyrus screeched. "That's what I based my knowledge upon. Then you sell short! You might have given me some warning, you ungrateful bastards!"

Slowly Clay shook his head, a grim smile lighting his eyes. "It has been common knowledge for over a month. Smart people stayed away from them."

Cyrus's voice again rose to frenzied shriek.

"Are you calling me dumb?" he cried. "From Vanderbilt we were going to get twice as much."

"Really," Clay grinned. "I was led to believe that he had no interest whatsoever in mess pork."

"That's all you know! I dine there almost nightly! He was very interested."

"How is your whist game, Cyrus?"

"What in the hell are you talking about?" declared Cyrus. "I have no use for silly games."

"Just like you have no use for fighting your own fights," he said quietly. "The next time you think up a lie, Cyrus, check your facts first. You see, I have been spending three and four nights a week at 10 Washington Place."

"I don't give a damn where you have been spending your time! What is that to me?"

"You don't recognize the address?"

"Hell no!"

"Strange that you don't recognize the address of where you dine nightly. Come, P.D. I hate to stand and watch someone eat crow!"

Philip Armour locked his arm in Clay's. His head went back slowly. Then the laughter came out in peal after peal.

Rage mounted up and beat about Cyrus's ears. He was not used to being made the laughingstock. Then, slowly, his anger subsided. Wasn't he the freight wizard? From the Chicago terminal Armour would have to ship on the Michigan Southern, or by ship to Buffalo and thence on the New York Central. Both routes were owned by Vanderbilt, with Jerome Plummer on the board of directors. He could still save face by recommending a sharp rise in freight tariff on mess pork. He would just see who had the last laugh.

Chapter 7

A Monroe family meeting—a Monroe family business meeting—had been called. But this was not a regular holiday assemblage. Nor was it called because the youngest son was home. Clay felt it had been called in spite of him or even to spite him.

Barrett Monroe presided, but no one paid the slightest attention to him. If in the old days he'd run his family with a growl, they now seemed to run him with heat and hate and contention.

Clay, sitting off to one side like an outsider, thought, each one wants his slice of the pie to be the most important.

Except for his mother and father, he hardly knew these people. They were rude, arrogant, spiteful.

Then, he had to remind himself, he hardly knew his parents.

Upon his arrival at the Milwaukee house, his father had been the first out to greet him—a painfully thin man with iron-gray hair and something of Jonathan's sensitivity of line about his face. He was stooped, and his hands trembled. What had happened to the giant? What was there to fear in this man? He had tears in his eyes at seeing his son. There was something else in the eyes that did give Clay fear. Death peered out of Barrett Monroe's tired eyes.

Then he heard the music of his mother's voice and put out his big hands.

He captured in his arms only a hundred pounds of skin, bone and pure white hair. Under the mass of wrinkles was still a hint of the beauty which had been, but here, too, were very tired eyes.

He hated Cyrus for making him look at their eyes again,

but it was true—watery blue and soft brown. Hardly a combination to make gray.

Afterwards, he was glad they had a few hours to sit together before the gathering of the clan. He could feel the slow warmth of love it brought, curling down to the tips of his toes. They wanted to know everything his letters had not covered in the twelve years. They were genuinely interested. His mother absorbed it like a sponge and kept looking at him as though studying an unusual problem.

"Bear," she said at last, "what position will you create for this child?"

The lumberman considered the question.

"Well," he said, "I thought we had him placed with Harv, Mother."

"That was my doing," she said honestly, "with your final blessing. His place is now here. I demand it."

Clay's big head jerked upright. He had never heard his mother demand before.

"Demand? Final blessing? My doing? I am no longer a child of twelve. Have I no voice in my own destiny?"

"The family knows best for you," Marti said curtly.

Clay looked at his father, his gray eyes hard.

"But do I know what is best for the family?"

"I hear you were most successful in New York. Of course, Cyrus would have us believe differently. You two never did get along, did you? Too close to the same age."

"We are straying," she snapped, anger mottling her cheeks. "We will have this settled before the others arrive."

"I ask nothing from the family, Mother," Clay said calmly, "though I thank you for the opportunity with Mr. Packer and Mr. Armour."

His father leaned forward, something close to understanding in his eyes. To Clay's surprise, his mother stood up and spat, very deliberately, upon the floor.

"I sent you away once before because you were insolent," she cried, "and I can do it again." Then she walked from the room as though Clay had done her great hurt.

Barrett got up at once, the veins in his forehead beating visibly. He motioned for Clay to come and take his arm. Clay slipped his hand under his father's arm and they went through the house together to the kitchen and out to the back garden.

"Your mother worries, Clayton. She makes herself sick worrying up one problem after another that don't need to be. In the old days, when we didn't have much money, she worried less."

"I don't recall those days."

"Long before you were born, Clayton. We lived in a tent until Hershel was born. It was more important for me to cut timber for the homes of others than for my own."

"Chicago was the only home I remember."

"I hated that house," Barrett said quietly. "There was never any 'welcome home' there."

"Is that why you visited so seldom?"

Barrett turned and appraised his son carefully. "I'm surprised you remember that. It was unfortunate that your mother and I did not see eye to eye for many years. The older boys knew, being mainly with me, but you were not of an age of understanding."

"Was there a reason for a problem between you?"

"With us the word should be plural," Barrett laughed. "When you have been married for twenty-two years, as we had been when you were born, you shall understand. Marriage is like a good axe. If you don't keep it well sharpened and balanced, it can give you all manner of fits. Ah, here we are. A bit of a surprise for you."

They had walked through the garden to the house next door. Where the Monroe house was stark simplicity, this three-storied structure, by comparison, was overdone with gothic lines and intricate gingerbread.

"Who lives here?"

Barrett laughed—a dry and crackling sound. "You never change. Always wanting to know what the surprise is before it is sprung on you. That's why your mother called you insolent. She doesn't take into account that your insolence came from her spoiling and your overly probing mind. Who? What? Why? I think those must have been the first three words you ever spoke."

"Is that why I was sent away to school?" he asked suddenly.

"I—I really see no reason to go into that old chestnut,

Clayton. We are all thankful that you were given the opportunity."

"Cyrus certainly isn't."

"Ah, Cyrus. I know he was resentful that you were packed off for England to study when he was supposed to have been included, although I didn't learn you had gone alone until my next return to Chicago. He insisted, at the time, that education was the last of his worries."

Clay's next question was stilled in his throat when the dark wood door came springing open with a single knock. A young woman in a sparkling white uniform greeted them.

"I saw you coming across the yard, Mr. Barrett," she said. "Himself was about to walk over for you, if you didn't come soon."

For no reason that Clay could see, his father roared with mirth. Something in the maid's voice made Clay take a closer look at her. It was, he realized, a very natural voice, but it bubbled with the joy of living. And, his scrutiny told him, she was quite natural and average. He first thought thin, but realized she was just small-boned with good lines and proper dimensions for her frame. He couldn't call her a redhead, it was almost the same burnt orange shade as the sprinkle of freckles on her turned up nose, which seemed to fight on the creamy complexion with the apple tint of her cheeks and the brilliant green of her eyes.

"And no need to tell me who this is," she chirped, waving them in, oblivious of Clay's gaze. "I can tell he is a Monroe by the size of him. Did you purposely set out to grow giants or did they just spring up like your trees?" Without a pause for an answer, she closed the door and marched to the sliding doors to the parlor. "Himself has ordered me to bring in a welcome home dram for the lot, but it will be only one dram, mind you. I'll not be having three drunken louts on my hands for the afternoon." Then she lowered her voice to a whisper. "And don't be letting him talk you into changing drams, or you'll be getting a bit of his medicine laced in."

Clay realized the meaning of his father's laughter at once. In the ornate parlor, before a blazing fire, even though spring was budding on the outside, sat a man in a high-backed wheelchair. Recognition was surprisingly instantaneous.

"Uncle Harry!" he exploded, running forward.

"Lord God!" Harry Hart Horner returned the bellow. "It did turn into a man!" He grasped Clay's hand and then pulled him down into a back-slapping bear hug. "Clayton! Clayton! Clayton! Stand and let me look at you again! My son, you didn't just grow handsome, you are almost ludicrously sublime!"

"Get on with you," the maid chirped, bringing from a side table a tray and three silver brandy cups. "Such words in this house are supposed to be reserved for me alone. Besides, H.H., look what you've done to the poor lad. Embarrassed him all the way to his root ends. Shame! And don't be making a face when you sip your dram. Medicated or no, I'll have it going down your gullet!"

"Bah! Don't mind the witch, Clayton! She's made my life a holy terror for the past three years. Fifty-seven years I did quite well without a woman in my life, except for those months I was obligated to support myself at my mother's teat, and now, at age sixty, I find myself browbeaten and wet-nursed at every turn."

"And loving every minute of it," she laughed gaily. "If I had been around when you were as young as this stallion, I might have made a proper man out of you."

"It is my legs which have gone bad on me," Horner tried to sound stern, "and no other bodily function above them. Keep that in mind, young lady, or your proud virginity might be vanquished."

"Mr. Horner!" she gasped in mock affront, and then pealed with laughter. "Not in front of a stranger!"

"Stranger? Barrett, you're a snobbish ass, as usual. I thought you would have done the honors at the door. Clayton, may I present the spirit who keeps me alive one moment and then tries to kill me off the next with her goddamn foul-tasting medicines. Miss Janellen Heubner."

"Nice to make your acquaintance, Miss Jane Ellen," he said.

She measured him with glinting green eyes.

"So that you never forget it," she said evenly, "it is simply Jan-ellen, Mr. Monroe."

"Most people have shortened mine to just Clay." He looked down at her and grinned. "Why don't we shorten yours to just Jan."

"Why don't you just sit and drink your dram like a good little boy."

She sailed away to a chair in the corner and took up her knitting bag.

Barrett cleared his throat, as though to warn Clay that young gentlemen of his station did not meddle with hired servant girls. It nearly made Clay laugh.

They settled into the usual welcome home chatter, with Clay looking over every few moments at Janellen. The moments between he was looking at Harry Hart Horner.

How proud, he thought, the tall, thin man sat the wheelchair, as though he would burst out of it at any moment. He reminded Clay of the London lions—haughty, with flowing white mane of hair, a chiseled granite face with lantern jaws and eyes as sparkling gray as quicksilver.

Because the tragedy of his legs was not mentioned, Clay avoided the subject, but greatly wondered. He recalled the man as a dynamo of energy—a self-taught architect who had always dreamed of building a whole city out of his own brain, rather than putting pieces of himself between the monsters of other men. Again, because it was not mentioned, Clay assumed the man was incapable of any more building.

It was almost two hours later that Barrett insisted that they had to leave. Horses had been clopping up to the house next door for the past twenty minutes.

Janellen had been ticking off their rhythms in her mind, but her thoughts moved in oblique tangents without any logical pattern.

He is certainly not like the rest of them, she thought. He's the gentleman of the clan. No wonder Harry Hart Horner called him his 'favorite' nephew, although the man was no blood kin to the Monroe children. Just an old family friend that Barrett Monroe had taken pity on after the building accident. Pity? She knew that was the wrong word. The man had ample resources to support himself and pay her a most decent wage, but Barrett and Marti Monroe had wanted the man to be in the vacant house next door to them. Why? she had asked herself many times in three years. Only when she wheeled him over for a family gathering did they see Mrs. Monroe, and those times boiled Janellen to a perfect steam. Granted, the man was an invalid, but did Marti Monroe always have to make such a big issue of it? Oh, how she detested the woman. Then she bit her tongue on the harsh thought. She could have held her harsher thoughts for the Monroe boys and their offspring. Not a one did she trust within an arm's reach of her, and especially Henri. It was not her fault that the forty-year-old man had married a shrew. What his own servant girl did for him did not mean he had the same license with her, even though he attempted it on every meeting.

But Clayton now, he was really a different sort of being. He was not only handsome, but big and healthy-looking—a man like H.H. must have been in his prime. And what joy he had brought to the patient. He had actually been controllable waiting for this visit. It certainly was going to be pleasant having him visit more often, especially for her—Lord save me, what gives you cause to think along these lines? Didn't you see the scowl Clayton got from his father? Even a leper would have gotten the message. And what would it have been like if it had been the barracuda next door hearing their prattle? She would have made a decent meal of a certain nursemaid, that's what she'd have done. For what it was worth, she was Milwaukee society, even though every German and Irish maid in town knew that the Monroes had lived apart for many years. She wondered how they now lived together. Although she never made it her business, on clear nights the arguments that filtered across the yard made the shanty settlement fights of her youth sound like a social gathering. Marriage, she thought bitterly, was God's worst creation for women. They got nothing but the short change. Doesn't He know that women can't afford to be short-changed? Well, being a man, she concluded, He probably does the same to Mrs. God.

After an hour he had to agree, if reluctantly, with Cyrus. His mother was a small, petty tyrant. How different things were through the eyes of a twelve year old and a twenty-four year old. It was now his father who seemed weak and loving and in need of protection. He saw with a sinking heart that the gray in his father's face was changing to white.

"Do you people really know what you want? You make Monroe & Sons sound like a half dozen companies."

"Which it is," drawled an unsentimental Hershel. "I get no better deal on barrel stays from Ivan than Jonathan gives to Ferguson & Fob in Chicago, and with freight added on. Henri, what about last month on your railroad ties and shoring planks for the copper mines? How did Bergstrom underbid you?"

Ivan, who ran the saw mills, now dropped all pretense of courtesy.

"You'd be all up shit creek without me, so get your facts straight, Hershel. Bergstrom's a smart Swede. He doesn't buy a board at a time, but in quantity."

Stubbornly facing the lot of them, Clay repeated words he had heard over and over again in New York, as though they presented a truth that made all argument useless.

"The South is a wasteland. Atlanta has been burned to the ground and hardly a plantation is left standing. It is going to need ready lumber to rebuild."

"Yes, Teacher," Hershel carped, "we are aware. You've been away so long you've forgotten we stayed for the whole war. Do you know what a depression means? It means that when Pissy Dandruff Armour sells off all his mess pork, there ain't going to be no more and that means no more barrels for me."

"All right, all right. But everyone knows, with the war over, they will really make a push on the western railroads."

"I don't know," Carter said slowly, speaking up for the first time. "The railroad men got nothing but a lot of paper. Even Harvel is in over his head, and you know that, Clay. Hell, everyone knows that Harvel Packer could be sold down the river tomorrow if his war bonds collapsed. Smartest thing Pa ever did was to take my advice and not buy any of that worthless Lincoln paper."

Marti Monroe cleared her throat, and it brought a deadly silence. "I'm sorry, Clayton, but you made your wishes known earlier on. We've got ourselves a family vote to take here and you seem prone to stay with Harvel Packer. Boys, what the vote says is family law. Time enough we cut our losses on this stupid scheme Cyrus got us into."

"I still think it has merit," Barrett said. "Like the hull of a ship, our hardwoods are right for making the carriers of that oil stuff."

"*Barrett*!" Bitterness twisted her mouth as she spoke her husband's name. "I find myself in the unenviable position of a wife trying to save a family's money, and I'm not about to throw good after bad."

Clay had three impressions tumbling over each other at the same time. He realized his father was too ill to control this mob any longer; he suddenly wondered what part Carter really had in the family business; and he was curious as to what manner of carriers they were discussing in connection with oil.

"I'm sorry, Mother," he said politely, "but you all seem to be talking in riddles. I don't mean to prolong your vote, but when you talk of oil, do you mean that Indian medication goop?"

"Exactly. It will never amount to anything, but back before the war great quantities were found back east—in Pennsylvania, I believe. Some foolish people thought it could be used to replace whale oil for lamps. You see how far that has gotten. Cyrus, because Jonathan couldn't figure out what to do with the pup, got together with one of those horrible Dole boys and came up with an old railway wagon they called a 'tank car.' Before I got wind of it, they had built ten of them and spent nearly eight thousand dollars. Just one more small reason why I pushed to get you home for Harvel and not saddle him with Cyrus."

Clay couldn't help but laugh. "And turn right around and try to force me back into the family business."

"Why else did we spend so much on your education? You proved your worth in less time than I thought. You owe, boy!"

Suddenly, she was no more than a Hammershell, Packer, Gould or Cooke sitting before him. "Perhaps," he said coolly, "I will repay that debt more effectively as an agent outside the family than within. What loss are you willing to take on their present plans, present rolling stock and any future plans a prospective buyer may wish to develop?"

"Lord a mercy," Hershel chuckled, "listen to all them big phrases out of Teacher's mouth, and I didn't understand a damn thing he said."

"I did!" Barrett Monroe spoke so quietly that they were all forced to turn to him. "Clayton, when it looked like a certain bust, Harrison Dole forced Cyrus to buy him out for three thousand dollars. Two young men who never should have been friends became enemies because of it, and caused us some shipping problems for a while. Understand?"

He nodded, and understood more than his father realized. So, he thought, that was part of Harrison Dole's questioning game: Who was Clayton Monroe and how did he fit into this scheme? He was growing more fascinated.

"Thereafter," Barrett went on, "their converted railway cars, which were to bring ten times their construction costs, sat moldering. Before we vote, what would be your recommendation?"

Clay gave his father a long, slow look. "You are out five thousand dollars, plus three to Dole, but are these inflated figures or actual cost to construct?"

"Inflated," Barrett said drily.

"Then, if someone paid five thousand, right now, you would be at a profit margin, less three in cash. Right?"

There was a deadly silence in the room. Most had accountants to do such heavy thinking.

Barrett nodded, hiding his grin.

"As you know I am an agent for Mr. Packer and others. I offer five thousand for the full purchase of the cars. Now you have something to put to a vote."

Even the voice of the most voracious was somewhat quieted and the vote was unanimous.

Clay had to get out of the house for a while. He felt guilty. It was business, but it was still family. But, he had to remind himself, they still thought in thousands, while he had been recently educated to think in millions.

But it was still thousands that worried him. He had just

put his last five thousand on the line and was broke again—the five thousand dollars extra Armour had given him when learning his profit would climb to two million. He associated with millionaires, but in a month he had squandered more than two men made in a lifetime on oil stock, railway stock and now rolling stock for the worthless oil.

If he was a fool, at least he was keeping quiet about his foolishness.

"Hello there, Clay."

He walked over to where perky Janellen sat on the Horner porch swing.

"You," he replied with a smile, "followed my order and called me Clay."

"I follow no man's law," she laughed. "I called you Clay because you remind me of clay."

He blanched. It was so like something Eugenia had said on the trip back from New York. He was clay that she wanted to mold into a loving thing.

He did not want to be molded. He still felt guilty over making love to her; it seemed so wicked. He had avoided her and had been horribly cruel to her. Nonetheless, she was everywhere on the train everytime that he moved. Finally, when she declared her hatred for him, he felt he had won.

"Not very flattering," he smirked, taking a seat on the step.

"Didn't God make man out of clay in his own image?"

"That's a little better," he said. "Was it you who were made out of one of my ribs?"

"Not unless you are Irish," Janellen laughed. Then she sobered abruptly.

"Clay," she asked, "why didn't you ask about his accident today?"

Clay frowned, looking up into her questioning face. He opened his mouth, then closed it again—grimly.

"Sorry I am," Janellen said. "Nurses shouldn't butt in, should they? But I am most aware of the long letter he received from Mr. Packer. He read it out to me—proud as punch he was of you."

"Then you know," Clay said, "and have every reason

to ask. Mr. Packer told me he had contacted an architect in Milwaukee, who would, in turn, contact me. I've feared it was Uncle Harry ever since."

"Why? Is he not still an architect?"

"He's crippled."

"Only from the waist down. Does that part of the body design a new home for a Chicago millionaire?"

"I don't know. It's a field I know nothing about. Is he capable?"

She rose and walked down the steps past him. "He calls me the spirit that keeps him alive with my jolly nature, quick laugh and joy of living. Do you know how hard that is to keep up day after day, month after month, and now year after year? He could roll himself to his drafting table, but there is nothing there for him to do. A great brain is dying and that is a horrible waste. Capable, you ask. Are a foreman and carpenters capable of building a structure without his designs?"

He rose and gazed down at her with wonder in his eyes.

"You're in love with him."

"Get on with you," she laughed. "It's no man I am loving. Respect and admire him, that is for sure. I was hoping you would feel the same toward him."

"Hasn't he done anything in the past three years? I recall him constantly building little models. One Christmas he made an entire little town under the Christmas tree. He was always building something or other for my father."

She looked away from him and back toward the Monroe house, as though she didn't want to comment on that statement.

"Do you know if Uncle Harry has discussed this with my father?"

She shook her head. "Why don't you?"

Instead of answering her, he followed a suddenly overwhelming impulse. Before she could move, he circled his arm around her small waist and drew her close. She opened her mouth to protest, but he quickly covered it, and his arms tightened. She worked her jaw closed, cold with anger that he was like every other Monroe.

Her instinct was to raise her hands to slap at his face, when suddenly she was aware of a vast difference. His lips upon hers were soft with tenderness and not cruelly demanding, as every stolen kiss had been before. Her unused womanhood inexplicably told her that he desired to kiss her, and no more. There would be no abrupt demanding for the rest of her body. A seed shell cracked and allowed a grain of mature growth to begin. Tenseness flowed away and she slackened against his giant frame. And just as impulsively as he'd kissed her, he stepped away.

"Sorry," he said. "I didn't mean to take advantage."

"I know," she whispered.

"Would you believe that you are only the second woman I have kissed in my life?"

"My first man," she laughed. "Though, mind you, others have tried."

"Will you be coming to Chicago with Uncle Harry?" he suddenly asked.

"How would he be getting along without me?"

He smiled a slow grin. "Well, good night. I'm sure I shall be seeing you tomorrow when I talk with him."

She watched him go back across the yard, her nerves singing a song she'd never heard before. She knew that it was not love, but the trembling excitement of having been desired in a full-blown and mature way elated her. Then a movement caught her eye and she looked at the Monroe's dining-room bay window. Marti Monroe had stood watching them, her mouth curling in a smile that was the cruelest Janellen had ever seen. The dropping of the lace curtain was as sharp and sudden as an exclamation point. Janellen could feel that the point was directed mainly at her and she could feel the tears start. Not good enough. She had spent twenty-one years of not being good enough. And for the life of her, she could not get the notion out of her head.

"So!" Marti said, stopping Clay in the middle of the foyer. "Is that all they taught you in England, to run after easy skirts?"

"My first time," Clay whispered, "but, perhaps, not the last."

"Over my dead body. For three years I have had nothing but trouble from that little snit. Every man in this family has panted after her like a pack in heat."

"Is that her fault or the manner of men you raised?"

"The point is, I will not allow you to be like them," she said icily.

Clay's head came up slowly, and his eyes, looking down at his mother, were clear with conviction.

"I am not like them to begin with," he said quietly.

She looked at him, startled. "Nonsense!"

"Then why does Cyrus call me a bastard, in the truest sense?"

"Bastard?" Marti was shocked.

"Yes: bastard. I look different; I act differently; I am treated differently. It does make one start to think."

"Then stop thinking! It's a wicked lie, Clayton. It will bring Cyrus nothing but shame and sorrow for having thought such a thing."

"I can't stop thinking about it," Clay said. "I've tried. Even today I looked at your eyes and father's eyes and my eyes. Mine are gray."

"Hush," she said sternly, "we'll not discuss this queer notion a moment longer. Your father is waiting to see you in his study. *Your* father, understand!"

Oddly unsatisfied, Clay spun down the hall. He stopped short, seeing his father standing in the study door with a strange look on his face. Then it changed, as the eyes went beyond Clay. Clay looked back. His mother was climbing the stairs and had her eyes firmly implanted on Barrett. Her face was filled with hate and dire warning.

"I should like very much," Barrett said suddenly, fiercely, "to be dead and out of this world!"

"Father! Don't say such a thing . . ."

But he had swung wildly back into his study.

Clay was surprised, when he quickly entered, to see that the man was crying.

"No, Clay," he whispered. "I'm sorry. It's true, though, sometimes. It has been a long life for me and I never get to see the forests anymore. They treat me like a very old, sick man. Well, I am old and sick, but hardly unthinking." He stood quite still, measuring Clay through his tears. "Sit down, my boy. There are many truths I suddenly wish to share with you.''

''No!'' came the warning wail from the hallway. ''I forbid it, Barrett! One word from you and I shall never speak to you again!''

''I should like that very much!'' Barrett bellowed back, going over and slamming closed the study door with a crash. ''It would return the sanity I had the last time—when you were silent for nearly twenty years.''

When he turned back, he was smiling oddly. ''A guilty mind can be a horrible thing, Clayton. Just mention the word truth and such a mind begins to fear that its worst secrets are going to be unmasked. She need not fear.'' He turned back to the closed door and raised his voice again. ''Did you hear? You need not fear, so go on to bed!''

''Her worst habit in life,'' he chuckled, coming back and taking a seat behind his study desk. ''The woman never thought a thing was a fact unless she heard it through the panel of a closed door. In the early days she could tell by the scratching of my ledger book pen the exact amount of money we had to the penny.''

Clay sat silent and stunned, not really knowing where this was all leading.

''Business! That's the first truth for you Clay. I loved the way you handled the louts today, and I say you are smart to stay away from them and the business. You notice I don't say *my* business, because it doesn't pride me anymore. Thirteen I was when I felled my first tree for profit, and every day thereafter I tried to improve upon that mark. Building, always building, for a dynasty of sons.''

''Which you did quite handsomely,'' Clay whispered.

''*Did*!'' he said testily. ''I reckon I did, but therein lies the greatest truth. They are not builders, Clay! They are little more than stagnatizers—if there be such a word—who are content to let it all start going back downhill.''

''But, Father,'' Clay said with gentle insistence, ''you are still the Monroe of Monroe and Sons.''

''A figurehead. Your mother was always the voice of authority. That's why she wanted you back, you know. She needs a younger figurehead to replace the old. When I am gone, she fears keeping this house of cards from becoming unglued. Hell, you can see for yourself that it is already asunder. I brought into the world a pack of jealous fiends who married even more jealous wives and between them produced a pack of wolves who can hardly wait to gnaw at my carcass."

Clay ran his tongue over his lips before he could speak.

"How do you know that I am not the same?" he mumbled.

There was, men of business always had claimed, a streak of truthfulness in Barrett Monroe that was as good as money in the bank. It beat now upon his brain like an angry tiger clawing to be freed from a trap.

"Because you are different. You have been educated and seen vast parts of the world. This bunch has never seen east of Chicago, except maybe for Cyrus. They are narrow and you are broad." He hesitated, still fighting to keep the tiger caged. "I never got to know you as a boy, and you came to manhood a long way from us. Your mother and I, perhaps, were not the best mating in the world. Too many wars have the German and French fought amongst themselves, and will probably continue to do so. Your mother and I have had our own wars. God bless her for being such a fighter. In that sense I could not hate her. No, it's the one thing I could really love about her. She would fight for the children, for the business, for her fancy French dreams. And if she did not get her way, then she would hate and feed on that hate until she was fully nourished."

Clay knew that the time of reckoning had come and had a strong impulse to get up and run.

"It was her hatred, not her dream, that sent you away," Barrett said quickly and defiantly.

"You'll regret it," Marti screeched from the other side of the door, and then they heard her running feet.

"I don't think I want to hear any more," Clay said, a catch in his voice.

Gloomily Barrett shook his head.

"Do you think this pleasures me?" he said accusingly. "I would have left well-enough alone, had I not heard what you said about Cyrus. That imp! Too bad that only saints are crucified! But shame I shall not let you bear! Nor will I now attempt deletions or abbreviations to lessen the truth. For a while before, and a long time after Carter was born, your mother and I lived separately. There was, Clay, another man in her life. I can say honestly that he gave your mother love for the first time in her life. Don't get me wrong—I also had a woman with me in the lumber camp, to care for the boys and myself.

"Then, when we learned that you were on the way, we patched things up and kept them more or less patched for the next twelve years."

"Why?" Clay stiffened suddenly. "Wouldn't her lover claim me?"

"He wanted nothing more, but your mother had very strong feelings about divorce. She and I made the choice and he was bound to go along with it. You were to be my son, and no questions asked."

"And I never to know about him?"

"That was the agreement."

"Then why did she send me away?"

Barrett sighed. "Her good fortune, Clay, was also her misfortune. You don't just stop loving. To her disgust, she could not stay away from the man. Purposely, she would come to the lumber camps each summer just to keep away from him. And just as purposely, she took that love and turned it into a hatred to cleanse her soul. But you were always there to remind her. She whipped education into your brain to make you a better product than the man or myself. She would not listen to the fact that she was making you hated and despised by the other children and, in Jonathan's case, by his children. We thought we had won a point with her when she agreed for you and Cyrus to go off to school. But the man, in all honesty, made a blunder. He offered to take you boys to London and be responsible for the cost of your education. In her way, she saw it as a threat to win you away from her, and her hatred mounted to such a degree that she sent you packing on a moment's notice—and without Cyrus."

"And kept me away for twelve years," he said bitterly.

"Out of love, Clay," he said soothingly, "and out of fear of losing you. He was becoming quite an important man and tried in vain to learn your exact whereabouts. Your mother and I agreed it shouldn't be. Whether you believe it or not, we did it out of our love for you."

"This whole family has a very strange concept of love," Clay growled.

"I wouldn't call it a concept, Clay; I would call it an unknowing. Love is an emotion taught to children by their parents. How could Marti and I teach what we did not know?"

"Finished?" Clay growled again.

"Yes, Clay, I'm finished."

"You've had your say. Now I'm going to have mine. For the first time in life, I respect you—not love you. You are right; I am still too much of a Monroe to be acquainted with that feeling. Lord, how I feared you. Now I wonder why. But to reverse the past is impossible. Thank you for letting me have my wings. I don't feel like being stagnant, if you get my point. Nor do I hate. If nothing more, this discussion has taught me what an energy-sapping emotion that can be. And on that point, I vow to you that I never want anyone revealing to me that man's name. It means nothing. He gave me life, yes. My mother gave me life, yes. But only for twelve years! What has transpired since has nothing to do with either of them. I am tired. Tomorrow is going to be quite busy and I am going right back to Chicago. Please forgive me if I now say good night."

He stood for a long time outside the study, fighting for self-control. There was no thought of tears. They had all been cried out of his system during his first two years in England. It was thoughts of the future he was trying to control. He did not, and would not, accept anything from this family ever again. Surprisingly, he didn't hate. It was more like pity. They were shallow. Within sat a great man that they were too stupid even to imitate. He was profoundly sorry that Barrett Monroe was not his real father, for he certainly now respected him fully.

Chapter 8

It was like a bad tooth. Once it was extracted and the pain gone, it was forgotten—except the cavity would always be there.

The country also had a bad tooth, but the pain of an assassinated President would not go away, and the cavity of the civil strife remained an open, festering wound.

Clay became a man of impulse and not logic.

While the business nation played caution with Andrew Johnson, Chicago pressed its advantage and Clay pressed those he advised to take full advantage.

The postwar immigrants came by the thousands, stumbling with weariness and straggling in a long line of human need, to be packed into small wooden cottages that sprouted like mushrooms and to accept any given job at any given wage.

"While labor is dirt cheap and you have additional cash capital, invest in the future of Chicago for yourself."

Philip Armour listened and quietly bought into the huge Union Stock Yards which were completed in the summer of 1865.

John Deere's plow and Cyrus McCormick's harvester could no longer be just cottage factory items.

"I feel bearish on this, Clay. The immigrants and the ex-soldiers can't afford such implements. Tell Deere and McCormick that my investment capital is spread too thin."

"Their implements would certainly help your Mason and Tazewell County property."

"What property?"

"The right-of-way land you gained in central Illinois with your railway stock. The tenant farmers never seem to have much to pay you back, although I hear it is superb soil."

"Clayton, Clayton, you handle it. My days are too filled with Harry and the building of the house. I promised Eugenia I would have it completed before she returned from Europe at the end of the summer. I leave everything in your hands."

Clay nodded with grim joy. This, he thought, was exactly what an associate should be doing.

Deere and McCormick rapidly expanded, mainly due to the large order placed by Harvel Packer. The tenant farmers were given a point-blank choice—change their idle practices by adopting the new equipment or move on.

Clay backed up their choice with a visual threat. He had taken with him into the central region a hundred immigrant farm families eager to work for a wealthy absentee landlord. It mattered not to him that he had to purchase farmlands to place most of them. Everywhere he looked, the fields swayed with rich, growing grain. And every farmer he talked with tried to hide their underlying panic. It would be a bumper season and the price of grain was still far too low.

Clay used Harvel Packer's money as though it were endless. He bought up the grain futures directly from the farmers by employing an old "tea clause" from India. The farmer was solely responsible for all loss in the event of "an act of God."

Clay was so certain that the grain trade would thrive, that he purchased a seat on the Chicago Board of Trade in Harvel's name and set about on a new scheme.

Jon Monroe's thick lips made a cavernous *O* in his face as he watched Clay march to him across the lumber yard.

"Hello, Jon."

"Clay? Haven't seen you since Milwaukee."

"No," Clay said truthfully, "I've been staying away from the family. I have some bachelor digs that suit me fine. Is everyone well?"

"Same. Same," Jon said cautiously, wondering why the sudden interest after months of silence.

"Lumber business looks good."

"Growing all the time." He shrugged.

Clay thought the shrug over, carefully, slowly. The stockpile was growing, but were the profits?

"Look, Jon," he said, "I've got to talk to you—right away. It's important."

Jon looked at him coolly. His grandmother had put almost the kiss of death on Clayton. He was not sure what Clayton had done to rile her so, but he could not afford to get caught in the middle. He had a family to support and his father still kept him only on salary.

"What's the matter," he demanded, "are you in trouble?"

"No. Packer keeps me so busy I don't have time for trouble. An opportunity is going to come our way by the end of summer—something big, something right down your alley."

"You trying to buy me away from the family business?"

"No. You could do this on your own or tie the family in."

"I don't have an awful lot of money of my own, Clay."

"Look, Jon, you've got what money can't buy and you won't have to ask your father for any. It's a business deal—one that can give you a private income of your own."

"Why me?" Jon asked, mockery in his eyes.

"Maybe because you're the last *working* Monroe. You're out here as a working foreman and not sitting behind a desk. Why? I don't go into a proposal unless I have looked at all the angles for Mr. Packer. I've seen the cost sheets on the mansion he is building. With what Ivan is now charging out of the sawmill, Illinois lumber is cheaper."

"Except for Uncle Harry," he scoffed. "Edict came down from Milwaukee this morning. Sell him all he wants, even at cost. With him getting the contract to design and build that new theater, it could put me under."

"Because you have so damn much land that you pay taxes on and it gives you nothing in return."

Jon smiled at him quietly, coolly.

"It takes time to cure lumber, Clay. Look at all the shanty houses that keep shrinking because they were built with green timber."

"I'm talking about the way you cure the lumber, Jon.

You stack it up like hundreds of little forts and the land in the middle does nothing but sit there and grow weeds."

"Shit, Clay," he growled, "there's nothing else to do with it."

"You could build grain silos in each center," he murmured.

"Impossible!" he exploded. "Where would I get that kind of money?"

Clay threw back his head and laughed merrily.

"Look around you," he said, "and think like a Barrett Monroe. You have the land, so there's no cost there. You have the lumber because you are not selling that rapidly right now. Labor? Jon, you have fifty-seven men employed here at present, and last week you had them all on half-time. I need a hundred silos to rent by the end of harvest time. I have a sketch of how I want them built. Say yes, and I will pay you one-twelfth of the annual rental on each in advance."

Jon's big face was puzzled; then he nodded. The funny part about it, he thought, is that it was Clayton Monroe who was thinking like Barrett. He might even be richer than Barrett some day. With that in mind, he thought it best to keep this business transaction strictly to himself.

As though Clay knew what he was thinking, he smiled at him softly.

For Clay it was a summer of content.

As the mansion began to rival what Jay Cooke was building in Philadelphia, Harvel spent more and more of his time upon it.

This gave Clay time to manage the growing portfolios in a dignified quietude. Each began to bulge with a neat sheaf of stocks, some so inter-linked that only Clay fully comprehended the pattern of the growing cobweb.

But in the banking and brokerage houses, he had formed the habit of appearing as little more than Harvel Packer's confidential clerk and secretary. Because he held himself on an equal par, he was accepted as an equal. Although he paid himself weekly, he astutely opened four separate banking accounts, to keep the clerks thinking he was on a monthly salary like them. Slowly, friendships grew and tidbits of business information were whispered in his ear.

None of it was really inside information that would help Harvel Packer, but it helped Clayton Monroe.

It took him until July to learn all he wished to learn about the personal finances of Harrison Dole. Then he plotted an appropriate meeting.

"These are not Mr. Packer's?" the broker asked.

"My own. I bought it from my family and wish to know its present worth."

"May I ask, why us, sir?" he sniffed curiously. "We do not have the privilege of handling any of Mr. Packer's affairs."

"You handled the original transaction between a Mr. Harrison Dole and my nephew, Cyrus Monroe."

"I say," Harrison laughed, sitting at the next desk with another broker, "did I hear my name mentioned? Why, bless me, my cabin mate. Clayton Monroe, is it not?"

Clay was quickly on his feet, all smiles and extending his hand. "Hello there, how good to see you again."

"I heard you were back in Chicago, but the summer boat traffic has kept me at the old grindstone. What was this matter that connected my name?"

"The rolling stock that you and Cyrus ventured into."

"I say," Harrison laughed, "wasn't that youthful folly!"

"I bought it up from the family."

"Rather a good sport, aren't you?"

For the first time the broker smiled, rather pompously. "I hope you have money to waste, young man. These aren't worth much."

"That's what I feared," Clay sighed. "Cyrus sold me a bill of goods. Well, Dole, nice seeing you again."

Harrison sensed at once he was taking it all too lightly. "A moment, while I finish signing this paper, Clayton. You're not going to vanish on me again. I hear you are placed with Harvel Packer. That certainly is some mansion he is building."

"Yes," Clay said, as though in answer to all.

"Come along and have a bite of lunch with me."

Clay looked nervously at the wall clock. "My half-hour is already half used up."

"Then grant me the fifteen minutes left." Harrison, as though they were old buddies, took him by the arm and started to steer him out of the office. He leaned over confidentially. "Are you really looking into that old scheme for yourself? The talk is that Packer is thrusting his fist all the way down to the blackbirds in the pie."

"Not here," Clay hissed, and made his voice genuinely angry. "I'm even sorry I ran into you. I hope that broker doesn't start putting two and two together."

Harrison Dole felt goose pimples crawl up his spine. He smelled something big and was elated over the chance meeting.

"Perhaps I should just walk you back to your office to save time."

"Time?" Clay acted confused. "Time for what?"

"Time for you to tell me why this old chestnut is roasting again on the fire. After all, I was one of the originators."

"And promptly sold out."

"That," he said mockingly, "was because of the idiot I was associated with. When he got cold feet I wanted nothing more to do with it."

"He tells a different story."

"Damned presumptuous of him, I'd say," he muttered grimly. "I was the one who wanted to hold on, but he was so lily-livered."

Clay smiled—a slow, enigmatic smile. "You should have held on. Mr. Packer is well aware that they are still struggling to haul the Pennsylvania oil away to the refineries in copper-lined barrels. Of course, this pleases him because of his copper-mines up north. But—" He stopped short.

"But what?" Harrison nearly choked.

Clay hesitated for just the proper effect to make the man think he was exposing another Packer confidence.

"He could not help but wonder why the two of you did not think of lining your tanker cars with copper."

"We did," Harrison lied, "but Cyrus would not go to your family for more money, and I had every penny available invested." He gulped. "I am a lot better situated now, however."

"However, I am not. It was all I could do to buy the rights and cars away from the family on the off-chance of selling it to Mr. Packer."

"I said, I am a lot better situated now," he repeated, his voice hoarse and unnatural.

"So?" Clay whispered, looking straight ahead.

Harrison Dole broke out in a cold sweat. "We each have something that the other needs—and possibly without including Packer. Can you extend your lunch half-hour?"

"I might get sacked."

"What difference does it make if you might possibly be going into business for yourself?"

Harrison & Monroe was formed before sundown, with Harrison Dole putting up twenty-five thousand dollars in working capital and promising that the Dole family would not learn of his involvement until the venture proved profitable. Clay also made him promise not to breathe a word of the matter to Harvel Packer.

With money in hand, Clay went and commissioned Pullman to revamp the existing ten cars.

As close-mouthed as he was, he still needed an escape valve for his volcanic activities. At least three nights a week he would have dinner with Harry Hart Horner, although they talked mainly about the mansion and the theater plans.

The man was so enthusiastic over his work that he would exhaust himself and fall asleep right at the table. It became a habit for Clay to put him to bed.

When he returned from the bedroom that night, he found Janellen washing dishes, singing softly to herself. He paused, listening. She sang beautifully, her voice moving liltingly up and down the scale.

"You sound happy," Clay said calmly, "although what will Mrs. Yost do in the morning with no dishes to do up?"

"That, Clayton Monroe," she said tartly, "is for the poor overworked woman to figure out."

"My, what happened to the happiness I just heard?"

"It's still there, because I know you are popping to tell me something. But what about Mrs. Yost, first?"

"What about her?"

"You know an awful lot about Mr. Packer's business," Janellen declared, "except on the domestic side. Clay, it's not that I am not happy in having her to do the cooking. It's a lot easier on me than in Milwaukee, but she goes from sun-up to sundown cooking for both houses."

"So?"

"So that snippity housekeeper over there is only paying her a single wage and no grubs."

"Grubs?"

"Meals and the leftovers to take home as her due."

"What about from here?"

"Get on with you," she laughed. "Three nights a week you hardly leave enough for a church mouse. Don't you eat the rest of the week?"

"Don't have time."

"What you need is a good wife to look out for you."

"Is that a proposal?"

"Clayton Monroe," Janellen snapped, "you're positively a caution!"

"I know. That's why you love me so, right?"

Despite herself, Janellen could not help but laugh.

"It's liking," she chuckled, "and not love. Liking, because you're my only friend here. Everyone else is cold and stiff—Harvel Packer being the worst. I keep away from his like as I would the plague. What's his daughter like?"

"Wow! You always go too fast. How did Eugenia get in here all of a sudden?"

"Eugenia? My, you are on friendly terms. I think we'll switch back to your good news."

"No way, young lady, or you'll dream up your own story. I've known Eugenia since she was ten and in pigtails. Hence, first name basis." Then, before she could probe deeper, he quickly told her about his day.

"Why have Mr. Pullman do the cars?"

"Because, you little snoop, I know nothing about such cars and P.D. taught me that experience is cheap at any price if you benefit by it."

"That's my point," she frowned.

"What point?" He had been lost again.

''Mrs. Yost's experience, which is being paid for too cheaply.''

''All right, all right,'' he laughed. ''I'll look into it. Next subject.''

''Was Eugenia the other woman you've kissed?''

''Lord help me, yes. Now, what does that prove?''

''Did you kiss me because she was in Europe?''

''Why?'' Clay grinned. ''Afraid of playing second fiddle?''

''I think,'' Janellen said coldly, ''that you are a user of women.''

''Granted! I have kissed me two in my life and so must be branded a user of them all. When you figure out that Eugenia left for Europe long after I came back from Milwaukee, you let me know.''

''You are excused for the night!'' Janellen snapped.

''My, my, and without a parting kiss.''

''I've only kissed you the once and you know it!''

''And afraid to kiss me again?''

''I fear nothing!''

''Nothing?'' he mocked. ''She fears nothing? Why is it, then, that you greet me at the door with such pleasure and then hide away from the dinner table? Why wait for these little chats and then hide your hands in dishwater? You're afraid, all right—frightened right out of your bloomers. You keep your hands busy so that they won't itch to be put about my neck!''

Janellen stood stiffly at the sink with her green eyes flashing. She turned very slowly and put up her dripping arms.

''Do you wish to dry them first?'' she murmured.

Chapter 9

It was not the kiss that troubled Clay as much as the question after the kiss.

"Does Eugenia kiss as well?"

He had answered it with a mocking laugh, but the question would not go away. How could he compare? Did he want to compare? Did he even want a woman in his life at that time?

Eugenia may have been out of sight, but she refused to stay out of mind. With each incoming lake ship and train were crates of her European purchases, along with hidden notes for her father and Clay. Without even knowing the scope of the mansion, she was spending a fortune to furnish it—piece by piece and object by object. Harvel was delighted she was taking such an interest and let her spend wildly. Clay read something quite differently into her notes. The princess needed a prince for her castle, and was laying out the treasure to dazzle his pauper's eyes.

Tears had flooded Janellen's eyes after the mocking laugh. She had turned and run from the kitchen, and he felt as guilty as he had felt with Eugenia in New York.

He climbed the stairs to his digs wearily, pushing both women out of his mind. But they wouldn't retreat. Eugenia was beautiful and would one day inherit a fortune. Janellen was pretty and had nothing. Eugenia drove him crazy and Janellen was a quiet relief after a crazy business day.

Hell, why was he working himself into such a stew? He, Clayton Monroe, had never had to worry about women before.

He put out his hand to unlock the door to his rooms, but

he held the key poised. Something disturbed him. Looking down, he saw what it was. The ray of light that stole under his door from the night gas-jet had been cut off abruptly.

Few knew his address. He was, therefore, fully prepared for an unwanted guest. He slid the skeleton key into the lock, as though he'd not seen the light go out, then swiftly pushed the door in and jumped to the side.

"Morrison?" a voice breathed from within. "Did you find him and did you bring food?"

Clay's jaw dropped. He stepped into the room, staring in astonishment at the guest as he turned up the gaslight once more. Then he began to laugh. Jay Cooke had grown a full beard, was clad in buckskins and smelled as though he had not bathed in a month.

"Have a good laugh," he warned, "for I hate you for not having proper bathing facilities. Where in the deuce is Morrison?"

"Morrison? If you stopped at Harvel's first, why didn't you stay there to bathe and get a change of clothing?"

"Clayton, do not make me curse, for you know I am not a cursing man, but this night has been a trauma. That witch, under the guise of Harvel's housekeeper, all but called out the police on me. I had to hide in the bushes until I spied Morrison within. But once I had rapped him to the door, she immediately burst upon the scene and screeched us out of the house. The 'nigger' was not to have his 'scum friends' enter 'her' house. When he tried to reproach her, she used language against him that was unforgiving and bolted us both out. Like the servant he is, he batted not an eye, but brought me right here and went in search of you and some supper for me."

"I do not keep a kitchen here," Clay said lamely.

"That was an obvious fact during my wait."

There was a light rap on the door. Clay turned to open it.

"Come in, come in!" he said, holding the door open. Morrison entered sheepishly.

"At this hour I had to go back and steal what I could out of the house. She don't know my quarters got a private entrance."

Clay smiled quietly and helped take parcels from his

arms. Morrison was trembling all over, as though the police would break the door down after him.

"Now, if you could fix Mr. Cooke something to eat, I am dying to learn some reasons behind all this mystery and frenzied activity."

"Mystery, I can solve," Cooke said, "Frenzied activity is due only to the witch. When one really seeks knowledge on a subject, Clayton, one must go in search themselves. The rise and fall of stocks can tell me at a glance the latest battle between Vanderbilt and Drew. It takes only a newspaper accounting to learn the progress of the Central Pacific, Union Pacific and Chicago Northwestern. Imitators and formidable rivals, Clay, pound the streets of Washington for railroad charters. The fight for the Erie has even made Andy Carnegie and Tom Scott jump in to get the construction charter for the Texas & Pacific Railroad. Ah, thank you, Morrison. As usual, you make a feast out of nothing."

He ate as though he were starved and left Clay mystified.

"Many, as you know, maintain interest in the northwestern quarter. I have just been on a most fascinating journey with an old mountain man. Two months surrounded by that pristine beauty, vastness and boundless riches. Not today, Clay, but in a few years hence, the wealth of that region will be staggering. Right now I am telling you that the cattle for the Chicago stockyards will mainly come out of Montana and northern Wyoming. As you know I have cautiously resisted the railroad fever, other than our small stock deal. I will continue that course, but keep my voice strong in Washington."

"Interesting," Clay said, as a listener.

"Clay, you have proven to me your worth as a young man of silence. No one is aware of my journey. America thinks I am in Europe purchasing for my new home. Now I ask for your friendship anew on several matters. First, a bath, if such is available in this building."

"Morrison, a favor, please," Clay said. "At the end of the hall is a boiler and tub. You should find the coal scuttle full."

"Coal," Cooke mused, as Morrison departed. "What a

beautiful word, and a part of my second request. Have you visited any of Harvel's copper interests in the north?"

"No, sir."

"My journey started near there at Fond du Lac. It is an old fur trading post of the Astor family and Bill Astor made arrangements for my mountain man guide. It no longer has value for their fur business, but some of the land around he thought would interest me as a private hunting preserve. There is a small white settlement nearby, called Duluth, that took my fancy. Astor property, of course. Tomorrow I shall talk with Harvel and have you go up to purchase the settlement quietly and the forty thousand acres around it."

Clay nodded his head, a knowing smile creeping into his eyes.

"For a hunting preserve?" he mocked.

"Yes," Cooke laughed, "for the hunting of coal and iron ore. I am just totally amazed that Carnegie never got wind of what lay beneath that land and thankful that John Jacob Astor was only interested in its pelts. But that is only the beginning. That settlement I see as the terminus of a rail line across the Northwest to the Pacific. On foot and horseback I have covered the route I favor and have recorded it all in a diary. Clay, I am going to entrust that book to your care. No one, not even Harvel, must know of it or my future thoughts. It may take me a few years to put this whole charter together, because we are talking about forty-seven million acres of land and the township building rights all along the way."

Clay was astounded. "That is an enormous responsibility."

Jay Cooke suddenly looked very tired and very old. "It hurts me, Clay, when even the President of the United States calls us robber barons. The real robbers are those who only take and give nothing back in return. The Commodore is right when he says that a secret shared by three is bound to be known by a hundred. We will keep the secret between us. Now, to my final request, before the water boils. I am going to do everything within my power to secure the next Republican nomination for Grant. The Illinois delegation will be important and I know few here.

You can do me a great service by starting a file on those you feel would favor Grant.''

''I am not political and know little about it. Only by chance did I learn that General Grant was born in Illinois and is quite popular hereabouts. A friend, Harry Hart Horner, the architect, is even thinking ahead to ask Grant to be here for the grand opening of his proposed theater—although some think it should be as grand as an opera house.''

Cooke roared with laughed. ''You see, my friend, you are a mass of important trivia. Grant has friends in his homeland and Chicago is due for a new theater. You have given me the notion that perhaps the convention should be staged right here in Chicago.''

Morrison came to announce the drawn bath and Clay found clothing for the man to change into. Without comment being made, Morrison found bedding to convert the sitting-room sofa for the night.

''What is her name?'' Clay asked softly, after Cooke had left.

Morrison knew exactly what subject they were back upon. ''Not really important, Mr. Clay. She has Mr. Harvel's ear in a way that we wouldn't be able to change.''

''Is he considering marriage?''

Morrison grinned. ''No, Mr. Clay, but she sure is.''

''Then I really don't know how to approach the problem.''

''No problem to approach, as I see it. Waiting for the water to cook, I set my mind. Mr. George Pullman has been after me since his car became so popular bringing Mr. Lincoln home. I said no, because of Mr. Harvel. Tomorrow I am going to say yes, because of Morrison.''

''You are used to serving one man, Morrison. Serving the public is going to be a lot different.''

''Not the public,'' he said simply. ''Morrison will have his own school to train the cooks and waiters to serve Mr. Pullman's public. I'm going to get me the finest black boys born and make them proud young men.''

''Then I will say nothing to Mr. Packer about the housekeeper.''

He hesitated. ''Do you think I am doing right, Mr. Clay?''

"If all of your young men become a Morrison," declared Clay with genuine love, "every railroad in this land will beat a path to your door to supply them with the same luxury service."

"Well, Mr. Clay, thank you. And until I talk with Mr. Harvel personal-like, it's our secret."

Clay's head was becoming too filled with secrets—his own and others'.

Duluth absorbed the rest of the summer. The harvest was bountiful, prices ruinous for the farmers and Harvel Packer considered a prophet in the grain market for having looked into the future and prepared with storage silos.

Packwood was finished by early fall. From that moment in time it was a Chicago wonder. Harry Hart Horner was the toast of the town. Everyone who was anyone now desired the same soaring towers, fairytale spires and leaded windows. The interior was Victorian splendor—bas-relief covered walls, massive chandeliers, curtains and furniture in red plush.

Society gasped at the hand-delivered gilt-edged invitations for the grand opening ball, some delivered as far east as New York. Others waited patiently for the knock on the door that never came. Wives began to badger their husbands, who in quiet embarrassment consulted Mr. Packer's associate.

Clay found it all rather amusing, for he was not among the invited either.

When he raised the subject with Harvel, the man smiled disagreeably, but with some shamed discomfort.

"The list was compiled by Miss Priest," he remarked indifferently. "But she ought to realize some things. Look into it, Clay."

Clay said nothing. He merely stared at Harvel gloomily. When he had raised the subject of Mrs. Yost, he had been told to stay out of domestic matters that did not concern him. Nor did he feel comfortable going to the new mansion. Eugenia had returned from Europe with a bevy of new friends that Clay had recognized at once as "minor royal leeches." Eugenia had not appreciated his attitude and he had avoided her.

Still, there were businessmen being overlooked that could not be insulted.

"My list?" Miss Priest said with formidable stiffness and majesty. "Why does it concern you, Mr. Monroe?"

"It concerns Mr. Packer, Miss Priest. Certain gentlemen have inquired as to their lack of invitation."

"So?" She looked down her bony Phoenician nose with a frozen haughtiness. "It is a social affair and not a business meeting."

"But some of those men are partially responsible for the business which acquired the money to build this vast, rambling structure."

She sat silent. Nothing, Clay thought to himself, would shake that stony woman, not even the business wishes of Harvel Packer.

He knew that Morrison had to be wrong about her. New York had taught him Packer's taste in women and LaVerna Priest, from her lathe-like back and front, her bony shoulders and sharp angles, did not fit the picture. She was a spinster in every quality of viewing—a grim gentlewoman, full of self-important breeding and severely lacking in any manifestation of affection. To imagine her in bed with Harvel Packer—with any man—bordered on the ridiculous.

She cleared her throat ominously as she stared rigidly before her. "You are putting me off my schedule, sir. This entire affair is on my shoulders and I have but ten days left. I'm sure that you have your own duties, as well."

"Yes, and one of them is to get a copy of the list."

Miss Priest lifted her head. In the cavernous expanse of the room, her tiny acidulous blue eyes glittered with eager malevolence.

"Once before, you tried to impose yourself upon my domain, Mr. Monroe, and only made matters worse for Mrs. Yost. Stick with your clerk duties and stay out of my household affairs. Good morning."

Suddenly her pressed lips broke into a thin smile, directed to the doorway behind Clay.

"You require something, Miss Eugenia?"

"Yes!" exclaimed Eugenia, in a tone of strong consternation. "The notes that were presented to each of my guests this morning."

"In a moment, dear. The gentleman is leaving."

Clay rose and turned.

"Oh, hello, Clay. Business?"

"To a degree. I was sent to get a party list for your father."

"Fat chance of that," Eugenia laughed drily. "Even my guests have been given eviction notices prior to that eventful day."

"Not exactly, Miss Eugenia," Miss Priest said in a severe and uncompromising tone. "But it is no concern of Mr. Monroe. I have already bid him a good morning."

"If you are leaving, Clay, may I get a ride downtown?"

"Certainly."

"Anything to get out of here," she remarked with a swift toss of her head and a sniff as she marched back to the foyer.

Clay followed, chuckling to himself. Even with Eugenia Miss Priest seemed to hold the upper hand.

"She is boorish and impossible, and quite rude," Eugenia said the moment she sank back into the carriage seat. "And why do you have father's rig?"

"To quickly get the boorish, impossible and rude list."

"Fat chance," she repeated. "She keeps everyone off it that she fears might commit a *faux pas*. How did you let father get saddled with such a beast?"

"Household affairs are not within my clerk duties," he said, mocking the woman's thin, nasal voice.

Eugenia erupted with laughter. "Oh, Clay, she is so gothic."

"Surely she doesn't lock you into one of those tower rooms at night," cried Clay with joking horror. "If not, wait until she is your stepmother."

Eugenia smiled darkly. "So you've gotten that impression, too. Father's a fool. You must have a sharp talk with him on the matter."

"He will be doing the sharp talking when I come back without the list."

Eugenia winked devilishly. "But you won't, Clay." She opened her purse and took out a sheaf of notes. "I have been doing my own detective work. Each time a batch was ready for delivery, I bribed Turner into copying down whom they went to. I'm only missing those out of town."

"Afraid you wouldn't be included?" he joked.

"Afraid my friends wouldn't be," she said with genuine concern. "And they weren't. Now they are going to be packed off to the Palmer House to make room for the out-of-town guests."

Despite himself, Clay agreed with Miss Priest on that point. But, to keep from having to comment, he rifled through the sheaf. Mentally, he began to think of names that were not included. He frowned heavily.

"Interesting, eh? Heavy on the church set, I determine. Well, why not? She treats the barn like a cathedral. Want to spite her?"

"Love to, but how?"

Again she reached into her purse. "My copy of the invitation. Do you know a printer who can duplicate it?"

"Better than that," Clay grinned. "I know the original printer."

Eugenia studied Clay curiously. "You've changed."

"You've just been gone a long time."

"No, you're more assured and stable. You're not even going to consult father about this, are you?"

"No reason," he shrugged. "Once I tell him I have the list, he will just tell me to see to its correction."

"Need help?" she purred.

"You might be useful," he said without conviction. "Especially if you want to get your friends back on the list."

"You don't like them, do you?"

"Not really," he said truthfully. "Saw too many of their type in England and India. They have avaricious eyes for everything but honest work. Watch out or one of them will try to marry you for your money."

"I've already told Tony Harcourt I would marry him," she said quietly. "We are keeping it quiet to announce at the grand ball."

A moroseness came over Clay that sorely puzzled him.

He was not in love with Eugenia, but the announcement quietly hurt him.

"Then that lets me out of the mold works," he said, trying to sound kidding and uncaring.

"I didn't have time to work with that much clay," she said lightly, but almost touched upon the truth. Europe had given her a different view on life. Why pursue life when money made it come to you? She didn't want to share the man in her life with the business world. Anthony Harcourt would have only one obligation—her constant pleasure.

Clay had been right. Harvel Packer left it all in his hands. The matter would not be open for discussion with Miss Priest until the last moment. A look between Eugenia and Clay put them in bond on a single thought. Harvel Packer was also intimidated by the woman.

In the next two days the list was nearly doubled. Names popped out of Clay's head or his massive files. He had a very good reason for each name added, which began to fascinate Eugenia.

"Who is Nolan Huffmeister?"

"A little-known nobody."

"Then why invite him?"

"For the future. He's the Republican precinct man for the area in which the mansion was built. In a grass roots way he gets his voters out to the polls."

"And will let his voters know he was included with the elite?"

Clay nodded and Eugenia took a different view of him. Actually, she had to admit, it was fun working with him and seeing how far he had progressed without her molding. She could not help but feel admiration.

Her admiration grew when Clay had to beard Miss Priest again.

"Now, that I will not allow," admonished Miss Priest in a severe and bracing tone. "No, I shall personally stand at the door and admit only those upon my list."

"Then there shall be no grand ball," Clay said firmly.

"Sir," she sneered, "I shall discuss the matter only with the proper person."

"Exactly," he said curtly. "Here is the revised budget I had Mr. Packer approve before he departed for Milwaukee.

If you have questions you may send your inquiry to the office via Turner. By the way, I soundly reprimanded the printer. He grossly overcharged you on the first set of invitations.''

Miss Priest gulped, then suddenly giggled hoarsely. From her it was a most odd sound. ''You are better suited to know such things, I am sure.''

LaVerna Priest was almost smiling by the middle of the evening. The grand ball was an enormous success and the credit was showered in her direction. Two things, however, commanded her attention throughout the evening: a close guard of the non-alcoholic punch-bowl to keep it pure for the 'church set' and the rumored fear of Miss Eugenia's announcement. She had hoped—no, dreamed—that Harvel Packer might have an announcement of his own.

One thing that not even Clay had taken into consideration was the necessity of Janellen having to attend with Harry Hart Horner.

''I don't believe I've had the pleasure,'' Eugenia said cordially.

''Because you don't accept dinner invitations,'' Horner got in first. It was intended as a light reproach, but came off bitingly.

''Ouch!'' Clay laughed. ''I feel that barb directed at me as well.''

''Nonsense,'' Janellen said mildly. ''We know how busy you have been of late.''

''Janellen,'' he enthused, ''I cannot get over this. You look absolutely bewitching.''

''Just the evening attire of a working nurse,'' she chuckled, twirling around so that the purple velvet of the gown rose and fell over the enormous tilting hoops.

''Jan,'' he said solemnly, ''You are, without a doubt, the most beautiful woman at the ball.''

''Even though hoops are becoming old fashioned,'' Eugenia whispered quickly.

Clay shot her a mean glance, then was relieved to see that Janellen had not heard. It was her first formal ball and she was enamored. Her thrill of the moment increased when Clay quickly took her by the hand and pulled her to the dance floor. She expertly glided into his arms, and her waltz was smooth and graceful.

"Hey, you've got hidden talents."

"Not bad yourself, Mr. Monroe. I'm amazed to find you even know how to dance."

"A social custom forced upon every English schoolboy, four-legged or not."

Eugenia saw the pleasure on Clay's face as the duo made quite a superb appearance on the floor. That he danced at all amazed her. Then she focused her attention on Janellen Heubner.

A rather pretty creature, she thought without envy, for she measured every female against herself.

"Don't worry," Harvel said, coming up beside them, "you'll find yourself another nurse, Harry."

"Now, Harvel Packer," Horner said, "don't fret yourself on that point! She's too smart to fall for a lad paid so poorly by his employer."

"You know," Eugenia said wonderingly, to herself, "I'm not too sure about that."

Throughout the evening she kept tabs on them. Clay danced and danced, but never with her. Several times she put herself in a position close enough to him to be asked, but never was.

When he was not dancing, he was introducing her father to someone or getting involved in a group conversation. To her amusement and yet displeasure, she saw that Clayton Monroe was the real host of the evening.

Oh, his humility was excruciatingly proper. It riled her, and she couldn't say why.

"Will he introduce us?" asked Tony Harcourt timidly.

"Why him?"

"Your father's man!" replied Tony vigorously. "Remarkable chap! Keeps everything going swimmingly and knows everyone down to their last button. Not one to cross wickets with, my dear."

She gazed at Tony and saw that he had a frightened adoration for Clay. It startled and confused her even more.

Then her father asked her to dance.

"My dear, you are quite the belle of the ball. Chicago

ladies are so dull and spiritless. Your Paris gowns dazzle them all."

"What's the catch, Daddy?" she asked quickly.

"You haven't called me Daddy for years, Eugenia."

"And did so now to get your full attention. Are you serious about Miss Priest?"

"And are you serious about your pale-faced snob?"

"I most certainly am!"

"Why don't we both consider it back-up time, Eugenia?" he asked, and in spite of his attempt at sternness, his strong voice was gentle and indulgent.

"Back up to what?"

"People with more blood and guts in their system and not all pomp and costume. Of course, that is easy for me, but difficult for you."

"Why difficult?"

"Because you are most obvious," murmured Harvel, overcome with the delight of being able to possess something his daughter could not. "He is beyond your reach, my dear. They do make a handsome couple on the floor, do they not?"

"Then it is Tony." Closing the subject, she turned with a stately solemnity and left her father alone on the dance floor.

But the evening wore on with no announcements. Quite overcome, and close to tears, Miss Priest kept her post to say goodnight to all the guests.

"Come, my love," Tony said, taking Eugenia by the hand. "The younger set will still find the shank of the evening."

"Only if Clay and Miss Heubner join us."

"I'm afraid I must see Mr. Horner to bed, thank you," replied Janellen with dignity.

"Run along," Horner barked. "Turner can wheel me home."

"Oh, may I go?" murmured Janellen, overcome with delight—but gazing at Eugenia, she knew at once the invitation had only been for Clay. "No, it has been a long evening, and there is still packing to do."

"Packing?" Clay asked, surprised.

"My fame is spreading anew," Horner exulted. "A Mr.

Henry Flagler has commissioned me to do a house in Pennsylvania.''

"What of the theater?" Harvel demanded.

"What of it?" Horner said demurely. "The designs are in the builder's hands. I am but a wheelchair in the way."

Clay frowned as he nodded agreement. The truth of the matter was he was elated. Five of the reconverted tanker cars had been sold to a Mr. Henry Flagler, with future orders pending his approval. Clay was scheduled to meet with the man after the trial run.

"Whatever!" Eugenia laughed, when she saw Janellen would not be included. "We'll just run along and have fun, like the old days, Clay!"

She deceived everyone except her father and Clay, and a very few others.

"I think I shall pass," Clay said.

"Good," Harvel said, slapping him on the back. "I had hoped for a nightcap, Clay. There is a Milwaukee matter I have not had time to discuss with you."

"Not business, Father," Eugenia chided. "Give the poor man a break."

"It's a family matter, my dear. Now, let me say good night to the rest of you. Harry, I will see you again very soon, so I won't say good-bye."

He nodded at Eugenia's friends as though wishing them to vanish forever. When Eugenia made no move to get a wrap, Tony gave her a motion of the hand.

"I think Clay is perfectly right," she said sweetly. "It is late and I think I shall pass, too. See you all tomorrow."

She locked her arm into Clay's and began steering him back to the parlor, automatically including herself in on the nightcap. Clay looked back to say good night to Janellen and Harry. Turner already had the wheelchair out the front door, with Janellen in the wake. She turned her head back for just a second and their eyes met. He saw the tears of hurt gathering in her eyes and he felt guilty. He wanted to break away and escort her home, but Eugenia pulled him back around and into the parlor.

"Oh, Clay!" she said, her blue eyes softening, "how can I ever thank you?"

"For what?"

"Making me see the truth about Tony. I can think of only one reward!" The next instant she was in his arms.

How long Harvel Packer stood in the parlor door, his face troubled, neither of them knew, but finally they heard the clearing of his throat.

Eugenia drew away her mouth and looked at her father. She smiled with knowing determination.

"We were saying goodbye to Tony Harcourt, Father," she said sweetly. "And hello to Clayton Monroe. I have come to the conclusion that he is the only man I shall marry."

"Impossible!" Harvel Packer growled.

"Father!"

"I mean it! There are reasons that make it utterly impossible!"

Eugenia stuck her tongue out and made an unladylike sound.

"Reasons, Father?" she laughed. "The only reason you would be able to muster is money."

"Nonsense! I have my own personal reasons that have nothing to do with his worth. Both of you just put this notion out of your head."

"I think you should know—" Clay started, but Eugenia cut him short, anticipating that he was going to reveal that he, as yet, had not even proposed marriage.

"We both think you should know," she said snidely, "that you may not have a voice in the matter. We have already known each other."

Harvel Packer collapsed weakly into a chair.

"When?" he gasped.

"In New York," she said proudly.

"Sir, let me explain," Clay stammered, ready to collapse himself.

"I don't want to hear!" Harvel shrieked. "And it changes my mind not one iota!"

"We both are of age, Father," Eugenia said gently. "We can always elope ."

"It is a matter," Packer said darkly, "that Clay should not consider without a deep discussion with his mother."

"Why should he discuss anything with them?" Eugenia

said confidently. "Look how they have treated him. Do you need their approval, darling?"

Clay did not answer. Instead, he stared down at Packer, his face grim. And through his mind ran a single word: *bastard*! Harvel Packer knew of his birth or he would have said a deep discussion with "mother and father." As good a friend as he was, he would not let his daughter be soiled by marrying a bastard.

"Clay!" Eugenia cried, grabbing him by the arm. "Say we don't need anyone to approve us."

"I think," Clay muttered, "I should do as your father says."

"Coward!" Eugenia's voice was thin with fury. "All you wanted to do was seduce me and then laugh at me. Well, I have had my last say on this matter. It's you I marry and no other."

Clay caught her by the wrist and held hard.

"Don't I have a say in the matter?" he said quietly. "It is usually the man who proposes and not the woman."

"Because you are so weak you never would have proposed. You were a cowering puppet for your family and now are a cowering puppet for my father."

He released her. "And now you want me to become your cowering puppet."

Her freed hand came up and slapped him hard across the face, then she raced from the parlor with her whole body racked by sobs.

"You hit her where it hurt," Packer said drily. "She can't face up to the truth."

"Maybe because she is like her father," Clay said grimly. "Can you face up to the truth?"

"About you?" he muttered sadly.

"Yes! You all but came out and shouted the fact that I am a bastard! How long have you known?"

Packer came fully erect in his chair. He stared at Clay with a face troubled and concerned.

"I have known since before your birth," he said truthfully. "Your mother had many long discussions with me at the time. I was the mediator who brought Barrett and Marti back together for your birth. I am sorry you had to learn in such a cruel way. Your father told me all during this visit of mine to Milwaukee. It was the matter I wished to discuss with you over a nightcap. Cyrus has learned of your tanker car purchase. He is under the impression that the family did not have the right to sell without his permission and will go to court if you do anything with it. Your father wanted you forewarned."

"Thank you," Clay said curtly. "But your statement brings another question to mind. I said to my fa- . . . to Barrett, that I did not want anyone revealing to me the identity of my real father. Do you know, sir?"

Harvel hesitated, his mind torn between the truth and telling a lie. Because he was Harvel Packer, truth won out.

"Yes," he said simply.

"And is it one of the reasons you do not want me to marry your daughter?"

"My reasoning on that point is more complex than a simple yes or no, but fundamentally, yes."

"I understand," Clay said through gritting teeth. "I also understand that it will now be impossible for me to remain in your employ. You would be constantly fearful that I was still after Eugenia, although tonight is the first time the subject became a matter of serious discussion. I, sir, would be fearful that you were keeping me on out of pity and loyalty to Barrett and my mother. I shall have all the books in proper order by your morning arrival. Good night, sir!"

"Good night," Harvel murmured.

Turner was waiting in the foyer to take him home in the carriage. He muttered his thanks, but decided to walk. He was in too much turmoil to go directly home. But his mind would not lock on a single topic long enough to fully solve it. Once he looked up to see that his feet had brought him to Harry Hart Horner's rental. Lights were still on in the kitchen and the bedrooms.

But he did not really feel like going in. He was in no mood for making up to Janellen. He wondered how she would react to learning he was a bastard. Suddenly it dawned on him that Uncle Harry must know, but the man was too full of love to let it matter and too gentlemanly to raise the point. The hour was too late for heart-to-heart discussion and what could he learn that he didn't already know?

What a turnaround, he thought! He had just quit his job, all but turned down Eugenia's marriage proposal and hurt Janellen—all in one evening! There wouldn't be any more Packer money for him to play with as if it were his own and no more tips to gain for himself by being an associate. He and Harrison had the tanker cars ready to show a profit, but Cyrus might tie the whole thing up in court. And to become rich as Jay Cooke—fat chance he had of doing that now. In nine months he had been able to squirrel away only a little over two thousand dollars. That might have to last him for quite a long time. Now he saw that his feet had brought him to the office At least work would keep him from thinking—and he was determined to leave everything in perfect order for his replacement.

Two hours later he was finished. He kept his files so current that there had been little to do but make a summary sheet for each one and then a complement of the whole. On paper Harvel Packer was worth forty-seven million. Clay had done very well for the man. He put the files back in the safe, extracted only the *Clayton Monroe, Personal* portfolio and clanged it shut. The portfolio contained the Coal-Oil Johnny letter, his railroad stock and Cooke's diary.

Not much, he thought, as he locked the office and shoved his key back under the door to be found by Packer in the morning. He walked along the street until a cab hailed him. He was about to wave it on, but then decided he had walked enough for one evening. It was nearly four o'clock and he ached. He sat mindless in the cab until the hansom stopped at his address.

As he alighted from the cab he looked up. A light was on in his rooms. He was in no mood to talk with anyone at that moment. He went up the stairs very quickly and, never locking his door after learning any skeleton key would open it, walked right in.

Harrison Dole was curled up on the sofa. He was already blinking the sleep out of his eyes.

"Must have been some party," he said, stretching and yawning.

"Been over for hours," Clay said curtly. "What are you doing here?"

Harrison pointed toward the table. "Telegram from Flagler. He's impressed, but a man named Rockefeller has doubts. Wants one of us the soonest. No way I can go without the family finding out. Will Packer give you some time off?"

Clay opened his mouth and quickly shut it. No reason for Harrison to know everything. "I'm starting an unexpected holiday tomorrow."

"Marvelous! Flagler will be in Titusville for another week, then goes back to Cleveland for the Christmas holidays."

Clay thought quickly. "I might still be able to catch the six a.m. eastbound."

"My, my," Harrison chirped, rising, "you do move fast."

"There's a reason, Harrison. Cyrus is furious with the family for selling to me. We need to strike fast before he can come back and get a court action to stall us."

"Court action!" he exploded. "I would like to see him try."

"Let's face it, partner. He is a sly, cunning devil who would try anything against me, and more so when he learns you are back in on the deal. The last thing we need right now is the expense of a lawyer."

"Don't worry. Harvel Packer would see that you were protected."

"What do you mean by that?" Clay snapped.

Harrison looked at him oddly. "Nothing, other than that he touts you as his golden boy. He told my uncle that you saved his neck on this grand ball thing. They weren't among the first to be invited, you know. Did they show up?"

"I think all of Chicago showed up, invited or not. Packer finally gave up on the gate-crashers. Everyone who had an invitation seemed to arrive with a carriage of extra people. You could have come with your uncle without an eyebrow being raised."

"Now I have to learn it," said Harrison with a sniff. "Well, this seemed more important. You're sure Mr. Packer won't mind you going? He regards you almost like a son, you know."

But will not accept me as a son-in-law, he thought ruefully. His next thought came so suddenly that he gasped inwardly and could not bear to think it again. He heard his own voice, far off and deep, saying:

"All right, Harrison, I must quickly pack. I'll wire you the news, as soon as I have any."

He was hardly aware of the stout man leaving. The thought groaned inside his heart and he knew it had to be true. It was so simple and logical that he could not hate Harvel for being so adamant against the marriage. He could not hate him for not fighting to keep him as his associate, for the truth had risen too close to the surface. Regarding him almost like a son was only a breath away from accepting him as the son that he actually was. The man could not allow an unholy marriage between a half-sister and brother. Then the full weight of the truth came crashing down upon him. He was already damned to hell, and the name of his sin was incest.

But there was no personal God before whom Clayton Monroe could fall upon his knees and beg forgiveness. Forced religion had turned him non-religious. Oh, he knew there had to be *a* God. But they had never been on a personal relationship. He felt it was the ultimate hypocrisy to pray for personal wishes or for personal gain. What God had time to sit and listen to such dotard drivel?

No, he had sinned—innocently or not, he had sinned—and he couldn't banish it from his mind or wash his hands of it. It was there, forever, and must be lived with. He would not feed upon it plaintively, like a child. False tears would make him falser. Boarding school had taught him that tears of self-pity only brought upon the victim further abuse.

He could not afford self-pity or abuse. Not a drop of Barrett Monroe's blood flowed in his body, but he felt very akin to the man at that moment. And suddenly he knew that it was not just respect, but love. For his sake alone, that man had come back to a woman he did not fully love just to give the child Clayton a respectable name in society.

If forgiveness was to be asked, Barrett Monroe was the starting point. Events had made him misjudge for too many years. But words were effective only as long as their echo lasted. Deeds were paramount. Deeds Barrett Monroe would understand far better than words.

Chapter 10

The stink of oil hung heavy in the western Pennsylvania air. It penetrated everything and was impossible to get out of the nostrils. Postwar platoons had invaded the oil-soaked region. Eight miles from Titusville several new wells had come in, around which had sprung up a tent and shantytown. Because of the manner of obtaining oil, it was named Pithole, but the manner of people who poured in to gain an oil strike soon made it one of the most pitiful holes on earth.

For five months Clayton Monroe was as nondescript as the next worker. The wooden tanker cars were effective from the railway spur at Titusville, but it was Pithole that was capable of producing ten thousand barrels a day.

"I can only use the five," Flagler said tersely. "If they come by barrel the eight miles, let them stay in barrels to Cleveland."

Clay swallowed his disappointment. In Cleveland he had measured Henry M. Flagler to be a bold and dashing fellow. He appeared rich, until Clay learned that they were in the home of his father-in-law, S.V. Harkness, the rich whiskey distiller and saltmaker. Flagler was deeply attracted by the possibilities of the oil business to make his own mark. Cleveland had thirty oil refineries. Flagler studied the manner in which each obtained their crude material and saw his opportunity. The supplier, not the oilman or refiner, was taking the middle chunk of the profits. Working on a modest scale, he went to the smallest refiner, Rockefeller & Andrews. By buying direct from the wells and shipping bulk crude in the tanker cars, he could cut their cost fifteen cents a barrel. Flagler had to prove himself, because John D. Rockefeller was a young man who ventured nothing unless totally sure he could defeat chance itself.

The tanker cars could supply him with three thousand barrels a week. It was sufficient for the refinery. It was not sufficient for Henry Flagler or Clayton Monroe, but each was invested to their limit.

Clayton looked at the Steele well rights and considered a quick sale. The McClintock farm was a forest of producing wells, but something made him keep quiet and not announce his ownership of the unproducing land. Instead, he gambled. He wired Harrison that an additional twenty-five tanker cars would be required by spring and gave him authority to withdraw his two thousand dollars from his savings in the Chicago banks. Going back to his lean-to cabin, he caught sight of his face in the shaving mirror.

"You stupid bastard," he whispered. "You're now a broke son-of-a-bitch and better go to work to get this damn slimy stuff to the railhead."

He walked to Pithole, moving past the mountains of oil barrels that awaited wagons, into the swarms of oil riggers, teamsters, shipping agents, gamblers, drifters, pickpockets and whores that filled the muddy streets of what, two years before, had been a quiet farm, asleep with the mineral of the century unnoticed beneath its plowed fields.

In a tent, next to one of the fifty so-called new hotels, he found the tall, enormously fat man he had heard about.

"I'm Clayton Monroe," he said. "What is that offer you are making for workers?"

"Two dollar day," the fat man beamed. "Fine offer, *nicht wahr*?"

"Reckon I'm getting a mite deaf," Clay drawled. "Didn't catch your name, sir."

"Mister Van Syckel, at your service." The fat man grinned. "As I wast saying—two dollar day, das ist goot, yes?"

"Still deaf," Clay said. "But before you go on, Mister Van Syckel, I better tell you I was part of an operation that brought a water line into the British compound in Calcutta . . ."

"Ach so?" Van Syckel said. "In that case, three dollar day for you."

"Never could hear figures under five," Clay said mildly.

"Five dollar day?" Van Syckel roared. "You crazy?"

"Nope—just know my worth."

"Ach, Gott!" the German declared. "You give me two days free to prove yourself."

"One day!"

"Done!"

"Then let me see your plan, supply schedule and labor force."

Clay was relieved to see the man had nothing more than a plan. He had not done the physical labor on the water pipeline, only handled the logistical paper work on supplies and labor. But from rumor he knew that the man was in trouble in those areas. He was determined to bluff his way through.

In the pre-dawn darkness, Clay trudged on the still-frozen ground that ran down a gorge to the railroad siding. He was all alone. In his gloved hand he carried a wooden mallet, but he stepped along calmly as though on a morning stroll. When he came to the next trestle, he tapped his hammer on the stout timbers. They were strong, strong enough to support the eight-inch gray snake that had been inched along mile by mile from Van Syckel's pumping station.

Clay put the hammer back into his belt and began the last climb down the gorge. It was still too dark to see the terminal of the pipeline, but he knew what would be there—the last five of the original ten tanker cars. In these months of labor he had nearly starved himself to be able to send Harrison five hundred dollars to have them shipped east. He had not informed Flagler, because Flagler had not been in the area since before Christmas. Nor had Clay seen Harry or Janellen. The houses and mansion that had been planned for a millionaires' row in Titusville sat in various stages of incompletion. Carpenters, when weather permitted, had to come the hundred miles out from Cleveland and then reported back to the architects. Nor was it just the weather that kept them away.

Whatever else might have been in short supply in the oil

region, hatred certainly wasn't. Jobs were so scarce that winter that some murders were attributed to it, but, stupidly, there were two jobs the unemployed would not accept: carpenters to help finish the mansions so that the oil-rich could start living in luxury and any job to do with the pipeline. Friends became instant enemies if one struck oil and the other did not, and the teamsters spread the rumor that the pipeline would put them all out of work.

The sabotage was at first minor. Then it began to cost Van Syckel so much that the project looked in doubt.

"Pithole," Clay told him, "has become the roughest damn hellhole on earth. Our workers' lives aren't worth a Confederate dollar day or night. It will be cheaper to hire some guards."

"From among these thugs?"

"From among *your* people who will only understand German and can't be bullied by the teamsters."

It brought a few days peace, until a guard was killed.

"Kill back!" Clay growled.

Only the undertaker benefited from the hammering back and forth by the warring parties.

"Stop this!" the sheriff screeched at Clay. "I'll put all your guards in jail if there is one more—"

"Murder? We are the ones within the law. A hundred feet on either side of that pipeline is a paid-for right-of-way and thus private property. Step upon it, even you, and I have the right to blow your head off."

"The next bullet will have your name on it, Monroe!" the sheriff warned.

That night fifty more burly German guards arrived from Pittsburgh. The sheriff quietly left the region.

"Is no goot," Van Syckel whimpered. "They win me out now or later."

"Is goot," Clay mimicked. "We begin filling your pumping station storage tanks now."

"For why? Months before they are needed."

Clay's purpose was dual. The refinery men were unorganized and operated on a dog-eat-dog principle. A barrel of crude could be a dollar different from well to well. New wells, just brought in, could run two dollars a barrel cheaper than wells starting to peter out. The teamsters were paid by the barrels they delivered. A mile or two run to the storage tanks gave them more round trips per day than the eight-mile run to Titusville.

Until the five fifty-thousand-barrel storage tanks were brim full, Clay had won over the teamsters. He had brought twenty-five days of peace and rapid advancement on the pipeline. But he had also brought panic among all the Cleveland refineries, except Rockefeller and Andrews, who were backlogged with tanker cars.

Suppliers screamed for crude barrels, which the teamsters didn't want to haul a full eight miles. Wells shut down, unable to fill more than the barrels they had on hand. Flat cars sat idle, but the tanker cars kept moving. The teamsters now saw their greatest hope in the pipeline, but only when it became operational.

"We must have the proceeds from the stored crude," Van Syckel fumed, "or Carnegie ships us no more pipe."

"Exactly," Clay answered, without saying anything.

Blood was on his hands and the stench of it reeked more than the oil. He stood on a perilous chasm. A few weeks more and the pipeline would make the need of his tank cars prime items. But the teamsters would not wait a few more weeks for the constant refilling of the storage tanks. They demanded more work now, and he had to be daring to keep them in line.

"No more bloodshed," he muttered, as he knew the course he must take. "Blame, yes, but no bloodshed."

He had never done such a thing in his life. Still, Titusville and Pithole had taught him many things he had never done before. He had never worked with his hands, but that had felt good. He had never starved himself to such a degree that rabbit stew tasted like a fashionable feast. He had never strived so for the success of a project.

The bleak winter months had turned him hard and cruel. He had been able to laugh boyishly at the New York prostitutes' proposals, but in Pithole he could put them in their place with a coarse retort. He considered the survival of Clayton Monroe and that was all.

He made the fuse long enough so he could get back to the pipeline office and wait. He did not have long to wait. The explosion ate cleanly up the side of the storage tank, just as he had planned. The wooden walls lifted as one and the hollow booming shook Pithole. Then, a second later, the crude oil flashed fire and the mushroom cloud rose with majestic slowness. It lighted the area like daylight, heated the surrounding snow banks into streams of water.

Fire Department? What was of value to save in Pithole?

Clay sat very still in the office until the air was no longer filled with the bits of wood and tongues of oil fire.

Then he stood up grinning. Outside, figures raced around the inferno like Druids at a fire ritual. Then he put on his more dire face and went out to them.

"Ruin us!" he bellowed. "Murder was not enough! Now they try to ruin us by burning us out! Who suffers by this dastardly trick? All of us!"

Clay glowered at them, seeing their jaws working amid the forest of their heavy beards. Of *whom* did he speak? Many had been the murderers, although no man would ever admit it to the next. They had been soldiers in the war and it had been kill or be killed. This had been no different. Survival in the jungle was the basic law. But Clay had not pointed the finger of guilt at them, or so each man individually believed.

"Well," he growled, "we will show them who is boss! They have given us light to work by. Let us empty these tanks into barrels and glut the market in Titusville. They want crude! We'll give them crude—at our price! Then we will refill the storage tanks and rebuild what has been burned. They do not become millionaires without our sweat and labor!"

They cheered his words and never once suspected their devious nature. Barrels could have been taken right from the wells, without filling them from the storage tanks and then refilling the storage tank from the well barrels. But he had given them an unnamed enemy to fight against and whoever questions the words of a demagogue?

And as though back in the employ of Harvel Packer, he was able to float these profits about on the waves of black oil and provide liquid funds for the pipeline completion. And that date, the most loosely guarded secret in local history, by design, was at hand.

Near the end of the pipeline Clay began to tap it with

the wooden mallet. The echo of each hit filtered back to Pithole to signal starting the pumps that would drive crude through the pipes.

"Ain't gonna do no good," a voice came from the trees.

Clay did not appear shocked in the least. His new-found cynicism had expected it before this time. Several suppliers had invested heavily in future barrel orders for the next day. Stupidly, in his opinion, they had shown their hand without the cards being called.

A big man, who weighed, Clay estimated, two hundred forty pounds, climbed upon the last A-frame trestle to look down upon him. It creaked dangerously under his weight. He had a stub of a cigar in the corner of his mouth. It was unlit, but he was arrogant enough to announce why.

"If the crude comes this far," he bawled, "the cigar gets lit to go in the end."

"Just like you blew up the storage tank?" Clay asked calmly.

"Never you mind," the coarse, whiskey-sodden voice came back.

"This time it won't work."

"It worked before, damn you!"

"Are you admitting the storage blast?"

"Damn right!" The man opened his coat. Beneath his armpit nestled two sticks of dynamite. "These are for your damn tanker cars."

"Too bad," Clay said, and the big man did not get his full meaning.

"*Jesus*!" the man gasped, as armed guards began to appear as if out of nowhere. "They said you would be alone!"

"Obviously not!" Clay said curtly and began to walk away.

Behind him he heard the shotgun blasts. He hoped the man died well. With dignity. With grace. He had acted quite properly. These were not Van Syckel's German thugs who had fired the killing shot. In a private meeting with a dour young man from Cleveland he had taken sound advice.

"Pinkerton. Chicago."

Although of near equal age, Rockefeller had made him

feel a minion and not a satrap. But the man had been a guiding genius of this present operation. *They*, as the Pinkerton operatives could attest, thought the man would be alone for cold-blooded murder, and he'd admitted, on *their* behalf, to the storage blast.

Unthinking, Clay began to hit the pipeline again. He stumbled blindly through the semi-darkness to the tanker cars, his eyes blinded by the rush of tears. He had brought about another death. Others may rape the land to become robber barons for money, but he felt himself the first to have taken human life in the quest.

It hardened him even more.

Spring covered the land with promise of summer. H. H. Horner found himself in the fantastic position of a builder who tries to convince his client that he should have his millions before acting the millionaire. Clay hammered at Henry Flagler from a different angle. He was conscious of a growing feeling of unrest in the world of oil. There were rumors, which a man could never quite pin down, of over-extended drilling and pumping.

"Look, Mr. Monroe," Henry said, "you've proven the worth of the ten tanker cars and pipeline, but twenty-five cars more I cannot afford."

"Wrong! You are being short-sighted and timid."

"Timid! Lord God, sir! You can see that I am only getting a few cents a barrel even at bulk. Rockefeller and Andrews are already screaming that we push it upon them too quickly."

"Which proves your first mistake," Clay growled. "The other refineries are in an angry mood because of your binding contract with Rockefeller. There is one sharp operator who suckered you right in."

"How dare you!" Flagler fumed. "If you are so much smarter, why are you not selling the twenty-five new cars to them?"

"Don't think I haven't tried." Clay's voice was flat and absolutely without fear. "Too many are short of hard cash and long on supplies. There's been too much oil speculation. Now, a man with money could corner that market for the future and almost force his way into an association with a refinery.''

''I am hardly that man,'' Flagler sniffed.

''Oooh?'' Clay drawled out the word. The portfolio-gathering for Packer had taught him the value of surrounding himself with facts on brilliant young men and the richness of old ones. Knowing the profit margin Flagler had made on being a supplier made him question the building of the mansion in Titusville. Afterwards, he called it a hunch, but accurate facts were more than a hunch. ''I can't help asking myself why Stephen Harkness would want to put whiskey money into a Titusville house for you.''

''I don't ask you your personal business, Monroe,'' Flagler said firmly.

''I quite agree, sir, but we are talking business. We're talking large sums of whiskey tax money that never seem to get into the pocket of the government.''

''I see,'' Henry said thoughtfully, thinking it best to find out how much Monroe really did know. ''Go on.''

''In his field Mr. Harkness is the personification of a success you hope to attain—shall we say the cornering of a certain large segment of the whiskey market? It seems time for him to invest in you for the beginning of that hope.''

''And?''

Clay shrugged. ''Just mirror in your mind how much crude could be stored away in thirty-five tanker cars and Van Syckel's storage tanks.''

''That could cause a panic and cause a lot of hardship,'' Flagler mused.

''I am only interested in selling the new cars,'' Clay said curtly. ''You should only be interested in making yourself important to John Rockefeller.''

''Good! I'll take the twenty-five new cars. Cash!''

''And say an additional fifty by December?''

''Why December?''

Clay smiled. ''By then the poor bastards will almost be willing to give you the crude for nothing.''

Flagler frowned. ''I'm curious. You seem to want no part of this for yourself.''

"Maybe I'm just crazy."

"Crazy like a fox," Flagler chuckled.

For all his hardship, Clay knew when to keep his mouth shut. He had come to detest oil. It was a filthy, dirty, catch-as-catch-can business. It was too unstable and fluctuating. To pare down the costs, it needed monumental attention to the little details. He had come to regard Rockefeller as a young man who could do such a task, given time, money and a corner on the market. Little did Flagler know that such a timetable had already been discussed between Clay and the man. Little did Rockefeller know that Clay had a hidden motive in wishing a panic developed.

The morning after the pipeline was completed, he thought again of the one hundred thousand shares he had in two hundred acres. Efficiently, but unobtrusively, he had the old wells quietly checked. They had never been drilled deep enough. Every indication was that he sat atop one of the rarest pools in the region. But a coming decline was not the time to glut the market with a bonanza strike. There was, Clay realized regretfully, a pattern that was developing in his life—the shrewd ability to put other men in the position of gaining vast fortunes, while he had to wait for future rewards.

In mid-June he returned to Chicago. He tried to avoid everyone, except for business purposes.

Harrison & Monroe was a definite success. Harrison Dole had overcome his family qualms and made a clean breast of his new venture. To his amazement they saw great future use for the tanker cars. Clay agreed and sent Harrison on an extended selling tour. After all, he had not promised Henry Flagler anything more than an additional fifty cars by December. There were other suppliers and refiners in the East. And Philip Armour wanted ten cars for a new project. For a few cents a hundred pound he was buying up all the waste fat from the Union Stock Yards. In Milwaukee he was turning it into soap.

Lumber was now almost a sideline for Jon Monroe. The riverfront lumberyard was now a near forest of closely packed storage silos.

And Chicago grew. . . .

And the Horner theater took on the look of a cavernous barn.

Clay did not ask after Harvel and Eugenia nor did anyone venture to supply him with information he did not want.

He paid a social visit to Uncle Harry and Janellen out of simple curiosity, but afterwards he was sorry.

One of the good things from the past, one of the things he truly cherished, was the illusion of Janellen's sweetness and down-to-earth gentleness.

There was nothing down-to-earth about their new rented house. It was Victorian regal, with a full staff under the direction of Mrs. Yost as housekeeper.

To his dismay, the rather unattractive maid reported his unannounced arrival to Mrs. Yost and not Janellen.

The florid woman regarded him coldly. "May I help you?"

"I've come to see Uncle Harry and Janellen."

"Quite impossible! The *invited* guests are due momentarily."

At one time Clay would have felt guilty for having barged in. Titusville had taken away a lot of his social graces. Now all he could think was that the human race was no exception to the rule that the female of nearly any given species is more deadly than the male. This was female-servant savagery at its naked worst, and he grimly understood the reason. He had not lifted a single finger to help the woman when she was having her difficulty with Miss Priest. He now wondered if LaVerna Priest may not have been in the right.

"I heard the doorbell, Mrs.—"

He looked up and hardly recognized the woman at the top of the stairs. Janellen was breathtaking in emerald-green satin with a lace overlay of pure white.

"I tried to explain to the gentleman, Miss Janellen."

"Sorry," Clay called up. "Didn't know it was party time. You look terrific!"

Janellen waved Mrs. Yost away and swept down the stairs. Clay could not help but think that she had become as regal as her gown and surroundings. Except for the face, she was not the same person.

As Janellen glided into the parlor, her thoughts were a near mirror. How much he has changed. The big boyo has developed muscles that make his frock coat look as though it is about to burst at the seams. Hard and healthy. But the greatest change was in his face. It, too, was hard. The boyish handsomeness had melted away to leave a skin-tight jawline and deep cleft at the chin. But the hardness in the gray eyes troubled her most. Then she pushed all of these thoughts aside.

She turned back mid-room, the chandelier light showing a strange mingling of savagery and hurt in her face.

"I presume," she said icily, "you're aware of your long silence?" Again she turned, then marched defiantly to the fireplace, her voice charged with a bravado that somehow seemed to lack genuineness.

"I'm at a loss to understand why you have done this to Harry, to your family, and mainly to me. You were treated very well by us."

"You knew where I was," Clay said evenly.

Janellen looked at him steadily, almost insultingly, with her green eyes, then laughed.

"And you knew where we were."

"I was busy," he said coldly.

She looked at him bitterly and said, "Busy running away. Do you think us stupid? Harvel Packer loves to gossip, and I know all about Miss Fancy Pants and how he stopped the marriage. That's the whole thing, isn't it? She got her bid in because she was afraid you were getting too interested in me, didn't she?"

He was filled with the same disgust for her that he had felt for Eugenia. He wanted to say something to hurt her womanly vanity. "Then why try to ape her in manner, dress and entrapment?"

She blushed angrily, blood coursing so through her face that the freckles popped out from under the powder cover.

"I dress to please Harry," she snarled. "He needs me now as a hostess to entertain his clients and guests. A new form of uniform, you might say."

"And new duties?" he mocked.

A scowl crossed her face, a harsh, belligerent scowl, and she could not kid herself into thinking that she was dealing with the same Clayton Monroe. He had become a hard man! Still, he was the only man she had ever wanted to love as her very own.

They stared at each other for some time, and he saw in those green eyes a flashing mixture of bitterness and confusion—and love. But as he continued to look at her, those attributes vanished and he saw only that she was not a happy creature in her new role.

"Harry will be gone for five days. We have a male nurse for him now. I'm sure that you will want to see him on his return. I would ask you to stay now, but it would embarrass you. Two of the dinner guests this evening are Harvel and Eugenia. Because of the money Mr. Packer has put into the theater, I must be gracious to them both."

"There's sense in that," he said thoughtfully. Then he grinned. "I didn't get a welcoming kiss or hug. Can I come back for it after they have all gone?"

"Please, Clay—let's not get it started again."

"Why not? You know damn well that I didn't propose marriage to Eugenia, even though Harvel cut me down about it. In the oil fields I thought a lot about that. I thought a lot about you. My silence has been one way of showing you that I could put my affairs back in shape and get ready for love and marriage. Oh damn! I've got no experience in these matters."

"Not now," she said gently. "I hear a carriage."

"Later?"

"Not here. Mrs. Yost thinks Harry is a saint. I will come to your digs."

"How do you know about my digs?" he grinned.

"I once tried to learn everything there was to know about you."

He suddenly remembered something Harry Horner had once said—an odd, fleeting remark? "We all know secrets about each other that can never be revealed. Like love. Too bad the timid don't have the courage to voice their true love. We learn everything we can about those we love and then stand like voiceless pets in adoration."

After Clay had gone, Janellen stood in the foyer thinking. Why am I frightened to tell him the full circle my life has come? When there had been little money and no fame, she had been just a nurse. Now Harry Hart Horner had borne new fame and with it a promise for her future . . .

As though he had seen them yesterday, Clay tipped his bowler at the couple ascending the stairs and skipped away whistling.

Harvel Packer growled deep in his throat. The new clerk had his affairs in a constant state of near disaster. He would never forgive Clay for deserting him. Never!

For all her vanity, Eugenia felt a startling thrill. What a man he had become! And without her molding. Because she could not have him now, he had become her Achilles' heel.

Then feminine vanity did return. She could not help but wonder why he had been to see Janellen, but was determined to find out.

Janellen, in pigtails, stood staring at the bed and the sleeping figure that appeared more dead than alive. There was no emotion on her face or in her thoughts. She sat down beside the bed in his bachelor digs, thinking: I said I would never let a man have me in this fashion, but you changed all of that, you great big puppy. I'd do anything for you—anything at all, except marry you. I'd do that, too, were it not for Harry. I can't leave him, can't you see that? There was no love in my past, till you succeeded in exposing it. No man has ever made me love before. This shall be the only time. In time I hope you forgive me, but don't ever ask this of me again. That I cannot do.

She rose very slowly and dressed herself in the everyday clothes she had taken from the maid's room. To her relief, no one had seen her enter, and the street was equally silent for her exit.

For five nights running she had played a cat-and-mouse game with Mrs. Yost to sneak out of the mansion and come to Clay.

The first night had been so fearful that she'd wanted to send a "repentant" message to keep from going again. Throughout that day and early evening she had put into effect a new stratagem. The male body was the most repulsive thing God had put upon earth. It was—and yet, wasn't it amazingly soft, despite the steel ropes of muscles under the skin, and the body hairs more like powder puff ends than scratching wool? And his maleness . . . No! That she would not think upon!

She lay tensely in her bed night after night after she'd return, unable to sleep but in snatches for the guilt throbbing in her veins. She felt momentarily deranged in not being able to stay away from him, but soon she must.

She was unaware that the Packer carriage sat in a side street night after night—or that Eugenia's nights had become as sleepless as her own. Ironically, Eugenia felt like a tigress protecting her cub. She proved to protect him in a very strange way.

When she told Janellen that she had been watching her nightly, Janellen laughed.

"I might have known. Are you now playing the protective sister?"

"Sister? Oh, really! Wherever did you get such a notion?"

"From Mrs. Yost."

"Mrs. Yost?"

"The woman heard much in that house. Her wealth of information, added to my Milwaukee knowledge, was quite adequate. Your father, it seems, was Marti Monroe's secret lover for years."

"Cleverly true," Eugenia simpered, "but foolish of you not to dig for the whole picture. My father, womanizer that he is, was hardly the only one smitten by her charms."

"But he all but admitted that he was Clay's real father."

"I know," Eugenia said, as though she were the one who had the confessing to do. "It came to me later what a kind man he was for playing the fool. If one counts accurately, Miss Heubner, I was not yet born when Clay came on the scene. Any affair my father had with Marti came after that time, although my thinking processes and memory might be questioned. Clay's father, to coin a phrase, had to come before." She looked at Janellen's peaceful, beautiful face until she saw the tremor start.

"Harry . . ." Janellen said, and then paused.

"I know," Eugenia said soothingly, "it shocked me, as

well. But I sit here with the facts. My father used that tool to keep me from marrying Clay. I no longer buy it."

Eugenia hesitated with pure daredevilry. "We, it seems, are in love with the same man. We both can't win, you know!"

It amused rather than angered Janellen. "The question, Eugenia dear, is not can we win, but whom Clay wishes to win."

"Yes," she sneered, "I had but a single night with him and you have had five. Oh, don't blush, my dear, I know. As you seem to have that advantage, let's look at the others. Do I shock you? Perhaps that is my intent. My father is becoming an old man and has only me. The next time I bark he will have to accept whatever son-in-law I put before him. Clay is ambitious, although starting to do fairly well upon his own. He wants the moon. I can give him the sun and stars as a bonus. You can give him nothing, my dear. But you can give Harry Hart Horner everything, and get everything in return. Give up Clay."

"And if I don't?"

With maddening slowness she draped her floor-length fur about her seductive form and arrogantly rose.

"How will you look in his eyes if you have known the truth about his real father all along?"

"How will you convince him that your father is not his?"

Eugenia stood, her throat and chest bursting to reveal the plans she had on that score, but too cagey to let the enemy know everything.

"Let me put it this way, Janellen. When I decide I want something, I convince everyone who stands in my way. I want Clayton Monroe."

Janellen remained silent. Their eyes clashed. Eugenia retained her smile, a little disdainful, and very removed and untouched.

Janellen was not convinced that Clayton Monroe wanted Eugenia Packer. But she would not admit to the woman that she had come to her senses and would never see Clay again. She was surprised and incredulous over the thought. It had tortured her and now was final. Still, she would not let Eugenia have the last say.

"Then you must fight for him." Immediately she knew the mistake of her words.

Eugenia's smile was unpleasant, its amusement malicious.

"I'm a very good fighter," she said, deliberately lowering her voice to a purr that was almost inaudible. "The man shall be mine."

Janellen doubted it, although she knew he could not be hers.

Three weeks later Harrison Dole came into the tanker car office, his fat face drawn with trouble. Clay took a single look and exploded.

"Damn!" he roared. "They haven't started to cancel, have they?"

"No," he whimpered. "I just sold ten more to P.D. Armour."

"He's in town? Why didn't you tell me? Where did you see him?"

"Going into church. He was on his way to a wedding."

"Just like him," Clay roared. "Get business in while you can. Who's getting married?"

Harrison stood up and faced him soberly. "Harry Hart Horner and Miss Janellen."

Clay's face paled, and then the red came back as he flushed with hurt anger.

"I don't like what I hear out of Pithole," he said grimly, the subject purposely changed. "I best get back."

"Not our business," Harrison reminded him.

"I'll make it my business," he growled. "I suddenly prefer the stench of oil."

"You're just getting upset because Janellen went off and married him."

Clay reached out and drew him close by the collar. "Keep out of my personal business," he sneered.

"Bull crap!" Harrison bellowed. "Wasn't it personal business when I sat here chewing my nails for you to do something positive in Titusville? Wasn't it personal business when I had to go to court and win out alone against Cyrus? I need you here and not weeping over a lost love.

Do like every other man does and just go out and buy a piece now and then.''

''Name a price and buy me out!''

''Clay,'' Harrison said sorrowfully, ''don't make foolish statements.''

''Name it! I want out!''

''Then out you are, you stubborn jackass!''

Chapter 11

At first it seemed good to be back in the filth and stench. It matched his ugly mood. Around him was roughness and he felt rough.

The summer progressed with breakneck speed. The oil barrels began to pile high again after the storage tanks were filled, and suppliers began to take futures on unpumped oil. In New York and Boston the wharves became jammed. The European market was also over-extended.

The tricky factor, of course, was the fluctuating price of crude oil. The futures looked bright, climbing to over fourteen dollars a barrel.

Ironically, in New York, the directors of an industrial bank specializing in oil looked to one of their biggest backers for sound advice.

"I've had one of my soundest young minds study the situation," Jerome Plummer told them. "First, it is a near-suicidal business run by non-businessmen. The results are chaos and disorder, waste and incompetence, competition at its worst. A hundred different wells produce a hundred different prices. Cyrus Monroe has learned that the producers at Titusville and other places are clamoring for a convention of interested persons to take some action to establish better and stable prices for oil. We should be those interested persons, gentlemen, but later. Cyrus has figured out a system whereby we can quietly obtain the overproduction slanted for the European market at four dollars a barrel under the prevailing future price."

"Why would they sell under to us?"

"Gentlemen, the wharves are packed with oil they have purchased at six, seven, eight dollars. They can't move their other supplies. At ten dollars a barrel they make a profit and Cyrus has found warehousing that will cost us only two cents a barrel until the first of the new year. With proper holding that oil will go to twenty dollars."

News of that nature was hard to keep quiet and was a banner headline in the Oil City *Register*. But that was oil already pumped and no help to those in Pithole.

Henry Flagler felt nothing but disgust. The man was filthy and unshaven. It upset Mrs. Flagler greatly to have the man in her home with its mansard roof and fifty thousand dollar conservatory blooming with orchids. Clay looked more desperate than the steadily growing number of jobless.

"Well?" he said. "And what is it you've got now?"

"An idea. A wonderful idea! Sam Andrews has perfected a process by which he can extract more kerosene from crude than the rival refineries. What will that do to the market if Rockefeller and Andrews announce it to the Oil City *Register*?"

"Send it through the ceiling," Clay said indifferently.

Henry Flagler's face darkened. It had nothing to do with that news.

"Monroe, you are one of the sharpest young men I have ever known. But look at you! If this is all because of a woman, it is not worth it."

Slowly, sadly, Clay shook his head. But discuss it, he would not. Ruefully, but only to himself, he would admit the fool he had been. Pride had gotten in the way of sound business sense. Fifty thousand dollars was a drop in the bucket compared to what he would have gained out of Harrison & Monroe. Anger had cost him his fortune. Never again would he allow the allure of a woman to so undermine his good sense.

He would burn her out of his mind, just as he would sit out this panic. He would blend with the ever-growing jobless ranks. He would suffer right along with them and guard his money like a miser. Even oil drilling, he reflected, had to be studied. When men were miserable, nursing along a pint, they were more apt to commiserate on the good days and reveal little secrets of the trade.

It was a fact that Clay could have saved some by telling

them not to sell futures to the suppliers, but it was also a fact that such an idea had never occurred to Clay. And once the new cracking process was announced, they would not have listened.

When the first frost hit the countryside, John Rockefeller gave the signal.

"Now's the time to cancel," he told Henry Flagler. "And since it was you who gave me the idea, you do it."

"Which has given me another idea," Flagler got in quickly. "With the new process you really should be thinking of expanding with another refinery."

"That takes capital."

Flagler stepped forward, his breath making an excited sound in the room.

"I have seventy thousand dollars on loan from my father-in-law to invest."

The dour, bloodless Rockefeller face cracked into a grin and then instantly sobered again. "I will be honored to have you as a partner, Henry, but let us be wise. Right now it would tip our hand. You be the pawn to create the noise, and I, as king, will remain silent. But in the meantime there isn't a single reason to keep us from quietly using your ready capital to purchase the other refinery. When the drillers get hungry enough, we will still be in a good enough position to start buying wells. Production and refining, Henry." The smell of success momentarily transformed him. His pale features literally glowed. "I'm bound to be rich! *Bound to be rich*! BOUND TO BE RICH!" Then he sobered again. "What we really need, Henry, is the third leg of this new giant—transportation. Oh, we have the tanker cars, thanks to Clayton Monroe, but they still charge us a tariff to use their rails. I would like to talk to him about that sometime."

Henry Flagler held his silence. That pawn, he determined, was best left silent and not noisy.

The cancelled contracts of Henry Flagler were like a spring thaw rivulet steadily increasing to floodtide. Rather than drown, the other suppliers began to sell, and the market nose-dived. By mid-September Cyrus Monroe sat with warehouses filled with five-dollar-a-barrel crude. A week later, with crude down to three dollars a barrel, the holding bank announced its bankruptcy. And rumor had it that Jerome Plummer was in personal financial straits.

One by one the four banks in Titusville and Pithole closed their doors. There was no more cash.

By December oil had dropped to $1.35 a barrel.

Clay sat back grinning. No one had expected that huge a drop. Even Flagler and Rockefeller began to curse, cry and roar out their rage. After the one-dollar-a-barrel government tax and transportation costs, new crude would cost them money.

Rockefeller began to lie awake nights worrying about the tanker car supply giving out. Public confidence in kerosene began to fade. Why should they continue to pay thirty cents a gallon for a product that the refiners could purchase for $1.35 a barrel to process?

A half-starved boy found Clay in his customary saloon and handed him the yellow square of a telegram. He laughed over the fact that the Cleveland refiner was asking him what to do. He took a few pennies from his pocket and gave them to the astonished boy.

"Go to Mr. Flagler's big house and tell him to answer this. Now get this straight: Mr. Rockefeller should expand with the calculated recklessness of an expert gambler."

The boy blinked. "Can't remember all them big words."

Clay found the stub of a pencil and wrote on the back of an envelope. The letter had been from Eugenia Packer. He had burned the letter without reading it, but for no good reason had stuck the envelope in his pocket.

His announcement had caused a few chuckles, as though he was pulling a very wry joke. That he wrote out the message raised eyebrows. They remembered him as the smart young fellow who helped to build the pipeline, but never considered him smart enough to know how to read and write.

"So—" a teamster mumbled at the bar. "You know that refiner Rockefeller?"

"Met him once."

"And Flagler? Sounds to me like you know him more than just once."

"So?"

"So, I say," he mumbled drunkenly, "it sounds like

you know more than we." He puzzled a moment. "And it seems you got pennies to throw away on messenger boys. I think we are due some answers."

Clay opened his coat. Beneath his armpit nestled a Colt revolver.

"Is that answer enough for you?"

The man backed away, but Clay knew he was the real loser.

Whatever else might have been in short supply in Titusville, whiskey certainly wasn't. But Clay always limited himself to two drinks, nursed along, and a clear head. Good thing for the clear head, he thought. He was now eyed with dark suspicion.

As he turned to leave the saloon, a soft hand gripped his shoulder from behind. Even as he spun, the toxic cheap perfume narrowed his nostrils.

"I could use some pennies," the coarse, whiskey-sodden voice said.

"For what you want to give him," the barkeep bellowed, "ask him for some of his *real* money. Only man here who has never tried to run a tab with me."

Clay felt trapped. The girl was absurdly young, and he had always assumed her to be the barkeep's daughter. She was more pitiful than pretty. He shook his shoulder to break the grip.

"And the only man who rations his drinks to two a night," he soundly reminded the man.

"You've only had one," she whispered huskily, "and I could be using the other."

He pushed his hand into his pocket and came out with all his change. He knew it would be just enough for a drink, for he wisely never carried more than his two-drink limit and a few extra pennies.

"Pour her a drink," he growled and made a quick exit.

To his surprise the leaden skies had opened up with a thick, blinding snow storm. It took him a moment to pull the earflaps down from his cap and tug his collar up around his neck. In that moment she was out beside him.

"Sir," she whimpered, tears gathering in her eyes, "me pa took the money but wouldn't give me the drink. I ain't turned a trick all week and he'll beat me for sure.

You don't have to do nothing. I'll do it all for both of us. Just take me along to your place."

Trouble, Clay thought, hearing feet come to the other side of the saloon door to listen. He saw their reasoning clearly. A man who had enough to drink each night had to have a little stash in his digs.

"Come on, Sophie," he said kindly. "No use standing in the storm."

He saw, when they rounded the corner, the drunken men come out of the saloon, each with something in their hands. He walked slowly to the next corner and then took off in a dead run, leaving the girl standing in the snow.

"No matter," he heard one of the men bellow. "I know his shanty!"

Fool, Clay cursed himself, stupid damn fool. You suffer along with them for months and blow the whole thing by trying to be smart-ass. He stumbled blindly through the storm, his eyes caking with the snow. He barged into his shanty. Even then, digging the leather money pouch out of the bottom of the coal scuttle, he knew it was no refuge. The gun was no help. He kept it just for warning and possessed no shells.

Buy them off? If they were thinking what he thought they were thinking, they were already in the realm of crazed animals beyond reasoning. A little would make them crave the whole lot.

He could hear them outside. A hard object hit the door with a dull thud. Immediately the shanty was bombarded with other flying objects.

"Burn him out!"

Clay's mind went as cold as the keening wind. He threw open the door and brandished the gun like an angry bull at the knot of drunken men. There was a hesitant surge forward.

"He won't shoot," someone shouted. "Remember, he had to have the Pinks do his killing before!"

A tall man darted to Clay and tried to bring a length of pipe against the side of his head, but Clay ducked quickly aside and brought the revolver butt up under his chin. The man sprawled out limply in the snow. The pause gave another man time to jump upon Clay's back.

He spun and the man went flying. Clay stooped to pick up the pipe length and with each hand armed began to flail his arms like a windmill. More black mounds fell to the snow, but it was now savage against savage.

Few heard the carriage come thundering into the street or paid attention to the licking flames that someone had set to the shanty.

Others poured from the neighboring shanties to determine the cause of the disturbance. The mounds in the snow called upon them for help. "He's rich!" "He sold us out to that bastard Flagler!" "He's a Rockefeller agent!"

Clay was aware, after a time, that someone was calling his name. For the first time he saw the closed carriage. Somehow he thought that Flagler had sent him help.

The others thought the same and new shouts were raised: "See, that proves it!" "They've sent him protection!" "Don't let any of them get away!"

The driver began to beat them away from the frightened horses with his whip, while screaming at the horses to keep moving. Clay broke away and tried to reach the carriage. He groaned under the weight of a fist smashing into his face. He tasted blood, but thought of death. Even though his limbs felt like solid lead, he forced them to run after the carriage and jump up to the running board. Slowly, stiffly, he got the door open and crawled into the dark interior. The mob surged behind, cursing and pelting the carriage with anything that came to hand.

There was a scream as a large chunk of coal cut right through the lowered storm curtain.

Clay turned slowly. His swelling lips came apart, but he said nothing. At that moment any refuge in the storm was welcome.

"What is all of this?" Eugenia cried.

Still he could say nothing. In a moment they were racing along millionaires' row and the gaslights from the street filtered into the carriage. Eugenia sat huddled in sable so silver that it nearly matched her hair and pale face.

"We just passed Flagler's house."

"The train will be safer," she gasped, a tremor in her voice. "I had to pay this heathen a ransom even to bring me from the siding. God, Clay, this is the end of the world!"

"Then why come to visit it?" he said bitterly. "This was really only Saturday-night sport. They riot to make them forget that they are hungry."

"Are you always their target?"

"We take turns," he laughed. "It adds a bit of blood color to the oil-black snow. God, I didn't know it would go this far."

"You could have gotten out at any time. Didn't you read my letter? No, don't even answer. I am here because you didn't answer."

"Which tells me nothing."

"Wait a moment. We are at the train."

Wordlessly, he got down from the carriage and helped her alight. The engine had been left at full steam, with only two cars behind the coal-tender. It was an escape route, but he suddenly felt the mob might be easier to face than any mockery from Harvel Packer.

"Father thinks I am in New York shopping," she said, climbing aboard. "I left him in Cleveland with Elliot and rushed on down here—Elliot Fairchild, of course, being your replacement."

"I see," he muttered and took a seat. Suddenly he was very weary.

Eugenia gave a gasp as she turned. "Your lips! Oh, my poor darling, they hurt you!"

"I am nobody's poor darling," he snarled.

"Don't get testy," she chided, taking off the fur wrap and going to pour brandy at the bar. "If you had read my letter, you would know that I have fully forgiven you."

"Forgiven me? As usual, Eugenia, you are confused. I have not forgiven anyone."

"And right you are," she said, handing him a brandy. "It is unforgiving what Janellen did to you."

"I don't care to discuss it, and especially with you."

"But I didn't know your feelings toward her. I just thought it was friendship because of your Uncle Harry. Not until you went off like blue smoke did I learn the truth from Harrison."

Once he would have been able to tell when she came

anywhere near a lie, but he was now too tired and too uninterested in the subject.

"Nor did I know the misapprehension you were under from Father. He is innocent! It was not he who sired you, Clay! I have proof; he admitted it to me himself!"

She had his full attention now. He looked at her, his battered face making it still appear suspicious.

"Granted, he was in love with her, but she became a woman who desired only to ruin love in others because her lover had thwarted her. Don't you see why Father denied us? He thought he was doing what Marti would want him to do."

"No," Clay said hoarsely. He did not want to see it that way. He did not want to see it any way.

"And look what she did to your real father," she said slyly. "Hardly ever went next door to see him after he became a cripple."

"No!" Clay got out the word strangling in his throat. The unspeakable had been spoken, the information he never sought unearthed. It was so obvious he could not believe that he had never though it.

"Oh my God!" she cried, forcing tears into her eyes. "I thought you knew. I thought that was why you flew into a rage over Janellen marrying him. Oh, Clay, I love you too much to hurt you in this way. Forgive me! Please say that you will forgive me!"

"Yes," he muttered. And in a very peculiar way he did. It was now obvious to him that Janellen would have known that fact before coming to his digs. She had used him like a male whore, because his *father* couldn't supply her needs. Eugenia had been an experiment for his unused bodily vigor. He had given himself to Janellen with heart and soul. She had killed them, just as his mother must have killed them for Barrett, Harry and Harvel. And the truth of the blasphemy was that her blood within him could make him feel as ruinous.

"But forgiveness will never make your father change his mind," he told Eugenia flatly.

"Oh, Clay, I wish you'd read my letter. Father is in such a mess. Elliott doesn't have your knack. He took the summer grain futures and put them up for three Cleveland refineries. That's why Father is there, trying to dump them."

"Fat chance he will have at this time on the market."

"That's the whole thing, Clay. He's proud and stubborn, just like you. You really are a lot like father and son, you know. Neither will bend and crawl, although he has come near to it. Jay Cooke told him he should come to you on his belly."

"But you came to get me to do the belly trick instead?"

She knelt down between his legs, her face tender and beguiling.

"On your feet, Clay, and make him pay a big price to get you back."

"Are you that price?"

She put her head down on his knee. "Only if you want me, Clay."

He stroked her silver-blonde hair lightly. Oddly, he could forgive her, but did he really want her? He knew, truthfully, that he could never love her as he had loved Janellen. No woman, he thought, would ever again be allowed to have his body and soul. He suddenly thought of Eugenia as a by-product of his desires. He certainly was tired of being poor. He missed grace, and dignity, and honor, and pride. And love . . . How did one miss what one had never had?

But for all he had been through, he could not strike a bargain on a lie.

"I must be honest," he said, his voice filled with unutterable weariness. "I come to you loveless."

"Only for the moment, my darling."

Eugenia mentally hugged herself. She had won! Janellen would never get him back. Her father would be forced to take him back. She would make him rich and powerful and feared.

Elliott Fairchild looked puzzled, but, to Clay's great relief, was hardly the hostile type.

As was normal, Harvel Packer was not yet in the office. He had muttered a half-hearted wrong-and-sorry phrase in Cleveland, then thankfully allowed Clay to solve the refinery situation. On the trip back to Chicago the young clerk was never informed of the guest's status.

"Sir," he stammered timidly, "those are Mr. Packer's private portfolios. However did you get them out of a locked safe?"

"By knowing the combination," Clay said calmly. "Lord, what a mess they are in! Are you a tobacco or licorice man, Fairchild?"

"Sir?"

"The smudges on the papers are one or the other. Not prone to either, I am unsure."

Clay was fearful the thin young man would faint dead away before he could answer. "A sweet after lunch, sir, it would have to be."

"While I am in charge of the office, you will eat your lunch and sweets away from the desk."

Fairchild nodded.

Then Clay pounced to gain full authority. "Are you a homosexual man, Fairchild?"

Because it had never been put to him so bluntly Elliott amazed even himself with his quick answer. "I'm afraid so, sir."

"Don't be afraid. I worked with many such in India and ask only that you keep your thoughts on your work and off of any possibility that I might be the same. Now, portfolio by portfolio, I want to be brought up to date."

"Yes, Chief!"

It was to be Chief thereafter.

Nothing about Chicago had changed and everything about Chicago had changed. The narrow streets in the poor sections were crowded with the surge of three hundred thousand people. Clayton Monroe walked the streets and tried to decide why the people and the city were different. Area by area he roamed, shopping in the neighborhood markets and listening to voices that were incomprehensible.

That was one thing. There were more immigrants. There was also about them, faintly and subtly, almost indefinably, an air of striving, of willingness to achieve, when the nation was suffering a reputation for slackness.

Still he was aware of a shabbiness about them. Men, women and children wore visible patches, though they were clean patches and worn with a certain pride.

The most important part of the strangeness hit Clay in a subtler, less obvious way.

He stopped a passerby.

"Pardon me," he said, "but I've taken a wrong turning. Close by should be Crenshaw, the jeweler."

"Never *heerd*," the man snapped, the nasal brogue heavy in his voice.

A street over he selected his informant with more care. The old man was obviously a rabbi with flowing gray beard, ankle-length smock and black rounded-crown hat.

"Crenshaw? Of course, my son. Just around the corner. You may say that Ben Zeev wished him a good day."

Clay felt a glow of warmth. Courtesy was not dead. Nor was craftsmanship. Jewelry he knew nothing about, but Avraham Crenshaw would not allow him to select just any engagement and wedding rings. He wished to know of the lady—her coloring, her size, her manner of dress, her manner of lifestyle.

Once the information was gathered, the man selected various stones and suggested various proper settings.

"Sir," Clay laughed, "any one of them sounds most regal to me."

"But it is the lady we must—" A man came into the shop with an air of important impatience. "Excuse me a moment, sir."

The jeweler went through a curtained doorway to a back room. The tall young man tapped impatiently on the counter with a gloved hand. For a second Clay thought there was something familiar about him.

"Here you are," Crenshaw said, handing him an envelope. "Right on time and all in order."

"We'll see." The man pedantically sniffed and silently counted the money within the envelope. Satisfied. he put it within an inside coat pocket and departed.

"He might have at least said thank you," Clay said.

Crenshaw shrugged. "The sign of a man unhappy in his work. Because the bank makes him go about collecting their rents, he looks down upon us as unspeakable swine. Now, may I suggest . . ."

Clay only half listened. Finally, he remembered the man. The name he could not recall, but the bank teller's face came back to him—always jolly and full of wry humor.

Absent-mindedly, Clay chose a design, and five minutes after leaving the shop he couldn't recall what it had been. His mind was a-buzz with a notion he couldn't shake.

"Fairchild, come into my office with me," he said, the moment he came through the door. "And be prepared to answer one question for me. What is Chicago? And don't you dare start off by saying a city."

Elliott stared blankly; then he took off his work spectacles. The moment he did so, his face changed. It became serious and studious.

"I am right behind you, Chief," he said, and matched the manner of Clayton Monroe's walk with perfect imitation. Because he was a shadow figure, no one had noticed that he had also aped Clay's hair style and form of dress. No longer did he cower and whimper out his answers, as he had done with Harvel Packer. He was positive and articulate, or readily admitted he did not know a subject.

"Chicago is," he went right on talking as he closed the inner office door and came to near attention in front of Clay's desk, "more than a city, Chief. I was born and raised here, you know. It is many little ethnic communities."

"Who owns it?"

"Would you give me time to study on that?" he asked politely.

"Sure. What do you think you are going to find?"

"Speaking only from personal experience, I still live at home with my parents and two sisters. Why? Because they need a portion of my salary to help pay the rent. I don't know of anyone in our neighborhood who doesn't pay rent—or in other neighborhoods, for that matter. That's why I shall have to study up on who really owns Chicago."

Clay sat back and grinned. "Can we do it quietly?"

Elliott puzzled a moment. "It seems to me that a friend from my bookkeeping class obtained a position at the County Recorder's office."

"How good a friend?"

Fairchild colored deeply. Clay knew he had made the question sound too personal.

"Sir," Fairchild said stiffly, "that is a subject I have been wishing to pursue again with you. First, you must realize my schooling was limited early on to night classes and apprentice-training as a bookkeeper. However, after your first day here, I availed myself of a dictionary at the public library. I fear that I confused two words in my mind, never having had experience with either. I am not what you first suspected me to be."

Clay put back his head and roared with laughter.

"I am not laughing at you," he boomed, "I am laughing with you. Most would not have even gone to the trouble to check up on their error. There is no such thing as lack of knowledge. But honestly, Elliott, sometimes you sound as though you had a dictionary of your own in your head."

He blushed even deeper. "One of the librarians, Chief, is from my neighborhood. I often stand and read the dictionary, just so I can keep tabs on her and have an excuse to walk her home. I—I think she likes me. As a soon-to-be-married man, sir, how does one get a woman to go from like to love?"

There was a silence between them. A long silence. "It's just something that happens," Clay finally said, his voice very low.

For six months Clay felt stifled by the heavy feeling of what it meant to be engaged to a princess. She was Eugenia Packer, after all, and the society editors had to wrack their brains to make Clayton Monroe sound equally romantic. An English education and years in India were made glamorous. Clay grinned at it, for he knew, from past experience, that it benefited him. To be an associate of Harvel Packer put him in front of a bank teller's cage. To be the future son-in-law of Harvel Packer opened the bank president's doors. Of course, with fawning servility, they turned over the opening of his personal account to a third vice-president. Fifty thousand dollars they considered his pocket money account.

There had been need for a personal account, for, as Clay said to Eugenia: "He still doesn't like the marriage idea and never will. He treats me more like a clerk than he does Fairchild. Nothing can be done without his approval."

"You got around that before," she laughed. "And we bowed to his wishes on the date. I don't think I can wait for you until June, Clay. Why don't you find a little hideaway for us to play honeymoon in advance?"

He shook his head. "Besides," he said demurely, "you make the society and gossip pages daily. Wouldn't they love to catch us in a love nest?"

"You are just too proper." She smirked and kissed him lightly on the tip of his nose.

But privately she was very pleased that he was being proper. Time and time again she would gaze with wonder at her engagement ring. That he had done it on his own had amazed and delighted her. She had broken instantly into tears—the first real tears she could recall shedding. Funny—in a way, as she had gone after Clay to spite Janellen and her father. The light of that reasoning was slowly turning upon her.

After the engagement party she came to realize that she was envied. He was so proper, so much a gentleman, so attentive to her, that nice girls could not help but have wicked thoughts about him. They flirted and giggled and fawned over him like perfect jackasses, she thought. But he was hers! It took a long time for her to come to that realization. She had framed the whole thing, but the actors had not stayed in character—mainly herself.

Clay had slipped back into the business and social life like a hand into a fitted kid glove. He worked at making it a proper courtship—flowers, candy, intimate little dinners at the Palmer House. They were able to laugh together again and talk for hours on any given subject. And compliments . . .

"What I have always respected about you, Eugenia, is your intelligence."

Respect! Well, it was better than nothing, even though the word love still would not cross his lips.

Harvel Packer, as actor and not father, was distinctly cool and absorbed in exposing his failing health as a valiant reason for her to reconsider the marriage. Because he had the helpless feeling that there wasn't anything he could do about changing her mind, his contempt turned toward Clay.

But Eugenia had to look at the only decent emotion she had in her whole spoiled life. She was having to wait quietly for something she wanted in life, and the more she waited the more she began to appreciate it.

Harvel Packer should have showed no contempt. Within that six months Clay had had his affairs back in perfect order and Fairchild properly trained to keep them that way. Then, a week before the wedding, Packer's contempt bubbled over.

Clay heard the tiger roar of Packer's voice the moment he entered the outer office, and the accusation he heard made his blood boil.

"You work for me and not that bastard!" Packer was bellowing at Fairchild. "You will tell me what these land acquisitions are all about! Is the scoundrel using my money even before the marriage takes place? Answer me or consider yourself fired on the spot!"

"Then ask the proper person," Clay said quietly, moving to the door of Packer's private office, his bulk filling the frame. "Stop cowering, Elliott. You've done nothing illegal or immoral."

"'Nothing illegal' he says!" Harvel fumed. "Then what do you call it, Monroe?"

"Money and land manipulation," he said cheerfully.

"My money!" he snarled, suppressing a dry cough. "My land! My office clerk's time!"

"Bullshit!" Then, a slow grin lighting his eyes, Clay stepped fully into the office. "My money to buy parcel after parcel, mortgage it to the hilt to buy more, and then use the rent money to keep up with the mortgage payments. Fairchild works at night, for a commission, collecting the rents. Fire one and you fire the two of us."

Clay could see the beads of sweat on the old man's

forehead and his fingers nervously twitching. Because the old man usually managed to avoid him, he was not aware until today of how terribly thin he had become. The bones showed sharply through the scant covering of his flesh. For a moment he felt sorry for him. The moment was fleeting.

"I say illegal," he coughed, quivering with fury. "Those parcels will be sold back into this company by nightfall or I will have the law on you. You both work for me. Everything you do will be done in my name so that I profit by it."

"Does that include future land acquisitions?" Clay inquired sweetly.

"Naturally," he barked and stalked to the door.

"Oh, Chief," Elliott gasped, near to tears, "what'll we do?"

"Spend a very, very busy day," Clay chuckled.

"And not have that extra money any longer," Fairchild said, crushed. "I had just saved enough to get up the courage to ask Miss Richardson to have dinner with me."

"No. It might even give you enough money to ask her to marry you."

Fairchild turned toward him wonderingly.

"It's a fact that he wants our land in the company name. Right? Don't answer! It's a fact that he all but gave us permission for future land acquisition. Right? Again don't answer. Just listen. We are going to divide up the banks where we have the mortgages, Elliott. From your records we know what other parcels they are holding. Buy them all with Packer credit. I will give you a letter of authority and no one will question that. They will think I have been very clever in smelling out the land market with my own money and a dribble at a time. How much land do you think we can swallow up in a single banking day?"

"We know that some of the banks are sitting on two to three million in foreclosed and rental property that they consider a great waste of their—" He stopped suddenly, for he had finally caught the import of the questions. "Oh, Chief, the company includes Miss Eugenia, doesn't it?"

"I *know* that fact. Now, to move quickly—before he

remembers it. I want all the parcels that are costing the banks a fortune each month."

Slowly Fairchild shook his head.

"It would take an army of collectors. The banks make the tellers do it as part of their duties each day."

"Suppose I tell you that I am thinking of an army—an exclusively trained army? Neighborhood businessmen who would know the problems and talk the language; Pole for Pole, Italian for Italian, German for German, Jew for Jew."

Fairchild's eyes widened in his face. His lips puckered in a whistle of admiration.

Clay continued calmly: "Get the picture, Elliott? Packer sits on his bony rear end and wants us to plunk down a million here and a million there. Profit, my ass! Eugenia's spending more on our wedding than he has gotten back on some of his stock deals. This will be a real steady cash flow. What do you say? Shall we go to work?"

"To work," he chuckled.

Early the next morning Harvel Packer was surprised to find Eugenia already at the table, calmly reading the newspaper. He considered discussing Clay with her, but he was in no hurry. He still had several days left to ruin the marriage.

"Your name in print again?" he began, with a reproving shake of his head, when she began to laugh.

"Your name, dear. It seems that your little coup of yesterday is being hailed as a stroke of genius and a landmark setter."

Packer's expression did not change. He was having trouble remembering what he had done the day before.

"You didn't tell me that you were going into the Chicago land business."

"I'm afraid you've been misinformed," he said gently. "I told your future husband to get out of such business."

"It seems that he has, according to this. His venture was considered a testing ground for the great Harvel Packer. A true believer in the future of Chicago and its people, you are being called. A record-setting four million in land and property purchases, my, my! And benefactor? Who gave you the idea for a standard rental schedule based upon et cetera, and et cetera and et cetera?"

Harvel Packer, at that moment, was stunned to speechlessness. He was unsure if he had been duped or made a saint. But he was not a man to give up. He brought on such a violent coughing fit that it scared Eugenia half to death.

"I don't care what you say," she scolded. "I'm calling a doctor."

His contempt for the medical profession was now suddenly of a lesser degree than that he held for Clayton. If nothing more, he could be so ill that the wedding could not go on without him.

Eugenia stepped to the head of the aisle and paused, as beautiful and assured as a queen on her coronation day. The music swelled triumphantly as six hundred pairs of eyes turned to get a glimpse of the gown that was reported to have cost over two thousand dollars. Eugenia hesitated to give them a good look and to let them know that she was master of the day.

As a bride, she did not need the presence of her father any more than the groom needed the attendance of his mother. Nor did either of them need some of the surprise guests. She would just ignore the wheelchair that was going to block part of the aisle, just as she knew Clayton would have to ignore the elegantly gowned and bejeweled woman sitting next to it.

To one side of the altar, Clay and Carter, in matching snow white tails with royal blue lapels, tried not to think of their family members present and not present. The invitations had been sent out of courtesy. Only Jonathan and Jon, Jr., seemed pleased to be there. Hershel, Ivan and Henri sat gloomily, without family, as though it were a great waste of their time and money to attend this funeral.

The surprise guest was Cyrus Monroe. Mary Louise had just automatically assumed that the invitation would include her son. Cyrus attended out of spite. He had always envied Clay; now he loathed him with a dark passion. The fall of Jerome Plummer had reduced him to Chicago and working for the family. Everything that Clay was gaining he felt should be his own. He now wished he had made his absence as conspicuous as that of his grandparents.

Eugenia raised her arm slowly and held it expectantly, letting the old world lace drape down from the gathering at the wrist. A hush fell. Old Harvel Packer had gotten out of his sickbed after all, they all thought as one.

Only Clay knew of the telegram Eugenia had sent the day before. Now his eyes brimmed with tears of utter pride and love.

Barrett Monroe stepped from the foyer and gently put his arm beneath hers. He was a rare sight in Chicago, but instantly recognized. Never had he been so proud of a last minute assignment and he glowed with happiness. For a moment they were not paying attention to the bride and her ancient lace train billowing about her like a diaphanous cloud or to the twelve maids of honor in royal blue and more lace. The groom and his lumberman father were for the moment the focal point. Perhaps it was wedding mist in everyone's eyes, but their handsomeness was equal in a young and old version.

The wedding reception included the four hundred who could not be packed into the church. The Palmer House had brilliantly combined the ballroom and several private dining rooms so that they all seemed like one big party. By the time the couple slipped up to a bedroom to change for their departure, no one was paying them any mind. Chicago had never seen a party such as this. Harvel Packer's dream had come true, but he was not there to relish it. Out of respect, the easterners had come to Chicago, like kings bearing lavish gifts. Although no business was openly discussed, several important appointments were set up for the next day.

Only one thing displeased Clay about the reception. He could not avoid or insult anyone who came through the receiving line.

There was a moment of silence; then Clay reached down to shake Harry Hart Horner's hand. His congratulation was so genuine that it came to Clay suddenly that the man was unaware of the knowledge he had gained. He was shaking the hand of his father, but he was little more than jolly Uncle Harry. For this day he would keep it at just that.

But how should he react to Mrs. Harry Hart Horner? They stood facing, looking at each other.

"Well, Janellen?" Clay said.

"I didn't know if you would speak," Janellen said. "Harry thought it important that he attend. I'm glad we did. She certainly is a beautiful bride."

"Thank you on her behalf," Clay said, expecting her to move on.

"Don't I get to kiss the groom?"

He quickly leaned forward and kissed her on the cheek. It gave her just a second to whisper. "I have so much to explain to you."

"No," he said wearily, "I don't think we can have very much to say to each other, Janellen."

She moved quickly to shake the hand of the bride, who glowered at her in triumph.

The next guest already had polite Chicago looking askance. Jim Fisk's passion for notoriety had already made headlines. While others arrived by rail, he had made the lengthy trip by water in his palatial new steamer, the *Plymouth Rock.* Somehow acquiring the guest list, he had taken it upon himself to play host for a bachelor party in the large gilded restaurant and white marble barroom of the floating palace. The entertainment was such that some husbands and wives were hardly on speaking terms the next day.

"Wasn't that some wingding?" he roared, pumping Clay's hand. "And now for the biggest news. Everyone listen to Jim Fisk's wedding gift. I'll take the train back to New York and turn the steamer and crew over to the newlyweds. I'm not about to tell you where it is going to take them, or for how long, but the honeymoon is on me!"

Clay and Eugenia stared at each other, unsure what to say. Elliott, hovering in the background, came quickly to pull at Clay's sleeve.

"I'm sorry, Chief. He had me take him to the house to see Mr. Packer and worked this out with him. I was sworn to secrecy, but didn't think you would mind."

"Who gets the last laugh?" Eugenia snickered. "Father

knows I can't abide the man and his vulgar display of riches. He expects me to cause a scene, you know."

"And what are you going to do?"

She smiled devilishly. "What he doesn't expect. You haven't been too hot on Europe, anyway. If his steamer can come up the Mississippi, it can go back down it. It really is a gracious gift, so let's accept it graciously."

Elliott let off a sigh of relief.

"What's this all about?" Clay demanded.

"The other part of the last laugh. When Mr. Packer made arrangements for you to go to Europe, as his wedding present, he had me book only third-class passage."

The *Plymouth Rock* was more than first-class. Eugenia had her choice of thirty-two suites of luxurious private apartments. The opulence of the floating hotel was overpowering.

"Bed her in a different one each night!" Fisk whispered, then winked, as he gave them the grand tour and introduced them to captain and crew.

Eugenia knew a vulgarian when she saw one and quickly selected a suite and ordered the luggage brought. She thanked him graciously again and slyly hinted that it was time for her to change.

In his unique way he was recklessly indifferent to her meaning and pulled Clay back to the glittering mirrored barroom for a nightcap.

Clay went almost gladly. He was suddenly shaking with far more nervousness than the first time he had been alone in a hotel room with Eugenia. She was to be his, and he still could not quite believe it. He had put this part of the marriage out of his mind for six months. The first time he had been like a naughty child playing a forbidden game.

After one drink he tried to excuse himself, but Fisk seemed unmoved to leave and have his luggage taken ashore.

"Hell, you've got the rest of your life to bed her."

"It's the principle of the matter."

"Principle?" he laughed, his belly flopping. "The only principle I have is none, Clayton. And I make damn sure that everyone knows it. They call me gaudy, pretentious, an upstart. I love it! I would much rather do business with a man who thinks me vulgar. Puts him off his guard. And you think me vulgar, don't you?"

Clay was taken aback. "But I have no business with you."

Fisk rose and went back to the bar. For one so florid and fat, he moved with an amazing grace. The candle glow made a million diamond sparkles in his heavily pomaded and carefully waved hair.

"You were really suckered into buying that railroad stock, Monroe. They haven't built a single mile out of Albany and probably never will."

"My loss, I guess."

"Glad to take it off your hands."

Rather than put Clay off his guard, it put him on guard. "Even in Chicago," he said stiffly, "we are aware that Daniel Drew went to the Commodore with tears in his eyes and begged his ancient rival for mercy. It's only a matter of time before Vanderbilt has all the Erie. I'll sit with a pat hand on that stock until then."

Fisk chuckled, rubbing his diamond studded hands together. "Gould said you were a sharp one. Pulled Johnny Steele's chestnuts out of the fire, too. Do you know where he is?"

"No."

"The rascal went back to his wife and has become a respectable farmer in Missouri. Saw him on the way up here. Says you're sitting with a hundred thousand shares of oil stock. Nickel and dime stuff."

Ah, Clay thought, we get to the real reason for his gracious gift. The *fait accompli*.

"I really do think it is time I join my wife."

"Man named Van Syckel told me where to find Coal-Oil Johnny," Fisk went right on as though Clay hadn't spoken. "Had some nice things to say about you. Got right down there in the muck and learned the whole producing and pipeline game. It's my pipeline now, and I'm going to extend it the full hundred miles into Cleveland. What do you think of that?"

No use not being honest, Clay thought. "It will still

only handle about a tenth of the daily pumping. The railroads will still get the bulk."

"Do you mind telling me what you paid for that hundred acres in Pithole?" Fisk asked softly.

"Ten thousand dollars," Clay said without hesitation, knowing full well that the man was too audacious not to know already.

He saw the look of surprise on Fisk's face and realized that he didn't know.

"*Jesus*!" he wheezed. "You're not only sharp, but calmly wise. You've just sat back and let it sit there. Do you know what it is worth?"

"To the penny," he said gently. "The question, Mr. Fisk, is what it is worth to you?"

Shrewd as he was, he did not realize he had been had. Steele had added an extra zero to the figure he had heard. No wonder Monroe had been able to afford to sit on the untapped land for so long. Still, he had certain buyers who would be gleeful to get it for one hundred thousand dollars.

"I think a dollar a share," he said grandly.

"A dollar?" Clay echoed blankly. "Why, Henry Flagler was furious that I wouldn't sell at ten before leaving Titusville."

"He was wise. No fool is going to go over ten."

Clay stood, yawned and stretched. "Then this fool will just sit on it a bit longer."

"All right," Fisk barked, "so we both know you are in the driver's seat. You can afford to sit back and wait, now that you are married to millions. But are you? Packer had his lawyer with him when I went to call. You will still be nothing but a salaried boy. He's got you sewed up with every legal twist he could muster. Mrs. Monroe is still going to want to live like a Miss Packer. Just look at the bundle she dropped on this wedding, if you think otherwise."

"Funny," Clay sneered, "I don't ask how you can afford to keep a mistress, so why should you question how I am going to support a wife? If you will excuse me, I think we shall go back to our original honeymoon plans."

Fisk was angry. With a muffled "damn!" he threw his

glass at the marble fireplace, his heavy face frowning. This was not how he had planned it.

"What do you want over the ten a share?" he snarled.

"Oh," Clay said quietly, "I will accept the ten a share for the rights to the land, but want a six percent royalty on every barrel of crude pumped out of it. As you say, I can't count on any Packer money, can I?"

"Robber!" Fisk snorted.

"Really," Clay said with a show of calm. "We both know that there must be at least fifty million in crude under that land. Good night!"

Eugenia turned as he entered, her blue eyes flashing danger.

"Ah," he grinned, "before your infamous tongue beings to wag with accusations, your husband will have his say."

"You're drunk!"

"Possibly! Possibly! But not from the grape! My dear wife," he said, bowing grandly, "history repeats itself!"

Despite her anger, Eugina couldn't help but laugh. "What ever are you talking about?"

"It is the Continental Hotel all over again, but slightly in reverse. Your horny-handed, great-thewed husband has just amassed his first million. You need not fear starvation or going about in rags. Although that little number you are wearing leaves little to the imagination. You look lovely!"

"You would look lovely, too," she smirked, "if you were dressed like the Continental Hotel. Shall I turn away, like before?"

He didn't answer but started turning down the gaslights in the suite. Without comment she got into the enormous bed and, when she felt him slip under the cool sheets, let the sheer nightgown fall from her body. Without reservation she climbed into the comfort of his strong male arms.

"You're supposed to be asleep."

She giggled. "This time I want to be awake for everything."

She curled her hands into the ringlets of his brown hair, while caressing his eyes, cheeks and mouth with her lips. There would be no sleeping and no waiting for his hesitancy.

She had waited too long for this intense, delicious capriciousness.

It was her turn to explore the furriness of his chest and stomach hair, to be captivated by the muscular torso and rock hard legs. Before, she had not responded to the growing heat in her loins. Then she had been trying to capture him subtly, but now she had to captivate him wantonly. Janellen had stirred fear in her heart that day. She knew, or thought she knew, what animal passions a woman of such low birth would possibly possess. Why else would Clay have had her back to his digs so many nights running, if she had not been a sexual wanton who utterly thrilled him? She would take the massiveness of his manly assault and turn it into a wild, passionate blissfulness for them both.

Tony Harcourt had been no challenge for her. He had been as exciting as his wet noodle. All she had learned from him was boredom.

Clay was hers alone. He was her husband. She would burn Janellen out of his system with her fiery meshing.

Clay was stunned with wonderment. This was not how it had transpired in the Continental Hotel. Nor had his senses been assaulted with so many alien feelings with Janellen. This was . . . this was . . .

"God," he thought, "I am—finally—a man!"

Then a new sensation came hot upon his cheeks—scalding tears of immeasurable happiness.

Chapter 12

A man struts a certain way coming into puberty, a different way after having gone beyond it.

Clayton Monroe never strutted. He marched like a field general before his troops on parade and, some said, just as mean and savagely.

But fate kept placing Clayton Monroe in the line of progress.

"Rents," he told Elliott sourly, "cannot be paid by non-working men."

"You're up to something." Fairchild smirked.

"No, down to something." He scowled. "Get me a ticket for Milwaukee and tell Mrs. Monroe I'll be gone for a couple of days."

It was a week later that he came in dirty, grimy and happy.

"Clay, for Lord's sake what have you been up to?"

"Turning waste into my second million, darling. P.D. has been showing me the slaughter business from the inside out, you might say."

Waste put three thousand men to work in small-scale satellite industries around the packing houses. Men, of course, who rented from Packer & Company. Horns for buttons and knife handles, hoofs for glue, bones for corsets, hides to the shoe tanner, intestines for sausage casings, wool to the cloth mills, blood and trimmings for fertilizer.

These men called Clayton Monroe a saint.

By the date of his first anniversary, he, indeed, was worth two million. It nearly caused Harvel Packer to have a stroke.

"What am I paying you for? Just to make you rich?"

"If you will check the books," Clay said indulgently, "you will see that for every dollar of my own I invested, I invested two of yours. If I made two million, then you made four. No, you actually saved money, for I now have to support your daughter's lavish habits."

"Rubbish! It should all come through the company. What in the hell do you want, Fairchild?"

"A message from the Republican National Chairman."

"What in the hell do they want?"

"Mr. Amos Cruthers has just suddenly passed away. They want an immediate replacement for Arrangements Chairman. It seems that he has accomplished nothing to date."

"Why ask me?" Harvel said fiercely. "My health is worse than Cruthers's."

"They are not asking you," Elliott said, supressing a smile. "They are asking Mr. Clayton Monroe."

"Why me?" Clay said with a show of alarm, but Harvel could see his chest expanding. This was not just for Chicago, this was for delegates from all over the nation.

"Don't ask, just accept," Harvel barked. "Fairchild can run the office. He already does. As an Illinois delegate, I want a damn fine convention!"

Clay found two drawbacks at once. Nothing had been done and he would have to work closely with Harry Hart Horner on converting the theater into a convention hall—which meant having to work closely with Janellen.

"I just don't think I can do it," he honestly told Eugenia.

After a year of marriage she didn't fear Janellen. She could still close her eyes and see him on the Havana beach. He was a golden god in the water making every woman present aware that she would give up all her worldly possessions just to possess him for a single night. And for a year, when she whispered "Love me," they melted into an unspoken union of equal giving.

"Is it Harry?" she asked.

He had expected an argument over Janellen and was glad that was sidestepped.

"Yes and no. Oh, I know I can work with him, but this is so out of my realm."

"Blasphemy," she warned in mock alarm. "Something

that the great Clayton Monroe can't do? Oh, darling, don't be foolish. When you don't know a thing, you find out from someone who does, then turn it to look like you were the genius. What you really need is another Elliott."

"Like me," he grinned, "they are one of a kind."

The one of a kind he was offered didn't please him.

"Even if I say so myself, it's an ugly barn," Harry was saying. "We've got to start all over. Did you bring those sketches?"

"Yes, darling," Janellen said. "I have them right here in your case."

"Tomorrow," Clay said. "Tomorrow I will look at them. Right now I am due for a meeting with the carpenters backstage."

"Janellen, go tell them he will be a few minutes late. Besides, what can they start building without my plans?"

Clay could buy that, but knew it was a ruse for them to be alone. He really had nothing to say to the man, except on convention business.

"You know," Harry announced. "No, Clayton—no denials. I am what you think me to be—but I should be the one carrying the title of bastard. I've made two grave errors in a very long life. My arrogant inability to bring myself to marry the woman I dearly loved and the denial of the seed she carried of mine. Too late I tried, but the ship had sailed without me. I smile, but there is no peace in my soul. Janellen has given me a tranquil moment, but my withered body has given her nothing but an unconsummated marriage. Is it too late for me to express the pride I have for you?"

He put out a hand that was quaking with fear that it would not be taken.

"Is it too late for a prodigal father to be forgiven?" he murmured.

"What's the catch?" Clay said warily.

"The catch is that we must work together and with Janellen. She is scared of you, because of your little affair."

"You know?" Clay gasped.

"Yes. She was most honest with me before our wedding. I, of course, suspected it. Even rather helped push it along, thinking of you as a chip off the old block. But you are not. You are unique. You are going to be a giant walking this land, Clayton Monroe. I just wish I had the guts to shout to the world that I had a small part in bringing it about. But my lips are sealed. Is that proof enough?''

Clay took his hand.

''We've got a lot of work to do in two months.''

''And a lot of political hype to overcome. Cruthers was set on this 'Home Town Hero' theme.''

''So? Galena is not that far from Chicago.''

''No, but Grant didn't go to work for his father there until 1860. He was nearly forty when the war broke out. Cruthers all but has him born in a log cabin.''

Clay frowned. ''I don't see the problem, Harry. The Twenty-first Illinois Infantry are planning a big welcome-home bash for their colonel and the DAR want in on the planning of the Nomination Ball. This is a theater and that is a stage. Isn't that really what we are putting on, a big stage show with the politicians playing actor? They want Grant, so let's give them Grant.''

''Bigger than life,'' Harry chuckled.

There proved to be plenty of committees for a convention of that size and magnitude—plenty of chairmen and no workers, which made Clay feel he would fail.

''What is this going to mean for Chicago?'' he asked Harvel.

''What I had always dreamed. Every delegate will be a man of influence and standing.''

''Then I need Chicago money to make Chicago look good. I need you to twist some arms and get me that money.''

''Delighted, my boy! Utterly delighted to participate!''

Clay already knew where he could get his army of workers and now had wages to pay them. He let the committee chairmen think they were doing the work, but scoured the town to find the right artists, decorators and carpenters to report directly to him.

''Harry sick again? Then, Janellen, we will have to meet on the—''

"Not today. I have to meet with the women on the ball. Besides, I can't make decisions for Harry."

"We have to or I'll have men standing around doing nothing tomorrow."

"I confess I'm badly fitted for this role."

"You seem to have the ready answers when Harry is around. We have got to meet no later than tonight, and that is that!"

She looked at him a long time, thinking: I'm a fool. I should not be afraid to be alone with him. We are both married and proper.

"All right," she said crisply. "Tonight. Say about eight?"

"Why don't we go out for dinner?" Clay said.

"No, thank you. When you think about it, you will see that was not a very good suggestion. I'll have dinner with Harry in his room and will meet with you afterward. Now, the women are waiting. They are so excited having a part to play."

Clay was given just a second to say hello to Harry, but refrained from asking him any questions. The man was miserable with a summer cold and could hardly breathe.

At home Janellen had reverted to wearing simple nurse-like frocks. It highlighted her youth and beauty.

For two hours they worked diligently in the study, with Mrs. Yost popping in and out as though she felt the responsibility of playing chaperone.

"Why," he said slowly, when they took a coffee break, "did you do it?"

She knew exactly what he meant. "Let's get back to work."

"Were you not the one, at my wedding, who said she wanted to explain?"

"I did," she said. "Hundreds of times. I no longer see why it is necessary."

"Because I found out about Harry?"

"No," she said, "because you seem to be a happily married man."

Clay looked at her. Seeing his face, his eyes, she had to look away. Her fingers ached to reach out and stroke his hair, to feel his lips lovingly melt upon her own. She stifled both impulses and sat there, waiting.

"And are you a happily married woman?"

"Yes," she said bleakly, then hated herself for sounding so glum.

"At least Harry is honest, Janellen."

"But—"

"It doesn't matter now. We both got out of our marriages what we wanted—a certain form of security."

"My God!" she cried. "What kind of a woman do you think I am?"

"Enough of one to do that. But, no matter. You had it all planned. You knew you were going to marry Harry even as you were giving me your virginity, didn't you?"

"Yes! Yes, yes, YES! Satisfied? He made me feel important and wanted and needed. What did you make me feel like? A scullery maid that the master had the right to sneak off to his bed! You reckoned without considering my sensitivity. I might have said no to Harry right up to the altar, but you didn't speak. You took me in your arms and . . . made love. But it wasn't love. You didn't have the proper words, but you really only wanted a mistress. I—I even considered that, which is a horrible thing for a woman to have to consider. At least I didn't spy on you. Eugenia knew of our five nights and then threw in my face that she had been granted only one. Oh, how cheap that made me feel. I no longer feel cheap. I leave that feeling for Eugenia. She fought for you and won."

Clay stood there, looking at her. Even his lips were white. All color had vanished from his face. He didn't say anything. He turned and crossed to the doorway, pushed the door open and went down the hall.

He heard, dully, the patter of her footsteps racing after him. She caught up with him, seized his arms, whirled in front of him.

"Oh, Clay!" she sobbed. "You didn't know! I never should have let you know! I was just being a mean, vicious bitch!"

"Don't worry," he said gently.

She clung to him, crying. "Clay," she got out. "Don't hate her. She was only fighting for what she wanted—you."

"No, Jan," he said. "I can't and I won't, even though

it makes me see things differently. I'm just as much to blame, I reckon . . ."

"Blame?" she whispered.

"You came near the truth on the security bit. I was wicked, selfish and thoughtless. I thought I hated you, but I don't. When Eugenia came to get me in Titusville, I thought I could hurt you back by marrying her. But it didn't work—not for you, anyhow. For myself, it was a disaster, because I still love you so!"

She looked up at him a long, slow time.

"Thanks, Clay," she said, "for telling me that. But you mustn't. We are—"

"The property of others! Even if we weren't, I'd love you still—"

He kissed her quickly. She freed herself gently from his clasp.

"Good night, Clay," she said.

"I—we—still have work to do. Will you come to the theater tomorrow?"

"Yes," she said, "I'll come."

He started toward his home, but her words were like a phantom swirling about him. He raged at Eugenia. Their year of romance was chilled with the recollection of her spying on him. The infamy of it beat on his mind and heart like a ceaseless rain of blows.

He knew, even as he thought of her infamy, that he was little better. He stood apart from himself and examined that thought. He had purposely set about to marry a dollar sign and not a woman. His relationship with women had never been on the basis of outright honesty—not with Janellen or Eugenia. If they had not been honest with him in return, why should they be the first blamed? And then, suddenly, inexplicably, he knew what he must do.

Oh, not against Eugenia. They deserved each other. They used each other and gained a certain happy harmony from it. He didn't think that Eugenia was any more capable of loving him than he was capable of loving her. They were a beautiful couple—socially correct, smartly dressed, elegantly elegant.

What he proposed to do was a violation of all of that and his own vein of puritanism.

An hour later, after a visit to the office, he was inspecting one of the rental houses. He walked from room to room, the feeling growing in him that he should stop this foolishness now. It was dangerous and worse, his mind told him.

"Very shabby furnishings," he said.

"Rents unfurnished," the blowsy neighbor woman carped, casting a shrewd glance at the quiet richness of his attire.

"How much?"

"Twenty the month," she said. "And in singles, if you will, so I can be paying the Land Office their eighteen and keeping my two for collecting."

Clay took out a sheaf of bills, well aware in advance of the rental charge. "Here is a year in advance, Mrs. Burleigh. The man who will occupy the house is very ill and shouldn't be disturbed. As his doctor, I shall call frequently and a nurse will come in and out for his needs."

"Well, Doctor," she said with new-found respect, and the commission already spent in her mind, "you can be counting on Ellen Burleigh. I'll be warning off the neighbors, I will."

She gave him the key and waddled out in an elephantine counterfeit of grace. She started to turn back and then thought better of it. With the rent paid for the full year, she had plenty of time to get the name of the occupant. Besides, when she turned in her money to that nice Mr. Fairchild, he only asked for the names of those who had not been able to pay.

On that thought she sighed. Once she had been a carefree woman without an enemy to her name. She had not been reluctant, or ashamed, to assume the role of rent collector. It had given her family free rent, plus her commission. The obligation rested upon her shoulders to report the non-payers. She closed her eyes and ears to their cries and wails when the Land Office men came to move them out onto the street. There was always someone waiting to move in the vacated house or flat. But how nice it would be, she thought, if everyone in her four block area would pay a year in advance. It would certainly save on her bunions.

Clay got her to the house on a ruse. As he had done, she walked from room to room.

"It really is in good order, Clay, except for the dreadful furniture."

"That's where the woman's touch comes in. I really don't know what to order to make it presentable. And before you say it, I will say it first. I will not allow Eugenia to smother it in rubber plants and horsehair."

"But, Clay," Janellen said with gentle insistence, "no woman can decorate without knowing the taste of the people who will live here."

"I shall live here!"

"Oh, for God's sake—you didn't . . .?" She paled.

"No, I didn't. This shall be a hideaway, unknown to any."

"But I know of it, now."

"You are not any, but the special nurse who will come to visit the recluse patient who lives within."

The color slowly left her cheeks so that the freckles stood out vividly against her pale skin. At the corners of her mouth a little tremor started. She stood still, looking at him, then all at once was against him and clutching his shoulders.

"Clay," she whispered. "Oh, Clay, we can't do this—"

He bent down and sought her mouth, deep pink, soft-fleshed, wide and generous. He was surprised, when he opened his eyes, to see that she was crying.

"Didn't you say you had considered being my mistress?"

"Yes," she said, suddenly, fiercely pulling away. "A very rash statement made in a very rash way."

He tried to pull her back. "I am not being rash!"

Again she pulled away from him wildly. "I wonder? You're doing this to spite Eugenia, aren't you? Do you realize that at the same time you are cheapening me again?"

"No," he said, dejected, "that thought never entered my mind. Foolishly, I thought it was maybe my bachelor digs that cheapened things. It was no more me than rubber plants and horsehair. Neither were you, either. Let's be honest. We are really no more than middle-class chintz and bone china, rocking chairs and hooked rugs. Comfort and loving."

Two days later Mrs. Burleigh looked at the heavily laden wagon and the furniture-movers and sighed: "I wish I was ill enough to live with such furniture."

In the three weeks before the convention the "stomach disorder" of the patient became so frequent an occurrence that the "doctor" and "nurse" were in daily attendance.

"Never has a man had such care," Mrs. Burleigh boasted to the neighbors.

"What is he like, Ellen?"

"He likes to be left alone," she said importantly, as though she saw the man daily. "I've me instructions from the doctor and nurse, I have. Leave the poor soul alone. And that will be going for you, too, Mrs. O'Leary. Don't be trying to knock at his back door with any of your watered-down milk."

"Watered-down, my sainted mother! Now you listen to me, you rent collector—"

"Ah, yes," Mrs. Burleigh cut her short. "A point well raised. 'Tis due again, is it not?"

In mid-August, 1868, Chicago became a circus. Every lamppost and storefront was festooned with bunting and a likeness of U.S. Grant. You could get a cigar with every Grant bourbon-and-branch drink in town. Potter Palmer revised the menu of the Palmer House to consist of every dish the General was supposed to covet. Bands paraded and then came back to play on every street corner.

The rich, the famous, the politicians came in on every train. The former quietly went to their hotel suites; the latter made sure everyone knew they were around. Senators, congressmen and governors almost outnumbered the bootblacks in the train stations.

Clay was in the limelight. If favors were sought, men found their way to his office off the theater lobby. It was not always for convention business.

"Hello, Clayton. Nice to see you again."

"Mr. Morgan! Welcome to Chicago!" Although the banker was only thirty-two, Clay still couldn't bring himself to call him Pierpont or J.P.

"Clayton, let me introduce you to a New York delegate, J. H. Ramsey."

"Pleased to meet you, Mr. Ramsey."

They seemed an unlikely pair. Ramsey had a glass eye and the other wandered persistently. He was massive and the burnished hair was going bald. Standing there, he looked like the suit of clothing he was wearing was the most uncomfortable hair shirt ever spun. At his side, the young Morgan was a London fashion plate.

"This the man?" Ramsey said.

"Yes, J.H.," Morgan said.

"Very well, may we have the door closed?"

Curious, Clay went to close the door. "Will you have the goodness to take seats?"

They sat and Clay came back behind his desk. Clay knew he was being studied by the one good eye. Very slowly, the man smiled.

"I did not take the liberty to seek you out before, Mr. Monroe. Certain men have been over zealous in watching my movements and business contacts. Also, I have been busy building the hundred miles of rail between Albany and Binghampton. Interesting?"

"Very," Clay said.

"I'm a railway president in name only, Monroe. Coal miner all my life. Know nearly every man jack of a miner in those new hard-coal fields and want that freight line so they can profit from their labor. Others want to profit at their expense. An obscure coal-mining corporation has been chartered as the Delaware & Hudson Canal Company. You aware?"

Clay frowned.

"Or damned careful to make it appear you're unaware. Which, Mr. Monroe?"

Clay looked at the burly man with interest. Whatever else he might be, J. H. Ramsey was nobody's fool.

"I," Clay drawled. "could hardly say it was a clear-cut matter either way, Mr. Ramsey. I am aware that, in lieu of cash payments on certain oil royalties, I gave permission for them to be paid in corporation stock. They are so minor, I am not aware what the company may or may not be about."

"You're very right on that point, Clayton," Pierpont grinned. "I had their issues checked from the original files of incorporation. Your holdings, which you say are small, are small—but the voting rights are retained by Jay Gould and Jim Fisk, along with every other voting right for the whole corporation."

Clay shrugged. "That is not really illegal."

"But," Ramsey resumed imperturbably, "they are using that as a lever to seize back the Albany & Susquehanna and make it a spur of the Erie. You are a stockholder of that line."

Clay threw back his head and roared with laughter.

"Who is just now being made aware that the line has been built and, I might add, also is just a small stockholder. I never dreamed it would be built."

"Then why hold onto the stock?" Ramsey asked a little snidely.

Clay sobered. "I'll tell you, even though it is none of your damn business. I had a chance to sell that stock to Fisk a year ago, but was sentimental. That's the first stock I've ever owned in my life. Then, five thousand dollars was to me a vast fortune. Now I can afford that sentimentality."

"You," Ramsey said, "were smart to hold onto it for whatever reason you had. All right, let's quit fencing. You are one of the private promoters of the line, but the cost came from state and county subsidies and from stock sold to the townships along the route to underwrite part of the building cost. When I say private promoter, I mean that you were one of only eight men who ever bought that stock. Today, you and I are the only ones with original stock."

"Which really makes me a minor stockholder," Clay quipped.

"Damnit!" Ramsey roared. "I was told you had a head on your shoulders, Monroe. Don't think in terms of dollars; think in terms of shares."

"Clayton," Morgan soothed, before he could flash back, "may I say first that, to support Ramsey in his resistance, a rival coal company, the Delaware, Lackawanna & Western, has quietly bought out the other private promoters. They would rather break the Erie than let the A&S fall back into their hands."

Clay stared at him a long, slow time. Then he smiled.

"Interesting observation. Number one, you have all but just stated that the rival coal company must be under the shadow of J. Pierpont Morgan. Number two, stock watering, for argument's sake, seems to have been involved. If it were, then my original fifty thousand shares must have been splintered to the nth degree, for resale to the townships. So let's drop that subject, shall we? Number three, I am not for sale, so why else are you here?"

"You, Monroe," Ramsey laughed, "are a man after my own heart. You buttoned everything down one, two, three. You are worthy of my steel. I want a fighter to help me fight them."

"When and how?"

"The first when is here. Gould and Fisk's political henchmen and Boss Tweed already have the Democratic nomination locked up for former Governor Horatio Seymour of New York. To cover their bet, because they fear Grant, they will try to get Huggins in as the Republican vice-presidential nominee."

"They're crazy!" Clay said. "The Speaker of the House has it sewed up as good as Grant."

"Nope. Gould alone has spent two and a half million to woo the New England and mid-Atlantic state delegates. Transportation, hotel, food, booze—all in the name of Lester Huggins."

Clay was puzzled. Amazingly, none of this had reached his ears. "A lot of money for what? Certainly not just for this railroad?"

Morgan chuckled. "It started with a railroad, yes. The Commodore has learned that it does pay to kick a skunk. Drew, Gould and Fisk are being called the Erie Ring, now that they have defeated Vanderbilt. They will now work unceasingly to exploit their opportunities. Through Boss Tweed they control New York. Their contempt is such that they feel they have the power to do the same with the whole nation. Everything, in their opinion, is for sale."

"Except us." Clay grinned. "I think I am going to like this."

* * *

From the marble-paved theater lobby at the street level—its politically frescoed walls illuminated by great gas chandeliers with a thousand pendants of cut glass that had been painted red, white and blue, and ornate with buntinged balustrades—a grand staircase ascended to the private boxes of the second floor. Here sat the rich and powerful in the splendor of silken hangings, gilded chairs, marble statuary of past presidents and national heros and uniformed servants in powdered wigs to bring them refreshments.

The Arrangement Chairman had a private box that was little used until the final day. Eugenia had shown little interest in the long days of long speeches and dull debate. Clay had not pressed her, because his days and nights were packed with every little problem that no one else seemed to be able to solve.

He was not even aware that she had arrived to watch the round-shouldered, bearded, sloppily-dressed, medium-sized man accept the nomination on the first ballot.

But then, he had little time even to look up into the boxes. Ten minutes after the first ballot for vice-president began, the troubles started. Delegates suddenly found their seats taken by alternates that they didn't know. Fights broke out and Clay was everywhere trying to soothe tempers and check lists. He had never thought to have extra police around. He was being pulled in so many directions that he had to press Janellen into service to help him.

Up and down the aisles they struggled, as the convention became a near mob scene. Most of the time he had to hold her about the waist to keep her from being crushed.

"Get that damn woman off the floor," the Vermont chairman wheezed. "It's a scandal."

"That damn woman," Clay growled, "is a lady, sir—a lady who has spent several days checking in the delegates from an official list. The scandal, sir, is your making. Your delegation is padded with unofficial people. They will leave the floor or I will have Vermont polled with each vote."

By the time of the third ballot, the Huggins supporters were making an issue of Janellen and it was reaching the boxes. Without understanding the real issue, the woman guests began to feel scandalized because Janellen would not leave the floor and Clay fought to keep her by his side. Those who thought they knew Eugenia intimately came to her box to cluck and wonder over it all.

Eugenia could only wonder. She knew she would only make matters worse by causing a scene—but Clay was certainly doing his damnedest to embarrass her. When she could no longer appear indifferent, she sent the uniformed servant down to the Illinois delegation with a note for her father.

They were into the fourth ballot before he returned with a verbal answer.

"Sorry, Mrs. Monroe," he hesitated, "but your father said not to think of her as a woman. She—she's Mr. Monroe's assistant and helping them put up a damn good fight."

She didn't bother to ask what the fight was about. She hardly cared. All that echoed through her mind was her own suggestion that Clay get himself an able assistant. Janellen seemed to be able and all too willing. She fought to keep her eyes off them.

Toward the close of the fifth ballot, they were right below her box with the Indiana delegation.

"Mr. Chairman . . . Indiana is proud to cast the winning votes for its own favorite son, the next vice-president, Schuyler Colfax!"

The theater erupted into bedlam.

"We did it!" Clay shouted. He picked Janellen up by the waist, swung her gleefully around, and kissed her neck, cheeks and lips as he let her down. "Baby, we just beat Gould and cost him a couple million. Oh Lord! I think I've fallen in love with politics."

He felt her hands fiercely pushing him away. He followed the line of her up-tilted head.

Eugenia seemed the only one of the thousands who was not cheering and applauding. Her hands were clutched above her breast. Her face was as pale as snow, but the blue eyes were smarting fire-red.

When he looked back, Janellen had disappeared. When he looked back up to the box, Eugenia had vanished.

The political victory suddenly had the taste of ashes.

* * *

He steeled himself for a barrage of accusations. To his amazement, they were not forthcoming. Eugenia was already gowned for the ball by the time he had arrived back from the theater.

"Everything is laid out on your bed, darling. Father is picking me up shortly for the Newberry affair. Really, Clay, you have missed all of the social fun of the convention. Tonight, relax and enjoy the ball."

He couldn't relax. He knew she was up to something, but couldn't pinpoint it.

She was sparkling, sweeping through every dance with partner after partner. She was gracious, taking her bows with Clay when credit was heaped upon his shoulders. She even applauded when he shared the credit with all the committee people and workers—including Janellen.

Janellen took a simple bow of recognition and sat immediately back down next to her husband. She was not fearful, just disgusted with herself. She had made a public display of herself and given Eugenia reason to hate her. Oddly enough, she was rather glad. Eugenia had been the first to draw the battle lines over Clay. It was easier to fight an enemy when you knew they hated you.

These past few weeks had given her back a spirit long dormant. Born a street-wise child, she had sensed this fight coming sooner or later. She had refused once to fight Eugenia for Clay. No more! The smile and graciousness did not fool her.

Eugenia was an actress. Tonight she was in the spotlight. She was Mrs. Clayton Monroe and ready to bask in the glow of his accomplishments. She would have played the fool to do otherwise. But what of tomorrow . . . and tomorrow?

Chapter 13

Eugenia had been wickedly sly. Following the ball, she had conned Harvel Packer into arousing his servants to prepare a breakfast at three in the morning, for a select few who wished the night to last until dawn.

To Clay's amazement, Harvel thought it was a marvelous idea and was far more chipper than Clay had seen him in years. In that setting Harvel and Eugenia were host and hostess and Clay gladly took a back seat. He was weary. The months of work were over and this was an anticlimax. Suddenly, he was responding to people—and then questioning what he had responded to.

"What was that again?" he said to Fielding Smathers.

"Your wife is a genius. I love this house and she will set up an appointment with Harry Hart Horner for me before I return to Dover. I am on the ocean and want him to create for me the sweep of its . . ."

The man talked on, but the words didn't focus for Clay. Faces and voices mingled, overlapped, fused. Somewhere in the back reaches of his mind he recalled that they stayed the night with his father-in-law.

Still, when he awoke, he was in his own bed, with only his half seemingly disturbed. He rolled over and went back to sleep.

The next time he opened his eyes, Eugenia was at the dressing table brushing her hair.

"You've slept twice around the clock," she said.

Clay sat up, running a hand over his beard stubble, as though disbelieving her.

"I said," Eugenia began again, "you—"

"I'm awake!" Clay snarled. "But I had a million post-convention things to see to."

"Seen to by your able assistant and staff," Eugenia said flatly.

"So! We finally come to that—that—"

"Situation," Eugenia supplied. "And properly seen to, without giving it its proper name. Horner has accepted a contract in the East and so you are without your—"

"Bitch!" he spat.

"Really, darling, aren't you being unkind calling her that?"

"It was directed to you. You take a single high-spirited moment and turn her into a tart over it. A girl who's good and pure and honest and hard-working—"

"And no more fool than I," she cried, throwing the brush at the mirror and cracking it. "We both wanted the same thing; I won the first round and she the second, or so I presume."

"What do you presume?" he demanded, seeing a small chink in her armor, "What, what, what?"

Miserably, Eugenia shook her head. "That's just it, Clay. I wanted to catch you both in the worst kind of scandal and you both come off like working saints. Even my own father is starting to call me a jealous shrew."

Clay sighed. He gathered her spying, if any, had not been as effective as it had once before. "I really want to commend you, Eugenia. You thought the worst, but did not act the worst. This convention business over Janellen will evaporate—just as their votes for Huggins evaporated. As a woman, you should be proud of her as a woman. She bowed to no man."

"Because you constantly supported her by the waist!" she said angrily.

"But did I seduce her in front of your eyes?" he said quietly. "Is that what you wanted? Are you so bored that you want to go back to those New York days when nothing but an orgy surrounded you in the Continental Hotel? I am no longer naive, Eugenia. It took me a little time to figure out, but you were no more a virgin in New York than you tried to pretend to be on our honeymoon. If we want to look at guilt, look to your own first. If you love me enough, you will erase these thoughts from your mind."

"I will not play second fiddle," she wailed.

"Then learn to sit in the first chair," he said sourly.

"All right," she whimpered. "Maybe I will."

Why did I say that? she thought, after he had gone to take a bath. It was a sign of weakness and she knew it. She had never been weak before, and it was his fault. Her love for him had weakened her. Could she put faith in his scruples? He had admitted nothing. Had she read too much into the guilt upon Janellen's face? Would she have looked just as guilty being hugged and kissed in public like that? No woman could not have. Still, something edged her mind with doubt.

Clay was unsure if he had won or lost until later that day. The Horner household, including Mrs. Yost, had gone east. There he had expected no message left for him.

At the rental property the message more amused than angered him.

Janellen, as he suspected, took full blame upon her shoulders, but was staunch in her declaration of love for him. Then, in the next sentence upheld her responsible duty to go with Harry, while pleading for Clay's understanding. She knew how Eugenia would feel, if their positions were reversed, then oddly declared she saw no sin and sinning in her love for him. She never wanted to see him again, but longed for the day he could hold her in his arms. Then she made him promise that he would not try to contact them while they were building a house for Fielding Smathers. Address: Park-Hamton Road, Dover, Maryland.

"She should have put a 'p' in Hampton," he chuckled, and went to knock on Mrs. Burleigh's door.

"Who is it?" she barked, and then brightened. "Doctor! Ain't seen you about."

He painted a very serious expression on his face. "Because we've had the patient in the hospital, Mrs. Burleigh."

"Ain't serious, I hope." Then she turned cautious. "Mind you now, a year is a year, and there be no refunds if he be dead and gone."

"No fear, dear woman. He will be back. I just wanted to warn you that there would be no lights there for a while."

"Good on you, Doctor," she said, and promptly closed the door.

Clay grinned, and thought to speak to Fairchild about her. She gave no quarter and he liked that. Then he wondered how long that while without lights would really be. He wanted Janellen back in that comfortable little world with him. He desired nothing more.

Wants and desires? So alike, and yet oceans separated the two words. Like the intake and exhale of breath. The same, yet so different, but each connected for living. Eugenia and Janellen: the same, yet so different, but each a part of his living.

Then he arrogantly shrugged. Why was he letting such a petty matter as two women consume so much of his time? Hadn't a man, no less a personage than J. Pierpont Morgan, come to him to thwart the crafty Gould and pugnacious Fisk? Hadn't the lofty of the land risen in a standing ovation to his recent deeds? Would not the next President of the United States remember the name of Clayton Monroe? He could not forget that a new love had come into his life—politics.

But, for the moment, he went back to being the most loving husband around, until Eugenia began to wonder why she had worried about Janellen.

Then a new worry began to beset her.

"Where is Clay off to this time, Father?"

"He happens to be your husband, my dear."

"And your general manager," she said slowly. "A month in Duluth for Cooke, over a month with P.D. Armour in Milwaukee, and then down to Kansas City."

"What the blazes are you driving at?"

"Just a question," she said sweetly. "Once upon a time, you both discussed business with me. Now I know very little of what is going on. You don't seem to take much interest either."

"No need," he said, surly. "Clay and Fairchild see to the day-to-day matters."

"But is it always to *our* best interest?"

"Daughter," he chuckled drily, "you are fickle. You want your husband to be king, as long as I still have the balls!"

"*Father*! Your language!" She hesitated. "Still, he grows, while you only stagnate."

Which Harvel Packer didn't mind, he told himself. My God, how bored I am with life! What challenge was there to sitting on the Chicago Board of Trade and shuffling paper? Clay was out doing the things he had done just a few years before. He envied his son-in-law. No, he corrected himself, he was jealous of him—that's the whole damned trouble in getting old and sick. His body and mind would not respond quickly enough for him. His eyes would look upon a beautiful woman, but his body would not react. Of late, he had come to comprehend, dimly, what a horrible waste that was. He had looked upon many beautiful women in his day, and usually his looking had been satisfied with conquest. Gone. Those days were all gone.

"Still," she repeated, "we're overlooking an important fact. He does have a knack for doing things for other people and not getting properly rewarded."

"True!" he snorted, as though to end the matter, but made a mental note to speak with Clay.

"A knack?" Clay exploded. "She also has a knack of spending money faster than I can make it. Reward? Duluth is not my idea of a fun place, but just look at your iron portfolio if you think I was up there just doing things for Jay Cooke. Milwaukee? Kansas City? I have P.D. convinced that Chicago should really be his main headquarters. Sure, he has interest in the Union Stock Yard, but who will he come to for the purchase of land to build a packing plant? Who will have the rental housing for the Negroes and Slavs he will hire? The opportunities are there, Harvel, but they don't bear fruit by sitting behind a desk and being home for supper every night."

"So I remember," he laughed lightly, then turned to the large wall map. "Those railroad lines inch closer and closer, Clay. I would love to see San Francisco one more time before I die."

"Not me! I mean to live always in Chicago. It's my town, and I love it better than anything on earth—except money. And we will bring the West here, just as we have been doing with the East.''

Harvel Packer sat up straight, his mind clearing. ''Clay, whatever happened to that damned cattle ranch I won from Alban Foster in that poker game?''

''Still there. Still losing money. Still asking for loans every once in a while.''

''Bah! Cowboys or not, they're all a bunch of thieves. What did you say about Armour coming to Chicago? Seems we should look even farther ahead and be ready to supply him with beef.''

Clay started to say that the time was not right, but had a different thought.

''It's going to take time. You don't just pluck cattle out of the ground like you do iron or oil. Plus, we need a good ranch manager to make sure we turn a profit.''

''Then let's take the time. Who just said that opportunities don't bear fruit by sitting behind a desk? When can you leave for Wyoming?''

Clay frowned. ''I have nothing pressing at the moment.''

''Nothing pressing?'' Eugenia screamed. ''Clay, you are very inconsiderate. We are almost into the holiday season. I have a tea planned, twenty-four coming for Christmas dinner and you promised we could have a New Year's Eve ball.''

''Blame nobody but yourself, my dear,'' he said sourly. ''I was not the one to put the notion into your father's head that I am always off doing things for others. As he is the one sending me off to Wyoming, then he is the one who will have to play your host.''

Eugenia blushed scarlet. ''I didn't mean to imply . . . Well, I will just talk to Father and have him change his mind.''

''I don't want it changed,'' he said brusquely. ''It's quite simple, if you have the brain your father gives you credit for. You were very clever, Eugenia, to discuss *our* interest, meaning his and yours. Funny, your husband was not included. I have given you a nice house and a lot of comfort. And you—you go out of your way to make sure that you do not ha child that would—''

''You have never once said you wanted a child!'' she flared back, cutting him short.

''Did it require a business discussion?'' he said bluntly. ''I have never heard of a husband yet who did not look forward to becoming a father.''

''Then that is a simple matter to solve,'' she shrugged. ''Just stay home and we can start work on it.''

''You say it would be simple, but in fact it could be rather complex. My child will require a mother and not a social butterfly. Think on it, Eugenia, and we will discuss it again when I get back.''

''How long will you be gone?''

''For as long as it takes.''

A child, she thought—the very last thing in the world that she desired. She pouted. It would ruin her figure and she wouldn't dare face a single friend for at least a year. And what was a child, but a nuisance? Then, in her clever way of always seeing things only as she wished to see them, she pounced on a new thought. Clay really didn't want a child. He had even said once that he could not stand children. He was just raising it now as an issue to spite her because she had talked with her father. Well, he might be gone long enough for the subject to die in his mind.

The subject was not on Clay's mind—nor Wyoming. The train had borne him east, not west. Harvel Packer had given him the perfect excuse to vanish in such a way that his tracks could not be traced.

His route took him from Chicago to Binghamton to Nineveh, then to Masonville to Oneonia to Collierville to Westkyrd to Central Bridge to Voorheesville to Albany.

''Have you gone daft?'' Joseph Watson growled, almost running to keep up with the mayor's furious stride. ''You've probably cost us every cent we might have made out of that stock. And for what reason? Your refusal to sit and discuss his simple desire to buy. Damn! It took us months to get the council to buy in the first place.''

''And a shorter time to sell—to the right party. They will crawl when they see the slick deal I have made.''

William Morton entered the Nineveh train depot and

went to the cage to prepare a wire. He had been expecting, and had been paid, for just this moment.

Across the street Clay stood smiling. He waited until the mayor and local banker had departed, then sauntered over to the depot.

"Oh, good evening, Mr. Monroe."

Harry Stillwell had been the first person Clay had met upon arriving from Binghamton. It had been by careful design. J.H. Ramsey had wired ahead to the stationmaster that one of the "big boys" of the line would be stopping through. Harry Stillwell had not found Clay to be a "big boy," as he had feared, but a very gracious gentleman who took the time to be friendly and ask "right proper" questions about the depot operation.

"Evening, Harry," said Clay, grinning as he pulled out a roll of bills and peeled off two fifties. "I would like to see that wire before it is sent."

Harry's glasses nearly fogged over looking at the bills.

"It's a company matter, Harry," Clay said. "You, being a company man, might as well know that Erie wants this line. They would move in their own men, of course."

"I'm a company man," Harry said happily, handing over the yellow blank, "but it don't say nothing more than 'On the move'—whatever that means."

"Code," Clay grunted, while memorizing the addressee. "We got anything through yet tonight?"

"Ten-ten coal freight. No passengers."

"I'm hardly a passenger. Caboose will do me fine. What're its stops?"

"Night freight only fuels and waters at Westkyrd before Albany, Mr. Monroe."

"I get it, but I'd rather no one knew I left town until tomorrow."

"My lips are sealed, Mr. Monroe," he said, starting to push back the money. "And I don't feel right taking this."

"Everyone gets a Christmas bonus, Harry. That's what makes us a company."

Loyalty, he knew, could not be bought—but a little seed money would help him earn it faster.

Once he had made up portfolios on the rich young robber barons. Now he mentally made them up on brakemen, firemen, engineers and stationmasters—where they lived, how many children they had to support, what life was like on that railway line.

In Westkyrd he avoided the mayor, banker and any council members. He wanted to get to know the town and what the railroad meant to it. He also wanted to see what one Maxwell Mumford of Albany would do with the message that the A&S was "on the move."

Leaving some of his "holiday cheer" behind, he caught a local to Central Bridge. It was over the mountains and thought little about getting the Pennsylvania coal to Albany and New England. Poultry and eggs were more important. Voorheesville looked to its milk, cheese and beef. Albany abounded in state politicians and little else.

The Susquehanna office, as it was locally called, was on the second floor of the depot. The sign on the door told Clay all he needed to know:

Headquarters
Albany & Susquehanna Railroad
Maxwell Mumford, General Manager

The fox was already in the hen house.

The office was coal-dusty and nearly barren. There was a clerk's high desk and chair, a roll-top desk and chair, a hatrack and an extra chair. The walls were blank, the windows curtainless, the floor unswept.

"Monroe to see Mumford," Clay said curtly, taking in many things at once.

The clerk seemed hesitant, even though the general manager sat but five feet away. The clerk was also a fool. He had been dipping his pen into an inkwell that was dry to put figures upon a page that was blank.

Mumford turned to greet Clay with the most extraordinary amiability and evident pleasure.

"Unexpected, sir—a most unexpected pleasure."

"Didn't you receive the wire that I was on the move?" Clay asked drily.

For the barest second there was a savage expression of the mouth under the walrus moustache; then the tiny pinpoints of eyes began to sparkle with amusement.

"Frankly, sir, we have some very lazy men down the line."

Clay didn't comment. He looked at the extra seat, but it was not offered.

"Who is paying you your larger salary, Ramsey or Fisk?"

Mumford laughed gently, as though the question was asked daily and was not an insult. He shook his bald head modestly. "You do me an undeserved wrong, Mr. Monroe; that you do. I'm a chap as must make do with this miserable job. The road is not wealthy, as you must know."

"I don't know," Clay said with a mock grimace. "I came from Chicago to learn if this was an investment worth keeping or not. I have not been impressed coming up the line."

Mumford smiled lovingly, as he contemplated strangling the idiots in Nineveh. This could not be the man they had been warned about, although he seemed to know about Jim Fisk. But around Albany men said that Maxwell Mumford set the best trap in the world.

"No new line is all that impressive, sir. When one has the highest admiration for profits, one seldom looks at railroads."

"I was looking at coal," he said coolly. "That's why I asked if you really worked for Ramsey or Fisk. Ramsey doesn't seem to be doing much with my rail investment and my broker's doing little better getting my Delaware & Hudson coal over the line. If I could get ahold of Fisk, I would tell him to chuck it all, but he seems to be out of New York."

"Chuck it?"

"Would you let your money go to rack and ruin because the owners of the railroad are fools?" he asked virtuously. "I am an investor, not a benefactor."

"There you are right," said Mumford with a wink. "And the townships will feel the same, sir. Ain't no good having money lest it can make money for you, says Maxwell Mumford. Would you be liking for Maxwell Mumford to pass your feelings along?"

Clay sniffed. "It is news only for the ears of my broker."

Mumford lifted his eyes piously to the barren ceiling, as if caught in a cynical suggestion.

"I meant only for the ears of Mr. Fisk."

Clay immediately assumed a grave and businesslike expression. "How soon?"

Mumford laughed with loud and vast enjoyment as he slapped thighs like pillars. "He will be in Albany on the 8:05 with many of his associates. I will let him know that you are here by 8:06."

Clay's expression became graver. "I'm not one who is frivolous with another man's business time, Mr. Mumford. You seen to have your finger on things. Do I sense that Mr. Fisk might be interested in this line to make my coal investment more secure? He certainly protected me well when Mr. Drew and Mr. Vanderbilt were fighting over the Erie stock."

"He does protect those who look out for his interest, sir," Mumford said shrewdly.

Clay allowed himself a momentary grim smile. "Then it really does seem a waste of his time to discuss a matter that he has in hand. To make a long story short, forget that I bothered you."

Mumford twinkled. "Still, wouldn't you like to meet the man more than your broker?"

Clay had purposely saved the best for last. "My dear sir, my wife and I were given, as a wedding gift, a two-month cruise on the *Plymouth Rock*. He knows my oil interest better than I do."

"I was unaware." He was suddenly quite impressed. Clayton's age and manner had led him to believe that he was just somebody's playboy son with extra money to throw around. Hell, he had a hard time getting a thank-you out of Fisk and this pipsqueak got a two-month cruise on his steamer. "I'll now tell Mr. Fisk whatever you wish, sir."

"Ah," said Clay, suddenly alert, and scowling. "I suddenly think it best that you not even tell him, or bother him, or mention my visit. He would only try to interest me in further investment in this line, and, frankly, many of us in Chicago are questioning why we cannot have our own stock exchange and forego the outlandish New York Exchange fees. Do you see me going about in a private steamer, or railroad car, or owning an opera house? No! But my broker certainly can afford them."

Mumford studied him long and thoughtfully. Then he

said suddenly: "This stock of yours? Would it put you in a better position if you owned more of it?"

Clay regarded him with simple bland honesty. "Naturally it would. But I am not about to pay the moon for it and Fisk's commission."

Mumford smiled broadly. "I'm a man as knows his way around these parts, you might say. Bundles of money are coming in from New York to be spread around the countryside. Your stock, sir, has been run into the ground along with the rest, in order to buy it up cheaply and watch it skyrocket after tied to the Erie tail. I could be the first one down the road to get you a nice piece of the pie."

Clay nodded gently. He began to laugh softly as he took out the roll of bills and peeled off ten fifties.

Mumford was not embarrassed; he thought it was an advance for his services. He joined Clay in his gentle laughter.

"Mumford," said Clay, "you are the most conscienceless rascal I have ever encountered. Why, blast you, you are almost artistic. Look at this place! Coal dust weeks thick and not a record in sight. Your nephew, whom I know to be totally deaf, doesn't even have ink for his quill. Had you been minding the store, instead of waiting for Jim Fisk to pull off his coup, you would have known, if nothing more than rumor, that I have been coming up the line with Christmas bonus money. There it is! The General Manager's share! Ill-earned, until this moment." Then he turned hard. "Now we will see if your ruthlessness and chicanery is bold enough for me to pay for. You will find that I can be very crude, compared to your methods. I have nightmares sometimes because there is blood on my hands. I don't mind adding to it."

Mumford was momentarily nonplussed. "I've given them information, sir. I admit it. Nothing criminal, though."

"Just jacked up the freight rates for the poultry farmers and never let it show on the books sent to Binghamton, wasn't it, Mumford? Who puts butter, milk and cheese on your table out of pure blackmail? Do you have a goodly supply of coal to last you through the winter?"

Mumford perceived that he had indeed met the man that

they had expected. He coughed delicately. "Do you not see those as bold strokes?"

Clay said nothing. His face was impassive. If he had made a single move, it would have been to kill the bastard. "Business. You will be paid well. You will not leave Albany, but you will keep me posted, up and down the line, on every move that Fisk and his henchmen are to make. I want to know his every scheme."

"That I already know. And a lot of it is already done. He's already paid out bounties to those who can sway a town councilor's or mayor's vote on selling the shares. You are going to have to be more highhanded than that."

Clay smiled musingly. "Well, Mr. Mumford, I can match his hand on that and beat him with the ace of resolution. But you shall be my trump of skillful skull-duggery. Every bastardly thing you have done to workers or shippers on this line I want. No, not to use against you. I shall probably end up making you look like a gilded saint while painting Fisk for the devil that he is. But don't think you are getting off cheap. When this is over, I pray that you were smart enough to save what I am going to pay you, because you will no longer need this office."

Clay had developed a sense in determining a man's touchstone. In a city man, the lust for money and power led normally to one instinctive goal: a woman. He renewed his brain on every aspect of Jim Fisk and his womanizing ways.

In these villages and hamlets he was sure that men also lusted for money and power, although, by ratio, on a much smaller scale. And with gossip being the best form of communication within a village, a man was not likely to have a mistress, as did Jim Fisk. But each of these men, up and down the line, did have a woman—a wife who was the mother of his children, and worry centered on their livelihood.

Going back down the line, he spent time getting to know the merchants—and their wives; the parsons—and their wives; the farmers—and their wives; and the wives and family members of the railroaders he had already met.

He was quiet, reserved, unassuming and considerate in answering their every question. Behind him stormed the political henchmen with their bundles of money. He gave them a wide berth, while carefully planning his travels for just one chance meeting in Oneonia.

"Clayton!" Fisk cried in disbelief. "My God, man, what a shock to find you here!"

The fat man was actually dressed all in pink, like some sort of exotic tropical bird. He came down the length of the general-store counter and hugged Clay like a long-lost brother.

"Hello, Jim. I might say the same at finding you here." Then he remembered his manners. "James, may I present Mrs. Calhoun and her daughter Jane. Mr. Jim Fisk, ladies."

Mary Calhoun nodded coolly. Jane curtsied, but she felt like a rag picker being introduced to a prince.

Fisk gave them a slight nod, but Clay saw his eyes quickly appraise the beautiful young woman. His voice brimmed with enthusiasm. "What luck, dear old friend. Is it coal or railroad business that brings you to this place of beautiful women?"

"Some of each. You know me, I never buy or sell unless I check a matter out."

"Which is it to be?"

"I am unsure."

"My dear boy," Fisk said expansively, pointing out the door to an expensive horse-drawn carriage, "this line is so badly built and operated that I travel in that rig rather than put my private car on their rails."

"But it is still good enough for coal freight cars?" Clay laughed.

"That pirate gives us no other choice," Fisk scowled.

"But his rate is cheaper than what the Erie charges from Albany on."

"Hardly a fine line of difference," Fisk scoffed.

"To me, the difference is quite a fine line, old friend. Take Mrs. Calhoun here. When her husband was alive, they wagoned their goods from Albany. They looked on the A&S as a boon. Now she finds herself paying a premium rate to the Erie on the merchandise that has to come on down the A&S line."

"One more example of their stupidity, Clayton. If the Erie owned this spur, the rates would be standardized." Then he blinked. "I am remiss, dear lady. I came to say how sorry I was to learn of your recent widowhood. Mr. Calhoun was certainly a far-sighted man to push for the bonds to bring the railroad to Oneonia."

Clay stood silent. He was fascinated, as always, by Jim Fisk. No political henchman was assigned to approach the widow, as Clay had reasoned out. The villain, himself, would do that charmingly.

"Short-sighted fool!" Mary Calhoun corrected sternly. "I would be packing for debtors' prison if this kind gentleman hadn't come to my aid."

Fisk was astounded. "Bond buying, Clayton?"

"Only on a personal basis."

Fisk's hazel eyes were dancing. He had come to believe that this whole operation was going to be a boring coup. Clayton, if only on a personal investment basis, would put some spice into it. Calhoun had purchased nearly half the bonds sold in that town.

"I shall stay the night here, Clayton. If you do not attend a small dinner I am having for Mayor Johnson, then I shall be mad." Then he remembered his social duty. "Ladies, of course, I meant the invitation to include you as well."

"We are still in mourning," Mary Calhoun said a little too quickly. The man's presence was making her very uncomfortable. She had business to finalize with Mr. Monroe. For two days the man had kept her on tenterhooks as though wavering in his offer.

"Oh Mama!" Jane protested. "It's been nearly six months and I have never eaten in the hotel dining room."

Mrs. Calhoun shot her a warning glance. "It is foolish to pay people a steep price for food we sell them in the first place."

"And I must beg off," Clay said quickly, delighted at how things were going. "Tomorrow is Christmas Eve and I have made plans for the holiday season. I really have to catch the next train or I'll never get to my destination on time."

Mary Calhoun's heart leaped. "But—but it comes through very shortly, Mr. Monroe."

"Oh, our business! My partner and I are prepared to pay any sum for the bonds. He still has not determined a fair price for the business, but has promised to get up from Binghamton over Christmas week. Here, however, is a down payment until I return from Maryland right after the first of the year."

He could see that his words had deeply troubled the woman, as he had wished. He chuckled that Fisk struggled to keep his face expressionless. This was the exact angle he had wanted to employ. Let Fisk feel the way was still clear to bid on those bonds.

"Have yourself a merry Christmas, Clayton," Fisk said sweetly. "Maryland? Not back to Chicago?"

"Harry Hart Horner is in Dover," Clay said, as though that would explain everything.

As he hoped, Jim Fisk's evil mind was quick to pounce on this tidbit. It was really Mrs. Horner he would be going to visit and he might be able to manipulate that information to serve his ends.

"Give him my regards. Oh, there is the train whistle. Let me run you to the station in the carriage. Ladies, my invitation still stands. Mrs. Johnson will be with her husband, as well as their daughter Betty. She must be about your age, Miss Jane. And we gentleman promise not to discuss railroad business all through dinner."

Sly fox, Clay thought, seeing Mary Calhoun waver, but he would tip his own hand by encouraging her.

"Well," she stammered, "seeing as I don't have to pay the hotel price, I can see no harm."

In the carriage Jim Fisk already felt the victor. "Clay, are you really going to fight me all the way down the line on this dinky little railroad?"

"All the way."

Fisk roared with delight. The reaction fully satisfied Clay. He was being told that he did not have the money or the power to fight the Erie Ring alone.

"Tell you what, Clay," Fisk chuckled. "Let's call a truce until after the first of the year. Business should be put aside when there is holiday fun to be had."

Clay agreed. He and Jim Fisk might agree to a truce, but that would not keep Fisk from keeping his henchmen busy in the countryside. Fisk was too ambitious to let a week slip through his fingers. Nor did Clay really want them out of the field. The dirty cesspool tricks they were pulling in their vulgar corruption to gain the stocks and bonds were the subject of rumor up and down the line, moving faster than the trains ran. They had no traditional moral standards and he would let the church-going folk in each community judge them by their exploits. Clayton Monroe, as they all knew, would respect the holiday with dignity.

"Why the about-face?" Jane Calhoun asked, as the carriage had rolled away.

"I have my reasons."

"Was it because you heard Rita Johnson would be there?" Jane put in rudely. "Mother, the woman is always so horribly rude."

It was the wrong thing for her to say.

"Normally I would not let that worry me," she replied angrily. "But I will not let her say in the days ahead that they gained more for their bonds than I. I am furious with Mr. Monroe." She tore open the envelope. "Down payment, bah! If Mr. Fisk makes a better offer, I shall jump at the chance." She frowned. "There is also a letter in here from Hiram Fester at the Oneonia Bank." With an involuntary start, she handed the letter to her daughter after quickly scanning it.

"Well, that settles dinner," Jane relented grudgingly. "How can you talk sale when the man has left on deposit with Mr. Fester the full value of the bonds plus ten percent over? The deposit is only for the business."

Mary nodded to her daughter. She was not aware of Clay's game, but she sensed he was up to something with this ruse. Whatever it was, she wanted to be in on it to spite Rita Johnson. "It settles nothing, Jane. We have an invitation and shall keep it. However, put out of your mind this letter."

"What are you up to, Mother?"

"You may laugh if you like," she said with a sly smile. "Your father fought hard for the railroad, while our mayor was laughing in vacant and meaningless derision over how it could only fail. As the mayor, he now sits with control over the other fifty percent. Didn't the letter say I could draw on the account at any time?''

''Yes, but—''

''Oh, don't worry. The man hates me more than his wife. I just want to force him into having to take Mr. Fisk's lowest offer and then have to explain it to the people of this town—when they later learn what I received from Mr. Monroe.''

Janellen had described the house as a ''hideaway'' cottage for the owner, a man for whom Smathers had only acted as agent to keep his identity secret.

It was hidden down a long lane of towering oaks, winter bare. But the forty-eight room, twelve-staff house was hardly a cottage.

Janellen had been fearful of his visit, and then embarrassed. The owner of the house was not to take possession until mid-January, but had suddenly appeared an hour before Clay's arrival. Janellen was all for sending Clay back to a hotel in Dover, but Harry calmly put the matter to the owner.

''I remember Monroe,'' William Vanderbilt admitted. ''One of the few men ever to beat my father at whist. No problem. I shall just return to Staten Island.''

There was no need for that, as there were thirty bedrooms available.

Clayton barely remembered the fortyish man. The Commodore was handsome and erect. Billy was homely and stout. A timid creature of routine, he allowed the three their Christmas Eve together and reluctantly agreed to dine with them the next day.

Unbeknownst to Janellen, he had already let the staff know that he was a hard-driving man, and to make sure it was going to be a perfect meal, he'd sat often upon a kitchen stool to watch them—or would suddenly appear in the pantry or dining room to harry the maids from their idleness.

While the gentlemen waited for Janellen, the butler served champagne.

"Wouldn't sody-water do instead?" Harry chuckled.

Young Vanderbilt blushed, knowing that to be a famous utterance of his notoriously stingy father.

Clay, for a reason he couldn't explain, thought it had been unnecessary and very cruel.

"I don't recall you being much at the Washington Place house, Mr. Vanderbilt," he said quickly.

The man smiled. "Mainly because I was relegated to living upon the family farm in Staten Island for health reasons."

"Or because your father thought you to be sluggish and stupid," Harry snickered.

Now Clay thought Harry was being cuttingly cruel and frowned.

"Don't frown, Mr. Monroe," Billy said. "Harry is being honest. I have been patient and submissive to parental abuse and many taunts."

"Why not," Harry laughed, "when you stand to gain a fortune of one hundred million?"

"Damn!" Clay seethed.

"Oh, it is not that much," Vanderbilt quickly said, expecting Clay at once to take advantage of the knowledge.

"The figure doesn't matter," Clay said. "It was the manner in which it was stated. Some *parents* should never be allowed to bring children into this world. They put price tags of accomplishment upon them, no matter how old they become."

They heard footsteps upon the stairs and the subject was left dangling.

Janellen, in a froth of green lace, swept into the room, almost a little too theatrically. William Vanderbilt was captivated with her, as he always was. Without giving it a second thought, he raced to the door to escort her in.

Janellen was a little chagrined. She had prepared herself mainly for Clay—curling her hair into the crown that he always admired; wearing the green of dress that he said complemented her hair and eyes, and of a cut that accented her slender figure and fullness of breasts.

Vanderbilt was making everything so formal that she

hated him. Clay was almost like a stranger. Harry seemed remote. Clay took her hand to guide her to a seat. The touch thrilled her through. But when she looked at her husband, she started. He sat in his wheelchair, seething with fury.

Harry's voice had an edge of temper that he did not attempt to conceal. "You just missed the first part of Clayton's lecture on parenthood, my dear."

"Which is really not worth repeating." Clay blushed.

Harry glared as though he were ready to start playing father and order Clay off to bed without his supper. The moment of silence was long enough for Janellen to become extremely uncomfortable.

"But a point I enjoyed." Billy Vanderbilt smirked. "I used to get my fertilizer from my father's Fourth Avenue stables and take it back to the farm on a scow. One of the grooms complained to Father, because he had a friend who would buy it. My father, never one to pass up a business dime, wanted to know the next day what I would be willing to pay for ten loads. I told him that it was worth four dollars a load to me on the farm. Father quickly agreed to this, because I was the stupid son who had just offered twice the amount per load as the poor groom. He was, in Mr. Monroe's words, going to put a price tag on my inexperience and teach me a lesson. The next day, when I had the scow loaded and ready to be towed to Staten Island, he came and asked how many loads I had on the scow. The answer was obvious, but I pretended surprise. I had but one, of course. 'One,' he screamed. 'Why, there's at least thirty loads!' I was very calm in explaining to him that I never put but one load on a scow—*one scow load*!"

"I don't get the point," Harry growled.

"If you had a son, you would." Billy said. "My father didn't know whether to be struck dumb with chagrin that I had outsmarted him or gratified that I had. Look at this house, for example. It is a secret, yet you let every one of his agents scrutinize every bill, check and voucher to its building. It is my money, yet you cater to him because he is my father."

"Ah, dinner is served," Janellen pronounced curtly.

Everyone tried too hard to make it a light, happy holiday meal.

Clay scowled. He had noticed quite a change in Harry Hart Horner. His drive and his burning zeal were gone. Not only that, he was sharp and rude. For every compliment Billy made over the house, he would find fault with this workman or that workman.

"But the house is greatly to my liking," Billy insisted. "What you need to do is forget it and get on with your next project."

Unknowingly, Billy Vanderbilt had come close to putting his finger on Harry's restlessness, which had grown with each final touch put on the house. There was no new project. Cornelius Vanderbilt had dangled a carrot, a central railroad station for New York on a grand scale and design. The building figures had shocked the Commodore, even though he was enjoying an income of roundly twenty million per annum. The project was put off. It had been a devastating blow to Harry's ego and pocketbook. He saw that the only way he could win Janellen's full love was by amassing a fortune. He knew he was being fickle. The incident in Chicago had pierced his heart. He now feared losing Janellen to Clay, and he had no weapons with which to fight. He did not revel in having to fight his own son.

At first he had taken the Christmas plans calmly, but had been surprised at Janellen's reaction. One day she would be quite ready to answer Clay and invite him down, and the next she'd think it a very bad idea. On those days she would keep to her room, pleading illness, but as much as she would try to hide her true emotions from Harry, he sensed them all the same. And just to ease his mind, he had a long talk with Mrs. Yost. The cook feared the worst—Janellen was pregnant.

Harry studied the problem calmly. Of course, it hurt that Janellen had not come to him, but it did make the Chicago rumors out to be fact.

"It's odd," he told Mrs. Yost, "the way the Creator plays his chessboard. I can see now why Marti Monroe could have loved and hated me, all in the same instant. Poor Janellen is much the same."

"But loves you, to keep you from this worry."

"Doesn't she think I will have to know, sooner or later?"

Mrs. Yost smiled. "You would have to be a woman to understand, sir. I was that scared telling Mr. Yost about our first."

"But you were man and wife."

"Not at that time. I carried the child for six months before I had the courage to get Mr. Yost to a preacher-man."

Harry hung his head sadly. "In this case, there can be no preacher-man. I suppose we could find the proper doctor for such matters."

Mrs. Yost was aghast. "I am not partial to Mr. Clayton Monroe, sir, but refuse even to think of such a sinning thing. I've raised five children and two grandchildren and can help with yet another. It still is your flesh and blood, sir!"

Harry was stunned. He had not thought of that aspect. Then he felt remiss on an entirely different subject.

"Janellen and I have been selfish, Mrs. Yost. We have completely overlooked the fact that you are a family woman and should be home for the holiday season. You have done a splendid job in getting a staff trained for this house and Mr. Vanderbilt. Our Christmas gift will be to send you home. Then you can get the house ready for our mid-January return."

Mrs. Yost was elated at the news, but darkly suspicious as well.

"You're not thinking anything foolish are you, Mr. Horner?"

"No," he sighed. "I will just wait for Janellen to tell me in her own good time."

The subject had not come up and Harry had anguished over Clay's arrival. There was still no decision in his mind.

Chapter 14

The plot of Janellen's game kept changing as the days slipped away. With Mrs. Yost gone, Billy delighted in retraining the staff to his personal desires. To their chagrin, he haggled over pennies on the grocery bills. He even sent a maid back into Dover because there was a pound of coffee on the grocery bill that had not been included in the order.

But these things made Clay revise his impression of William Vanderbilt. As he spent more and more time around him, he saw that the "mistrusted prince" was a laborious, methodical fellow.

"It's not fantastic parsimony," he told Janellen, on one of the few occasions she allowed them to be alone. "I understand his position and his family. All they have ever given him is a run-down farm and then a small, bankrupt railroad on Staten Island. To make both prosper, he has had to watch over every little detail, all petty expenses, and scrutinize the books daily. Those pennies and mills multiplied many thousandfold and made a momentous difference in making each project successful. He offered to come back to Albany with me and give some advice on running the A&S."

"Good. I was afraid I would have him under my feet until we departed."

"I suggested to Harry that the two of you spend a few weeks in New York."

"What did Harry say?"

"Nothing. He just sat sour-faced, staring at a blank drawing board."

She didn't comment.

"I'm worried about the subject he did talk about, though," Clay continued gravely. "With the central station idea put aside, he has no immediate project."

"I know."

"It doesn't seem as if he really cares. I kept bringing the conversation around to projects that I might be able to uncover, but he ignored them. He sat most of the time mooning about something else." Clay hesitated, looking sideways at Janellen.

"I've noticed that, too," she mused.

"Is it us?"

"No," she said curtly, wanting to avoid the subject. "Chicago never comes up in our conversations. Nor do I wish it to." She frowned. In no way did she think it possible that Harry could know about the child. That was a subject a long time down the road. And in thinking about the child a dreamy look spread over her face. "No, there are some subjects that it is best not to worry Harry about."

So, Clay thought, she is resigned to her life with Harry Hart Horner. The idea was a painful one. Damn! Nothing but wasted days and he was due to leave in two. Why didn't he have the courage to grab Janellen up and haul her to his bedroom? He wanted her so desperately that he ached. But he had to put such madness out of his mind.

A low whistle brought him out of his pensiveness. In the door, motioning for silence, was Billy Vanderbilt.

"Billy! What are you up to?"

He looked at them with a wild grin. "I am trying to get rid of you two." He playfully pretended to roll the wheels of the wheelchair. "I've a little matter to discuss with himself. Each morning I've been taking an early morning ride over these four hundred acres. I should have done that before building here. It is not the proper spot. I've made you a map and have the one horse shay ready at the door. Please go see if this new spot on the St. Jones River is not better suited."

"You're crazy," Janellen laughed. "This house is just completed."

He looked around and bowed grandly. "And that is part of my plan, dear lady. Jon Dryden owns the property next and is very taken with this house. He has offered me a purchase price that will more than pay for the new structure I have in mind, plus all of Harry's commission. Now, am I going to get some help in this project?"

"Oh, you're impossible. Let me get a shawl."

Janellen gasped in delight when Clay produced a basket filled with food from the back of the shay.

"Where did you . . . Clayton Monroe, this was no spur-of-the-moment lark! You and Billy planned this all very carefully, didn't you?"

"Honest, I didn't, and only knew of this when Billy whispered the fact while you were getting your shawl. However, you might have noticed on his hand-drawn map that he indicated 'dining area' for the location of the house."

Janellen laughed. "And the location he is quite correct about. Oh, this is so beautiful."

"Not bad for the dead of winter," he laughed. "I would much prefer to see it five months from now when it is spring-budded and green. Well, maybe I shall. If I get the proper invitation, I shall come back in May and see how this house is coming along."

"Yes," she mused softly, and was suddenly frightened by how short a time five months really was. The baby was due in May. As little a time ago as yesterday that had seemed centuries away. She let a silence fall between them as he spread out a blanket on the winter-brown grass knoll and prepared the food. She accepted hers without comment and sat staring down at the frozen river. Her mind was just as frozen. A hundred different ways she had planned on how she was going to tell Clay and then not tell him.

As she sat brooding over whether this was the proper time, neither noticed the hunter who came up the river road, passed by the shay and continued on. Quickly he darted into a stand of oak and squatted down to watch them.

The day was unusually warm for the last day of December, but Clay felt himself shiver. He, too, had a million words to say to Janellen and they strangled in his throat. He looked down at the river in desperation, as though their equal line of sight might produce a conversation topic. He was running out of time. Tomorrow was the first day of 1869 and he wanted to be back in Binghamton by the evening of the second.

"Do you think I am wrong in fighting this railroad battle?" he ventured.

"I don't think that is any of my business!"

"You always took an interest in my business, Jan. You seem so different now, not like you were before."

"I don't want to be like I was before. We were selfish and unthinking of those we hurt."

"Hurt?" he scoffed. "What if I told you how much it hurt dear Eugenia? What if I told you that I want this Susquehanna thing to be successful enough so I no longer have to be the business whipping boy for Eugenia's father? What if I told you that Eugenia has been purposely keeping from having a child? What if I told you that I am sick to death of that marriage? What if I told you how desperately I am in love with you?"

"What if I told you I wish to hear none of this?"

He laughed drily. "There is one more 'what if' I had in mind—but it would mean divorce for each of us."

Janellen gasped. But before she could say anything, he had put his arms around her and tilted back her head with a long, hard kiss.

After a moment he pulled away and whispered, "Oh, my dearest darling, will you agree to it and marry me?"

Janellen had gone pale. His embrace had brought back too many memories, all of them too pleasant. Desperately she tried to convince herself that she did not love him and that she did not need him. But she couldn't lie to her heart. She had tried that during these months in Dover and it hadn't been effective. The only time she had ever felt excitingly alive was in their private little nest in Chicago. That had been marriage and could never be again.

He took her chin in his hand and raised her head.

"Will you?"

Janellen shook her head wildly. "It is too late, Clay. It is too late for you and me."

"Never too late! Put aside your pity for my father and think of your love for me."

"It is not pity," she whispered, "and I shall never forget the happiness of being with you. I do love you, Clay, but believe me when I say it is too late for us."

There was, Clay decided, only one thing to do about this. He scooped her up in his arms and started for the shay. In Dover the privacy of a hotel room would change her mind. He dumped her on the seat, forgetting the blanket and lunch basket.

Janellen searched his face, her lips trembling, and knew the moment had come.

"I came to you a virgin," she murmured. "I am now with child."

"But Harry is unable . . ." His words trailed off as the full realization came. He crawled up into the seat and slumped back. This was not at all what he had expected.

"That's why I have avoided you," she blurted out. "To get up the courage to tell you that."

"Does he know?"

"No. That will take more courage than this time."

"Like father, like son," he scoffed.

"That will never be! I will never come to hate you as your mother came to hate him. Now do you see why it is too late for us?"

"Why?" he asked tartly. "This will now free you from Harry. It is my child and my responsibility. Eugenia will rush to get a divorce when she learns of this. I will not force Harry into having to become another Barrett Monroe. He is too old to become a father, anyway."

"But not too old to be hurt." she said acidly.

"Perhaps this is his just reward."

She began to laugh, but when she saw the fierce look on his face, she sobered. "I will not let you use this child for the sake of revenge, Clay. That would be wicked."

"Any more wicked than you being my mistress to produce it? I took you away from him then and you didn't have such pious feelings for the old boy. Any other husband would have known at once that his wife was cheating on him, but he isn't a normal husband."

"Take me home," she said, near to tears. "I think you have made yourself quite plain. I never realized until this moment that you were really using me to hurt him. How could you do that, Clay?"

"Don't be stupid!" Hurriedly he tried to think of the proper words to say. Her words had shocked him. He had married Eugenia to a degree to hurt Janellen. Had he then taken her as a mistress to spite Harry?

When he said nothing further, it was for her an admission of guilt. She held her silence until they were back in front of the house.

"Goodbye, Clay," she said, climbing out of the shay. "I shall not join you gentlemen this evening, or until you depart."

"Don't you want me around when you break the glad tidings to Harry?" he demanded snidely.

"I don't see why," Janellen replied calmly, turning back to him. "After all, he has been through this scene before."

"Then have Billy bring my things into town," he said, his voice now cold and formal.

Without a good-bye, he turned the shay sullenly about.

After he had left, Janellen oddly smiled to herself. Half of her fearful battle was over. She now realized it was the worst half. Clayton Monroe was not ready for fatherhood—or husbandhood. He mouthed words of love, but they were self-serving. For the first time in days, she was calm.

Clayton Monroe was not calm. After he had found a hotel, he went into its tavern. He sat blaming everyone but himself. It was a holiday eve but he sat and ate a tasteless meal alone. The spirit of the evening livened around him, but he still sat quietly alone. At midnight he ignored the well-wishers, including the drunken hunter who tried to interest him in one of the rather obvious women he had in tow.

When the tavern closed, he was amazed that he could stand and walk. For the first time in his life he had wanted to get blind drunk, and he had failed.

In the hotel lobby he found Vanderbilt sitting with his luggage.

"I saw the new year in with them and then brought your things," Billy said, a little embarrassed.

"Thanks and Happy New Year. The horse and shay are in the livery for the night—paid in advance." He stumbled a little and for the first time had trouble in keeping Billy's face in focus. "Sorry. Well, good night."

"Of course," Billy said, "but may I have a word with you in private first?"

Clay looked around. The lobby was vacant, except for the hunter who had collapsed in a chair and was snoring. Clay grinned sheepishly. "I just may need some help to my room—with the luggage."

"Whatever." He threw out a farm-toughened arm and let the big man use it as a support, then took up the two pieces of luggage with the other. As they crossed in front of the hunter, Billy purposely tripped over the man's legs.

"What the hell!" the man roared, instantly awake.

"Sorry, friend," Billy apologized, and then started. "Oh, it is you! I have still to see my share of your bag for allowing you to hunt on my property."

"Didn't get a blasted thing," the man growled, rose and walked away quite stone sober.

"And is out the cost of two tarts without any benefit," Billy chuckled.

"What?"

"My reason for privacy. But it can wait another minute until I have you in your room."

The effects of the night were catching up with Clay. He was farther gone than he realized. Never had a room seemed such a safe haven.

"Good old bed," he grinned, collapsing upon it. "I've had one hell of a day, Billy."

"So I understand," he said coolly, pulling a chair up to the bed and sitting down. "They were both quite without embarrassment in discussing things in front of me this long evening."

Clay shrugged and tried to focus on a crack in the ceiling.

"So . . . the bastard father knows his bastard son has produced yet another bastard offspring . . ." He tried to grin, but it was not a laughing matter.

"This was not the discussion I wished to have with you, Clay. That hunter—did he try to interest you in one of the women he was with?"

He giggled. "That I think he did." Then through his fog came a flicker of understanding. "Were you spying on me for Harry?"

"Hardly. But I think the hunter has been spying on you. He has been on the property and around the house every day since your arrival. I recognized him at once when I looked into the tavern for you. He had the two women at your table at the time. I waited, not knowing if that was to be your desire for the evening. But shortly thereafter he was paying off the young ladies in the lobby and then pretending to sleep. I averted my face so that he would not recognize me."

Clay sank back onto the pillow, laughing. "Well, I'll be damned. I thought I saw a hunter on the road, but paid it no mind. A Fisk henchman, I will bet."

"Then I suggest we leave first thing in the morning. I have checked. We can get a train to Philadelphia at 6:10. There is a one car-passenger freight that goes to Wilkes-Barre and Scranton at 10:00. If we are lucky we can catch the afternoon run up to Binghamton."

"There are no such routes."

Billy laughed viciously. "I was made to learn every railroad timetable before my numbers. I am forty-eight years old and doing the same with my sons."

Clay waved a drunken hand. "Every little boy loves trains."

Billy's face darkened suddenly. "My little boys, Clay, are but three and six years your junior. I was married off quickly at an early age to keep me from sinful and money-wasting ways. My parents will see that their grandchildren are directed along the self-same path."

Clay sat up on his elbow, a look of puzzlement crossing his face. "Then why didn't you spend Christmas with them?"

Billy pounced on the comment like a cobra. "Because my father, for all else that he is, is not a stupid man. His agents are most aware of your coming little foray with the Erie faction. He will sit this one out. He does not wish to get burned again by the illegal printing press in the basement of Fisk's Grand Opera House. He knows they will pull the same stock-flooding trick on you. They own the State House in Albany. They will rub you into the cinders and then stomp on you!"

"What has this to do with my question about Christmas?"

"Everything! I sent them all to New York so I could come down here and meet you. If I am going to get in on this fight, I wanted to know something about the man I would be fighting with."

Clay sat up, stunned. "You only wanted to help get it running on the right operational basis."

"Which it needs, desperately. And I desperately need to make it so. One does not jump from managing a few tracks on Staten Island to the New York Central. I will prove to my father that I can be pugnacious."

"Even with a bastard?" Clay sneered.

"Had you gone with one of those women," he said quietly, "you might not have found me in the lobby."

That was a measure of honesty Clay could understand and yet not understand. "Why would my actions with one of those whores be any different than my actions with Janellen?"

"Do you look at them as the same?"

"Do I? Do I?" Suddenly he was quite sober and rational. He put his feet on the floor and sat looking at Vanderbilt as though the man had asked the most illogical question in the world. "No! Naturally not! But I can't live down the facts at hand."

"Then live up to them."

"Worry," Ramsey grumbled. "The man runs off for a week and tells me not to worry. Fisk is determined to leave nothing to chance. If you had to run off, Clay, you might have been more discreet. You've played right into their hands with your tomfoolery."

With a mischievous grin playing at the corners of his mouth, he laughed. "You speak, I take it, of the man who spied upon me in Dover?"

"Now, Clay," Ramsey began with a reproving shake of

his head, "you are taking this matter too lightly. Such things may be big-city ways, but these are all God-fearing little towns. The reports that man sent by wire burned even the operator's ears to crimson. The one that came through this morning has tongues wagging all the way to Albany."

"Did anyone, including yourself, consider checking the validity of his reports?" Clay beamed. "The man that I visited, Harry Hart Horner, is my natural father." He paused, and re-phrased the next words in his mind, for he had never really thought of it in this light. "Therefore, the woman in question is my stepmother and is with child."

"Damn," Ramsey gasped, "what then is all this business about making love on a winter picnic?"

"Lies and more lies, and lies upon lies. I kissed her upon hearing the news of the child." It was near enough the true version, but sounded a little cheeky. "Billy Vanderbilt was there and can vouch for each of these facts."

Billy nodded his head. As stated, the facts were the truth, without all the truth being revealed.

"Well," Ramsey sighed, "the harm is already done."

"I would disagree, sir," Billy grinned. "Let he without sin answer the charge as to why he sent the man to spy. Those who wish to believe will believe, no matter what. If Clay is right back in the fray, without reason for guilt, it will be answer enough for those who do not wish to believe."

"And we will have gained over this and not lost," Clay insisted. "It will strike Fisk dumb to learn that we have a Vanderbilt as a consultant."

J.H. Ramsey smiled quietly. "I think that will please Morgan, too. It will make us appear to have ample resources for a long fight. What will it take to get rid of Mumford?"

"Little more than the truth that he has been a double agent."

Ramsey puckered his lips and whistled softly. "I would not like to be in his shoes when Fisk learns. Well, no matter. To work. Here, Mr. Vanderbilt, are my records of the line, and you will find it accurate nearly to the last lump of coal in each tender. These books here, sir, are a similar reckoning of the line as made up by Maxwell Mumford of the assets—and the figures that the Fisk men use to sway people to sell and jump ship before it sinks. Just look at the difference on the balance sheets."

The two tallies left Billy gasping with wonder.

"I am utterly amazed," he stammered. "Without even checking I can smell out the false areas." He flipped back a few pages. "Look at these rebates back to the Erie. They are enormous and unneeded. Clay, why isn't the trunk line we came up on used?"

Clay looked to Ramsey for the answer and he seemed puzzled over the question. "It is used to get the coal from the coal fields and on up through here to New England."

"But below the coal fields are Scranton and Philadelphia. They, too, possess wholesale merchants for your clients. The Erie business through Albany would dry up immediately if these people were offered a proper freight rate."

"Who owns the line?" Clay asked.

"It's a holding company quietly owned by the New York Central," Billy said, as though it were common knowledge. "Mr. Carnegie has tried to buy it several times from Father for his Pennsylvania line. I am now glad that Father was stubborn in his refusal. Do I have your permission to wire Father to work out a freight agreement?"

Ramsey thrust out his beefy hand. "You're the acting general manager," he chuckled. "You do any damn thing you please to save this line."

The next day, when Billy had heard back from his father, they started up the line to restructure the system.

"You're a mystery, Billy," Clay said. "The Commodore sends you a three-word reply and you can immediately make a rate schedule out of it. Do you have some secret family code?"

"Hardly." He smirked. "The first word—'You?'—is really a thousand words of amazement. Father knows I am normally easily frightened and prone to compromise rather than fight to the bitter end. Well, this does frighten me, but I shall leave all the confrontation for you. 'Lake Shore' was something that happened a few months back. The

Lake Shore Railroad is a part of Father's New York Central System. A refining firm, Rockefeller, Andrews & Flagler, came to the Cleveland offices of Lake Shore and demanded a rebate of ten to fifteen cents a barrel on crude oil shipped from the oil fields and another on kerosene shipped to New York. Father made me go to Cleveland with him as an object lesson. It seems this Rockefeller is only thirty years old, although he acts ancient."

"I know what you mean," Clay said. "I have met the man and his partners. Of course, the Commodore turned them down."

"Oh no, they got their rebate."

"Might I ask the reason why?"

"Of course, because that was the object lesson that I think he wants applied here. The rebate will enable that firm to knock out the local competition, thereby reducing the number of Cleveland refineries from thirty to ten in this coming year. Lake Shore will have the exclusive shipping contract, a saving in manpower from having to deal with and handle the books for thirty companies, and the rebate can be made up when the kerosene is shipped to Europe on Vanderbilt ships."

Clay wanted to roar with mirth. John Rockefeller was squeezing in on the third leg of his dream—transportation. But he held back his mirth. He wanted to see how Billy would apply that lesson to this situation.

"So, but that doesn't very well apply to the general merchants and farmers along this line, Billy."

"You are not looking at both sides of the coin, Clay. Those ledgers I pored over last night were like a history book of the region. Miners live in these lower towns and buy from those merchants. Whose side will they be on if the freight rates lower the price of their daily staples? Whose side will the farmers be on when they can sell their wares without all profits going out for freight. Of course, with more money available, they will buy more and the merchants will have to ship more. But we are really looking for good will here, to keep the wrong people from getting the stock."

He sighed deeply. Seldom had he talked as much as in the last two days, and never had he felt so alive. "Now, flip the coin and you will see the real homework. We will offer a rebate per carload of coal to Pierpont Morgan's Delaware, Lackawanna & Western Coal Company and tack that rebate onto every carload that the Delaware & Hudson Canal Company wishes to ship. It won't take long for their stockholders to start screaming."

"Granted," Clay smirked, "and I shall be one of the first to call for an accounting."

Working town by town, it took them nearly a week to get to Albany. Billy was methodical and wanted ironclad contracts with each party. He also spent time with each stationmaster and freight handler on the saving of pennies and mills. Nor did they resent it. They were conservative, penny-pinching old stock who talked the same language.

In each town Clay went directly to the parson and parson's wife. They were better than a fire wagon in smothering the rumors and tongue-wagging stories. But one thing was troubling Clay. Fisk had been very coy in his stock purchases after their meeting in Oneonia. If a man had been a director of the line prior to the purchase, then Fisk made it appear as though it were only an option to buy with the man retaining his vote on the board. A tally of the board of directors showed that it was evenly divided between the two forces.

Mary Calhoun was waiting for him, a young male clerk assisting her behind the counter.

"This is my nephew from Elmira," she said in her usual crisp manner. "I have exchanged him for Jane, who will live with my sister and get some schooling." She hesitated, feeling a little embarrassed. "I-I wish to speak to you about your offer . . . ah . . . and—"

"And don't wish to sell," he said quickly, saving her further embarrassment. "Then I shall just accept my money back."

He saw her stiffen, her whole body rigid suddenly and her face blank with incredulity. She had misunderstood him and he was delighted. The parson's wife had been full of more gossip about Mary Calhoun and Rita Johnson than about himself. He was almost sorry that he had missed the near brawl between the two women at Jim Fisk's dinner party. But now he needed to know if she were still a friend or had become a foe.

"All of it?" she gasped.

"What did you expect, Mrs. Calhoun?" Clay asked, scowling, "That I should pay you interest for using my money while I have been away? You have dipped into that account by nearly half."

"Mine to dip into," she rebutted, "and so the letter states. It is only the general store that I have decided not to sell and that deposit money is untouched."

"That sounds quite different," he said to win her support, "but what of the bonds? One only has to be in town five minutes to learn that you and the Johnson family are on the outs."

"You've heard already?" Mary said with mild surprise. Then she laughed. "It nearly made Rita Johnson ill on Mr. Fisk's food. The gross man made much over my Jane to soften me up and learn your price. Our dear mayor was furious that he was not being asked first. So, naturally, I lied and gave only a quarter of the original figure. Mr. Fisk, of course, called you some names that nearly sent Rita off with the vapors. Then, all sweetness and light, he began to bargain upward and I remained stubborn. Old Johnson, God bless his stupidity, had to jump in at that moment and start pushing the town's share of the stocks and bonds. I could see that Mr. Fisk was ready to dump the whole discussion until another time. I told the mayor to keep his mouth shut."

Clay chuckled. "Is that when the brawl started?"

Mary, who considered herself a perfect lady, looked hurt. "My dear Mr. Monroe, it was hardly a brawl. When Rita jumped on me like a fishwife, I just firmly informed her that I was there selling my own personal property and that her husband was trying to sell something that belonged to the entire town. If he was so anxious to sell, then it should be offered to a townsperson first. I'm afraid that I saw red when Rita scoffed that no one in town had that sort of money. I then made my offer, demanded a town-council meeting for the next day and departed without dessert."

Clay was astounded. "And how did the meeting come out?"

"Not to the liking of Mr. Fisk, who made a counter-offer after I had left." Then she frowned. "The council members are businessmen, Mr. Monroe, who, like my husband, invested their savings and taxed themselves for town money to complete the railroad. Even though my offer was less, they wanted Oneonia money to stay in Oneonia."

"What about my purchase of your bonds and stock?"

"Oh," she said simply, "that is a different matter. Everyone knows that you originally invested when no other outsiders would. You're homefolk." Then she scowled deeply. "I sit with the same amount of stock as before, but we have a problem on it."

"What problem?"

"Being a woman, I wasn't allowed to vote the stock after my husband died, so why would they let me vote this new stock?"

Clay let out a sigh of relief. He wished all problems were so easy to solve. "All you need to do is sign a voting proxy over to one of the male voting members and instruct him on your wishes."

"Then I shall sign it over to you, because I know your wishes will be the same as mine. Horace, I declare, you are worse than Jane. Don't make that stack so high, and dust off every article before you stack it. If I have to do everything myself, I might as well do it alone."

And Clay was quite sure that she could. He had never given it much thought before, but Mary Calhoun was a prime example of the waste that P.D. Armour always screamed about. Her agile mind had been clever enough to beat Jim Fisk at his own game, and no man in America could make that boast.

In the next month he wished he had a hundred like Mary to counter Fisk's henchmen. Every time he gained a block of stock, he lost a block of stock. The director count seesawed back and forth, but normally stayed about fifty-fifty.

In those days Harvel Packer's words came back to haunt him. In this battle he was having to meet force with force, bribe with bribe and duplicity with duplicity. It was draining him mentally and physically and financially, and he also knew that to be a Fisk ploy.

The only shining light was Billy Vanderbilt. By the end of January he had the road running like a well-oiled clock, had trained a battery of accountants and found a stationmaster he felt should be elevated to replace him as general manager.

Then the duplicity turned mean.

Billy stood shaking. "You can't just order us out in twenty-four hours," he quavered. "We have a lease on this depot."

"*Had*!" the sheriff whispered maliciously, waving the court order in Billy's face. "It is state land that was leased to the Erie without the right to sub-lease. You will vacate this office and depot by ten a.m. tomorrow or stand in contempt of court."

Billy got off a one-word message to Clay in Central Bridge before the A&S telegraph line was mysteriously cut.

The 6:10 Susquehanna freight came in the next morning on time, transferred the coal cars over to the Erie tracks, came back to its own depot to off-load the freight cars, reload and make its normal 7:40 departure.

At 7:45, as on any other busy day, William Vanderbilt walked from the Albany Hotel to the depot, climbed to the second floor and unlocked the office. In the next three minutes the four new account clerks came bustling along, already trained to the fact that Mr. Vanderbilt wished them on their stools at the first stroke of eight from the Legislative Building clock.

Then all became work-a-day quiet. The next A&S train was not due until 10:17.

Across the railyard, in the Erie terminal, Jim Fisk had sat by a window and watched it all. Behind him stood a dozen muscle-hardened Erie porters.

"I think they are going for the contempt of court, boys," he chuckled.

"Do we move in on them now, Big Jim?" a porter asked, smacking a freight-bar into his beefy palm.

"Steady," Fisk cautioned. "We have sufficient law on

our side and don't want to lose that advantage. Besides, Vanderbilt warned Monroe that he had 'trouble.' Well, we haven't seen him arrive during the night and it was only a normal crew on the 6:10. That leads me to believe that he will try to bring the 10:17 in early. But we don't move until that ten a.m. deadline."

"How many over there, if'n he don't show?"

"Count, you idiot, count," the Erie stationmaster growled. "Four skinny clerks and Vanderbilt upstairs, the stationmaster and freight clerk down."

"Lucky for you," the man sneered, as a way of getting back, "that you don't work for them. Their stationmaster had to work like a porter getting those big crates off the cars. Should make you appreciate us the more."

"Stop the chatter," Fisk barked. "Someone get me something to eat!"

No one wanted to remind him that they had brought him quite a sizable breakfast from his private railroad car just a half-hour before. In the next two hours he nervously ate everything put before him.

He was so bloated that he could hardly march the porters across the railyard at a minute after ten. But elation spurred him on. Clayton Monroe had not come to do battle.

At the size of his little army the stationmaster and freight handler took fright and ran.

He pounded up the stairs to the second-floor balcony, his weight making each step shake. Behind him marched his dozen bullies, belligerent sneers on each face. Two frightened away left only six to cower.

"Vanderbilt," he bellowed, stepping onto the balcony, "your time has expired. Surrender now and bring the stock books out with you."

Billy opened the door to the office. He appeared ashen. "You are not the sheriff," he stammered. "I do not recognize your authority." Then he quickly slammed the door.

"*Authority*!" Fisk bellowed like a mad bull. "I make my own authority when I have paid for it! Rush in, boys, and take full possession! Throw those pantywaist bastards the hell off my legal property!"

The other two doors on the balcony opened quickly and were just as quick in pouring out twenty stout A&S railroad men.

"Weren't you expecting company?" Clay asked devilishly, pushing through them.

"Where in the hell did you come from?" Fisk thundered.

"We arrived as crated freight," Clay grinned. "A little smuggling lesson I learned in India."

Fisk screamed his men into a charge. But Clay's men were already on the move. They bounced around Fisk like he was a punching-bag, grabbing up the porters and hurling them over the balcony rail or punching them senseless back down the stairs. In the cramped quarters the twelve were never given a chance to raise their arms to weapon level, and the fists that had a downward momentum were lethal.

Clay tried to get to Fisk, but at first there were too many fighting bodies in the way. Then he was able to corner him in front of the office door.

"Tell them it's over!" Clay shouted, right into his fat face.

Suddenly, in a lightning-quick move, Fisk spun, locking back one of Clay's arms, snatched a derringer from a shoulder holster and held it against his throat.

"Fisk!" Clay gasped. "What are you doing?"

"I am the law!" Fisk shrieked. "I own this state! You will obey me!"

Clay's men shrank back, unsure what they should do. The pounced-upon porters fled, wishing no part of gun play.

Clay had himself under control. "This is laughable. If you expect my death to solve everything, then you really are a fool." He had spoken so coldly and calmly that Fisk started, turning to the side to peer at his face.

"You aren't frightened, are you?" he roared with mirth.

"Hardly by you! Only a coward has to stand behind a weapon to give him false courage."

"Coward," he said slowly, drawing out the syllables. "Why you insolent little pup. I should have crushed you the first night I met you. You have become a bother I can no longer afford."

Clay felt the release of his arm and heard the cock of the derringer hammer. He swallowed hard. No matter which way he turned he was as good as a dead man. He had not heard the office door quietly open.

"Do it!" one of the young trainmen shrieked.

The cry was followed by motion, fury and noise.

Billy Vanderbilt obeyed, at about the moment the derringer exploded. Used to heaving hay bales, Fisk's body was little challenge. His fright washed away by cold wrath, he sent the rotund man crashing down the full flight of stairs. Then he mindlessly raced halfway down, to make sure the cursing figure did not countercharge.

Then a mournful wail from one of his clerks spun him back. He stood mesmerized, watching the dripping pattern of blood on the balcony wall. He did not need to be told that the crumpled body below the pattern was that of Clay Monroe.

"Murderer," Billy screamed, spinning and threatening Fisk with his bare fist. "Do you know the consequences for murder? I will see you hanging in Times Square for this action."

Fisk trembled, desperately trying to get to his feet. "No, you will not. I am the law!"

"My father once said, 'Ain't I the law,' and I don't think he was any more than you. Get out of here before I suddenly decide I am the law and turn this scene into a jungle."

Jim Fisk rose and quietly brushed himself off. He was used to cowards and fools. He gave not a single thought to Clayton Monroe. There was a more pressing matter now on his mind.

Because his bribes fell into the right pockets, the Albany papers screamed out only the Jim Fisk version of the shooting. Never once did those papers even check to see if Clay was dead or alive. Nor, because Fisk was too smart to mention it, did the name of William Vanderbilt get into the accounts. He wished only to shore up his Albany position.

But anything to do with Jim Fisk was bound to creep

down to the gilded, gleaming cesspool of New York. Here, some newspapers were developing new, startling moral attitudes that asked questions.

"Once before we asked why the Erie Railroad millions never reached the railroad's treasury, but remained in the pockets of the Erie Ring and Tweed Ring. At that time we had to come to the editorial reasoning that Mr. Fisk and his associates had done nothing that they could not legally justify, at least in the New York courts, several of which they seem wholly to own. Now we ask why these millions were not enough to take over a little line in the outskirts of the state? Was a bullet into the body of one of the stockholders who refused to sell out legally justified? Again Mr. Fisk seems to own wholly the upstate New York courts and sheriffs' departments. They know nothing, wish to know nothing and probably won't know anything. Well, we are back to editorial reasoning. Well, we leave that to you."

The Chicago papers left nothing to speculation. Clayton Monroe, for them, was news, and they made the most of it. When the New York papers learned who had been shot, the presses began reverberating again.

Jim Fisk pulled in like a turtle and began plotting a new angle of attack.

Billy Vanderbilt pulled out on his father's orders and went back to Staten Island.

From Albany down to Binghamton, people pulled closed their doors and refused to talk to newspaper men—some because they did not want their "side" known and others because they wanted to protect Clayton Monroe.

Among the weaknesses incidental to humanity is a reluctance to credit eminent persons with commonplace motives.

Billy Vanderbilt directed the spiriting away of the unconscious man on the 10:17, for he feared that Fisk would return with thugs to kill them all. At Central Bridge they took aboard a doctor and wired Ramsey to make hospital arrangements in Binghamton.

J.H. Ramsey was found in a meeting with Pierpont Morgan and Jay Cooke.

"Wire them back!" he roared. "I want full details!"

"What now?" Morgan was almost fearful to ask.

"Monroe has been shot. I am to make hospital arrangements."

In silence they waited, no man wishing to press fate with unknown speculation. From Collierville they finally got a report from Vanderbilt and from the doctor. The bullet had entered the left shoulder, above the collar bone, and was still within the body. The doctor was fearful of operating on the swaying train.

"Gentlemen," Jay Cooke said softly, then went to the floor on his knees. They joined him in prayer. As with all important things in life, Jay Cooke put it in the hands of God. The life of this very dear friend was very important to him.

Silently he rose and went to the telegraph room in the Binghamton depot. He had questions to ask and problems to solve.

Even with a green-light track, it took the 4-4-0 engine three hours to arrive, its four wheels and four drivers churning at full throttle.

The new Matthias Baldwin ten-wheeler, with ten drivers, had taken only two hours from Philadelphia. During the run, Dr. Henry Judson and his hospital surgical team had converted a Pullman dining car, on personal loan from Andrew Carnegie, into an operating room.

It was not a question of mistrusting the small mining town hospital or the doctor traveling with Clay. Jay Cooke wanted the best he could muster for Clay.

Everyone agreed that his next suggestion would be best also. All news of the operation and Clay's whereabouts should be kept secret.

Clay opened his eyes and thought of heaven. The rotunda-like ceiling was sky blue with angelic figures pulling garlands of flowers up to the chandelier fitting. The walls were also sky blue, with Doric door columns and molding of purest white. Everything in the room was blue and white. Everything was as still as death. But he could hear human breathing that was not his own. He turned his head, but it ached terribly. He closed his eyes against the pain and did not see that Eugenia was in the room.

Eugenia's gaze rested briefly upon the face of her husband, but did not respond to the opening eyes, the turned head or the pained expression. It had happened several times in the last two weeks, but didn't concern Dr. Judson. The man had lost more blood in the long, probing surgery than from the shooting. He was rather glad that the man stayed in a mindless, semi-conscious state, as it allowed his blood supply to replenish naturally from the liquids the nurses force fed him several times a day.

Then Eugenia looked up as well. The ceiling had become like her private cathedral and never had she prayed so much in her life. She knew every face of every perfect cupid. That was the main thing that troubled her about Ogontz. Everything about Jay Cooke's magnificent home was pure perfection—almost too pure. At times she had an impulse to move an article or a chair out of place, just to create an imbalance. But she stifled the impulse when she thought of the imbalance in her own life.

Three months without a husband and now she had to bear the thought of losing him altogether. Where does the blame start? she thought miserably. With herself? With Clay? With Janellen?

That had been her hardest decision since arrival: to let Harry Hart Horner know about his son. And in letting him know, it automatically let Janellen know. Learning that he had spent Christmas with them had sent her jealousy to new heights. It was almost becoming an incurable disease with her. But she had to let them know for Clay's sake. She said those words over a thousand times until Harry wired back that both he and Janellen were too ill to travel. She didn't think to question why they were ill; she concentrated on Clay. The pounds had melted off his big frame, and the bones showed through the ugly scar that crossed from left shoulder blade to the extreme right lower rib cage. When she looked at his face, she had the horrible idea that she knew what he would look like lying in his casket. A handsome wax death mask. Then she would shudder and look up at her little cupid friends.

"Where are we?" he whispered.

"Oh Clay!" She was instantly kneeling by the bed, holding his hand to her cheek. "We are at Jay's home near Philadelphia."

He licked his dry lips. "Always did want to see it."

"You will see a lot of it, darling," she said, swallowing the lump that kept rising in her throat. "Dr. Judson doesn't want you moved for a month or two. Then I will take you home."

"My—my work . . ."

"Please, Clay," she whispered, "please don't think of that now. We've got to get you well and strong again. That puny little railroad almost got you killed. You just put it out of your mind—forever."

She rose, bent over his head and kissed his mouth.

"I'll let the nurse know you are awake. Oh, my darling, thank God you are finally awake. I love you so! These days will just fly by, because I am going to become your private nurse. I will make you well, my dearest. And when you are home, you'll see, all of this will be forgotten. Father says you just bit off more than you could chew, but he's willing to forgive you."

He closed his eyes and his mind to her rambling. Forgive him for what? For getting shot and not dying? For not being there to wipe his ass? Puny little railroad? All will be forgotten? Bit off more than he could chew? Forgive? Forgive?

For the first time in his life he felt something inside him that was strange and frightening—more frightening than death itself. He knew suddenly the one thing Harvel Packer was forgiving him for, the thing that Harvel Packer forgave no man for—defeat! They were waving the flag of truce over his war. Generals make war; politicians make peace. It had been a one-shot war with a single casualty. Now rush him home to Chicago to hide away his great shame. He was not fit to play with the big boys. They had bloodied his nose. He wouldn't be allowed to play with them again, for defeat was just not permitted.

He lay there trembling, not even hearing the nurse's voice. The plump, matronly woman lifted his head and fed him spoon after spoon of scalding soup. He didn't even taste it. His mouth was too full of bitter wormwood. He was too weak to protest—too weak to do anything but accept. When the nurse lowered his head gently upon the pillow, he went back to sleep.

Every two hours they woke him to feed him, with Eugenia taking her turn with the round-the-clock nurses.

"I don't understand it," Mrs. Flynn told Dr. Judson a week later. "It was easier to feed him when we had to force it down his throat. If you ask me, he just doesn't seem to have the will to live."

"Nonsense!" Eugenia scoffed. "He has everything in the world to live for!"

Hattie Flynn had her doubts on that and was tempted to speak her full mind. The woman might have richness of clothes, jewels about the neck, rings upon her fingers, but she had no bedside manner. It didn't take an expert to see that the patient ate less when the wife did the feeding, or that he had a glassy-eyed, uncaring expression when she rambled on cheerfully about everything that she thought was important.

"What does he talk about?" Dr. Judson asked. "I can only get grunts out of him over his condition."

"Home," Eugenia got in, before Mrs. Flynn could speak. "He wants to go home and I think that would be the best place for him. After all, Chicago is not a wilderness, you know."

Henry Judson frowned. "I really hate to move him until I am sure that incision is fully healed. I had to go quite deep, you know. Let's wait another week. In the meantime, let's try visitors. That might perk him up."

"I forbid it!" Eugenia protested.

"Mrs. Monroe, it can do no harm. Jay asks me daily when he might be able to pop in."

"He needs to be home," she went on doggedly. "Worse than that, we have worn out our welcome."

"Another week," Dr. Judson said sternly. Mrs. Flynn smiled to herself.

Downstairs the doctor had a chat with Jay Cooke. He hated to go against the woman, but thought he knew best for the sake of the patient.

That evening, late, Jay was surprised to find the adjoining bedroom dark and vacant of a night nurse. Thinking that she was probably in the patient's room, he knocked softly and entered. The room was in shadows, illuminated only by the lowest flicker of a wall jet. He hesitated, reluctant to disturb Clay, but puzzled over the fact that no nurse was in attendence. He had just finished his nightly cookies and milk in the kitchen and knew that she was not there.

He started toward the bed, but stopped short when a figure sat straight up on the right-hand side.

"Who is there?" Eugenia demanded.

"It is I, Jay Cooke," he stammered.

"What are you doing here?"

He was too embarrassed to ask her the same. "There was no night nurse."

"I dismissed her. I shall take care of my husband at night from now on, and I demand a new doctor and new day nurse. You all thought you were so clever. Well, I followed him downstairs and I question his ethics."

"He was only doing what he thought best."

"Shut up!" she snapped. "I will be the judge of what is best until I get the opinion of another doctor. Now, good night, sir!"

Clay heard it all. It was near the same thing he had heard for a week. As always, Eugenia would have her way in everything. She had even tried to treat him like a loving wife that night, sitting atop him, careful not to give him pain. The first time she had tried it, on their honeymoon cruise, he had been amused. This night he had been shocked and too weak to become aroused. Eugenia had not relented. She had worked herself into a frenzy trying to excite him and jumped to her side of the bed only when she heard the footsteps in the hall.

"Damn snoop!" she sneered, when Jay had departed. "I think I almost had you going."

Clay nearly laughed. Not only had she told the man to shut up, but now accused him of being a snoop in his own house. Eugenia would never change and would never stop trying to change him. Perhaps she was right. Perhaps he would be best off back in Chicago. Here he could only lie and brood over his defeat, fearful even to ask how severe it had been. His mind had already conjured up the worst from what Eugenia had said and said and said and said. He might as well resign himself to that fate. He had already resigned himself to another fate. He had put everything he owned on the line for the "puny little railroad," and if Fisk now had it in Erie control, he had no hope but to get back more than a few cents on every dollar invested.

"Clay?" she cooed. "Shall we try again?"

He let out a big snore.

Eugenia shrugged and nestled down into her pillow. She was content; she had showed them all who was boss and would do the same with the doctor the next day.

Dr. Morgan Stern at least got one syllable answers out of Clay, but he totally agreed with Dr. Henry Judson. The patient should not be moved for at least another week.

Eugenia, being Eugenia, would bend but not break. She would accept his word, even though he had been retained by Jay Cooke, but she would still take full charge of the nursing duties.

Within the week she felt triumphant. She could not see that Clay's steady recovery had anything to do with his resigning himself to the fact. She gave herself full credit in being the better doctor and nurse.

But to her intense surprise and annoyance, she found Jay Cooke quite the master of his own house.

"I make up my own guest list for dinner," he told her with grim satisfaction. "If you do not care to dine with Mr. Morgan, you may eat in your room."

"We shall," she huffed.

"*You* shall," he said gruffly. "As this is Clay's first meal downstairs, I shall not have it ruined by your shrewish manner! Nor will I be dictated to any longer in my own home."

"As you have just made me feel most unwelcome," she said piously, "*we* shall leave at once. If you are a gentleman, you will make arrangements to inform the railroad yard that I, at long last, have need of my father's private car. The first train out will suit me fine!"

Storming into the room, she looked Clay up and down coldly.

"You may change out of that borrowed dinner suit," she hissed. "We leave for Chicago at once!"

''But Jay sent up word that Pierpont was coming for dinner.''

''What difference does that make?'' she demanded. ''We are going home, didn't you hear me?''

''But I want to see Pierpont!''

''Why?'' she growled.

Why, he thought bitterly, must you ask 'why'?

Wasn't it enough that, night after night, when his strength for recovery was more important, she had forced and forced until his manhood was capable of matching her womanhood? Wasn't it enough that she was his twenty-four hour constant guardian? Wasn't it enough that she was master and he slave?

''I need to know.''

''Know what?''

''Eugenia,'' he said huskily, ''I need to know how badly hurt I am financially.''

Slowly she shook her head.

''No, Clay,'' she said, ''you don't need to know. Father knows. Fairchild kept accurate track of it for him. You should be thankful that you have us to pick up your misguided pieces.''

''I—I guess I should, in a way,'' he said bitterly. ''Now if you would step aside, I should like to go downstairs. I would like to learn, on my own, how misguided were my pieces.''

Before she could scream out her fury, there was a rap at the door and he quickly jerked it open.

''Telegram for you, sir,'' the maid said with a curtsy. ''The messenger is sorry for its lateness, but he went first to Mr. Cooke's office in town.''

Eugenia saw his face darken as he read the message.

''What is it?'' she snapped. ''Oh God! It isn't Father, is it?''

''No,'' he said sharply. ''It's from Harry. They've rushed Janellen to a Philadelphia hospital and Harry is too ill to get here.''

''Well, thank heaven, that's all it is,'' she sighed.

Clay controlled his fury. ''Miss, ask Mr. Cooke to arrange a carriage to take me to the hospital mentioned in this telegram. Please hurry!''

Eugenia stood speechless until the door was closed. "I don't believe what I just heard. Your first night out of bed and you're running off to the hospital. Now I really put my foot down."

"Harry asked me to go and be with her, if possible."

"Well, it is certainly not possible and I think he has a lot of nerve."

"He is being quite logical," he said hoarsely. "She is having trouble with the baby."

"Baby?" she asked in utter disbelief. "I thought it was impossible for him to even—"

"She is having my child," he cut her short.

Eugenia stood there; her mouth dropping open foolishly, she stared at him as though he'd lied—then cruel hate glazed her eyes as the truth fully dawned.

"Go to her," she said acidly, "if you dare. I shall not be here when you return, nor shall I ever forgive you. I shall drag you through such muck and mire that a pig will feel clean standing beside you. I am no longer Eugenia Monroe. I am again Eugenia Packer, and proud of it! Prepare yourself, Clayton Monroe! You haven't tasted defeat until my father and I have finished with you!"

He pondered this, smiling softly and secretly to himself. His quietness gave her pause, and then an expression of quiet triumph glowed on her face.

"Well," she said with a smirk, "you need not say it, but your non-answer tells me that you have come to your senses. Now, forget that dinner downstairs as well. We can be packed and out of here in minutes."

"Out of here in minutes," he echoed, as though finding life pleasantly amusing again, "it shall be, Eugenia. Tell your father to stick it up his bucket! I've made him more damn millions than he can count, so I don't need his damn forgiveness or any of your vituperation! If I went down to defeat, I did it fighting hard and damn honestly! Nor do I feel shame in bringing a life into this world. I came into the world the same way. Maybe there's something to be said for bastards. They seem to have that greedy capacity to survive!"

* * *

But his boy-child bastard did not survive. The eight-month malformed infant had twisted and turned and strangled on its cords. It was draining away its mother's life and had to be removed—and still left her life in the balance.

As Janellen's strength waned, it seemed to renew Clay's strength so that he could share it with her. He cared not that Eugenia had carried out her threat to leave. He didn't have time to think upon it.

He could feel sadness over the stillborn infant as well as a touch of relief. It would never have been a fully functioning human being, so why wish it such an unfortunate life?

Then, in the days he paced the gray corridors of the hospital, he was able to take a measure of himself and those around him.

Harry had not asked him to look after Janellen just because he was the father of the child she bore; he had asked out of respect and trust and the knowledge of their shared love. Clay knew then, too, that she would never be his, but it did not stop his loving.

Jay Cooke had not asked him any questions about Eugenia or Janellen; they had become male friends who shared their feelings through the touch of a handshake, a gentle smile, a softly spoken word.

J. P. Morgan or William Vanderbilt would come and walk the corridor with him. They didn't need to discuss business to let him know that things were not a bed of roses. On the other hand, they were not the thorns of defeat either.

Now that Clay was back on his feet, J. H. Ramsey was no longer reluctant in sending him down reports. The A&S people were a strong, determined breed. They were hanging on by their teeth, but they were hanging on. The courts may have found the Ramsey-Morgan-Monroe party in contempt, but they still retained possession of the Albany depot.

Eugenia, for her own purposes, had waved Clay's white flag too soon. It had been but a single battle and not the whole war.

They stood on the platform, the private train ready. She seemed more childlike than he could ever remember. A month in the spring sun at Ogontz had brought out every freckle.

"Mrs. Yost has Harry already tucked in. You are going home in luxury."

"That's nice," Janellen said simply. "Thank Mr. Cooke for bringing Harry up from Dover." Her hand, however, was tense and frightened and shaking like a leaf on his arm.

"What's this?"

"Clay," she whispered, "come to Chicago with us! I fear for you!"

"What the devil—" he began.

"It's the talk of Philadelphia and the hospital, Clay," she cut him short. "Jim Fisk has taken over control of the Binghamton terminus and stopped all Erie shipping at Albany. He's vowed to kill the A&S—and you for sure."

"I won't give him the chance." He grinned. "Jan, take care of Harry and always know that I love you."

He took her in his arms and kissed her as though it would have to last forever.

Chapter 15

"Personally, Clay," Jay said on a troubled note, "I think this whole Albany & Susquehanna fight is a smoke screen being fanned by Jay Gould. The man is unfathomable. In the few years that he has had the Erie under his reign, he has increased its capital by sixty-five million and yet has not added a single locomotive, a train or a station. Where, I asked myself, is the money going and why?"

"Did you find out?"

"Perhaps too much," he said grimly, "and it's why I now believe you have got to win this battle at all costs."

"You really make it sound quite serious."

Jay began to pace nervously. "The whole nation may be at stake, Clay. I have been in and out of Washington a dozen times while you have been mending and looking after Janellen. I have come to believe that the Mephistopheles of Wall Street might even have President Grant in his hip pocket. The whole country knows of his alliance with Boss Tweed. What they don't know is that Tweed now has the strongest voice in the management of the New York City funds, which amount to between six and ten millions of dollars. My operatives have been able to learn that this money is *all* in the Tenth National Bank and all of its officers are Tammany men."

Clay whistled. "The Erie and Tammany money give Gould quite a liquid operating base."

"A gold base, Clay, a gold base. They want to be bulls on gold." He laughed. "On Wall Street they are being called the 'goldbugs' and worse. Because of my massive vested interest in government bonds, I oppose their scheme and have been pressing for the government to redeem their obligations in hard currency valued at the traditional gold standard, as we discussed so long ago."

Clay frowned thoughtfully. "Then why am I reading so much about the cheapening of greenbacks to move the western grain crops more rapidly to the European market? That will cause inflation and not deflation."

"More smoke screen? Still, you don't have to be a banker to know that the dollar is very close to its gold parity. Gould says gold must rise again and the dollar must fall. Why? I asked myself again. The gold market is such an up-and-down affair that the profit is not *real*, not in the classic sense that he likes to masterfully wave his Mephistophelean golden baton over."

"It could be real if you had sixty-five to seventy million to invest."

Jay looked at him, a deep respect creeping into his eyes. "Your illness has not affected your brain, my friend. I think you begin to envisage his scheme as do I. The Federal Treasury has holdings of some seventy-five to eighty million in gold. To *corner* the whole nation's currency, he would have to get his hands on that hoard or *neutralize* it. Either way, he could manipulate the price of gold to a tremendously inflated figure. Overnight he could *own* the United States of America!"

Clay's Adam's apple jerked in his muscular throat.

"And they call us the robber barons," he choked. "When do you think he will try to put this into operation?"

"It has already begun," he said grimly. "Several days ago Henry N. Smith drew out of the Tenth National Bank four million dollars of the Smith, Gould and Martin brokerage firm account, which he kept at home under lock and key. The next day he and Tweed came back in a cab and drew out the balance of that account and the Tammany account. But the bank shows their balance to be undisturbed. Now enters the master upon the Washington scene, but from what I have gathered, without a red cent of that money. His meeting was with Abel R. Corbin, a lawyer, speculator and lobbyist. In a tactful manner, I am told, because I have an operative who works in his law office, Corbin was persuaded to contract for the purchase of $1,500,000 in federal gold at 133."

"Who is this Corbin?" Clay asked.

Cooke grinned broadly. "He is wedded to President Grant's sister and considered very close to the White House. So close, in fact, and so excited over Gould's prospect, that he used his direct influence immediately. He was able to get General Daniel Butterfield appointed Federal Subtreasurer at New York. Butterfield, of course, is Jay Gould's personal choice so that he can be kept intimately informed of the government's day-to-day fiscal policy."

"I can see why that would be helpful for information, but for little else."

"Think again, Clay! The purchase contract to Boutwell at the Treasury was opened in the name of Subtreasurer Butterfield. It was so little questioned that a similar contract was opened in the name of General Horace Porter, private secretary to the President. That's why I say this scheme goes right into the Oval Office."

"How long do you think we have?"

"Gold is at 125. I don't know why Gould pegged the contracts at 133, but he never does anything without a reason. He is safe, of course, because there has been no payment on his part for either contract. I cannot openly fight him yet, because none of this is public knowledge and all of the evidence could vanish in a wave of his wand. Keep in mind that the bank books show no withdrawal and that he has a corral on the greater part of New York's supply of ready money. With those resources at his command, we are going to see him start to manage the floating supply of gold traded each day in the Gold Room of the New York Stock Exchange. That's his lever to get the gold up to 133. That's our time schedule. We must watch the rise and be prepared for his next move when it hits 133. I frankly think it will take most of the summer."

Clay shrugged. "I frankly don't think the A&S can last the summer."

"You will never know until you go and take a look."

The spur line had been barricaded off a mile out of Binghamton. A tent depot had sprung up, and the local farmers were making a few dollars hauling in what supplies were arriving. No supplies, on direct orders from Jim Fisk, could go by rail beyond Binghamton.

Binghamton was like an occupied town during a war. Everywhere Clay looked there were men bearing arms—sheriff's deputies, Pinkerton men, and men wearing green arm bands that proclaimed them to be "Erie Security Patrol."

The J. H. Ramsey house was deserted and all the windows broken out. The depot was barricaded on all four sides like a fort. On the tracks a flatcar had been bedecked like a speaker's platform. As though they were prisoners of war, the townspeople and miners were being gathered together by the armed men and pushed toward the flatcar. Having arrived dressed like a miner, Clay mingled into the crowd.

"More damn promises," the man next to him grumbled. "We don't need more promises; we need to go back to work."

Clay looked around. The faces all expressed the same simple truth. With no railroad to move the coal, the mines had shut down and the miners wanted work to keep from starvation.

"Keep quiet," another man hissed. "My son-in-law preached the same and a deputy took him down to the station for a beating and a warning. His broken arms won't mine coal for some time."

Clay's throat was taut with worry, for none of this terrorism was leaking out to the public.

A man jumped up onto the flatcar and Clay averted his face. But the voice was not that of Jim Fisk. He was smart enough to use the voice of authority to wage his propaganda war.

"Men, I've heard tell that the Ramsey-Morgan gang are planning to burn us out," Sheriff Homer Catwell bellowed. "Maybe toss a few bombs down the coal shafts! Well, you have the law on your side. We got the depot and every mine shaft guarded—and we got men you don't even know about walking around in plain clothes and they been ordered to see that those dirty A&S people leave our town feet first if they try anything."

"That's not putting food on my table!" a man from the back shouted.

"Shut up!" Catwell roared. "We all know who is to blame for putting you out of work. They ignored the court order and almost killed Mr. Fisk in Albany."

"What about Monroe?" someone right near the flatcar asked.

Catwell glared down, as though he was going to immediately order the man's arrest.

"Now you listen to me, Thayer, because I'm not going to say this again. I got the full report from Sheriff Hoag in Albany. That man was accidentally shot by one of his own people. If not, don't you think there would have been an arrest? If that hot-headed anarchist had not come in here to stir up this mess, we would all be living normal lives. But some, up the line, listened to his strange talk of the people owning their own railroad. Hell, we all know that the Erie owns it and the quicker Ramsey surrenders, the quicker you go back to work. He stands alone! Morgan is not pouring any more of his money down this dry well. Vanderbilt is so scared he won't let the spur line be used for anything but food supplies. Monroe is dead and buried back in Chicago. Ramsey stands alone! Now, for the last time, Mr. Fisk is asking for your help. Every damn one of you have miner friends and relatives who live up the line. Go to them! Make them put pressure on those town-council members and individuals who are holding out with Ramsey. Let them know that we know about their dark plots of blowing up trestles, warping tracks, burning depots and killing Erie men. Tell them!"

Clay prayed that some of them would go, so he could join them. This was worse than he had dreamed. Fisk was setting the stage, he knew, for tragedy. Catwell had planted these dark deeds in their minds so that when they happened, the miners would rear up in revolution and join Fisk's army. And who would question who had placed the first stick of dynamite? They had the law on their side and could twist the facts just as smoothly as Catwell had in convincing them Clay Monroe had been shot by one of his own and was dead.

Dead? He had never thought of it before, but it might be

a very wise move to remain dead in their minds. It just might mean that he could go on living—and fighting.

Only three men, with fire in their eyes, crawled over the barricade and started to put a handcart on the northern tracks. Clay started after them, but a security guard stepped in his way.

"Ain't seen you 'round before," he said suspiciously.

Clay coughed. "Been in Philly 'cause of me black lung."

"Who you know up the line?"

"An aunt. Mary Calhoun."

"Hey, Sheriff. Is there a Mary Calhoun up the line?"

Clay kept his back to the flatcar. "Yah! Owns a general store."

"She got a nephew?"

"Yah! He went down to Philly."

The man shrugged and nodded for Clay to go on over the barricade.

But Clay didn't go directly to Mary. He jumped off the handcart at Nineveh. He wanted to check things out all the way up the line.

Harry Stillwell nearly choked when he walked into the station. "We was told you was dead, Mr. Monroe."

"So I hear, Harry," Clay chuckled, "and why don't we keep it that way? Any idea where I might find Ramsey?"

"Hell, yes! He's back in the freight office. That's the new headquarters. Did you hear about his family?"

"No, but I saw their house in Binghamton."

"Yeah, 'lawmen' stoned them out of it and put Mrs. Ramsey and the girls into such a nervous state that friends had to sneak them out of town and get them here. Poor woman was in such shock that the boss took her on to Albany and sent her to his sister in Boston. What kind of a world has this become, Mr. Monroe?"

"A sad one, Harry. A very sad one."

Sadder than he realized. J. H. Ramsey was near the breaking point. There was no need to run any traffic on the Albany & Susquehanna route. Its affairs were in lamentable confusion, and the natives along the line were starting to put the blame on Ramsey. Fisk was winning the propaganda war on that side of the line.

"Perhaps you would have been better off dead," Ramsey said wearily. "These people are not only bereft of transportation and jobs but bewildered and frightened at all this terrorism as well. We only get a trickle of supplies in, but who has money to buy them?"

"Are Morgan's mines closed too?"

"Why not? He can't move the coal to sell it."

"It would keep just as well above ground as under it."

Ramsey shrugged hopelessly. "He has given up all interest, Clay."

"Do you know that for a fact?"

"No. Our telegraph lines are now cut at each end. I had to smuggle the reports out to you."

Clay dropped the subject and the thought he'd had. Now he really wanted to get up the line, but the germ kept growing at each stop. The passenger load of miners from Nineveh, Masonville and Oneonia was because the big mines were below Binghamton and also because the three Delaware, Lackawanna & Western mines on this side were small as they were still relatively new.

But each stop had a different subject to take his mind away from that one. He tried to keep the fact that he was alive known only to close friends.

In Oneonia he talked only to Mary. To his surprise, she was not shocked to find him alive. Her nephew had been making weekly runs into Philadelphia for supplies and checking at the Jay Cooke & Company office on Clay's health.

"But how does he get the supplies through Binghamton?"

"Same as my husband did in the old days. He off-loads at Johnson City ten miles below Binghamton and has two farm wagons bring them over the wagon road to Nineveh and on up. He keeps just enough to bribe Catwell into thinking he is bringing back food for just the two of us."

"Mary, I love you. I'll be back in three days so we can really look into this."

Summer was coming. The farmers were wondering about their crops and the dairy people were already in a stew over their lost Albany customers. Clay asked them, too, to give him three days' time. From Mary he had also gotten the wagon route to Albany that Calhoun had used.

But none of his strategems would work unless his original one was successful.

They may have still possessed the Albany depot, but the tracks leading up to it had been removed.

Big as life, he marched into the Erie station and up to the telegraph cage. He ignored the operator and wrote out his message. One of the porters thought he recognized the man, then shrugged it off.

"That will be twenty-seven cents."

Clay counted out the change as though each coin was precious.

"As you can see from the message," he said with a worried frown, "it is quite important." He hesitated and then added another dime. "The family would appreciate your courtesy for speed."

"I understand, pal," the operator said with genuine sympathy and sat right down at the sending key.

As though fascinated by the process, Clay stood in open-eyed amazement. He was actually waiting to see if the man would catch on and not send the wire. But the words were tapped out with speed and accuracy:

Jane P. Morgan
98 Sutton Place
New York
Mother Morgan desperately ill. Stop. Need you soonest. Stop. Will await you Albany. Stop. Can't send money to help. Stop. Mines closed. Stop. Brother Clayton.

"It's done, friend. Too bad about the mines."

"And the fact I had to walk all the way from Central Bridge to send that. Sure hope my sister-in-law brings enough money so we can rent a buggy to get back."

"With an address like that she should have a couple of dollars."

Clay was well-prepared for the man having knowledge of the city. "Not really, sir. She's just a maid there."

The man leaned close and lowered his voice. "Still, I'll wager she makes more than me. Skinflint that owns this line dropped our pay because we ain't getting any more business off the A&S line. Then you know what I read in the paper? Wasn't enough for him to have one big steamship for his Narragansett Line. Spent a half-million dollars, according to the paper, to build a new floating hotel that he calls the *Providence*. Sure ain't my providence to be working for him, but ain't nothing else around. Think you'll get an answer?"

"Probably not. What trains do you have coming up from New York?"

"About the only one she will be able to catch after getting the message would get her in here at 6:25."

"That late," Clay mused, although he had planned it that way. "Well, I'll just walk around to keep my mind off of things."

Poor guy, the operator thought. He wouldn't walk across the street to do anything for his mother-in-law.

There were many things on Clay's mind—and no time to waste if he expected to accomplish them all.

The train had already pulled in when he returned. Purposely he waited by the telegraph cage, his face growing longer as it became obvious that all the passengers were male.

"I guess she couldn't get off work that quickly," he said sadly, "and will come in the morning."

"If you're looking for a place, my mother runs a boarding house on Canal Street."

"Couldn't help overhearing, friend," the cherub-faced man broke in. "Barker's my name and canal barges my game. Would your good mother be taking in traveling salesmen?"

"That she does, sir, but is strict about no ladies in the rooms and smoking only in the parlor. If you both rush along, she serves a right tasty dinner table until seven. Oh, if two gentlemen share, the rate is quite reasonable. Mr. Barker this is . . . ah . . . Brother Clayton."

"Religious, eh?" Barker mused. "Well, Barker's the name, canal barges my game, and I snore like a billy goat eating tin. But, Brother Clayton, I'm a man who keeps a tight eye on my money. Come along."

"Oh, and gentlemen, if my mother hasn't sent my dinner pail along, tell her to speed my wife up. The name is Soames. Paul Soames."

Clay had a hard time controlling his laughter. The derby

was a size too small for Pierpont's head and the plaid suit was garishly loud.

"Don't you dare laugh," he chided. "What did you expect Jane Morgan to arrive in, a skirt?"

"I didn't even recognize you," Clay giggled. "Or your voice."

"It's the cotton I stuffed into my cheeks. Crafty, eh? My wife went into hysterics, although my black houseman didn't think it funny. I borrowed the suit from him. His Sunday best, of course." Then he turned serious. "I have not been idle, Clay. My lawyers had billy clubs thrown at them in court, so we've got the case shifted to Staten Island. Billy is working as hard on that judge as the Tammany boys."

"He should be working on his father."

"Oh no, I was the one who got the old Commodore to act frightened. Delaware & Hudson made a secret deal with Carnegie for their coal. This war is beginning to pinch them and Jay Gould is furious with Fisk. The Carnegie money would have kept them from dipping further into their own pocket."

That piece of the puzzle fit neatly into Clay's mind. Gould wanted all of his money for gold.

"It has helped make us look like the bastards, though."

"That was necessary," Morgan said flatly. "Clay, we were both schooled in England. The headmaster didn't give a damn if you were born a prince with a silver spoon in your mouth or a merchant's son. You were there to be taught, strict and proper. That's what makes a callous British businessman—the necessities of survival. That training is what has helped me be as crafty as Gould and more pugnacious than Fisk himself. In a war everyone must suffer so that the loyal troops rise to the top like rich cream. Now, you would not have sent for me unless you had something damn important in mind. What is it?"

"A time for skimming," Clay chuckled, "but in private."

After dinner they sat in their shared room and Morgan listened with avid interest.

"I like it, Clay," he said fretfully, "but it will make you a target for every hired gun that Fisk wants to send out."

That, Clay reflected, was God's own truth—though it was disconcerting to hear it expressed so baldly.

"And if you lose another million," Clay joked, "your father will cut off your allowance."

"And my balls!" He pondered a moment. "I was only able to quickly scrape together pocket money. It should get you started."

"How much?"

"Just a little over seven hundred thousand dollars."

Clay impulsively jumped forward and hugged the man. "J.P., we are not building the railroad over, just keeping it alive."

The man proved how crafty he had become. "I think I smelled out your plot from the telegram, Clay. The railroad is only a means to the end. Here is a list of the foremen and miners I trust. Give them full authority to open those mines to their fullest capacity and hire accordingly. We will turn Binghamton into a ghost town until we regain control. I approve of the land purchases. I think they are brilliant. I approve of the whole scheme and will back it financially until victory, but there is a flaw."

"And that is?" Clay's face was filled with astonishment. Clearly he thought he had covered every aspect.

"Jay Cooke is smart because he knows what the other man is thinking before he thinks it. He questioned me, that night you ran off to the hospital, why we didn't out-Gould Gould and issue our own fraudulent new stock. Oh, I can see your shock at such a suggestion coming from Jay and my even contemplating it. But, Clay, to beat them we have to learn to crawl in their slime and corruption. Which means, we need a few well-paid—*damn well-paid*—spies in their camp. I think my man Thayer in Binghamton has a very likely prospect."

"Thayer is your man?" Clay asked in amazement. "I thought he came off second best to Sheriff Catwell."

Pierpont shot back his head and chortled. "I'm beginning to enjoy being pugnacious. Catwell is the bird that we nearly have in the bag. Because of the bribes he has already accepted, he has to appear the sworn enemy of Thayer. But it gives us a listening post at that end of the terminus. Albany? I am at a loss."

"I, too," Clay fumed. "We can buy that land out of the limits to build a new terminal, which gives us a base. The merchants will even come out there to pick up the produce, dairy goods and coal supplies. We have an option on the land to build a spur to the Erie Canal and move your coal down the Hudson River. What we don't have—"

They both froze in fright as there was a rap on the wall between bedrooms. In their excitement they might have exposed all to the occupant next door. Their fear of such increased when a moment later there was a rap on their bedroom door. Morgan opened it, as though expecting to look upon the face of the devil.

It was only a broadly grinning Paul Soames.

"Gentlemen, I failed to expose another of my mother's rules. So that others may sleep, she keeps a pot of coffee on the stove for those who wish late evening business discussions. As my wife and I share the adjoining room, you have really disturbed no one, Mr. Morgan and Mr. Monroe."

"You know us," J.P. said in surprise.

"Not at first. It was my wife who really recognized Mr. Monroe while serving dinner. To make ends meet, we are a working family and she worked at the hotel when Mr. Vanderbilt was a guest. Mr. Monroe met with him quite often. Your name, Mr. Morgan, came to me after I started thinking about the telegram. My congratulations. It was clever trickery."

"Which you shall now use against us?" Morgan sneered.

Clay shot him a reproving look. His voice was soft when he spoke. "Perhaps Paul would like to join us in the kitchen for coffee."

"Thank you, Mr. Monroe," Paul Soames said. "That would pleasure me."

J.P. and Clay looked at each other. Their eyes glowed, for all their English-trained habit of self-control. An Albany listening post had just presented itself to them.

Like all wars, this one was waged on many fronts during the summer months. The shareholders remained deadlocked. The duel of legal strokes and counterstrokes went from courtroom to courtroom within the state. Within the little townships there were wrestling bouts for control of the stock books held by the town council. The bombings, the unnecessary personal attacks, the slander, the ruined public property did make many wonder which of the opposing captains was responsible.

The little country within a country would not give in—even though it had enemies within its hundred miles.

The Delaware, Lackawanna & Western mines did expand and turn Binghamton into a ghost town. The working miners had been neutralized as an army, until Fisk brought in a hundred Bowery thugs dressed as miners to stand in front of the flatcar and scream out their wrath at the still-closed mines.

Because they were vocal and because Jim Fisk paid for the right newspaper reporters to be on the scene, the rest of the country never read about the mountains of coal that began to grow on the outskirts of Binghamton and Albany. They never learned of the wagon train of supplies that daily traveled from Johnson City to Nineveh. They were unaware that the A&S trains again ran. The merchants in Albany really didn't want them to know that the produce and dairy products from the area were mixed in with their own and then shipped out on the Erie line at their own freight rates. The Erie Canal barges came from the Great Lakes and down the Hudson River Valley to New York, loaded to the water line with coal hidden under piles of general merchandise.

From Nineveh to Voorheesville, they began to forget about the world outside their hundred miles. Their prosperity was coming back. With the watered stock floating about like fleecy clouds in the sky, the pressure point had swung back to the Morgan-Ramsey camp. To keep that swing moving, Morgan devised a most uncommonly crafty stratagem.

The miners gathered around, utterly stunned that the owner they had been working for was only a thirty-two-year-old man. In Binghamton, the Fisk men had them believing that Morgan was a blood-sucking old vampire.

He seemed as afraid of them as they had been fearful of him and of attending this meeting with the big boss.

"Gentlemen," he said nervously, but with cold purpose as he wanted to appear very human in their eyes. He and Clay had gone over his words carefully to take out anything that would make him appear more educated than this uneducated group and yet to make sure he spoke as the voice of authority. "We are in the business of coal, and yet we find ourselves in a railroad war, because we need those bastards to haul it for us." He paused, but did not get the response Clay had anticipated. "Coal doesn't make money sitting in the ground for you or for me. You men who worked my mines below Binghamton know they have richer veins. But rather than keep you out of work, I opened these smaller mines to a larger operation."

There was a scattering of applause. "But that has cost me money and, frankly, it's cost you money, too."

"How did it cost us money?" Thayer asked sneeringly, right on cue.

"I don't claim to be a transportation expert," he replied, bristling indignantly, "but I do look upon myself as a fair businessman. Carnegie wants all the coal he can get for his Bessemer steel process. He's in Pittisburgh and we have to ship him coal by way of New York. Dammit, don't those added transportation costs take money away from me and away from you?"

"Maybe you, but not me," Thayer scoffed, again right on cue.

"Listen, mister," Morgan growled, using Thayer just as Sheriff Catwell had used him, "answer me this! Has Jim Fisk lifted a single finger to help you?"

Thayer shrugged and there was a mild scattering of dissent.

"Has the A&S an army of cutthroats like they have in Binghamton?"

A few more added a negative response.

"Was it Jim Fisk who opened the mines on this side?"

Now half a hundred men responded.

"And were any of you ever questioned on your past employment? Didn't we accept D&H men right along with D,L&W men?"

They looked at each other and had to agree that former Fisk miners had been hired right along with former Morgan miners. Men wishing to feed their families hadn't taken that into consideration.

"All right," J.P. said sternly. "I put my money on the line to put you back to work, and now I need your help to keep you working."

"Here it comes," Thayer snickered, on cue for the third time. "More Catwell-like promises."

"I don't know who you are, mister," Morgan exploded with realism, "but you are bucking to get yourself fired. I was just about to offer these men an offer on a ten-cent-an-hour raise, but you make me wonder why I even reopened the mines!"

"*Jesus*!" a chorus bellowed, "Keep your damn mouth shut, Thayer!"

"Thank you," Morgan said quietly, noting the shocked expressions upon their faces, including Thayer's. He had not been let in on this part of the gambit. "Gentlemen, we have with us tonight Mr. Horace Greeley of the *New York Tribune*. Now, Mr. Greeley, I apologize. We out here don't get your paper and my miners aren't well acquainted with your national name. But, boys, I trust Mr. Greeley and I wanted him to let the rest of the country know what we are up against and what I honestly propose to you. Which is this: I'm willing to give you the unheard-of ten-cent-an-hour raise, if you are willing to do the unheard-of and invest that back into a collective fund to buy up the railroad stocks so as to break up Fisk's hold on our future."

They all didn't fully understand, but the chorus of voices was overwhelming. The propaganda war had been reversed. Greeley could quickly calculate that ten cents an hour for twelve hundred miners would make little difference in the stock picture. But as the perennial friend and watchdog for the people, he would banner this story.

"Well, gentlemen," he said, when the hall was nearly empty, "I shall report from the war front."

"And here," Clay said, handing him a packet, "is a report from the home front. Mr. Cooke sent it by special courier from Washington City. He continues to make urgent representations to Secretary Boutwell and President Grant."

"Young man," asked Greeley, smiling, "could you put all of that in a newspaper headline for me?"

"Gladly. Denounce the Gold Conspiracy."

Greeley had suspected, but it was still a sobering shock to gain such world-shattering news in such a little hamlet.

He would have been further amazed at their intelligence and how these "little" events were all a part of a master timetable.

When gold was quoted at 133, they were amazed that Jim Fisk had not rushed back to New York. Then, after the President visited New York on September 2, 1869, and word spread like wildfire that he had ordered the Treasury not to sell any of the government's gold, Fisk stayed in Binghamton—even with gold marked up to 137.

Almost unbelievably it came to the minds of Clay and Pierpont that the inscrutable Jay Gould had disclosed none of his gold plan to Jim Fisk. Their plans and Jay Cooke's plans were doomed if the Erie money was left to do battle with them and not to be used in the gold battle.

Morgan had gone nearly to the limit of his resources in "floating" the area for the summer. From Cooke they knew that Gould had accumulated forty million in gold, or twice the available floating supply, thanks to the boundless credits opened by his banks. They had to shift public opinion from amusement or fascination to anger.

Step one had been to get J. H. Ramsey once more elected president on September 6th. The proxy votes of Mary Calhoun narrowly carried the election. He then allowed those who backed him to sell out control of the line at an inflated price to neutral interests. The sales went through Jay Cooke & Company. The neutral interest parties were never disclosed as Messrs. Morgan and Monroe. Step two was to get Paul Soames to devise a telegram for Jim Fisk that would travel to New York and back up to Binghamton and appear to have come from Gould. Step three was the pay raise and stock offer. It was little more than a publicity stunt for the ears of Horace Greeley. They wanted the public to determine who wore shining armor and who wore horns. Step four had to wait for the others to lock into gear.

On the morning of the sixteenth a ten-wheeler with a single car pulled into Albany. Its only passenger raced across to the A&S depot, triumphantly waving a *Tribune*.

"I've only a minute," Jay Cooke said breathlessly, "I want to get to Washington the soonest. Horace is as watchdoggy as ever, my friends. I thought he would tip his hand on the series of articles he has been doing on this battle, but yesterday he was a perfect fire-alarm. 'It has come to my attention who is behind the growing currency tension. Do Messrs. Fisk and Gould feel they can do with a nation as they have attempted to do with the Albany & Susquehanna Railroad? That memorable struggle, as I have been reporting, was waged by these unscrupulous usurpers with calamities of unusual horror, damage and death. And they will not relent. Why then would they relent over a vast gold conspiracy? Yes, a conspiracy to control the currency of this entire nation. I call upon the Treasury to . . .' The rest is for me to handle. It is time the President was made fully aware of all the facts."

Clay was puzzled. "Why did Mr. Greeley come out yesterday? I thought you wanted it to come after we got Binghamton back."

"I did, but their ploy seemed to change day before yesterday and I told Horace it was time for the green light. I think they are going to just sit tight and make no more waves up here. Fisk came into the Gold Room with his normal gusto and slyness. A rumor had been floated that morning that Mrs. Grant and her heroic spouse were caught in Gould's net. Fisk kept the rumors alive by queer winks, knowing tugs at his waxed moustache and wobbly little nods of his head. At first I thought he was just trying to prove that he had been in on the scheme from the start. But when I got a message from the Tenth National Bank, I knew we had entered the first day of the final battle. The Tammany boys have placed all the bank resources at the service of Gould. Their certified checks started arriving immediately in unlimited amounts and drove the price of gold to 141.''

''Then we don't need our final step?''

Cooke's face turned fierce. ''We need it more than ever. Tomorrow, if that is not too soon. If I have measured Gould correctly he will fight to get it to 200. That could come sooner than we ever dreamed. Grant has been slow-moving and wavering. We need this event to wake him up and stall the conspiracy.''

Clay smiled slowly. ''Then I think Pierpont had better go back with you, Jay. In the articles Mr. Greeley has made him universally respected as the able financier. Let's not tarnish that by having him involved.''

''Now just a minute,'' Pierpont protested. ''This was my plan and I want to see it through.''

''No,'' Clay said firmly, ''and I am not questioning your desire or your courage. This summer you have directed this campaign with a ruthlessness that has amazed me. You approved of things in this bizarre struggle that even made me squirm. But in no way should your name be connected with this affair. Your voice will be better used screaming at newspaper reporters when you start getting the wires.''

Morgan had to agree with a sigh. ''Sure would have been fun.''

Before dawn the bell-funneled locomotive began to couple up the empty coal cars. On the outskirts of Albany no one paid it any mind. It had become a normal daily event—just like the twice-a-day arrival of the freight trains at the barn-like freight depot and the return of the coal train in the evening to add to the mountain range of black that grew faster than the barges could haul it away.

''Are you ready?'' Clay asked as they left the boarding house.

Paul Soames nodded. ''This day will cost me my job.''

''I hope so,'' he growled, then grinned. ''Because from today on you work exclusively for me.''

''Thanks, Clay.'' He grinned back. They shook hands

and took different directions. Clay walked out to the temporary freight terminal and Paul to the Erie depot.

Paul relieved the night operator and scolded the porter over the sloppy manner in which he was sweeping the floor.

"What difference it make?" the man mumbled. "Ain't nobody ebber on the 5:10."

Paul smiled to himself and went about his early morning chores.

Ten minutes later the porter's eyes rounded in surprise and mystery. The 5:10 had twenty passengers that morning. The filthiest, most nondescript specimens of humanity that the porter had ever seen. Each one wore the green "Erie Security Patrol" arm band, and each was armed with a shotgun, rifle, or revolver.

He breathed a sigh of relief when only one of them came in on his freshly swept floor. The rest went directly across the tracks toward the A&S depot.

"You Soames?" the burly man growled, coming up to the cage.

"I am," Paul said a little nervously.

"Want this message sent down the line, so they can transfer it back up to Binghamton."

Paul let his eyes dart over the words. "You know, of course, that the New York Central will have to handle the message."

"Listen, buster," he sneered, "Fisk has already seen to that part. You do yours!"

The still morning air was broken by gunfire. The porter's black skin turned grey as he ducked behind a waiting-room bench.

"What in the hell is that?" Paul demanded.

"Never mind!" the man barked as he started to run out. "Just send the damn wire!"

Paul stood frozen looking at the porter, who likewise looked back at him. Together they crept to the window and looked across the tracks. The Erie thugs had taken over the opposite depot and had the stationmaster and freight handler outside. Someone barked an order for them to start running. Fearfully, they did, and the thugs shot at their retreating heels. The stationmaster fell, sprays of dirt kicking up around him, then rose and ran down the street screaming his lungs out.

Windows banged open and men rushed into the street in their nightshirts. Then, as the gunfire continued, they darted right back in.

Belligerently the motley crew began to march out toward the rising smoke from the engine.

"Mister Soames," the porter mumbled, "dem supposed tah be our men?"

"Yep!"

"Then I'm goin' home. I was in on that last shooting and I ain't goin' tah lie about this one."

"Charlie, I think you are right," Paul said, going back to the cage to send the message.

"You gonna send that message?"

"Yep!' Then he grinned. "And then some."

He began to tap at the key:

Catwell

Binghamton

Via NYC

Albany station and train taken. Stop. Coming down line. Stop. Open telegraph so wire can progress. Stop. Johnson-Erie Security Patrol.

Paul sat a few minutes, leaving the key open. In the distance he could hear more gunfire.

"What they doing, Charlie?"

When he got no answer, he knew the man had fled. He hunched back over the key, not needing to look out to know what was happening.

Then he tapped out:

Attention along the line. Gun fire here. On orders of Fisk Erie to take A&S by force. Engineer, fireman kidnapped and train stolen. I quit.

He closed and locked the key. Albany would be silent until the next train came in at 8:30.

It didn't take that long for an enterprising young man from the *Tribune* to rush from the New York Central offices to the fine brownstone residence of Josie Mansfield in back of the Grand Opera House.

"What makes you think him's here?" the sleepy-eyed maid sniffed.

"Come on, honey! Everyone knows Fisk keeps his wife at a convenient distance in Boston. Go get him out of Josie's bed and tell him the jig is up!"

Moments later a wild-eyed Jim Fisk came pounding down the marble stairway in a flaming red nightshirt. Without knowing it, the young reporter had put the fear of God into him. He thought the jig was up on the gold conspiracy.

Upon hearing what the reporter was really after, he returned to his usual aplomb and philosophic detachment.

"A stock buyer buys only an investment in a company and not the right to run its daily affairs. He has no authority to send out any forces, nor have I."

The reporter didn't even think it was a good quote; still, he reported it to Horace Greeley.

"Jumping Jupiter!" he stormed, nearly pulling out his side whiskers. "Get out to Binghamton and keep a wire open to me. I'm going to press with this much for the noon edition, even if the man sues me!"

"That's exactly what he said he would do," he said hesitantly. "Said we really should be looking into men who come back from the grave to pull such duplicity. What did he mean by that?"

Greeley looked at him narrowly. "Read my articles on the subject," he snapped. "And the next time hang around for a while. I would love to know what Fisk did after you hit him with this bombshell. I bet it drove him crazy."

Sheriff Catwell did think Jim Fisk had gone crazy. The two telegrams came right together. One from Johnson saying he was coming down the line on Fisk's orders and one from Fisk asking for information.

"How in the hell can I give him information when I've just learned? Barney, hook the damn telegraph wires back up and raise Albany."

Because he had taken the incoming messages, he already had the A&S line hooked back up. He tried and then tried again, but Albany didn't respond. Before he was even asked, he tried Voorheesvile.

"Son of a gun!" he giggled. "It's an Erie man answering."

"So? . . . So?" Catwell demanded.

Barney went back to tapping and the grin spread broader and broader on his face as the answers came back. The small force had taken Central Bridge by surprise, found everyone still asleep in Westkyrd. There had been a small gun battle in Collierville. Because he had been forewarned, Mayor Johnson of Oneonia had taken over the station with local police before they had arrived. The Oneonia police had then gone on to help secure Masonville.

"Well? . . . Well?" Catwell fumed. "Find out about Nineveh so I can wire a report to Fisk."

"Dammit! I'm trying to raise them. If you can do any better, do it yourself! Here they come on the line."

His face began to fall as his ears picked out the words from the Morse code. "The miners have taken up arms. They've got the Erie men and police trapped in the depot. They want help."

Catwell was momentarily silent. He was trying to think of the proper orders, but his disgust was bottomless. With Fisk around he had been forced to appear tough and mean, because the judges Fisk controlled wanted the situation tough and mean. But those were his people out there. He had done his damnedest to keep things from coming to a bloodbath. He despised the Bowery toughs in Binghamton, as he knew he would despise the Bowery toughs under fire in Nineveh. But the law was still on the side of the Erie gang. He had to go to help them.

"Fire up an engine!" he barked. "Take down the barricade and call out the Erie men and my deputies. Let them know we will be on our way as soon as we get up steam!"

Inside the Nineveh station it was as quiet as a tomb. Harry Stillwell sat nervously before the key-box and prayed for it to chatter back at him.

When it erupted, he nearly jumped out of his skin. His palms were so wet that he could hardly hold the pencil to write down the message. But others in the crowded waiting room could mentally pick out the code as it came in.

"So?" Ramsey spread wide his hands. "Catwell has taken the bait."

Clay frowned heavily. Men were going to die that day, he thought bitterly. It was a dirty, ruthless way to end it, but everything else had failed.

"We can still call it off," Ramsey said quietly, so only Clay heard.

He studied the man curiously and then looked out at the train on the tracks.

"We can," he said sadly, "but can they? Our 'thugs' were beginning to shake by the time they got to the train this morning, Ramsey. They feared that the Albany sheriff deputies would come out shooting and stop us before our little charade ever got started. Our twenty. That was to be it. But the word spread down the line. We preached and they listened. It's their railroad now. No one asked the dairy men to climb into the coal cars with their pitchforks, farmers to hop aboard with clubs and spades. Mary Calhoun passed out every firearm and round of ammunition she had for sale. Those miner axes should be chipping out coal. The fraud has backfired. In a simple way we wanted them to believe the Erie men had taken over, had run into trouble, and get Catwell out here to surrender. It's no longer simple. That's an army of over four hundred on those coal cars. Call it off? Will they go back to the way things have been? Can we go back to the way things have been? The mountains will take no more coal. Cooke holds my paper for your stock. The summer season is over for the farmers. We do it now, or we walk away forever."

"We do it now," Ramsey sighed, and strode sadly away to warn the engineer.

Harry Stillwell caught Clay by the arm. "Mr. Morgan left a message with me, Clay. If it came down to this, you were not to go."

"Harry," he said slowly, "you can't kill a dead man twice."

* * *

The men huddled down in the open coal cars. The wind whipped around them as the 4-4-0 climbed to full throttle. They could gain a faster speed because the other train would have to climb through the hills, cross a dozen trestles and switch back before entering the long tunnel, fifteen miles out of Binghamton.

Because this had not been a part of the full plan, Clay had to run it over in his mind as they raced along. He was still not sure of a plan when he rose to inspect their progress. The long tunnel entrance lay ahead, but already the engineer was whistling and tooting his bells in warning. An equal warning came from the far distance and Clay looked across the valley to the switchback on the opposite hill. The Binghamton train was breathing fire and fury to make the long sweeping corner to enter the tunnel from the other end. The belching engine carried behind it five flat-cars with a formidable body of Erie's Bowery toughs and sheriff's deputies. Clay tried to judge their speed. Neither fireman was giving a quarter in stoking the steamer full. Neither engineer was going to give up the track, he also quickly realized. But where would they meet?

Suddenly he began to shout. "Jump off! When we enter the tunnel, jump off! Pass it forward to the other cars!"

The Nineveh train came barreling out of the tunnel, just as the Binghamton train was coming into the straightaway from the curve. Frantically the engineers used their steam whistles to warn each other off. Neither would give ground to keep from a head-on collision.

"This is madness!" Catwell roared, as he saw the Nineveh engineer and fireman jump from the cab of their locomotive. "There's not a damn living soul on that runaway! Jump for your lives!"

The enemy engines came together with a deafening roar and momentarily churned against each other before the Nineveh locomotive started a slow, grinding climb into the air, its still pistoning front wheels eating away the other's cowcatcher and striving to get high enough to chew at its headlights.

Each was spewing steam from its ruptured boilers like hissing dragons. The Binghamton dragon now had the advantage of attacking the enemy's underbelly and toppling it off the track. But the weight of the still-coupled coal cars would be its undoing. These dirty chariots of industry had the honor of divorcing the headlight, smashing the bell smokestack and piling one atop the other until there was no engine in sight.

And even before that thunderous sound became an echo, the interior of the tunnel exploded with a frightening yell of defiance that left Catwell and his men open-mouthed. Clay's army poured out upon them in mind-boggling numbers. Immediately they began to fall before they could even react.

"Stick men to the rear!" Catwell commanded. He felt betrayed and he was furious. The dynamite men were quite glad to grab up their wooden boxes and run back along the tracks. Already men around them were sprawled in thick pools of blood.

Clay kept his men in knots, firing, then running forward and regrouping. They had the Catwell force in a panic. The issue was already decided, but Catwell didn't have the sense to order his men to lay down their arms. He ordered a retreat, a tearing up of the tracks, and the blowing up of every trestle and bridge.

But Clay's men were better armed and made a slow and murderous advance. The Bowery thugs had not been paid to be killed, only to kill, and they zigzagged off into the hills while Clay's men knelt and fired. But, although many would claim differently, Clay's men now only shot into the air over their frightened heads.

Sheriff Catwell went momentarily insane, and perhaps his deputies did as well. They destroyed everything they could get their hands on in their frantic desire to get back to Binghamton. To a man, they claimed they had been fired upon all the way back to the barricade. To a man, they claimed that Sheriff Catwell was correct in immediately wiring for regiments of the National Guard to come to their rescue. To a man, they would swear that they had been a force of one hundred against over four thousand. Look at the figures! They had left twenty-seven dead and dying out in the hills.

But no longer was this an affair that could be kept under a bushel. The bushel had been toppled.

"Damn right!" Pierpont Morgan screamed, when asked if the National Guard should be called in. "It's about time

Hoffman started being the governor of all the people of New York instead of just two or three. My lawyers already have a petition going forth for the state's Attorney-General to operate that line until this affair is ended. I challenge the Erie to do the same."

"Mr. Morgan, are you not afraid what the National Guard might find in their investigation?"

"Afraid," he snorted. "I welcome it! Justice, though tardy, is on the right track at last."

The reporters greeted that statement with applause.

Pierpont Morgan could make the statement without fear. He already knew what the National Guardsmen would find when they traveled from station to station. Nothing. Not a man wounded or dead, because they had been lucky. Not a man who would claim to have been away from job or home, because they were loyal. Not a man, woman or child who would oppose being under the National Guard, because that was the first step back toward sanity.

And Erie did join in the petition, because Gould discreetly felt this minor retreat would get his name out of Horace Greeley's newspaper and mind.

And he was relieved that it did, without knowing that was part of the plot.

For five days certain men knew every time he sneezed. They also knew every time U.S. Grant took up a new cigar or poured a nervous glass of bourbon. They also knew the moment Abel Corbin, removed from all connection with the President and paralyzed with fear, left to communicate that message to Gould in New York.

Friday, September 24, 1869, would later be called "Black Friday" for the gold ring's campaign.

It was a very black Friday for Clay. Barrett Monroe was dead.

"Pack!" he told Paul Soames sternly. "You and your wife meet me in Chicago when I return from Milwaukee."

As he took train after train, he cared little that it was a day of pandemonium. From Boston to San Francisco banks and brokerage houses closed their doors, and panic filled the streets. Gold at 165 made a catastrophic fall to 138 when the government swung into action.

The question would always remain: Had Grant saved

Corbin and then the nation? For Corbin's forewarning to Gould had certainly saved his and Fisk's neck.

Hate that day could be bought for a penny a scowl.

Clay found that a cheap price by Milwaukee standards. He was not even treated as family for Barrett's funeral. Harvel Packer and even Harry Hart Horner were honorary pallbearers. He was nothing. Death was not cold, only the people who surrounded the corpse.

His mother had given him only a cheek to kiss, his brothers only a weak handshake and nodding indifference. The biggest hurt came from the very cool attitude of Carter, Jonathan and Jon. From Cyrus he expected the leering hate, but from nieces and nephews he didn't even know he resented it and frowned right back.

At graveside he stood apart. He was not saying one last farewell to a coffin, a mummy within, or those who falsely mourned. He turned and started walking away, content to live with the memories of the man. He heard footsteps and felt a hand on his arm.

He turned with a smile, expecting to find Janellen.

"They are being very cruel" Eugenia said.

"You should know," he said curtly, "you're an expert in the field."

"I will ignore that," she said sweetly, "because we are at a stage in our lives when we need each other, Clay."

"You have your father," he sneered.

"And you have just lost yours."

"Don't you mean stepfather?" he said with disgust. "They all went out of their way to prove that point, so don't be kind."

"They went out of their way to show their mean fear," she said simply. "The moment he was dead they couldn't wait to tear at his will. What a shock for them to find out that he had left you as executor with full control over the whole family fortune."

He took a step backward, glancing warily at the knot of people around the casket, then again at Eugenia.

Slowly he shook his head.

"Oh no," he said huskily, "I've got no fight left in me for that kind of battle."

"I know," she muttered. "You will have your hands

full with the problems Father is creating for you. He's out to ruin you, you know."

"You are so kind with the warning. Am I remiss in questioning why?"

"My maternity dress might give you the first clue."

He looked down at her round belly, confused. "When?"

"You should be able to figure out that it was at Jay Cooke's. I didn't bother you, because you have had a busy summer—and a most successful one—from what we all read in the newspapers. Now, as husband and wife, we have a few things to discuss."

He struggled furiously with a million things he wanted to say, feeling oddly like his boarding-school friend caught in a similar situation. But it was not similar. He was already married to this woman. He was the father of the child no matter what. But what a thing to spring on him at that time.

"I will have a word with you," his mother barked, racing up to them.

Clay wearily shook his head.

"No," he muttered. "Eugenia has explained. Just have the lawyers bring the papers and I will relinquish all."

"No fight?" Marti asked in amazement.

Again Clay shook his head.

He had just waged a victorious battle and won. But that had been for a real family. These people were strangers. He owed them nothing and he wished nothing from them in return. The moments of love and respect he had gained from Barrett Monroe could not be measured in a will. He was honored to be named executor because of the man's fear of the future for what he had built. But no, he had just been handed a different future. He had handled the child situation very badly with Janellen. He would not handle it the same with Eugenia. She was his wife and carried his child. Love was no longer the issue.

For nearly half of his life, he thought slowly, bitterly, he had been surrounded by men who had not loved their wives, but had produced happy children—by men who had been the most callous, cruel businessmen it had been his misfortune to work with.

Chapter 16

Sitting across from Clay was a little intimidating for Carter Monroe.

In the two years since the Barrett Monroe funeral, the Chicago business community looked upon Clay as serious, protective of his privacy and the kind of restrained businessman who might answer a potentially resonant business question with a simple "yep."

At thirty, he was molding his own image from past clay—a mixture of good looks, scalding anger and rueful humor. He played the social lion, and yet his private life suggested deep vulnerability.

Once before he thought he had found immeasurable happiness. Christopher Barrett Monroe gave him immeasurable love. From the moment he first held the baby in his arms, he knew a creature had been born who had a stranglehold on the emotions he never showed outwardly.

Ironically, Christopher was born two years to the day of his return to Chicago. How long ago that seemed.

The arrogant associate was skilled enough to be the best for others. Self-assured but hollow, he was driven by the ravaging demands of intense ambition.

Two years had mellowed the image. He was a charming husband, comic and shrewd in turning Paul Soames into a cattle foreman, and icily reserved toward the fretting, swearing and devious ploys of Harvel Packer. He was quick to hire Elliott Fairchild on the day of his firing, although Harvel's new "associate"—Cyrus Monroe—vilified them both in a careless and reckless manner.

In the meetings to sort out his personal affairs from those of Packer and Company, Clay played the washed-up businessman who was going to be forced to dig deeply for one last shot at self-redemption.

Cyrus had cut deep for every pound of flesh he felt his due. Clay took it all very quietly. Too quietly, Elliott thought.

"Chief, that carping little thief took everything but the bones."

"Yep!" Then he grinned. "Because he doesn't know the real value of 'buried skeletons' and we do. Fairchild, do you know that three-quarters of P.D.'s money now comes from what was thrown away just five years ago? Cyrus thinks he has put us face-down in the offal."

"And Mr. Packer?"

"Have pity," Clay said with genuine understanding. "He lost his battle with Eugenia over me. Gone is the penchant for kicking the legs from under eastern money men; gone is the financial intelligence that made him millions. All that remains is fragility and a warped sense of revenge. He thinks he is hurting me in hiring Cyrus."

"That hurt will back up on him," Elliott said jokingly.

"Given time. Given time."

Clay had the time. Experience had taught him that time was a very important calculation in the business world—even when the businessman had considerable clout.

But all time is in the hands of God. The chessboard continued to have its pieces moved about in strange patterns.

"He just never woke up from his nap," Janellen whispered.

"But he was fine when I drove out to see him this morning," Clay protested, to make it unreal, a strange lump rising in his throat.

Janellen placed her fingers across his mouth.

"Don't cry, Clay!" she wept. "He wanted only joy in his passing."

"I should have guessed this morning. I've got to tell you about it, Janellen. He said all he could very well afford to ever give me are the plans for his dream city. All that land, all that Great Northern Railroad land, needs cities built upon it. His city. His dream. I'll talk to Jay

Jay still owes me a favor. He knows that Harry was the best designer ever, I guess . . ."

Harry Hart Horner had requested and received a private service. Even though private, it brought forth a strange mixture of enemies and friends.

Marti Monroe stood so long before the open casket, shaking all over with weeping, that the anguish made Clay act on impulse.

He went to stand beside her and put a protective arm about her thin waist.

She stilled and looked up at him quietly.

"I was praying," she whispered, "and remembering his grace and gentleness and love . . . and my years of foolishness."

"Hush, Mother," he wept. "He wanted only joy."

"Just like him." She hesitated. "Did you come to love him, Clayton?"

"If respect has anything to do with love, I guess that I did."

"How is the mouse holding up?"

Clay had to smile to himself. Even at a moment such as this, Marti Monroe was still Marti Monroe.

"She's holding up."

She asked no questions about anyone else and let Clay return her to her carriage. Marti Monroe was tired and wanted a quick return to Milwaukee. Within the month she had joined Barrett and Harry.

The "boys" gathered as though duty-bound for the funeral of a neighbor woman. Out of respect Clay and Eugenia attended, and Harvel Packer was civil.

For Clay it was like a long-held sigh and prompted a new sense of freedom. For twelve years he had read her letters; she read his. The letters had bled off into other areas of his living, his school life, his enthusiasms and his impulses. He would now let them molder to yellow. He was free of the last bond from the past.

"It is beautiful, Clay!" Eugenia gasped. "The most beautiful structure to come out of Harry's mind. And the location! With Humboldt Park as a backdrop, it looks like a grand English estate. Who did you say Janellen sold the plans to?"

"Us!" he chuckled. "Happy Fourth Anniversary!"

Eugenia looked at him in wonderment as the carriage pulled off North Avenue and onto the brick-paved lane. She put her head out of the window and her blue eyes widened. It was breathtaking.

"I shall be hated eternally," he laughed, "if not already, but except for the interior and roof, it is all red brick. Jonathan is livid that what lumber was needed did not come from him."

It was a perfect opening for something that had been on her mind, but common sense made her back off. Another worry was more pressing.

"It seems a long way from town, Clay. From shopping and your office and . . ."

"Your father?"

"Well . . . now that you mention it."

"It shall delight LaVerna Priest," Clay growled in mock wrath. "She will have the old boy and the house to run without you popping in every five minutes. You can still badger her at least once a day."

She let it pass. At that moment she just wanted to marvel at the new house. She laughed with delight as Clay suddenly lifted her into his arms and carried her through the massive double front doors. She looked into his face, thinking: Other than the engagement and wedding rings, this is the first real gift that was given with a sense of love. He is trying hard to erase the past. I know it angers him when I see Father daily . . .

She also knew that she had done it out of spite because he had seen Harry Hart Horner daily—and thus Janellen. But Harry was dead and she would make him forget Janellen yet! She bent her head and kissed him.

"Thank you, my darling. It's a grand present."

He put her down, his big face flushed with contentment. "I have left it bare for you to furnish as you see fit. Why don't we just rent the old place furnished and start here anew?"

"Oh Clay!" she gasped. "Can we afford it? Father says his business affairs are at a point of ruination."

"Mine aren't," he said flatly, "because I don't have

a Cyrus Monroe bringing it to a point of ruination. Understand?''

Eugenia's face, as she went through the house floor by floor, was a study in joy.

''This wing, of course, will be Christopher's,'' he announced proudly. ''Harry put a child's wing into the plans when he first developed them in Dover—'' He stopped, glancing warily at his wife.

Eugenia's head came up. There was a flare about her fine nostrils.

''The right house, but for the wrong child?'' she said.

''I don't live with ghosts,'' Clay said ominously. ''The plans were for sale, and frankly she needed the money. Harry always rented, as you know, and didn't leave her a hell of a lot to live on.''

''Widow's mite?'' she sneered. When he ignored her, she decided the time was right for the other matter. ''Speaking of people who need help with their problems, Carter dropped by this morning. He would like to come by the house this evening to see you, but is too embarrassed to ask you directly.''

''What in the hell does he want?'' he growled.

''I didn't pry.''

He looked at her, his face taut and still. Why did people feel they had to lie to him? he thought. He had been in such a good humor that day. He had been pleased to pull off the surprise, and then he'd ruined it with a stupid statement. He did worry about Janellen, even though she tried to lie to him about her finances. Had Mrs. Yost not been honest with him over her back pay, he might never have learned of Janellen's plight. He had pried, just as he knew Eugenia would have pried with Carter. It was no secret that Carter visited Eugenia. He had never questioned it, because there was nothing to question. Carter and Eugenia were old friends and he could understand Carter's embarrassment in having to face him. But there was no need for lies.

''Then we had better go back,'' he said curtly and marched from the bare room.

Eugenia started after him, aghast at the new problem that came to her mind. She hadn't fully inquired into

Carter's reason for wanting to see Clay. She knew he was in deep financial troubles, as was normal for Carter. To keep him away from Clay, she had been giving him small loans. But that morning Carter had hinted that it was time to approach Clay with the truth about his situation and she had encouraged him to meet with Clay. Now she knew precisely the truth Carter wished to reveal and she was suddenly very afraid.

Sitting across from Clay was a little intimidating for Carter Monroe.

Even though he knew everything that Clay had accomplished, he felt they were strangers. And Clay, listening to his long, sad tale, felt he had been listening to a stranger's woes.

"Although they have now split the company, since Mother's death," Clay said sternly, "my business intuition tells me they cannot survive."

"I hope so," Carter said with a sigh. "It was a great relief to let it all unravel . . . to someone who had been treated likewise."

"Hardly!" Clay corrected. "I wished nothing to do with them, you included. You were a part of their blemishes, their indecisions, their vulnerability and the wreckage they made of a giant industry. You say you are now in the pits. I certainly have been there a couple of times in my life. It would be cowardly and hypocritical to set myself up as perfect, Carter. But, I ask you, what did you ever do to help keep it glued together?"

"Glued together?" he mimicked. "That's a fine thing! I was never more than an errand boy. That was not much fun. Everyone had a reciprocal trade agreement on what assignment they could next give to Carter. And you thought you were treated badly?"

"The law," Clay said slowly, patiently, having come to realize that Carter was as childish as ever, "gave you a portion of the estate. But you let them steal you blind. If you went through every court in the land, if you laid your evidence end to end, they would still have the upper hand. Why did you wait so long to fight back?"

"Listen," he said dully, "it was Eugenia's theory. I'm hiding behind her skirts, you know. She has been my only friend in life—the only one I ever loved and respected, the only one who never made me feel dull and witless."

"Enough!" Eugenia stepped into the study and abruptly closed the door behind her. She came forward, walking slowly, awkwardly—and the fear in her face was like a thundercloud.

"You left out a few sentences in that chapter, Carter," she said gently, although her face remained fierce. "He never fought back, Clay, because they took away his fight. They made their own laws after Cyrus seduced his bride-to-be. Left at the altar? A fable! Jonathan bought off the harlot and put Carter into a mental hospital!"

"Don't!" Carter wailed. "I never wanted Clay to learn of that."

"I'm sorry, Carter, but he needed to know."

And Clay wondered why he needed to know at this point in time.

"Needed to know?" Carter exploded, his face growing dark and angry. "You are the one who said keep it a secret from him. I did. You don't love me! If you did, you wouldn't reveal this secret. You don't even understand what love means . . . I've kept all of our secrets."

Eugenia glared at him with warning and pity.

"We have no secrets, Carter. You do not have to fear Clay as you have the others. He loves you just as I love you—maybe more. You fear going back to the hospital, don't you?"

She saw him stiffen, his whole body suddenly rigid with the fear she had implanted on his mind, and when she looked at Clay for backing, she saw what she wanted. His face was blank with incredulity.

"Never!" he gasped. "I would never let him be sent there!"

"I—I don't fear that, Clay," Carter stammered. "I fear the real punishment. The kind that I used to get whipped for doing. That's what I've been doing, Clay. Do you understand?"

"No, I don't understand."

"Why," he said with mild surprise, "don't you understand? Eugenia said we have no secrets and I shouldn't fear you. I thought that meant that you knew everything."

"He does know everything," Eugenia said without hesitation, although, the moment she had said it, she knew it was wrong. "And now give me a moment alone with Clay," she added quickly.

Carter chuckled, rubbing his fat, pudgy hands together. He left the room quickly. He could always count on Eugenia. They were friends. He would do anything for her, just as she would do anything for him. He felt safe in her hands. She had abundantly demonstrated her ability to take care of him. The careless and indiscreet favors she had asked in return were only a measure of his love. Never had he felt so alive as when she took him to her bed after coming back from Philadelphia.

"Do I know everything?" Clay asked stiffly.

"No," Eugenia said, her face frowning as she turned. "You are not aware of how sick a mind his has become. He clings to me because there is no other. I am the only rock to keep him from drowning."

"A sure sign of maturity."

Eugenia glanced at her husband. Was there a note of reproach in Clay's voice? She couldn't tell. Clay's emotions were so hard to fathom of late.

"All right," she sighed, "let's face the issue squarely. A return to the hospital is the only answer."

"For you," he whispered, "but I wonder about poor Carter."

"Why wonder about him?"

She saw the expression of surprise on Clay's face.

"You really amaze me, Eugenia. The minute you go about changing facts to suit your own mold, you consider everyone else blind and stupid. My habit of collecting portfolio information on people did not exclude my own family. They, too, were very much involved in business with Harvel Packer. I have been very much aware of Carter's past problems. I never considered them a problem to himself, until now."

"Good!" she sighed. "Then you will have him put away."

"No," he said patiently, "that would only solve your

problem. I shall send him away, quietly and discreetly. Perhaps out to the Wyoming ranch."

"That solves nothing!" Eugenia flared. "And what do you mean by my problem?"

"Between you and me, Eugenia," he said, as cold as ice, "I shall say this one time, and one time only. We are husband and wife, until death do us part. I am no fool, unlike my brother Carter. I can read between the lines and count upon my fingers. So enough of your arrogant, spoiled games. You were not a virgin when I married you, so I am not shocked that you could not remain faithful. I just question your weird enjoyment in twisting poor Carter's love for you. And don't think of divorce. Christopher is *my* son and I will fight to the bitter end to keep him from the hell that has been my life. No child deserves that, no matter which parent has been errant. I will keep you as wife and he as my son!"

"And if I don't agree?" she flared with true Packer spirit.

"I wonder," he snarled, "if you would like to be proven as the first unfit mother in this land. The proper candidate for that honor, my own mother, is dead."

"You're a beast!" she screamed. "I will cry from the church steeples of every church in this land that you are a beast!"

"Who will listen, Eugenia? You entered motherhood out of revenge. Not even my own mother was that daring. She at least started with love. I will end with love—for *our* son. I don't think there is a woman in the world who would call me a beast for that decision."

"Not even Janellen?" she sneered.

"If that decision were mine alone, Eugenia, I wouldn't give you the benefit of my answer."

"So!" she said angrily. "You are using this as a little game so you can run back to her!"

"You are very obtuse, Eugenia," he said quietly. "I said I will keep you as wife and Christopher as son."

"All right," she said, just as quietly, "but I have said nothing on the subject!"

"You have nothing to say," he said grimly. "On certain matters you have nothing to say, in my opinion. We have each produced a child, not together but by different parties. One survived and the other did not. I am at a loss to say which was the blessed. But Christopher is the survivor."

Miserably, she knew she was defeated, but she would not give in. "I will not move into that damn house."

"All right," he said quietly, "but Christopher and I shall by the end of the summer. Now, my dear, if you will call Carter back in, I will make arrangements to take him to Wyoming."

Clay was not being obvious; he was being subtle. He knew that Eugenia dared not mention openly her lack of scruples, but any overt action on his part would certainly prick the ears of Cyrus Monroe. The man would certainly have meat to grind if Clay were to put Carter in a mental hospital. Brother helping brother could not be turned into a scandal. But he was not really helping a brother, but a child—and not Christopher. Carter was a child and needed the love and protection necessary for a child.

It was sweltering. The last day of September was like the middle of July. There was no escaping the drought's heat, for even the shade was like a brick oven.

Clay followed the ice wagon down the street, the waterfall off the tailgate drying almost as quickly as it hit the street. The two-hundred-pound blocks were melting into odd forms before the iceman could pick off the ten- and fifteen-pound chunks to be hurriedly rushed into the dwellings' little ice-boxes. Only for the children was it a delight. When the wagon stopped, they appeared from nowhere and darted among the waiting women customers to snatch up the chippings and suck on them as if ice were the most marvelous candy in the world.

"A fifteen and a twenty-five," Clay said on a sudden inspiration as the iceman jumped down from the wagon.

"You've no carrier, Mister."

"Little will that matter," Clay laughed. "It will dry on my clothes just as quickly as it melts."

"Saints alive," a voice said behind Clay. "It's nice to be seeing you again, sir."

"Hello, Mrs. Burleigh." He smiled and tipped his hat. "I trust you are weathering this long drought."

"Barely, sir, just barely. Me endurance is near reached the limit."

Ellen Burleigh had come to know his true identity when he purchased the majority of the "cheaper" rental dwellings from Packer and Company and hired her away from them as a collector. Her loyalty was such that she forgot he had ever been a "doctor" or the nice young widow woman a "nurse," and in public she never referred to him by name.

"As it is with most folk, Mrs. Burleigh, and not just here. Each day you read of a new cyclone raging with dreadful destructiveness through the South and Southwest. I just returned from up north and saw a flood of flame destroy a three thousand-acre forest. Tinder dry. Everything is so tinder dry."

She pulled him a little aside, suddenly trembling with apprehension. "Sir, I'm that glad you are back. I've spoke me piece to young Mr. Fairchild, but he thinks it's not a worry. Fire is a fear to me, sir, and I've been alert over *our* property. But the world does have evil-minded creatures, bent on plunder the minute an alarm sounds. A week ago, a block over, the McHenry family were burned out. The hoodlums had the place ransacked almost before the pump wagon was on the scene. My nephew, sir, works out of that fire station and says the back of the building was piled high with combustible refuse."

"Was it one of our buildings?"

"No. Still a Packer house. I do me best to warn our people, but some are irresponsible. I wish you would take it upon yourself to upbraid Mrs. O'Leary, sir. She still keeps cows in her barn and the hay has not been cleaned out the whole of the summer."

"I'll look into it," he said, paying for the two cakes of ice. Which really meant he would have Elliott look into it.

He had to bang on the door with the corner of the ice cake. When it came open, joy and misery mingled in Janellen's green eyes.

"Clayton Monroe," she whispered. "You promised never to visit here if I promised to move in."

"Exactly," he said testily, "but I never promised not to

come as the iceman. Now quickly, let me enter. My hands are beginning to freeze."

"Just to deliver the ice," she said with gentle insistence, "and I might ask why so much. The box only holds fifteen pounds and I got a chunk just the day before yesterday."

"The rest is for me, if you would be so kind as to fetch the washtub from the back porch and then do something clever with this little bag I am having trouble holding under my arm."

She took the bag and marched sternly before him back to the little kitchen. "You may put the ice in the sink, Clay, and then explain yourself. I will not turn this back into a house of guilt. We agreed, Clay. We agreed that if we had business to discuss it would take place in your office. It's bad enough that I have to feel guilty just shopping in the neighborhood."

"Why guilty?" he demanded, pumping water to run over his numb hands.

"Cyrus," she sighed. "Harvel is making him do their collecting and I had the misfortune of running into him one day. He was his normal mean and nasty self. Now I feel compelled to look into each shop before I enter. I don't want him to know that I am living here or renting from you. He would run immediately to Eugenia."

Clay stood silent next to her. He was quite sure that Cyrus had probably said something to Harvel and thus Eugenia. It made their biting conversation of half an hour before quite clear. He had not planned on that entering their discussion.

"She knows that I was going to have to see you today," he finally said. "Now, would you get the washtub?"

She looked down at the rapidly melting ice. "What does the washtub have to do with Eugenia knowing you were going to see me today?"

"Because I intend to sit and soak my hot feet in ice water. If you care to join me, I promise not to let as much as our big toes come into seductive contact. Or would you prefer that I call Mrs. Burleigh in to chaperone?"

Color rose in her cheeks and the spray of orange freckles stood out vividly on her nose. At the corners of her mouth a little smile started. Then, all at once, she turned to him and threw her arms about his neck.

"Goose," she chuckled. "Oh, you silly, silly goose . . ."

He bent down and sought her mouth, but she quickly turned her head and offered him only a cheek.

"No, Clay," she said gently. "Everything is on a strict friendship basis. Come, let's cool our feet."

"I'll take care of the tub. You take care of the sack."

"I've already sniffed. Where did you get lemons?"

"At P.D.'s warehouse. His brother has been experimenting in shipping whole sides of beef in railroad cars that are like giant ice-boxes. In reverse, they have been trying to bring some items back from the East. Those lemons, my dear, came all the way from South America, where it is winter. We certainly are living in a marvelous time. Which also brings me to the reason of my visit." He continued to talk as he went to the back porch for the galvanized tub and filled it with the larger hunk of ice and a few buckets of water from the pump. Janellen listened indifferently as she chipped ice from the other chunk and made the lemonade.

"Your invitation came in care of me, because the Commodore's office had no address for you. Billy especially wants me to attend. He says the Grand Central Station is magnificent. Of course, it is not all Harry's plan, but enough so that he is still being given some credit."

Janellen put the pitcher and glasses on the kitchen table and sat to take off her shoes and stockings. Clay already had his pant legs rolled to the knee and his feet in the tub.

"When is it?"

"Monday, October ninth. We would like to leave on the fifth or sixth."

"We?" She grimaced, and it was not from putting her feet into the icy water. "You can't be serious?"

"You have just about echoed Eugenia, my dear. I told her I was being practical. My new hotel-car has everything in one—kitchen, dining area, sitting room and sleeping accomodations for twelve. At present we are five. You, Eugenia, Christopher, his nurse and myself. Harvel, naturally, will go in his own car."

"Naturally," she echoed blankly. "You make it sound like a family outing."

"Good Lord! Do you and Eugenia compare notes? We are all civilized people. We are all friends."

Janellen wanted to laugh, but not at Clay. He had come to view the world only as he wished to view it. Everything was falling into place for him. Where once everything he touched was for the benefit of Harvel Packer, it now came directly to Clayton Monroe. It had been a very prosperous summer. He could look at his books and know that he was equal in wealth to Harvel Packer. He was happy. His absence most of the summer had allowed Eugenia to accept her defeat in a ladylike manner, even though she was taking her own good time about completing the interior of the house.

"Besides," Clay went on, "you must go with us. We, meaning you and I, have an invitation to meet Will Ogden at Boscobel. That's his country estate on Fordham Heights, just outside New York City. He's retired as a railroad president, but not as a dreamer. I'm in partnership with him on his Peshtigo village in Wisconsin. Imagine, Jan, those Indians are making quite a showing for themselves in the timber industry. Thanks be to the Lord that all of their land was spared from those fires. Hershel and Ivan weren't so lucky. They were totally wiped out. Maybe I'm getting soft-hearted, but I told Henri in Milwaukee to have them come and see me."

She only nodded, knowing that it was more shrewdness than soft-heartedness. The massive forest fires would send lumber prices booming.

"But, back to Will. He owns a lot of the right-of-way land with Jay Cooke. They want to look at Harry's city plans for purchase. I want you to hold out for a right stiff price."

"They belong to you, Clay."

"I have them only for safekeeping, just as I kept Jay's diary for so many years. The right price will get you out of this house and keep you for a long time."

Again she only nodded, but she did not know what she would have done without him. She did not, however, regret that Harry had spent his money as fast as he'd made it. It had given him so much happiness in his last few years. Of course, she missed the fine houses to live in, the fun of playing hostess to the great and near great, the joy of being pretty in fine clothing. She didn't mind the little DeKoven Street house, except on the day of Mrs. Yost's weekly visit. All they had to talk about were memories, and it put Janellen into a depressed mood, rather than raising her spirits. And now this visit was beginning to depress her. She did not want to make the trip, but couldn't find the right words to tell Clay.

Eugenia, as usual, had all the right words against the trip. Clay put her acid comments out of his mind. It was too filled with another gnawing worry.

On the afternoon he left Janellen, billowing smoke and fire alarms drew him to the Chicago, Burlington & Quincy Railroad yard. A hundred-and-sixty-five-foot-long warehouse was burning with irresistible rapidity and quickly ignited the next warehouse and Burlington Hall and station. The firemen poured their water on the hall and station to save them. They had already determined that the warehouses, owned by Sam Nickerson, President of the First National Bank, were a total loss. By evening they had determined that the fire in the warehouse was incendiary. What no one knew was that Sam had a silent partner—Clayton Monroe.

On Sunday, October one, a new double brick residence on Prairie Avenue was accidentally set on fire by boys who were playing in the vicinity. The building was owned by Michael Mortimore on land leased from Clayton Monroe.

Monday saw a carpenter shop destroyed on Twenty-first Street, a row of rental dwellings on Burnside Street, the Rice & Johnson bone-button factory on West Randolph, and a box factory on West Twelfth Street. All were attributed to malicious persons. All had spider webs that could be traced back, in one way or another, to Clayton Monroe.

By Tuesday Clay and Elliott were both concerned. Of the sixteen fires that day, eight were Monroe properties and all were incendiary.

"I don't even want to think evil," Clay insisted, "but

the insurance company is beginning to give us a fishy eye, Elliott."

"They're not happy, that's for sure. The warehouses alone were $350,000 on claim. We are rapidly closing in on three-quarters of a million."

"That's only money," Clay snarled. "Who can give Charley Stearnes back his life? I want guards on all the rest of our property and a tail put on Cyrus."

"You don't think . . ." Elliott gasped.

"I said I don't want to think evil, but I am also not a damn fool. If that idiot bastard is up to something, I want him caught red-handed!"

On the fourth there were only three small fires, none of them at Monroe properties. On the fifth there were four, and again none at Monroe properties.

Clay began to think he might have been wrong and Elliott was carping over the added expense as though it were his own money. It was taking one accountant alone to pay the guards each day.

"All right," Clay ordered, "call it off. I've got to get ready to go to New York. Send one of the boys over to the Michigan Southern roundhouse and have them get my car out. If we leave in the morning, we might still make New York by the ninth."

But the news sent Eugenia into a tirade.

"On again, off again, on again. Clay, you are not being fair. You know Father doesn't like rush trips. At this late date how in the world are we going to sleep each night on the siding?"

"Part of the way we shall have to go straight through," he said quietly, sitting down at the dinner table.

"Father will cause a scene, Clay," she pouted. "He wanted to leave days ago and take me with him. I wish now that I had listened to him."

"Why didn't you?"

All the inherent snobbishness in her soul came to the surface. "Really, Clay," she sniffed. "Isn't the answer to that question quite obvious?"

"Ah, Janellen," he said, sipping at the hot soup, because Eugenia had broken him of the habit of blowing on it. "Well, my dear, your sensitivity on that subject would not have been put in danger. She is not going. She claims illness, but I can see through it as a bald-faced lie."

"Really, Clay," she sniffed again, "perhaps you are the insensitive one. If a nurse says that she is ill, then she must be ill."

"Except I don't hoodwink easily, not anymore. As this is Friday, and her note came to the office yesterday morning, then I have every right to question truthfulness."

Eugenia blinked. "Perhaps I missed the logic somewhere in that statement."

"I didn't," he said, pushing the empty soup bowl away, a little amazed that the gaunt butler of Eugenia's choice was not there immediately to snatch it away. "Thursday afternoon is Mrs. Yost's afternoon free. She would have bustled her little fat bottom right in from the kitchen if Janellen had as much as a sniffle. Ah, there you are! As you can see, I have finished all of my soup, like a good little boy."

"I was detained taking a message at the door, sir," Murdock the butler said coldly, handing him a folded square of paper. He did not like Clay any more than he sensed Clay did not like him. Without a rattle he cleared the soup plates and went to bring in the next course.

"Damn!" Clay exploded, as he read. "A mysterious fire broke out in a freight car on the Michigan Southern track. It was right next to our car and they want me to come and inspect the water and smoke damage. They want me to come at once and see if it will be ready for travel. They can't seem to find Elliott."

Eugenia was quick with a suggestion, as though she had it thought out in advance. "Don't worry. We can always go in Father's car. I'm expected there after dinner and can easily arrange it."

"We shall see," he said, rising. "Tell Mrs. Yost to put my dinner in the warming oven."

Eugenia didn't protest. She had not found the right moment to tell Clay that she had fired the woman the day before. The butler and cook had not seen eye to eye, and she had opted to retain Murdock. After all, he was a proper servant and did not have his big nose in family affairs.

She waited until she heard Clay's carriage depart before she rang the bell.

"Murdock," she said evenly, "you may tell cook to put a portion away in the warming oven for Mr. Monroe. He shall be returning quite late, as I understand the situation. Now, reset his place and start again with soup. Mr. Cyrus Monroe will join me shortly."

Murdock didn't think; he just responded. That the uncle and nephew were not on the best of terms was really not his concern.

The hotel-car was a complete shambles. The heat from the freight car had warped its windows and the interior was a sodden mess. Clay simply walked away from it and started back toward the office to look for Elliott. To his amazement he found one of the accountants still laboring at his desk.

"Ritchard, isn't it?" Clay said. "Have you seen Mr. Fairchild?"

"Not since closing, sir. I had the fire guard accounts to close out, sir. Being a Friday, he and his wife usually have supper with his parents."

"I suppose," Clay mumbled, but his ears were really on a distant sound.

"Another fire alarm," Simon Ritchard said. "Sounds like the Canal Street area, Mr. Monroe."

"Damn!" Clay fumed. "We have a lot in that area, don't we?"

"Pretty much everything from the 200 to 700 block, as I recall."

"If you see Elliott," Clay snapped, "tell him I will be down there."

Simon Ritchard nodded and waited until he heard the big man pound down the stairs. Then he quietly closed his ledger, which he had not been working on. The schedule had been nearly as perfect as Cyrus Monroe had planned it—the freight yard fire, the arrival of Mr. Monroe, his rushing off to Canal Street on the merest suggestion. Simon could have told him that the fire would be in the basement of 561 South Canal Street. He also could have told him that Elliott Fairchild was in a meeting in the Banker's Exchange Building with a group of very nervous insurance men. But Cyrus Monroe had only been paying him for one-way information.

He closed the office and patted his fat purse. He really deserved to treat himself to a lovely dinner, a long, lovely dinner with wine. He knew it would be many hours before Clayton Monroe would get back to his dinner, and by then he might have totally lost his appetite.

"Lucky we were, Mr. Monroe," Fire Captain Herman Flood wheezed. "Those that fear have developed a right smart nose for smoke."

In the basement of 561 South Canal Street, Clay took a poker and pried through the huge pile of rags and papers and half-burnt debris. Flood had said it was possibly spontaneous combustion. Lem Saldeen, one of Clay's bill collectors and fire guards, said the women in the building had complained all afternoon about the invasion of rats into their apartments. Clay poked until he got to bare basement floor, having unearthed several empty rat's nests in the process.

"Flood," he growled, "that sure as hell is no mystery to me."

The portly fireman squatted down and ran his fingers over the ground. "Gunpowder," he gasped. "Undetected, the fire would have sent this up like a swoosh!"

"And spread to every building around. Lem, I can't find Mr. Fairchild, but I want the guards back out."

"Why, he's at a meeting, Mr. Monroe. An insurance meeting."

"How do you know that?"

"I was in the office getting my pay from that insolent snot Ritchard when the messenger came. Elliott went running out and told Ritchard to send a messenger out to your house in Humboldt Park."

Clay filed this curious information away. Right then he wanted to find Elliott quickly. "Do you recall the place of the meeting, Lem?"

"Sure. You were to come to the Banker's Exchange Building. Hell, I thought you had already been there."

"No, but I'm on my way. Lem, get the guard out, even if you have to spread the word block by block and hire new men."

"I don't know all your pieces of property, Mr. Monroe."

"To hell with just my property, Lem. I'm worried about the whole damn city."

He knew the twelve insurance executives on a first name basis, but they sat and regarded him as an enemy.

"Back down!" he growled. "I wish I knew where Mr. Fairchild was as well. I just learned of this meeting by accident."

"And well you attended," Joseph Bates sneered. "You not only have policies with each of us, we learn, but with almost every underwriter in the city. To a man, we are ready to cancel you out, sir!"

"We are not back in the days of heedless speculators, Joe." He stared the man down. "I worked just as hard as the rest of you to weed out the shaky companies and demand a statistical test of those who were stable. Damn! I own stock in half the companies represented in this room. Cancel me and I'll sell my stock short and ruin your patronage."

"Now, Clay," Charles Case said soothingly, "let's look at this from a different angle. You must admit that you've had a very strange run of mysterious fires."

"That I will admit." But he was not ready to admit that he had suspicions as to the origin of their mystery. "But you admit something in return. Why would I burn down a warehouse that you would only insure for $350,000 and will take me twice that amount to rebuild. Sam, as a banker and insurance man, tell them what we lost. Our renter lost over $600,000 in stored goods and is holding us responsible."

"Six hundred thirty eight thousand, to be exact," Arthur C. Ducat intoned. "He has put in his claim with me as well."

"This is getting us nowhere," Gurden S. Hubbard, Jr., snapped. "Clay, the Hubbard family and Monroe family go back to the '50s with insurance coverage. My father took out a policy on your life when you were sent to England. Now, when this marathon session started this evening, I made a simple suggestion. I make it again, now that you are here. Until this fire craze calms down, would you consider underwriting your own policies?''

''Naturally,'' Clay said with a show of calm, but Gurden could see that he was seething. They had all but accused him of setting the fires. ''But I wonder if the same should not apply throughout the city. Harry Hart Horner put it quite nicely before the '68 convention, when you self-same gentlemen jacked up your insurance rates because you feared the destruction that might come about. He wondered then what you were really insuring. Buildings tumble down, because walls of a hundred feet or more in height are built of a single brick's thickness. Our infamous wind brings down magnificent cornices, because their seemingly beautiful stone carvings are only ingeniously molded and skillfully painted sheet iron. Our stately Gothic church towers topple over because they are tin and not the massive stone they are painted to represent. Solid stone? We are a fake city of stucco upon wood frames and yet, because you all base your rates on eastern standards, we pay as though these were Ionic, Corinthian, Renaissance and Elizabethan structures built for the centuries. We are a sham and a cheat, a sand trap snare and a lie.''

He stopped for a second, because his truth showed in each embarrassed face.

''But no city,'' he went on, quieter, ''has a chance to start anew. Yet, I still have faith in the spirit that distinguished our Chicago of a few years ago, and not the debauched state we find ourselves in now. So, yes, Gurden, I will underwrite. I had planned on leaving for New York in the morning, but I will postpone for a day and work out all the papers with Mr. Fairchild tomorrow.''

There were murmurs of assent, except from Maynard Stocking.

''Gentlemen,'' he said sternly, ''I hope your greed has not gotten in the way of your better judgement. If the public hears one word of what we have forced upon Clay, we will need lynch-mob insurance upon ourselves. God help us if a real disaster strikes."

Clay was too tired to think beyond his own worry. He put the horse in the stable and left his personal buggy in the drive. Food didn't cross his mind. The house was already dark and he just wanted the comfort of his own bed.

His own bed, he thought, as he climbed into it. Eugenia was furnishing the house a stick at a time and he was lucky to even have a bed. Her bedroom he had never looked in upon, so was unsure of its complete condition. With Christopher long since weaned and Miss Dawson in full attendance, she had taken up the habit of spending the evenings with Harvel and sleeping late of the morning.

Thus, when the carriage rolled in at the wee hours, it did not disturb his sleep. As he rose at five, a hangover habit from P.D. Armour, he left as quiet a house as he had entered.

When in town he would breakfast at the Sherman House at Clarke and Randolph, a half block from his office. It was not only the location of the six-story structure that attracted him, but the fact that, as a part-owner, he could eat in the kitchen an hour before the dining room opened for early rising guests.

"Well, the lost is found," he said, sitting down at the staff dining table. "You better have some coffee, Elliott, it is going to be a long day and you look terrible."

"I feel even worse." Elliott sneezed. "That wind was terrible last night. I wish the heat of the day would have stayed around last night." He sneezed again and blew his nose. "Chief, we've got a problem."

"I would say several, but let me hear your gem first."

"We have a spy in the office."

"Simon Ritchard!"

Gloomily Elliott shook his head.

"Do you always have to know everything first?" he said accusingly.

"No," Clay replied, accepting the steaming plate of breakfast from a waitress. "I just happened to fall over one of his lies last night."

"And I fell over more than that," Elliott said wearily.

"I rushed off in such a state that I forgot our insurance portfolio. But coming back to the office, I saw Ritchard in the street talking to a man in a hansom cab. The man was Cyrus Monroe."

"Go on," Clay said, calmly eating.

"When Simon went right back up to the office, I thought I better keep an eye on Cyrus. He went down to South Canal Street and had a short meeting with his bill collector in that area, one of the last ones Harvel lets him pay. Then it was strange. He went to your old house on Michigan Avenue, let himself in with a key and came out an hour later dressed to the nines. Did you know he was living there?"

"Nope," Clay said, chewing on a sausage. "I gave Eugenia full authority to rent it out for her pin-money account." He looked a little amazed, but not over the facts. "Aren't you eating?"

"I can't, Chief. I am so sick over the rest. It'll make you stop eating, too. Don't hate me, but it's got to be said. Cyrus went out to your house in Humboldt Park. I didn't see your buggy about, so I crept up and looked in the windows. Big as life, he was sitting having dinner with Eugenia."

The fork didn't even pause as Clay scooped up a quarter of an egg. "I'm amazed that Mrs. Yost served him."

"Mrs. Yost?" Elliott exploded. "She came in for her final pay voucher on Thursday. Had a run in with starched pants, she did."

Clay pushed his plate away. He did not stop eating over the news; he was finished. Over a fresh cup of coffee he would listen further. He could forgive a mistake but there was no excuse for carelessness. Eugenia had been foolish and careless.

"Well," Elliott gulped, "after dinner they both went back to Harvel's house. A couple of hours later they came out laughing and went up the block to your old house. Then . . . then . . ."

"Then they did not leave until the wee hours?" Clay prompted.

"Only Eugenia left," he said sadly. "She came back to

the Packer stable to rouse the groom to take her home. I came right here, because it was already near five.''

The hurt was like a heart attack, but there was no show of outward emotion on Clay's face. Enemies without he could fight recklessly, but enemies within had to be handled with stealth.

''It is time to go to the office, my friend,'' he said calmly. ''I want Simon Ritchard to be kept very busy and unaware of our knowledge. You, and you must lie over your looks, will have had a spat with your wife.''

It was a difficult day and a longer night. As though he smelled trouble, Cyrus remained in the Michigan Street house throughout the day and night. Nor did Eugenia make her normal daily visit to her father.

Simon Ritchard left the office at the normal closing hour and went directly to his boarding house.

Clay and Elliott were puzzled, but Simon was quite pleased with himself. Because the fire had been a fizzle, his orders were to make no contact that day if they were putting out the guards again.

Cyrus thought he finally had Clay where it pinched. He thought he was quite sly in reminding Harvel Packer that the Gurden Hubbard notes were long overdue. The suggestion had been so simple and yet so devious. Hubbard really should protect that note before Clayton Monroe ruined him with insurance claims. Having known Harvel longer than the Monroe family, Gurden never knew he was being used by taking the friendly suggestion. After all, Harvel was Clay's father-in-law. By the morning, Cyrus thought, he would have ruined Clay, as Clay had ruined him twice.

But nothing had happened by ten o'clock.

''All we are burning up is money, Chief. We've got guards everywhere and runners at every alarm box.''

''Give it another hour,'' Clay mumbled. He could feel this in his bones, just as surely as he felt the men had to jump off the train in the tunnel. But he prayed mightily that he was wrong. The wind was blowing so fiercely from the south that men had a hard time standing up on the street.

Then, several minutes later, a boy came racing down Randolph Street and Elliott quickly threw open the office window.

"Box Number 248," the boy screamed against the wind. "Boiler explosion at Lull & Holmes planing mill!"

Clay and Elliott looked at each other aghast. They had never considered fire striking two nights in a row in the same area. They had even agreed that Cyrus would not be that foolish. But the mill was at 209 South Canal Street.

Before the firemen reached the address, the mill and its contents were consumed. By the time Clay and Elliott reached the scene, the fire was unparalleled in rapidity. The strong wind drove the flames with terrific force upon the wooden buildings to the north. The pumped water just turned to steam vapor in the heat and evaporated. The block square was a mass of darting, roaring flames.

"Holy Jesus! Get back!"

The warning came at nearly the same moment that the devilish wind veered into the southwest, bringing the wall of flame right back at the firefighters. They had to flee or be cremated.

Within those minutes of change, the area between Jackson and Adams Streets and between Clinton Street and the river was ablaze.

A dozen leads of hose—all that could be worked to advantage—flooded water into the blazing pile. The firemen fought with gallantry in the midst of the intense heat.

Never had Clay known such fear. The whole city was going to go up in flame—and all because he judged wrong. They needed help and he felt so helpless.

Then he turned and the animal screamed out of him. Hundreds of spectators were fighting to get into a building on the corner of Canal and Adams, while across the street the roofs of the Pittsburgh & Fort Wayne Railway freight and passenger depots were ablaze.

He screamed and shoved his way through the throng, with Elliott trying to haul him back by his coat tails.

"Idiots!" he cried. "Your help is needed!"

Either no one heard him or no one cared to hear him. When he got to the door of the building, his stomach churned with disgust. It was a saloon and the owner, convinced that his place was lost, had thrown open the doors for free use of his stock of liquors and cigars. Several hundred men were having a gay old party.

Clay pulled a man around by the arm. "What's more important, a drink or your damn life?"

"You're crazy! My life, of course."

"Then get some of these bastards to help save your life and theirs. If we demolish some of the P & FW sheds, we can control the spread. If not, this damn saloon will burst like a tinder box."

Twenty followed Clay and Elliott. Twenty was more than enough, because they were met by a frightened stationmaster who knew the inevitable. He took them to the dynamite shed and opened it as freely as the saloon.

Up and down the two blocks between Adams and Van Buren they raced. Coaches, locomotives, warehouses, storage sheds and depot went booming into the sky behind them. The explosive draught sucked the flames across Canal Street with a fearful velocity and smothered a great portion of it under a lurid cloud of flying debris. The river was now a natural fire break.

All night and far into the next day, the firemen, with too damn few volunteers, struggled to extinguish the smoldering fires. Their lungs filled with the oppressive odor of smoke and the emitted gases; they were hardly aware of their own exhaustion.

Through red-rimmed eyes Clay had to look at the man who spoke to him twice before recognizing him.

"It's relief time, Clay," Captain Flood repeated. "I've got some volunteers to poke around the coal heaps and cool them down. Elliott's gone to fetch you a cab. He went up Clinton toward Madison. Most of the curious have gone home from our terrifying spectacle."

Clay blinked. Never had he felt so exhausted and painful. There were hundreds of little burns on his hands, face, head and, through his clothes, on his body.

"Over," he murmured. "You have a heroic crew, Captain Flood."

"Not just my men, Clay. We had to call upon every department throughout the whole city. This was the biggest thing to hit Chicago. I never want to live long enough to see a bigger fire. Only one blessing. No lives lost."

"Blessing," Clay mumbled, as he stumbled up Clinton Street. "A real blessing . . ."

He hardly felt Elliott hoist him into the cab. He was not aware of the ride to Humboldt Park, only half aware that someone helped Elliott get him out of the cab and into the house.

"Fine stew he has put us in," Murdock said indignantly, for he looked on Elliott as just another servant. "Mrs. Monroe has been furious. He might have at least let us know where he was. Just put him in the study. I am not about to carry his bulk up the stairs."

"Where is she?" Elliott demanded.

"Mrs. Monroe is with her father," he said coolly. "They are most upset that he has once again ruined the New York departure. I was to let them know the moment of his return."

"Then why don't you do it, you stuffed pig! You can take the cab waiting for me. I'm going to get some coffee and see that he is all right."

"Cook does not work Sundays," Murdock sneered.

"Go to hell!" Elliott growled. "I know how to make coffee, so get lost."

"I shall file your rather earthy statements with Mrs. Monroe, sir. I hope you have enjoyed your employment, for it is very short-lived."

Elliott ignored him and went down the hall toward the kitchen. He was more hungry than tired. Ever since his wife had become pregnant, he was starved all the time.

Chapter 17

It was an unusually rowdy Sunday evening on DeKoven Street. Mrs. Catherine McLaughlin wanted her newly-arrived nephew from Ireland to see what a fine place was America and the lovely friends her six sons possessed.

"Hey, Ma, its Simon Ritchard. He's the fine lad that's been getting me the extra-pay jobs of late."

"Well, I'm thanking thee for that, Simon Ritchard. Takes all a widow body can scrape together. And what's this you be bringing along with you?"

Simon smiled expansively. "I thought a couple of pails of milk might be making the oyster stew a mite more gargantuan or might do for a touch of milk punch. I knew you had a supplier in the neighborhood."

Mrs. McLaughlin pursed her lips intolerantly. "Your intention is sound, me boy, but the McLaughlin family does not allow a single of the coppers to cross the palm of Mrs. Patrick O'Leary."

Simon winked. "Perhaps the cow gave me the commodity without a financial discussion with Mrs. O'Leary."

Catherine McLaughlin giggled. "I'll be showing you the way back to the kitchen."

Outside Ellen Burleigh was scurrying back from evening mass, having a hard time keeping her bonnet on in the wind.

"Good evening to you," said Cyrus, with a quick tip of his hat and a dart around her on the narrow sidewalk.

"Evening," she said a little tartly. "Does himself make you collect on the Sabbath?"

Cyrus laughed as though he didn't have time to stop and chatter. "A different matter. By word of mouth one of your renters has a complaint against one of mine. After last night I thought I'd best look into it at once.''

He knew he had her attention with that. ''Might I be so bold as to ask the particulars, Mr. Monroe.''

''Not at all. A neighbor saw the Harridan boy and three of his friends sneaking into the O'Leary barn with pipes and tobacco. As the woman is not on speaking terms with Mrs. O'Leary, the matter came to my ears. I shall point out to the boys the evil of such a practice and the danger of a pipe ash falling in the hay and smoldering to flame.''

''Another needs fresh warning on that,'' she said accusingly. ''I myself have a hard time talking with the woman, her habit being to hide out at rent-due time—but you are well acquainted with the likes of that, Mr. Monroe. Give a body a perch and they think they can lay eggs forever. Like behind us, if you can hear the noise. Them that can give parties and not pay their rent on time, and on a Sabbath eve to boot. Humph! Wouldn't have attended if invited. But my point, sir, is the O'Leary barn. The woman has a nasty habit of milking at dusk by lantern light and leaving the lantern behind while she carries in the pails to do the skimming. I fear every time I see the light shining through the barn slats, I do.''

Cyrus painted his face with a worrisome frown. ''I do say, I don't like the sounds of that. With your permission I should like to have a chat with her on the subject, after I have talked with the Harridan family. After all, we must look out for each other.''

A young man came tearing out of the McLaughlin house, mumbling and feeling in every pocket. ''I know I had my money purse when I left the board house! I just know it!''

Ellen Burleigh didn't know the young man and Cyrus Monroe pretended not to, but he smiled to himself. Simon had planted one of the many fables Cyrus wanted planted that evening and made his excused exit on schedule.

''My permission you have, but she's a hard one. Brrr! That wind is chillier by the moment. It's right between the blankets for me. Good night to you.''

Cyrus tipped his hat and went around the corner to Jefferson. He slowly walked the two blocks to Ewing and turned down the street to walk right by the Harridan house.

He had already made that visit earlier. Timothy Harridan had denied being in the O'Leary barn, but could not deny the practice of learning to smoke. Cyrus had left it as a family matter, because all he wished to do was plant a seed.

He continued slowly to Clinton and back again to the DeKoven corner. There was no rush. He had done his homework well. It was eight-thirty and the O'Leary house dark, as he surmised it would be. Had the neighbors been on talking terms they would have known that the woman had been in bed for several days with an injured foot and the milking of her cows had been left to her daughter.

Cyrus quietly went to the back of the lot and entered the barn. The days of having Simon come to buy milk had paid off. He was able to walk through the litter and around the junk piles as though he'd been there before. Because the stable was kept indifferently, he had no fear that what he sought would not be found.

Behind a crate he found the lantern that Simon had hidden while Catharine O'Leary had drawn him a fresh pail several days before.

It took but a single lucifer to bring the wick to life. He placed the square based lantern down on the earthen floor and then took a plank to smash the glass globe container and topple it. Even as a finger of flame spread to the spilled kerosene, he examined the lantern to make sure that it looked like it had been kicked by the cow.

But, he thought sadistically, the evidence would never be found or the fables ever needed, if he'd ever thought the fire of the night before would have been confined to four blocks.

Never once did he think of life or limb. His mind was too warped to consider even a single victim.

Except for the party, the neighborhood was abed.

The fire went undetected as it raced across the littered floor and crawled the walls to the loft, which had recently been filled with drought-dry hay for the winter. The cows and calf did not low, because they had the freedom of the fenced yard during the day and had vacated the barn at the first whiff of smoke.

The high wooden fence ran from the barn to the alley

and then the entire length of the alley to Jefferson Street. Backed up to the fence, on the contiguous lots, were sheds and old barns used for storage. Piled against the fence in the alley were masses of dry refuse susceptible to combustion. Cyrus had picked a most suitable place and time for the perpetration of his crime.

It was fifteen minutes before a drayman came along Jefferson and saw the strange bright light coming from the tunnel-like alley. When he looked down the alley, the fire had extended to the adjoining sheds, barns and dwelling roofs toward the north and northeast, and it was consuming them with terrific rapidity.

It took another fifteen minutes for the overtaxed firemen to be routed from their beds and brought to the scene. It had only been a few hours before when they had been given relief. The equipment had not been cleaned; large quantities of their hoses had been damaged or destroyed; two of the nearest pumping wagons were incapacitated.

The fire was beyond their control and they shouted for the people to evacuate.

Clay felt that he had just barely closed his eyes when a sharp object kept poking him in the ribs. The voice screaming at him was just as sharp, but it took him a moment to gather the meaning.

"Get off of that brand new sofa, you filthy beast," Eugenia screamed, jabbing him with the fireplace poker. "Murdock said you looked like a pig. Get upstairs and bathe! You are not getting into Father's hotel-car in this condition!"

"I'm not getting into it in any condition," he said wearily.

"I thought that would be your answer," she sneered. "I should have listened to them and left yesterday."

"*Them*, meaning Harvel and Cyrus. I didn't know that you were still living most of the time in the old house—with Cyrus."

It was out now. He had said it.

Eugenia was calmly still. She stood above the sofa and her mouth tightened slowly into a bitter line. Clay realized that she was not going to deny it—that she was really rather proud of it.

He ran his tongue over dry, swollen lips.

"You may go," he said simply and stretched out on the sofa. "And I will use this as long as I paid for it."

"With money you stole from my father!" she snapped.

"Do they have you believing that again?" he demanded, but with no real intent on wishing an answer.

"You don't understand," she purred with malice. "They can prove that you forged Father's name on documents for years."

"How true. My congratulations to you all. I'm sure it will make a fascinating discussion—" He sat up on the sofa and looked Eugenia full in the face. "At the divorce proceedings," he added softly.

"Thank you," she snarled, "exactly what I had in mind. But I am in the driver's seat, so don't act so high and mighty. When Cyrus finishes testifying on Carter's condition, who will ever believe your insane theory?"

"Leave Christopher out of this," he said heavily.

Eugenia bent forward mockingly, her face ugly with hate.

"That is precisely what I will not do, Clayton Monroe. I had that child for one reason and one reason only. To make you suffer for the hurt you caused me over Janellen. Why do you think we have never had another child? Because one was all I needed. Oh, you narrow-sighted fool!" she said bitingly. "How easily you took the bait on the Carter story. His mind has become so simple that you can plant any thought and it starts to become a reality. I knew I had you when you took that bait. At last there was something in this world that you loved that I could take away from you. Your *real* son!"

Clay sank back on the sofa, his mind dazed. Was Eugenia playing tricks on him again? Christopher was really his?

"Then you are in for a real fight!" Clay finally bellowed, then an unusual sob caught in his throat. "No," he got out. "I won't drag him through a scandal that would haunt him the rest of his life. Name your price for him, Eugenia."

She smiled wickedly. "By tomorrow morning you won't have the price for anything, Clayton!"

"And what in the hell is that supposed to mean?"

She continued to smile, ever so slowly, draping the floor-length furs carefully about her body.

Miss Dawson came into the room and stood looking at them, her pinched face filled with dread.

"Ready, mum," she whispered. "But I'm most fearful."

"He will do nothing—to you!"

"Ain't afraid of Mr. Monroe, mum. From the third floor nursery window, the whole eastern sky is orange with fire."

"The fire has nothing to do with us," Eugenia said cruelly. "Now get the child to the carriage."

"Oh my God!" Clay cried, stumbling up. "I understand about tomorrow. What crazy madness have you helped Cyrus bring about?"

"To the carriage!" Eugenia barked, ignoring him. "We have to pick up Father and get to the train!"

Elliott burst into the house, gasping for breath. "Chief . . . Chief, there's fire from DeKoven all the way up to the river! It'll jump it sure!"

Clay was momentarily stunned.

"It wasn't supposed to be that large," Eugenia said, frowning, as though her statement would stop its march. "River?" Then she gasped. "Father! Father will be right in its path. I must get him to the station."

She spun and raced for the still-open front door. Miss Dawson hesitated, but Clay quickly stepped forward and pulled her back.

"To the nursery," he whispered. "I will see to Mrs. Monroe."

But by the time he reached the porch, the groom had the carriage careening away with Eugenia screaming at him to go even faster. Elliott stepped up beside Clay.

"It's a madhouse," he said sadly. "The people are trying to flee north to Lincoln Park and jamming the streets. I fear there has already been death. I took the liberty to go by the office and grab what records were of most value."

Clay was still in a state of shock and fatigue from the

night before. He just stood and looked at the orange halo growing larger and larger in the sky.

"DeKoven?" he said dully.

Elliott knew the exact thought that Clay did not want to face.

"I tried to get into the area by coming down Halsted. The police have it blocked off because it's just one big inferno all the way to the lake. When I got back to Madison, carts and wagons were everywhere. I left my wife with the cab and told the driver to whip any man who tried to steal it. Coming back from Randolph Street I spied the McLaughlin family. All they knew of Mrs. Horner was her refusal to attend a party they were giving this evening because of a prior engagement."

"Engagement?" Clay mumbled. "Mrs. Yost? That would be her only other engagement, Elliott. But where in the hell does she live?"

"I'm afraid, sir," Elliott gulped, "I do not have that information."

Clay spun toward the stable. "I'll go to Lincoln Park and work my way back down."

Elliott nodded gravely. "You'll be fighting against thousands upon thousands. Thousands more are fighting to get west. I doubt that Mrs. Monroe even gets through to her father."

"Take your wife in the house," Clay said, turning back and grasping for one logical thing to do and say. "I feel so helpless."

His mind wanted to rush forward to help, but his lungs were still seared from the night before and his body in great agony.

It was terrible and frightening. When he heard wagons rumbling on North Avenue, he walked out to his brick gatepost. It was like a scene from hell. They seemed hardly human as they staggered along—their hair and eyebrows singed, their blackened faces covered by handkerchiefs to keep out the smoke, their clothes full of holes from the hot sparks driven by the cyclone-like winds, their eyes red from the acrid smoke, their legs tottering from exhaustion, their arms clutching a few possessions.

Without giving it a second thought, he began to wave

them into the drive and told the women to take over the kitchen and cupboards.

From the men, as the night wore on, he got fragments of what they had left behind. It was near the unbelievable. In the brief space of six and one-half hours, the fire had run the distance of two and one-quarter miles, and still it raged.

The fire raged for three days. And each day the news grew bleaker and more dreadful.

Clay had only a hazy idea of those three days. A few moments after turning the house and grounds into a refugee center, a soldier came galloping down the street and swung off the horse in front of him.

"Sir, would you please tell me where I might find Mr. Clayton Monroe?"

"I am him."

"Sir, I am with the Department of the Missouri, under the command of Lieutenant General Philip Sheridan. We have been informed that you have a private telegraphic service within your home."

"Yes, I have."

The young officer let out a sigh of relief. "Sir, it may be the last one in Chicago. The general asks your kind permission for its use as his communication headquarters."

At last Clay felt of use.

Over the strong objections of Elliott, he stayed day and night with the soldiers in the message room. With them he gulped mouthfuls of food and swallows of coffee, then returned once more to the hundreds of messages flowing in and out.

Room by room the house filled with more and more soldiers, until it was more general headquarters than message center.

Then, on the afternoon of October eleventh, the house was oddly quiet and nearly deserted. No one dared speak as they waited. Then the explosions began to rumble—one on top of the other. Sheridan's troops had done the only thing left to them. In a semi-circle around the fire, a wide path of mines had been laid to blow out a fire-break. They waited for word of its success.

"Sir," the soldier said politely. "The telegraphic key."

He touched Clay on the shoulder, but there was no response.

Elliott came in and silently motioned for help. In those moments of waiting, sleep had finally caught up with Clay.

It remained a headquarters for another week, but Clay was hardly aware of the hustle and bustle.

Elliott made sure that he was right in the center of the hustle and bustle. The army was very protective of their facts and figures, but Elliott had learned from a master.

He put down the coffee cup and clucked. "You've got too many blocks drawn in there, Jellison."

"Damn, Elliott, I can only go on word of mouth. Did every damn map of this damn town burn up with it?"

Elliott chuckled. "Lieutenant Eastlake on your ass?"

"You said it. 'Get the North Side done yesterday, Jellison.' 'Why isn't the West Side done, Jellison?' 'The South Side is the most important, Jellison!' Hell, Elliott, look at that stack of notes. I'm supposed to weed through them and figure out what building was where and what it was. The lard-asses in Washington are scared to death that everyone is going to claim we blew them up and put in for compensation. Don't blame them with so many insurance companies screaming they're bankrupt. Hey! What are you doing? We were told not to mess with Mr. Monroe's private office."

"I'm allowed to mess. Come here and keep your mouth shut."

Jellison was flabbergasted. Section by section the Monroe maps revealed who owned every piece of property in Chicago.

"Get Eastlake out of the house and I'll help you use these."

So, before anyone else in Chicago knew it, Elliott knew that the burned district on the South Side was four hundred fifty acres. As Jellison worked, so did he with secret little marks on his maps. Three thousand six hundred buildings destroyed, including one thousand six hundred stores, twenty-eight hotels and sixty manufacturing plants. Twenty-one thousand six hundred people had been burned out of their homes.

The burned acreage on the North Side was one thousand three hundred, with over ten thousand buildings in cinders and seventy thousand left homeless. Only six acres short of two hundred were burned on the West Side, representing five hundred buildings and two thousand five hundred rendered homeless. $196,000,000 in losses.

Elliott tried to control his emotions as another list had to be pinpointed. The Army wanted to know exactly where the three hundred people lived who had perished—especially those who had foolishly refused to leave until it was too late.

He breathed a sigh of relief when Janellen Horner's name did not appear, although even Jellison figured the three-hundred count was inaccurate at that early date.

Three names for one address Jellison troubled over.

"Tell me I'm wrong about this, Elliott."

"I'm afraid you're not. That's his cousin, wife and father-in-law."

"Poor man!"

Elliott held his silence. There was even worse news to break to Clay. Will Ogden had rushed from New York to help with the fire, only to learn that the Peshtigo village and timber region had been destroyed by fire with the loss of over one thousand lives.

"Mr. Elliott," Miss Dawson said, sticking her head in the door. "There's a very nasty man down in the foyer insisting that he must see Mr. Monroe. Would you be seeing him?"

Janellen got up stiffly, thinking: Harry doesn't live here anymore. But was she living? The house might just as well have been as vacant as the Monroe house next door. For two weeks she had sat feeling sorry for herself and was not bothered. Nobody bothered a widow woman in a gingerbread house that was dark each night and used but a single chimney each day. She wondered if Clay had been by the little house yet and found it just as she had left it? It was true what Mrs. Yost had said—it was, it was! Eugenia was out to ruin Clay right under his nose. Couldn't he see it? She could—now that Eugenia's lawyer had put it in such brutal terms. She had felt so cheap and vulgar. Oh, I hate her for this! She was not now Clay's mistress, but the lawyer's face had told her how difficult it would be proving that fact. Didn't he own the house in which she lived? Wasn't his name on the check that had passed through her bank account? He wouldn't even let her explain the reason for the check. He was only there to protect Mrs. Monroe and her son. They did not want a legal battle, if it could be helped. Mrs. Monroe was even willing to be quite generous.

That was the only moment of pride she had felt. She had asked the current price for selling out the man she loved and, at the same moment, realized it was also a near admission of guilt. But she couldn't fight Eugenia Packer Monroe.

"No," she said coldly, going to put another log on the grate, "you ran like a coward. And don't tell one lie after another. You didn't do it to protect Clay. You've been afraid of that woman since you first heard of her. Afraid and madly jealous. And just listen to yourself. Twenty-seven years old and talking to yourself like you were seventy-seven."

As she put the log on the fire, the old log hissed and spit back at her. "About time we got some snow."

She went to the window to see if it was really snow or just a green log. Suddenly she stiffened, then pressed her nose against the cold glass, shading her eyes with one hand so that the reflections would not hinder her view.

"Fool!" she breathed. "He will only make matters worse for himself!" She banged on the window and motioned for Clay to come in out of the snow. Then she ran to the front door, her heart fluttering.

"Hello, Clay," she said. "How did you find me?"

The truth of the matter was that he didn't know himself. After Elliott had awakened him, he had been a raging bull. For the shyster lawyer to try blackmail on him, after what he had been through, was pure infamy. In simple syllables and with no disguised allusions he let the man know all the facts he had against Cyrus Monroe, Simon Ritchard and his late wife. As two were dead and the other oddly missing, he had only the lawyer to question as to their conspiracy. As for the allegations against Mrs. Horner, the man better have solid facts or stand to face charges of character assassination. Then, to Clay's surprise, Corporal Jellison, who had not been able to avoid overhearing from the next office, stormed in berating the man, bodily seized him up and hauled him from the house.

"I said," Janellen repeated, "how did you find me?"

"I don't know," Clay answered truthfully. "I think I just came back to the first place that I kissed you."

"That it was. Go sit by the fire. You must be half-frozen."

"Not really," he said, going into the parlor and taking off his great coat. "I would have come sooner, but I had to wait for the memorial services."

"Memorial services?"

"From the fire."

"But Mrs. Burleigh told me there had been no deaths."

He looked at her wonderingly, as though it were impossible for anyone in the world not to know of it. Then he understood.

"I'm aware that you had a visit from a rather obtuse lawyer," he said. "I can now surmise that you left Chicago directly thereafter, and are unaware of later events."

"No!" she groaned. "I don't want to hear! Haven't I given you enough trouble in your life?"

"You must listen," he said simply, "because I think I must speak it aloud to know that it is really true and not a nightmare."

An hour later they sat over coffee in the kitchen. Once it had been their room for their second stolen kiss. That had been several lifetimes past. Slowly Janellen could feel the anguish inside herself come under control. She felt the slow upsurge of a tremendous wave of pity for Eugenia. The woman had owned the world for the asking, but planted the seeds of her own destruction by demanding the moon. For the moment she didn't even want to think about Cyrus and Harvel. They stood before another judge.

"I once said I wanted to be as rich as Jay Cooke," he mumbled. "Elliott says it will take months for the banks to get things straight. No matter, I have accounts in New York for the brokers to draw upon. Should tide us over. And those plans. No use wasting them on Montana. They are perfect for the rebuilding of Chicago, don't you think."

Why can't I lie? she thought miserably.

"Do what you wish," she said quietly, "but I never wish to see Chicago again."

"Never is a long time."

"I wish you could listen to yourself, Clay Monroe!" she flared. "This plan! That plan! This account! That account! Have you forgotten the story you've just told me?"

"That's the whole point," he said grimly. "I'm not going to dig in the ashes! For the sake of Christopher I will let their deeds lie in their ruins with them. Who benefits by unmasking them? No one! And no one will be able to point a finger at my gain. Sam Nickerson has already been named as executor of Harvel's estate. It will all go for the rebuilding of schools and hospitals. I wish none of it and never have."

Janellen looked at him wonderingly.

"I can agree to all of that," she murmured. "Now I wish to tell you one thing about us. Never have I loved a man as I love you. Suddenly, for the first time, we find ourselves free at the same time. I don't want to dig in ashes, Clay. For the sake of Christopher I will not let our deeds ruin him. Who benefits by our being discreet? We do! Go back to Chicago, Clay, and begin to rebuild. When the mourning period is over, we shall speak of our time for marriage. Until then, we won't do anything wrong. I won't and I won't let you. So kiss me good-bye until then."

Clay kissed her and her sigh was soft with contentment.

The gingerbread house in Milwaukee sprawled as the family expanded.

Christopher and his brother had been too young to understand the financial disaster of 1873—and too well insulated to know if their family wealth had diminished or not.

Clay never knew how well insulated, until he took the

family down to attend the 1893 World's Columbian Exposition in Chicago. It was also to be a family reunion. Christopher was coming home from his second year of medical school. He did not seem as thrilled as after his first year.

"The blood and gore getting to you?" Clay asked.

"The social life," Christopher answered truthfully. "Father, are we rich?"

Clay sensed it was a girl that prompted the question. Seriousness flickered over Christopher's lean, handsome face, and the dreams of every young man glowed half-hidden in his blue-gray eyes.

"As rich as whom?" Clay answered jokingly.

"As any of the robber barons!" Christopher said harshly.

"What the devil do you mean?"

"It came up as a topic in a social gathering. Names I heard as a child were flying all over the place, and not kindly. I wanted to counter some of the charges, but had no knowledge. I felt so stupid that I began going to the library to read up on the subject. I'm afraid, sir, that I became so absorbed in the subject matter that I was spending all my time in the library or in social bull sessions fighting a lost cause. To get to the sainted truth, as mother says, I'm afraid I've flunked out."

"I see, all right," Clay growled. "I ask but a single question. Why fight a lost cause?"

Christopher blinked in amazement. His father's attitude was right, but the question was wrong.

"Sir? How do you answer when they say you used cheap labor freely during the depression to fortify against competitors when the flush period returned?"

"You answer honestly, Christopher, and with the facts, as I gather you dug them out. Because I had money during the panic, I used it on cheap labor to keep them working and not starving. I forced my competitors out, but bought their factories because they were idle and I could put more men to work. Robber baron, my ass. If that is robbing, then it is bloody damn hard work." Then he laughed. "And here I thought your long-faced problem was going to be over a girl."

"Little time for that in medical school, Father. With this

flunked semester, I shall really be behind. I shall be ancient before I can start practice and even think of marriage.''

''Then I take it that you plan to go back.''

''Naturally. The other was just a curiosity to see where I came from. I always knew where I was going. Each day I can see things in the classroom that the professors have not even thought of looking into. More challenge there than you ever dreamed of. Oh, here's mother and the girls. This Exposition is just great!''

Clay smiled to himself. He was fifty-two years old and was being told about challenge. Whenever again, he thought, in the history of the world, would young men in their twenties and thirties be given the challenge and opportunity of individual fortune to change so radically their own station to such a degree and to shape so dramatically the nation they served?

''Naturally,'' he repeated Christopher's words under his breath. ''The other was just curiosity to see where I came from. I always knew where I was going.''

''What are you mumbling about, old man?''

''Challenge, my dear wife. More challenge than you ever dreamed of.''

''You'd best get your challenger to the elevator,'' Janellen laughed. ''You have five daughters who think every man in Chicago is the biggest heart-throb they have ever seen.''

''Is that true, now?''

She came to him quickly, and when she was close he could see a million miles down into her green eyes.

''They don't know that I captured the best first.''